MW00809955

AN ANGEL'S CRY

AN ANGEL'S CRY

The Last Eulogy Series Book Three

A Novel by

ANTHONY DIVERNIERO

gatekeeper press™
Tampa, FL

An Angel's Cry

Published by Gatekeeper Press
7853 Gunn Hwy, Suite 209
Tampa, FL 33626
www.GatekeeperPress.com

The editorial work for this book is entirely the product of the author. Gatekeeper Press did not participate in and is not responsible for any aspect of this element.

Library of Congress Control Number: 2022952020

ISBN (hardcover): 9781662934858
ISBN (paperback): 9781662934865
eISBN: 9781662934872

Dedication
Ruth Mullen
Gone way to early
A wonderful person and an exemplary copy editor

Acknowledgements

First and foremost, to all my readers of my novels Messenger From God and the Third trumpet. Thank you! Thank you! I hope you enjoy the conclusion of the series, *An Angels Cry*.

Thank you to my editor, Alice Peck. I am so grateful to you for sharing your wisdom, and insight in completing An Angel's Cry.

Thank you, Duane Stapp, for the cover design. Your artistic talent is beyond compare.

Thank you, Crystal Shershen my copy editor. Your insights and thoroughness were superb.

Thank you, Stephanie Scott for your wonderful ability to proofread and your comments.

Thank you, Jennifer Clark at Gatekeeper Press, for your patience and understanding.

Special thank you to my Barnes and Noble family in North Haven. Frank, Ellen, Marjorie, Clive, and Diana. Your support during the years is so appreciated. To the marvelous employees who allow me to spend countless hours writing and drinking Espresso's. Especially, Noelle, Nye, Rob, Kevin, Adam, and Jay thank you for the morning smiles and cheerfulness.

To my longtime childhood friend Bunny as well as Sharon, Ellen, Lynn, Ben and, Lisa thank you for reading the manuscript and your valuable input.

Debbie Abrams and the book club babes, Diane DuPont, Cindy Gilhuly, Nancy Labanara, Sue Croce, Susi Zuse, Carol Cusano, Kathy Mitchell, and Gina Hart. The zoom call was wonderful.

Pamela Slagle and the book club, The born to Read Group, Brenda Kay, Sue Meister, Janice Spector, Karen Ennis, Anne Weimer, Ann Comeau, Marie Vitale, Laverne O'Boyle, Rachel DiGiovani, and Kathy Halligan. The evening in New Jersey was spectacular. Thank you so much for your hospitality.

Corinne Schioppo and the members of the book club Karen, Laurie, Joyce, Stacy, Diane, and Robin. Thank you for the wonderful evening and questions.

Prologue

The Fiftieth Anniversary of Paolo DeLaurentis's Death, January 23, 2054

Snow covered the ground as icicles glistened in the late afternoon sun, emitting a prism of rainbow colors. Pine trees cast dark shadows on the virgin white crystals. Inside the English Tudor house, the owners had transformed the sunken living room into a bedroom. An expansive area containing a hospital bed, TV, couch, and living space with a lounge chair allowed the guest to live his remaining days in comfort. Two brothers and their spouses sat on the sofa watching the famed novelist.

Tony's eyes opened, then closed as he contemplated his words. He addressed the two boys—men now. "My buddy, Steve—God rest his soul—and your grandfather were best friends. We had a unique bond with Paolo. I don't know why, but he trusted us. He said we were old souls." The storyteller pondered and smiled.

"And let me tell you…," his eyes fluttered open as he squinted and his tiny, withered hand pointed at the twins. "When he gave you the look, it was as if God x-rayed your being. The gift he had was beyond our comprehension…*shit*…it was beyond the world's. His unconditional love for mankind was outside our intellectual capacity. Even though your grandfather never met you, he knew you and loved you both. His ability to see and witness the future was God-given."

Tony reached for a tissue. His frail arm tremored as he dabbed the corner of his mouth.

"Paolo and Arnaud, I see the skepticism in your eyes. Be patient, you'll understand soon enough."

The author's eyelids closed as he inhaled for a moment, coughed, and, with a renewed vigor, his eyes flashed open.

"In January 2004, days before he passed, Paolo called Steve and me to his house. This was the first time I doubted your gramps's sanity. His brain wracked with cancer..." Tony's voice trailed off into a sigh. "Seems like yesterday, but so long ago, the years gnawed forward for your father and aunt. Backseat drivers tried to manipulate humanity. But your *grandfather*...let me stop before I get ahead of myself." Tony struggled to position his fragile body in the black leather reclining armchair, his feet up, a blanket covering him.

"Can I help you, Mr. D?"

"Sure, but don't think I can't kick your ass. I still got it."

Tony reached forward and touched Arnaud's face. "Life holds a promising future for you, young man. Harbor no prejudice in your heart. Honor your brother, your wife, and most of all, have compassion for your fellow man. We are a kind people. Love was the battle your grandfather fought. I believe his overwhelming, unconditional devotion to humanity killed him. How he wished humankind could see the heart, the soul of one another. Your grandfather was an architect of life who saved the earth."

Arnaud cradled Tony with one arm under his legs and the other supporting his back. With a fluid movement, he repositioned the author.

"Ouch...damn, kid. What are you trying to do—kill me?"

"I'm sorry."

"Yeah, yeah..."

"Arnaud, he's smiling. I think he punked you," Paolo said to his twin brother.

"Gotcha, kid. Now, are you gonna let me finish the story before I die?"

"Yes, Mr. D."

"I love you guys."

"We love you too," Paolo's wife said. She rose from her chair and tucked the blanket under his arms, then kissed him on the forehead. "Are you comfortable?"

"I am, thank you…Paolo, she's a keeper."

Tony reacted to the couple's gaze with a smile.

The narrative of how humanity's history changed through the actions of Paolo DeLaurentis needed to be explained. The tattered journals chronicling Paolo's visions and his mission to transform the world lay on the table by Tony's side.

"When we met your grandfather…that day…I'll *never* forget his words."

Brewster Estate, January 20, 2004

Paolo's breath was shallow as the cancer progressed to his lungs. Mornings and evenings proved increasingly difficult with each rotation of the earth. The desire to maintain life diminished with every gasp. He prayed for the day that the gripping agony would disappear. Time dwindled with each fleeting moment. *Days, maybe…*he reflected. Death loitered before taking him home.

Sydney, his soulmate, departed the house at eight to go food shopping. A necessary break to ease the pain of watching her husband wither away. Paolo's recollection of their wedding replaced the tortured thoughts of his demise. Married less than a month, the newlyweds' love never ceased. Whenever Sydney entered the room, his heart skipped a beat.

Marge, his nurse, sat nearby reading a book while Paolo adjusted the hospital bed to better see the snow-covered pine trees on the grounds of his Brewster Estate. A moment of solace. Two weeks prior to his rapid health decline, he signed over the deed of his sanctuary to his daughter, Rio. Paolo pictured his last hours, loved ones gathered by his bedside as his pain-ridden body eroded into the peaceful realm of Heaven.

Before his soul departed his temporal existence, he needed to make right the wrong he had done. Today, Paolo waited for his longtime friends Tony and Steve to arrive to help rectify the misplaced act of his playing God. Troubled by the visions that haunted him since he was a child, he believed he now had to act on the divinations. Paolo took matters into his own hands. He foresaw their last meeting, and at the conclusion of his pleas to convince Tony and Steve to correct his errors, the dreaded final heartfelt exchange of their last goodbyes to one another, concluded with, "*Until we meet again in a place where suffering no longer exists.*"

Concerned his thoughts overwhelmed his rational thinking, Paolo kept his mind focused. Alternate realities of space and time intensified his visions. He questioned the validity of the revelation he had in Ottati, unable to distinguish between prognostication and hallucination. Was his premonition a result of the brain tumor or his gift? Could he trust the predictions? What choice did he have? He decided to have faith in his buddies.

"Marge, do you have the new journal?"

"Yes, Paolo, it's here." She lifted it off the bedside table to show him. "Can I ask you a question?"

"Marge, please, have I ever said no?" Paolo propped the journals on his lap and read, saying, "I have to get it right this time."

Chapter 1

The Papal Palace, Vatican City, January 5, 2024

Giacomo rose from the table, walked to the window, threw open the sash, and took a deep breath. A blast of the chilled Italian air filled his lungs. The widower gazed upward to the gray, cloud-cluttered sky. Snow covered the grounds of Vatican City. Wisps of the white powder danced in the breeze. Saddened, he reached into his pocket and seized the small envelope. Inside was a bronze key. He fiddled with the metal object.

"What does this unlock, Dad?" he said aloud.

Perplexed, Giacomo outlined the sequence of events of the past five days. The love of his life whisked away into God's kingdom. *Who was the priest with no name?* The afternoon walks with Emily around Piazza Dante Alighieri. The sniper who killed his wife. *Was the bullet meant for me?* Then the devious mortar attack on the old city of Grosseto coupled with the death of his father-in-law, Arnaud Chambery. *Why didn't the police stop Arnaud from killing the man who murdered Emily? I should have been the one to kill my wife's murderer in the bell tower.* The incessant thoughts fueled Giacomo's anger, now set on an irreversible course of revenge that could never heal his pain.

Giacomo grappled with the vivid pictures of watching his wife's wedding band slip off her finger, clinking to the ground as she succumbed to the bullet's wrath. The memories struck horror in his heart. *What did it all mean?* Amid the chaos of the recollections, the sound of the gold ring hitting the concrete sidewalk sent chills down his spine. Etched in his soul was the realization that a murderer's hand stole Giacomo's wife and twin sons. *My family destroyed by a piece of lead—* His computer chirped, breaking his train of thought.

Still troubled by the revelatory video of the Dean Essex interrogation, he walked to the desk and advanced the footage to where the traitor had died. He watched again as confusion overtook the room as a medical team performed CPR on the turncoat. A doctor placed a sheet over the disfigured, suicidal nurse who lay dead in a pool of blood. Another physician entered the frame to call the time of death. Giacomo paused the replay and, with his finger, tapped the frozen screen.

"What the…?" He tilted forward. "What is he doing there?"

"Do you enjoy wasting the Vatican's heat?"

Giacomo jumped, startled.

"Sorry, I didn't mean—"

"It's fine, Andrew."

"How are you, my friend?" Andrew's question was rhetorical.

"How am I? Shitty. I apologize, forgive me."

Pope Andrew waved a pamphlet he held in his hand. "I've heard worse."

Giacomo closed the window. "Have a seat. I woke up this morning, and Em wasn't in bed. It is a strange sensation. My consciousness expects Emily to be there, and she isn't…my arm flails, searching an empty mattress. Two nights ago, I slept on the couch. I thought I could trick my brain."

"Did it work?"

"No. It's not like when my father died. The emptiness is surreal, the void so devastating…I want to die."

"You were husband and wife—you became one and the death was unnatural. Do you know what I mean?"

"Yeah, I do, but it doesn't help."

"This might." Andrew slid the pamphlet across the table.

He grabbed the paper. "Stages of Grief." Giacomo riffled through the pages. "I have two: anger and revenge."

"Read it."

"This is a bunch of crap."

"Let's have supper tonight?"

"Sorry, I can't. I'm taking Mom and John out for dinner. You're more than welcome to join us."

Andrew's eyebrows raised.

"Sorry, forgot who you are…security."

"What about yours? Is it safe for you to travel outside these walls?"

"Ask me if I care," Giacomo challenged.

Andrew nodded. "Let's not get carried away. I'll arrange for the Swiss Guard to handle your transportation and protection."

"Andrew, please, no. Security won't be necessary."

"Do me this favor, please? I don't feel like attending another family member's funeral."

"Fine, fine."

Andrew pointed to the wall and glanced at the plaster on the floor. "Nice hole."

Giacomo's face blushed in embarrassment. "Sorry…"

"Don't be. I did it once."

"You?"

"How many times have I told you, Giacomo? I'm just a normal man."

That evening Giacomo sat near the Christmas tree, transfixed by the sparkle of the lights. A dim lamp on the coffee table cast an eerie glow upon the room. The shadows of the night filled his heart with emptiness. A tear welled, falling down his chin as the cruelty of life gripped his soul. His hand lay on the pamphlet Andrew had given him. Through his tears he read the seven stages, acknowledging his disbelief, shock, denial, guilt, pain, anger, and depression. As he read further, his chin wobbled and his sighs grew louder. The seventh step was acceptance.

"No, no, no!" he screamed. "They can't be dead—my wife, my Emily." As his groans got louder, he cried out, "My boys, my sweet little boys. I will never accept this!" He threw the pamphlet across the room.

Chapter 2

Adinolfi walked to his office within the Grosseto military hospital. The hallway was stark and cold, and painted in a putrid green. His shoes clacked on the black asbestos tiles as he passed the records room and the entrance to the morgue, where a gurney with a deceased body lay. He reached his office at the end of the corridor and glanced at the stretcher again. A flashback of his test subjects crossed his mind. A hidden voice echoed in his head: *You will pay for what you have done.*

Father Alphonso Adinolfi was fifty-four with peppered gray hair and a matching close-cut beard. Orphaned at seven, his relatives had placed him in the care of the monks at the monastery of Monte Cassino. He entered the seminary at fifteen and was ordained as a priest twelve years later. Adinolfi enrolled in medical school and by the time he reached thirty-five, he was a licensed physician of neurology.

On his desk was a medical file containing a report on the condition of the twin baby boys. Amused by his accomplishment, he tapped the red folder just as the alarm on his watch sounded. *One hour until he had to leave for the monastery of Monte Cassino.* Located sixty-seven miles northwest of Naples, he was not looking forward to the ninety-minute drive.

Father Adinolfi's scheduled visit required him to fast forty days before the annual meeting of the leaders of his order of Imitatores Spiritum Sanctum—Followers of the Holy Spirit. The society used the

acronym FHS. Their purpose: to abide by the rule of God. His job: to
unite the secular and those members guided by the mystical voice of
the Almighty.

The schism within the FHS occurred during the turbulent 1960s,
when morals declined and God was replaced with money, greed, and
selfishness. God's gift of free will backfired. The human spirit of love,
forgiveness, and giving was replaced with pleasures of the self. An
attitude of *me first* overcame the needs of others.

The organization's religious influence waned over the years. During
this time, the secular unit purchased property and medical research
companies throughout the world. The international group was now
worth eight hundred billion dollars and included dynamic individuals
from the corporate and government sectors, including politicians from
the United States.

FHS became a prominent global conglomerate, all the while
keeping its identity hidden beneath layers of dummy corporations.
The association's membership exceeded five million people and was
governed by seventy-seven men and women entrusted to manage and
promote the organization's philosophy. These elite individuals held
various jobs within the top echelons of the world's governments and
corporations. Committed to their beliefs, they fed information to the
thirteen board members.

Although the technology and leadership of FHS had changed over
the centuries, its values remained the same: prayer, fasting, church, and
giving to the community. Founded in the ninth century, they believed
in the one true Church. In the year 1054, the Roman Catholic and the
Orthodoxy at Antioch split. The believers abhorred the schism and
vowed to reunite. The dictum still held true for the religious sect: *not
by man's mind but by the will of God.*

Father Adinolfi recalled the time he was approached by a member
of the FHS; a moment that forever changed his life and built upon his
hope of a Christian revival among the people of the world.

*   *   *

"Mass has ended, my brothers. Let us now go forth and spread the good news." The 253 monastic clerics rose and exited the church. The priest cleared the altar and entered the sacristy. He removed his vestments, unaware of the person who sat on a nearby high-backed wooden chair.

"Excuse me, Father Adinolfi?"

The unexpected voice startled him. "I'm sorry, I didn't notice you sitting there."

"Spiritus Sanctus Vobis."

"And the Holy Spirit be with you. May I help you?"

"I was wondering if we could go somewhere and talk."

"Do you need confession, Father?"

"No, no. I thought we could chat."

"Anything in particular?"

"Let's say, an idea that could expand your horizons."

"Sounds intriguing. We can talk in my office, a short walk to the infirmary. I have an hour before my first patient arrives."

They entered Adinolfi's workspace. Adinolfi walked to a small desk by an open window overlooking the grounds. An additional doorway to the left led to the examination area. "Please, Father." Adinolfi motioned for his visitor to sit in a brown leather chair.

"Thank you."

"What can I do for you?"

"Have you heard of the FHS?"

"No."

"We are an organization controlled by priests and the religious. In fact, Imitatores Spiritum Sanctum…"

"Followers of the Holy Spirit?"

"Yes, we govern ourselves by our Christian faith and a firm belief that God guides us in everything we do. Can I interest you in joining the organization?"

Adinolfi asked three questions: Do you believe in the one true Church? Do you believe in a global rule governed by the Church? And his final question: Do you believe that the Holy Spirit communicates with his favored priests? When they were answered to his satisfaction, he agreed. Seven years later, the seventy-seven governing members elected Adinolfi as chairperson of the board of directors. However, Adinolfi's twenty-year tenure eroded as the FHS pursued a secular path, a journey that gave the organization a global stronghold. Adinolfi was scrutinized and criticized for his belief that Christian principles, not the secular viewpoint, should govern the FHS. Guided by his religious fervor, Adinolfi vowed to reclaim power over the institution. The hidden voices informed him that it was the will of the Father.

* * *

A knock on Adinolfi's office door shook him from his reminiscence.

"*Pronto.*"

"We need to talk," the irritated visitor said.

Adinolfi glared at the man. "You're not supposed to be here. You violated the rules."

"What are you going to do? Kill me like you killed my son?" Sergio hissed.

"Sergio, we talked about this…we had no choice. What's the problem?"

"My cousin, Anne Fortunato."

The name caused the priest to sit back. He became more attentive. "What about her?"

"She's not happy."

"Yeah, yeah, yeah. What a complaining bitch. Tell her not to worry. We have things under control."

"Under control?"

"We have similar interests. Your cousin was more concerned with her personal vendetta, and she carried it to a detrimental extreme."

"What do you mean?"

Adinolfi, exasperated, slammed his fist on the desk and stood. He quelled the anger that surged through him. "In her quest to seek revenge, she jeopardized our operation."

"I don't understand."

"She's the one responsible for the attack at Grosseto. It was her terrorist gun-for-hire organization that killed the wife of DeLaurentis. It wasn't the FHS. We need Giacomo alive to deliver us to the remaining prophecy."

"I thought…"

"You thought wrong."

"And Rio?"

"Sergio, listen to me. You understand the implications—our church needs to survive. We're accountable and must ensure that the leaders of the nations align with the one global rule. It's dictated by God himself."

"So, we altered the minds of Paolo's daughter Rio and Eten Trivette? It makes little sense to me. Why her?"

"We are going to finance her presidency. And then America will be ours."

"Hm, well, there is another problem."

"Yeah, what now?"

"Giacomo has a copy of the interrogation."

"Care to tell me how he got the video?"

"I don't know, but he recognized you."

The priest shot a gaze of disbelief at Sergio. "He'll never see me again."

"Are you sure?"

Adinolfi said nothing.

"What about the twins?"

"They're fine."

"Where are you going to send them?"

"None of your business."

"I have a right to know."

"You have no rights. You're too close to the situation. Besides, you're better off not knowing."

Sergio left Adinolfi's office. Fueled by grief at the death of his son and wracked with guilt at his betrayal of Giacomo, he pledged to correct the wrongs he had committed.

Chapter 3

Eten Trivette swiveled his chair and gazed out over the streets of Paris. He watched a tourist boat cruise down the Seine past the historic sites dotting the horizon of the City of Lights. Eten clutched the physician's report as he searched for a hidden memory. Confused, he mumbled aloud.

"I'm sorry, Mr. President. What did you say?" asked a nurse, seated on a nearby couch. The petite, red-haired woman dressed in blue scrubs scrutinized the anguished face of her patient.

"Nothing."

*   *   *

A week earlier on New Year's Day, by happenstance, a janitor found Eten prostrate on his office floor, struggling to breathe, between his brown leather chair and the floor-to-ceiling windows overlooking Paris. He awoke in a private Parisian hospital renowned for protecting its patient's anonymity. Medical personnel performed a battery of blood tests and CT scans. Trivette studied the comparison of his previous three years of health reports. Mystified by what he read, the shocking revelation—an uncharacteristic and unrecognizable cell that did not adhere to his genome.

"How could this happen, doctor?" Eten's voice trailed as he sat up in the hospital bed. Weakened, his bodyguards offered to help. "Get away, I'm fine."

The physicians nodded to the men, and they withdrew. "To be honest, sir, you've been undergoing gene therapy."

"Gene therapy?"

"Yes. Your DNA has been, what we call, edited. Within the past decade, science has made impressive strides in using the technique to treat metabolic diseases. In reviewing your medical file, I found no reference to any illness or disease that prompted this type of treatment. I must ask this question, so please don't take offense. Are you being treated for a genetic defect?"

"No, this is nonsense. It's absurd. I'd never allow such a thing."

With a curl of his lip, the physician's face wrinkled. He touched his chin while his forefinger tapped his cheek. Eten Trivette was no longer the person created by the sexual union of his biological parents.

"Am I going to die?"

"No. We've isolated the abnormal cells not associated with your genome to determine what impact the modification will have on you."

"What do you mean?"

Hesitant, the doctor elaborated, "Your human characteristics have changed. A scientist altered your genetic code. Mr. Trivette, your thought process is no longer your own."

"Are you crazy? How is this even plausible?"

Eten's wrath took hold. His face was red with his eyes bulging, he screamed incoherent babble. The physician touched his shoulder as he glanced at the bodyguards, who gave an approving nod. A medical aide injected a dose of valium into his IV, and the body of the President of the EU surrendered, falling into a restful sleep.

*   *   *

After his discharge from the hospital, Eten visited the National Center for Scientific Research, located in Marseille, for answers. Back in his Paris office, Eten swiveled his chair and placed his elbows on the liver-shaped glass desk, watching the nurse on the couch file her fingernails. He reached forward and grabbed a document titled "DNA Editing." To understand what had occurred in his body, he made a point of studying the process.

Defiled with a virus that transported billions of proteins with genetic instructions, Trivette's mind stewed in anguish. He felt violated at the thought of a scientist tampering with his genetic material. Without thinking, he rubbed his arms, trying to rid himself of the impurities traveling through him. Nauseated and incensed, Eten threw the article across the room as he struggled to overcome the transgression.

Troubled by a recurring nightmare of a doctor opening his eyelids, he concluded the dreams were real. For the past eleven months, Trivette had been receiving anonymous phone calls, often in the early morning hours—the threatening voice of the speaker commanding him to abide by the wishes of the FHS. His broken memory ushered the conversations in and out of his waking thoughts, his actions often triggered by a word texted to him during the day. An unconscious act he could not control. The ominous voice on the other end of the line fueled his desire to track down the person responsible for altering his genome. With an imperious decree, he demanded his chief of security review all available footage from his office and home video surveillance. An unpleasant death awaited the enemy who drugged him. Eten vowed to be persistent in his quest of those who manipulated his mind.

"*Bonjour,*" Eten said, answering the phone.

"Don't be stupid enough to think you can destroy us."

The hairs on his neck rose as a rumbling fear traveled through his bones and caused him to shudder. Eten reached deep inside to rid himself of his dread. He struggled to force the words out of his mouth. "Who...?" Eten perspired. Dread swept through him as he fought to overcome an eerie sense of being both Dr. Jekyll and Mr. Hyde. He felt confused, but he resisted the thought of compliance. *Where was he? Who was he? What were the voices?*

"Are you there, Eten?"

"Yeah, sure… Who are you?" he screamed.

Eten stood and pounded his fists on the desk. He mumbled as spit erupted from his mouth.

Alarmed, the nurse rose from the couch, reached inside her bag, and pulled out a syringe. Eten's eyes were glassy, and his empty stare told her he was moments away from a catatonic state. She approached the President of the European Union and plunged the hypodermic needle into the artery in his neck. Incapacitated, he went limp. She placed her patient's head on the desk and grabbed the handset away from him.

"What happened?"

"Just like the others, doctor." She described what she observed.

"Damn it! Where are his bodyguards?"

"Outside the door."

"Alright, give him an injection of epinephrine. Get him to the hospital. I'll call our colleague. He will meet you there."

Without a pause, Adinolfi telephoned Jackson Rift, MD, PhD of Biomechanical Engineering.

Chapter 4

Brother and sister walked the hallways of the Papal Palace in silence. Muffled voices traveled through the corridors. Giacomo opened the door to a stairwell for Rio, and they descended, stopping at a window that overlooked Saint Peter's Square.

"I'm sorry, Rio."

"Why? I didn't lose a spouse. Sometimes you're such a moron."

Giacomo rolled his eyes. *Will she ever recover?*

"What did you say, Giacomo?"

He tripped over his words. "I said, I'm sorry."

"No issues, big brother, at this stage of my life…love comes and goes." She gave a weak smile.

Giacomo wrapped his arm around her.

"Why the hell are you touching me—I'm fine." His sister brushed him aside and scowled. "Essex is dead?"

"Yes."

"Screw him. You know, Giacomo…" Rio's voice wavered, "I'm not angry."

"You're not?"

"Why should I be? It's your wife and children who are deceased, not mine, you damn fool."

His sister's insensitive words pierced his heart. Giacomo's fury swelled; his hands tightened into fists. Teeth clenched, he refrained from punching the wall.

"Did I say something wrong? You appear to be upset with me."

"A little. Do you understand what you said?"

"What? Are you all right, Giacomo?"

"The question is, are you?"

"Of course, I am. I'm alive."

"Yes, you are, my little sister."

They continued their descent, exited the building into the sunshine, and walked through the Vatican gardens. Giacomo zipped up his blue jacket against the cool, crisp winter air. Rio, dressed in brown corduroys and a tan cashmere sweater, looked to the sky as she took a deep breath.

"I have dad's gift," Giacomo said.

"What do you mean?"

"I've been having visions, and the day of the funeral, a globe of white light enclosed me."

"What the hell are you talking about, Giacomo? Did the mothership take you away?" She giggled.

Whether in judgment or jest, Giacomo couldn't tell. He recognized her confusion as Rio's eyes darted left then right, followed by a rapid movement of her eyelids. "Rio, how're you feeling?" Sympathetic, he softened his voice, cognizant of her internal struggles. *What happened to my sister? Were her injuries a type of schizophrenia or another psychological illness?*

She ignored his question and said, "You mean like the one Dad told us about when he was a kid?"

"Yep." *What the hell is happening to her?*

"Did you see the light?"

"No, Andrew and a few Cardinals did."

"Wow."

"Yeah. Tell me about it..."

"How are the boys doing?"

"Rio? I don't understand. What boys are you talking about?"

"Paolo and Arnaud."

Giacomo's heart broke as a moment of grief swaddled him. "My children are dead."

"You're ridiculous, Giacomo. They're alive and well."

The fateful day of the shooting erupted in his mind. The sound of the gunfire and Emily's wedding band falling off her finger shook him to his core. His dying sons suffocating in her womb as the nourishment to their bodies ceased. Tears dangled from his chin before tumbling to the ground in slow motion—time suspended.

"Giacomo, Giacomo are you... Oh my, what have I done? What did I say?" Rio dropped to the bench, her head in her hands as she wept. "Oh, my God. I'm so sorry, I'm so sorry." She stood again, saying, "Let's go for a walk."

Giacomo bowed his head, turning left, away from his sister as the sorrow gripped his heart. He overcame the momentary loss of emotional control and allowed Rio to move ahead of him. He touched her shoulder as he chose his words. "You need to be examined by a specialist back home."

"No, I'll be fine. I'm going to Ottati to recuperate."

"Is that a good idea?"

"Damn, Giacomo, stop telling me what to do. I'll not be dictated to. I can make my own decisions." She scowled, her eyes darted, and her eyelids fluttered. Then, the tone of her voice became despondent as her head bowed. "When do you plan to return to the States?"

Dismayed, Giacomo shook his head in disbelief. *Who was this woman?* "Within two weeks, when I get the nerve to bury Em and the boys."

To avoid the dread of the impending burial of his family, Giacomo diverted his attention to the blank look on Rio's face. An argument lay on the horizon if he continued to pursue the suggestion of her returning to Connecticut. Tired of conflict, he remained quiet as thoughts of Emily engulfed his mind. His sister touched his arm.

"Do you believe we are safe now?"

"I hope. We have answers, but there are still lingering questions."

"Like what?"

"Trivette concerns me."

"The man is a bumbling fool."

"Rio, how can you say that?"

"I've spoken with him enough to understand that his chief priority is increasing his power and wealth. There is no connection to us."

Giacomo thought otherwise. The bastard stole his father's journals. He used the prophetic information they contained to capitalize on the tragedies that unfolded. Eten Trivette's shrewdness and business acumen enabled the European Union to expand its global reach. In his possession was the second journal with its words of doom and gloom. With Arnaud, his father-in-law, now dead, Giacomo didn't know how he could recover his father's writings. But Rio had been told all this. For whatever reason, she couldn't remember, and Giacomo decided not to push the issue.

"Don't start acting like Dad with all his secrets."

"I won't."

Giacomo responded without thinking, but truth be told, he was keeping information from her. What choice did he have? Rio was not herself. His family had perished at the hands of a sniper. And now the circle of friends he could trust had dwindled down to President-Elect Tom Maro, Pope Andrew, Sergio, and Jason, his second-in-command of the BOET forces—the United States Black Operations Elite Team. More than that, Jason was a confidant—a loyal, trusted friend. Giacomo relied on him to handle the minutiae of day-to-day tasks of managing the select group of personnel who, under the direct command of the president, were deployed throughout the world.

Rio interlocked her arm with his as they walked back to the papal residence. Giacomo thought about, but didn't share, his knowledge of the bronze key he had received in Grosseto or his belief that Eten Trivette was a puppet. Although a part of him wanted to isolate in his deep grief and let the dominos fall where they may, he couldn't resist his drive to uncover the answers and prevent his demise. Could

Giacomo move forward to expose those who were involved, or would he be thwarted by his own sorrow? He prayed that the light at the end of the tunnel was not a freight train.

Chapter 5

Giacomo's Apartment, Vatican City, January 14

Giacomo dreaded the journey home to America to bury his wife and sons. After the funeral Mass he isolated himself within the walls of Vatican City. Verbal communication was limited to voicemail, as he never once answered his phone. Sergio corresponded with him via email. Rio texted she had arrived in Ottati…that was the last interaction he had with her.

Grieved, the widower listened to his messages.

"Hey, Tony here. My plane will be in Rome on the fifteenth to take you home. I hope you're okay…"

"Giacomo, my staff has made arrangements for Emily and the boys to be returned to the States. Call me back, I'm concerned… It's Andrew."

Disheartened, Giacomo ignored the other messages—from President Richardson and President-Elect Thomas Maro.

Overcome with disbelief and shock at the death of his family, Giacomo's eyes strained to focus on the Christmas tree. His thoughts overrode his involuntary responses. Evergreen-infused air stirred memories of his childhood. The white lights shimmered in the darkness of his Vatican apartment. Dressed in blue jeans and a hunter-green sweater, he sat by the Yule sapling. Outside, the gardens echoed with the sounds of shovels scraping sidewalks as the maintenance personnel cleared away the snow. The noise refocused his mind on the handwritten pages before him. He shook his head in disbelief as he spoke to himself. "How is this possible?" He turned over the lined white paper and read.

Be still and not afraid. Your sacrifice was great. Fear not.

Seven people were before me. Their faces blotted out. Five were men and two were women. I can hear their voices, but not their words. One by one, they disappeared until one remained. An unseen person spoke, 'This is the one who will cause many to succumb.'

I was whisked away to a meadow, and there stood a massive tree, its branches hung over a cleared area of bright green grass. The leaves reflected the fall hues of orange and red.

By the trunk, a young boy sat, his knees pulled to his chest as he gazed out over the pasture. His twin approached him and whispered in his ear as he pointed to Giacomo. He stood, and the boys climbed the oak, perching themselves on one of the thick, strong limbs. The brothers waved to him as a familiar voice resounded, 'The Gemini will be my final warning to humankind.'

Then I flew over the earth, and as I peered down below, darkness cloaked the nations. After three global rotations, the lights of the favored countries flickered with an abrupt pulsating movement across the horizon until they appeared brighter than the stars in the sky. The fallen ones disappeared in explosive mushroom clouds that dotted the skyline. I gazed through a mist covering the kingdoms of the world. The vapor confused the people below as they squinted toward the stars, their eyes blinded.

The nemesis of man straddled the continents of the earth. Written across the heaven: 'His time approaches a time no one knows.'

Giacomo read the words again and again as he tried to decipher their meaning. Curious why the point of view changed; it was as if another person were describing the vision. He glanced at his watch, folded the paper, and placed it in his shirt pocket. Time for his evening walk. He turned the Christmas tree lights off and grabbed his jacket. As he was about to step out the door, his cell phone rang. The caller ID showed that the call originated in Paris.

"*Bonjour,*" he said.

"General DeLaurentis? Eten Trivette."

Chapter 6

The caller's introduction—*Eten Trivette*—stunned Giacomo. *What the hell?* He paced the apartment in a stupor. His mind surged with anger and hate, the internal upheaval causing his military physique to sweat.

"Hello?"

The characteristic French accent with the nasal whine made his skin crawl. Giacomo scowled and his jaw tightened as he forced himself to say, "What?"

The manner in which Eten spoke sounded strained, he struggled to find the right words. "I am sure, Giacomo." He paused. "Your distaste… for me…is unwarranted. I must tell you…you are mistaken."

"Go straight to hell, you bastard. After I'm done with you and whoever your people are, you'll wish you'd never heard my name. Rot in hell."

Outraged, Giacomo struggled to take command of his emotions. The sinister sound of the Frenchmen's twang caused him to pull a chair out from the kitchen table and sit before his body reacted to the unfathomable consequences of losing control. Then all thought stopped. Within an instant, his senses heightened, and he entered what seemed like a spiritual realm.

He stood on a gravel pathway, surrounded by brilliant colors of an inexplicable brightness. Vivid green trees covered a snow-dotted mountain range. Red, purple, and yellow flowers filled a rolling meadow to his right. The vibrant hues caused him to catch his breath. His skin tingled, and his being overflowed with an extraordinary joy. Confused about where he was, a conflict arose in his mind. The beauty disappeared. In the field lay a hospital bed. He thought he recognized the patient. Was it him? He heard a voice. 'We can never change our fate.' Dad, is that you?

The searing, nauseating intonation of Eten's voice escaping from his cell phone pulled him out of the vision.

"Hello, Giacomo? General DeLaurentis?"

"I'm here. What do you want? Better yet," Giacomo sneered, "why don't we meet someplace so I can beat the shit out of you?"

"You…you have it wrong…"

"I doubt it. My wife and my children are dead because of *you.*"

Eten's labored breathing surprised Giacomo. *Why was he speaking in fragments? Who was this man?*

"No, I am…not responsible for their…" With a fluent quickness he responded, "Yes, I wanted your father's journal, but I was not culpable in the death of your wife and children."

As Giacomo stood and walked over to the sink, the distraught widower allowed the man to continue his discourse.

Eten's disjointed speech continued. "I know it looks bad…there is more to this story…a shocking account with global implications. It's the seventy-seven…disaster will strike." Once again, he paused and then continued, "I can't talk…lines are unsecured. I'll be attending your president's inauguration. Why don't we meet in Washington…at a place of your choosing? You have my number."

The phone call ended. Giacomo didn't move, his muscles frozen. His arms held him upright on the counter as he leaned his forehead against the cabinet. The conversation had dumbfounded him. A paroxysm of hatred surged through his body as bile traveled up his throat. He wretched the burning liquid into the kitchen sink. Giacomo placed his head under the cold-water faucet, grabbed a towel, and sat at the table to contemplate revenge. Fired up with the sole purpose of bringing justice to those responsible, Giacomo called Jason, his second-in-command.

"Where's Tony's airplane?"

"Standing by for you in Rome. Tony left a message for you."

"Right, I forgot. Who are the pilots?"

"Danny and Pat. When do you want to leave?"

"Tomorrow. And, Jason? Prepare yourself for the worst."

Chapter 7

A throbbing emptiness dominated Giacomo's heart and mind. An inexplicable void, a cataclysm of sorrow and pain. Moments like thorns pricking his wounded soul replaced the recognizable passage of time. The cascade of torments and recollections imbedded within him became a permanent state of mind. Numb and disillusioned, the deaths of his wife and unborn sons engulfed him in an immense sadness.

Traumatized, Giacomo shook his head as he tried to escape the dreaded emotions. Emily plucked away from the world; here one day, gone the next. He grew bewildered. *How could this be? What meaning does my life have?* The questions never stopped bombarding him. *What could I have done to prevent the deaths? Their deaths are my fault. I failed.* He strove to push the thoughts to the back of his mind. His psyche attempted to accept the morbid fate. But it was to no avail.

Awoken in the night by the ghost of Emily's face, he lay awake for hours. Distraught, he waited for the time to pass and the pain to diminish. He prayed to a God he hoped heard his bellows. "Damn it! When will these musings vanish and when will my agony cease?" Desperate, the days struggled forward, and his life slowed to the beat of his grief-stricken heart as memories antagonized his troubled existence.

Giacomo wandered among the gravesites in this city of the dead. Out of respect, he circumvented the burial plots. The gray-and-white headstones replaced the towering buildings and homes where these people once lived and worked. *Why the need to visit the deceased? Did the visitation ease the grieving process—the closure of life?* For him, it brought back the nightmarish recollection of the horrific murder of Emily. He approached the corner of Saint Matthew and Barnabas, the ground under his feet hard from a fourteen-day cold spell.

A brown mound of sand crested above the snow-covered surface of the gravesite. Fresh tracks from the caretaker's backhoe creased the soil where Giacomo's beloved family lay. The winter sun kissed the blue sky as a jet aircraft added decorations of white contrails. A remote-controlled drone hummed in the distance, its roving eyes scanning the boneyard. Giacomo sensed the camera's lenses tracking his movements. A secret service security measure implemented by the president against his wishes. In a long, heated conversation, President Jerry Richardson left no doubt in Giacomo's mind that the commander in chief had his best interest at heart. Giacomo acquiesced to the president's wishes for twenty-four-hour security.

Twenty sorrow-filled days passed with agonizing slowness for the commanding officer of BOET. Dressed in a below-the-knee, chocolate-colored leather coat, with his hands buried deep in its pockets, Giacomo's appearance was deceptive. The long brown hair and well-trimmed beard were uncharacteristic of a general in the US Army. Back in Connecticut less than a week, he avoided his home and the haunting memories. He opted to stay at the Omni Hotel in downtown New Haven. Dazed, Giacomo recalled the words his father had written: *There will be hard choices and sacrifices which you will have to make and endure.*

Giacomo heard footsteps crunching the ground behind him.

"You been here long?"

Lisa's whisper trailed in the winter air. The melody of her tone struck his heart with a memory from his younger days. He smiled; it was a good remembrance.

Giacomo didn't move. He continued to stare straight ahead. "No."

"It's cold today."

"What brings you here?" The frigid air crystallized from his mouth as he spoke.

"Came to visit Mom." United States Senator Lisa Hill was the daughter of the late Sydney Hill, Giacomo's father's second wife.

"Sorry I wasn't here for her funeral." His stance remained stoic.

"I understand. Giacomo, you can turn around, I'm not gonna bite."

"I just want to be alone."

"If you need anything, please call me. It was good to see you, Giacomo…be safe, see you."

"Yep, tell your hubby I said hello."

"I will." Lisa's husband, a physician with a PhD, was the world's leading researcher on bio-fabrication.

The sound of a car door opening, then closing, broke the eerie silence. It came from a black SUV parked at the corner of Saint Marks. The sunlight silhouetted the person in the back passenger seat. Giacomo bowed his head in acknowledgment of the passenger's wave as the government vehicle crossed his line of vision, driving the curved roads to the cemetery's exit

He kneeled, patting the hard, brown burial dirt. "I love you, Em." He stood; another car door opened, followed by another. Giacomo walked the ten steps, his eyes welling with tears.

"To the hotel?"

"No." Hungry, he read the time on his cell phone. "Take me to Katz's. We'll have lunch."

"Yes, sir."

"Please, Sam, my name is Giacomo."

"Yes, General."

Chapter 8

Katz's Deli, Woodbridge, Connecticut, January 19

The ride from Saint Lawrence Cemetery to Woodbridge took less than fifteen minutes. Traffic wasn't as congested as it was when he was a young boy and fuel prices were reasonable. The man smiled at the considerable number of cars as they pulled into the parking lot of his father's friend's restaurant.

"Giacomo, over here."

The eatery had evolved over the years. Steve had franchised his business to over fifty establishments, spanning the Eastern Seaboard from Washington, DC to Massachusetts. For Giacomo, it was the place where his dad, Paolo, met his cronies every Tuesday afternoon. Today, Steve, Warren, Tony, Wayne, and his son Blake were all seated at a table in the eatery's corner. Other than Blake, the men were now in their late fifties to mid-sixties. Giacomo walked over to the welcoming friends. The five men hugged and offered their condolences.

"Sit," Warren said.

"Thanks."

Steve waved over a server. "What do you want to eat, Giacomo?"

"I'll have a pastrami on rye with a Pepsi, please."

"It's good to see you, my friend. When did you return?"

"Three days ago."

"You're always in my prayers."

"Much appreciated, Wayne."

"We missed you at the pig roast."

The annual event occurred on the Sunday before Labor Day. In its heyday, over six hundred people attended the festive affair. The amount of food and love the occasion generated had astounded Giacomo's father Paolo. The event was more than a get-together—it was a joining of souls, an openness to share, to love, and to enjoy one another's company. Giacomo relished the barbeque and attended whenever he could. As the years progressed—and now, with a weakened economy— the pig roast was held for relatives and close friends.

"I wish I could've been there. Emily and I were in France to celebrate her father's birthday." Giacomo paused for a moment. "I promise I'll be there next year."

"How's Rio?"

"She is doing okay, Warren. She has a long road ahead of her. Rio's a fighter, she'll recover."

"That she is," Tony replied.

"We read the news about her home being robbed."

"Yeah. They made a freakin' mess. I have to go clean the place."

"If you need help, call me."

"Thanks, Blake."

"He must be here for you," Steve pointed.

Giacomo's driver approached the table with a phone in hand.

"General, the White House is on the line."

"Thank you, Sam."

"Hello. Good afternoon, Jerry."

Warren elbowed Wayne in the arm. "Jerry? He calls the president Jerry—*shit*."

Giacomo smiled. The four men rose and saluted.

"Sorry, sir. I'm having lunch with friends, and they thought it amusing that I referred to you by your first name… Yeah, sure, I'll see you then." He handed Sam the phone and, as his duty officer, the army sergeant exited the restaurant and stood guard by the door.

"My apologies, guys."

"No problem, Mr. Big Shot I-Know-the-President. *Damn*, what is this world coming to?"

"Funny, Blake."

"Excuse me," the server said, as he placed food in front of Giacomo.

"Did you catch the son of a bitch who killed Emily?"

"Not yet, but I will. I won't stop until I do."

"Giacomo, if you need any help in tracking those bastards, I'm available."

"Thanks." He hesitated. "Be careful what you ask for, Warren. To answer your question, the investigation is ongoing."

Warren was an old friend of his dad's. A solid, muscular man who stood six feet, three inches tall and weighed two hundred pounds. Even at sixty, he was hard as nails. Giacomo's father, Paolo, often told him tales of Warren's exploits and his generosity to anyone who asked for his help. A trusted ally, his dad said, a person you can depend on.

The men nodded their heads in understanding. Blake, a spoon in his hand, leaned forward and scooped Katz's homemade chicken soup. His eyes darted upward. "Oh boy, you got a problem now, Giacomo."

Giacomo didn't have time to react. The firm grasp of his friend's hands on his shoulders caused him to smile and say, "Frankeee!"

Giacomo and Frank graduated from West Point together and served side by side in Delta Force, the army's elite combat applications group. After six years, Frank opted out, to pursue his lifetime passion for music. During the last decade, he toured the world playing his saxophone. The two friends often tried to meet, but their schedules never matched up. Aside from a brief conversation the evening before, they hadn't spoken since last September.

Giacomo stood. Frank was three inches taller than Giacomo, bald, and had a goatee. He was broad shouldered, with arms so muscular he could crack a walnut between his biceps and forearm. A handsome man, he'd been married to his long-time love, Mary Beth, or MB, for the past twenty years. The old friends hugged. There was nothing left to say; they had cried the night before.

Steve summoned a server to bring another chair. "Sit down, Frank. Do you want something to eat?"

"No, a glass of water with lemon, please." He shook the hands of everyone around the table. The musician had attended high school with Blake and knew his family well.

"Congrats on your Grammy nomination."

"Thanks, Warren. It surprised me when I received the call. I didn't expect it."

"It's a wonderful tune. Maybe a potential Oscar," Tony chimed in.

Steve smirked at his friend.

"What? Okay, okay, forgive me…I'm a little prejudiced."

Hollywood adapted one of Tony's books for the movies, and the music director for the film was an associate of Frank's. The two collaborated on the theme song, which became an international hit. His saxophone interpretation of the love story captured people's hearts around the world.

As the men ate their food, they joked and bantered. Giacomo tried to join in, but the ache in his heart overcame him. He slid his chair back.

"What do I owe you, Steve?"

The restaurateur shook his head in disbelief. "Nothing."

"Giacomo, we're playing poker tonight. Why don't you come over?"

"Thanks for the offer, Blake. I have to be in DC tomorrow morning. Frankeee, I'll talk to you later." He patted his friend's shoulder.

As Giacomo walked out the door, he looked back at his friends conversing among themselves. His last glimpse was of Tony handing envelopes to Frank and Warren.

Chapter 9

*T*he air is icy—snowflakes float to the ground. Tens of thousands of people are gathered. The Capitol stands in the foreground— soon-to-be President Tom Maro and the outgoing President Richardson flash Giacomo a smile. Fighter jets fly overhead in formation, their afterburners glowing bright. A commotion ensues...

Giacomo awoke in a sweat. He jumped out of the king-sized bed and struggled to catch his breath. Anxiety cloaked his entire being, the unsettling sensation trapped in his body. Unable to escape the tortuous emotion, Giacomo scrambled toward the bathroom. Leaving the door open, he entered the shower and turned the faucet on. Still dressed in his briefs, the cold water cascaded onto his head and down his back, shocking his senses. He tried to break free from the suffocating insanity. His heart raced as the walls of darkness closed in on him. His vision became tunneled.

Giacomo hurried to step out of the tub and slipped on the wet tile floor. He caught himself by grabbing hold of the sink. Back in the bedroom, he sucked in deep gasps of air as he fumbled to locate his clothes. In a panic, he tossed clothing out of the closet and clutched a pair of jeans and a shirt in confusion. He rushed to dress—to be free of his smothering fear—anxiously placing sockless, dampened feet into shoes and scrambling out of the suite. Could he shake what had overtaken him?

Giacomo ran past the receptionist in the lobby, barely hearing the words, "Are you okay, sir?"

Once outside in the frigid New Haven, Connecticut night, the claustrophobia vanished. He stood in the darkness on Temple Street in front of the hotel. The streetlights illuminated the empty road. A breeze swayed the blinking red stoplight at the corner of Chapel. Stars shimmered in the black sky; the Milky Way lay on the horizon, too low to view.

"General DeLaurentis?" A soldier spoke from the shadows behind the concrete pillar near the entrance to the parking garage.

Giacomo turned as two members of BOET scrambled out of the blackness, their guns drawn.

"Stand down, gentlemen, I'm fine. A minor panic attack, that's all. Nothing to worry about. I'm going for a walk."

One man spoke into a microphone on his wrist. Within seconds, a black SUV arrived in front of the hotel and shadowed the three men as they walked down the sidewalk toward Chapel Street.

Giacomo's heart ached. Tired and distraught, his purpose in life seemed to have disappeared. The winter breeze had no consequence for him as he ambled in the predawn chill. His mind replayed the events of the last fourteen days. His wife and children nestled in the cold-soaked ground. "Damn it, why didn't you take me? I should have died, not my family. This is a dream. It can't be real," he muttered. He lowered his head in despair. *What significance does my life have now?* How he wished he could change his past.

He remembered what Emily had once said: *I don't want you to be a picture on the mantel. A memory faded away by time.* Now her photo stood on his bedside table. He vowed never to allow her memory to fade. In his mind, he knew his wife and his sons were in another place, a different world perhaps—soon he'd be with them. For Giacomo, it couldn't happen soon enough.

Chapter 10

January 20

Giacomo crossed the street with his hands tucked in his jean pockets. A police car's siren refocused his mind to the impending meeting with Eten Trivette. He stopped in front of the New Haven library. The SUV pulled up beside the curb on the corner of Elm and Whitney. The click of the flashing yellow stoplight caused Giacomo to turn. A bodyguard opened the passenger door. Giacomo entered the warm vehicle.

"To the hotel, sir?"

"Yes, have the men standby. Time for me to move back home."

"Yes, sir."

The soldiers hopped into the Jeep. The front-seat passenger called ahead to the security team who guarded Giacomo's house.

*   *   *

Two hours later, as the sun rose over the city of New Haven, General Giacomo DeLaurentis packed his bags. The Presidential Inauguration was the following day. To his dismay, a military aircraft waited to take him to Washington National Airport. Although he was humbled to be an honored houseguest of outgoing President Jerry Richardson and President-Elect Thomas Maro, Giacomo dreaded the forthcoming dinner conversation at the White House residence that evening. The topic? His disturbing vision of an assassination attempt on Tom Maro. *Can I prevent the tragedy?*

His heart remained empty. Giacomo had witnessed his fair share of death: friends lost in combat, his father dying of cancer. But this—the heartbreaking loss of his wife and children—the pain never ceased. A knock on the bedroom door startled him. He closed his suitcase and removed it from the bed he and his spouse had shared four months earlier. Now, the house sat vacant, except for the BOET security team that slept in the six spare bedrooms.

"Enter."

In the doorway stood a five-foot, seven-inch, square-jawed, broad-shouldered Army corporal. "General, sir." He saluted. "Your car is ready. May I take your suitcase?"

"Yes, thank you, Corporal."

"Sir, if I may, I was sorry to hear about your family…I know what it's like. My wife and I lost our nine-month-old son last year."

"I'm sorry to hear that. A parent shouldn't have to bury a child. Was your son ill?"

"No, sir. My wife was carjacked, and the bastard drove off with my son in the backseat. A police chase ensued, and the car crashed."

Giacomo watched the man's eyes as they grew sadder. "I hope they caught the bastard."

"They did. The trial was two months ago. They sentenced him to life."

"That's good news. You must've been relieved?"

"I wish I was. At first I wanted him dead, then I realized I was wrong. A friend of mine told me I should forgive him…I couldn't do that. My marriage fell apart, my life was a mess. Then, prior to the sentencing, my wife and I stood before the judge. The fury within us was ready to explode at this barbaric son of a bitch. My wife looked at me. The anger in her eyes disappeared, replaced with a somberness. As she wept, she looked at the defendant and forgave him. I did the same. A peace fell over us that day that allowed us to repair our marriage and move forward with our lives. We found out today that my wife is pregnant."

Giacomo was at a loss for words.

The corporal pointed to the suitcase. "May I, sir?"

Oblivious, Giacomo recalled his conversation with Eten Trivette six days earlier. *"You have my number."* The phrase echoed in his mind. An earworm, the repetitive recall of a song, but instead of lyrics it was, *"You have my number."* His planned meeting with Eten was hours away and the thought of revenge hung in the air. "I can't forgive you, you bastard."

"I'm sorry, sir, what did you say?"

"I said, 'I can't…'" Giacomo registered the soldier's puzzled expression. "I'm sorry, you're a better man than I am. I want my family's murderer dead."

Giacomo noticed the sadness in his subordinate's eyes. "Thank you, Corporal. I will take your words under consideration. Here's my suitcase. I'll be down in five."

"Yes, sir. I'm sorry if I caused you any pain."

"No issues. I'll see you downstairs."

The young man saluted and exited the room. Giacomo sat on the couch in the corner by the windows, shaken by what he heard. *How can I forgive the people who murdered my family? It's impossible. All I want is Emily and my boys. Soon I will be with them, if not by my choice…*

Chapter 11

Giacomo boarded the antiquated United States military Gulfstream Five. The captain of the aircraft stood at the top of the stairs and saluted. Giacomo returned the gesture and handed his firearm to the pilot, who placed it in a locked box. He turned left and isolated himself from his security team in the back of the corporate plane. An F-22 Rapture orbiting the skies of Connecticut was on the ready to escort them to Washington National.

The flight attendant approached. "Sir, can I offer you a drink?"

"Pepsi and a copy of *The New York Times*?"

"Yes, sir."

Giacomo opened the newspaper to the op-ed section. His attention drifted to an editorial about bio-fabrication, written by Doctors Paige Leavitt and Jackson Rift. The latter name gave him pause. Rift, a physician with a PhD in biomechanical engineering, was married to Lisa Hill. Giacomo pushed the not-unpleasant recollection of the sound of her voice at the cemetery out of his mind as he read the editorial.

"Reading anything interesting?"

Interrupted halfway through the essay on repairing human body parts via DNA editing and cell regeneration, he folded the newspaper and smiled at his old friend. "Jason, glad you could make it."

"What's with all the secrecy? You have me drive to Connecticut and then I have to stay in the most uncomfortable jump—"

"Oh, stop complaining. It's because what I need to tell you I can't say to anyone else." He motioned for his number two man to sit opposite him.

Colonel Jason Vandercliff's right eyebrow rose. "I'm listening."

Giacomo opened the table stowed to his left. He placed a yellow notepad on the makeshift desk and wrote. They huddled in quiet conversation, their words a spoken acknowledgement of what each had written on the pad. With a ding, the seatbelt sign illuminated as the Gulfstream started its final approach.

Twenty minutes later, the airplane arrived at the executive terminal. The air-stair door lowered, causing a cold winter draft to sweep through the cabin.

Jason exited first and descended the stairs, where two BOET members greeted him. The three stood guard, waiting for Giacomo. Nearby, the line crew marshaled another aircraft as it taxied and stopped to the right of the government Gulfstream.

The flight attendant gave Giacomo his brown leather coat. "Your firearm is in the right pocket, sir."

Giacomo nodded his head. "Thank you. Right on time, 11:56," Giacomo said, as he glanced at the TAG Heuer on his wrist. He stepped down onto the tarmac, and the men saluted their long-haired commander. Jason pivoted toward the other plane coming to a stop.

Giacomo stared at the overcast sky. The light of the sun peeked through the clouds. His diamond-stud earring sparkled in the daylight. A breeze caused his coattails to flutter as his hair flowed with the wind. He placed his hands in the leather pockets and closed the garment. His right hand touched the nine-millimeter Beretta.

Chapter 12

"Giacomo, the door is opening."

The United States Gulfstream 5 shielded Giacomo as the stairs of the Dassault Falcon Ten X kissed the ground with a light thump. A diplomatic limousine with French flags attached to its front bumpers stopped short of the corporate jet.

"Let me know, Jason, when it's safe to meet the bastard." His finger rested on the trigger.

He watched his men walk to the Frenchman's plane. Four immense bodyguards hustled down the stairs. Two more of equal-sized proportion stood at the doorway of the cabin.

"We might have a problem. We're outnumbered."

"Don't worry about it," Giacomo quipped.

Eten Trivette descended and paused halfway down the steps as the American military men walked toward the plane.

Jason nudged Giacomo. "He stopped. I think he's spooked by our guys."

"Trivette's too arrogant to be frightened. My guess…he's disappointed the president is not here to greet him. Not gonna happen today."

"My friend, don't do anything stupid," Jason replied.

"Yeah, yeah, yeah…are we ready?"

"He's on the ramp."

"Our men?"

"Looks like they're making introductions."

"Guards?"

"Total of four, two with our group. The others are standing behind Eten. The limo doors will open as discussed. You enter one side; he enters the other; I'll be in front."

A nearby helicopter started its engines. The high-pitched whirl and the *wop, wop* of the blades sliced through the air. Giacomo rounded the nose of the Gulfstream and faced Eten's aircraft as the chopper became airborne. The rotorcraft pitched forward and began its flight into the restricted airspace. Giacomo stared at the flying vehicle. He had an uneasy feeling. *Why is the helicopter door open?*

"Jason!" Giacomo screamed over the noise as he drew his Beretta. He took aim at the whirlybird as it rotated on its axis and swept over the Ten X.

An assassin with an automatic weapon tethered to the helicopter hung outside the door and opened fire. Three of Eten's bodyguards tumbled to the ground, their torsos shredded by the fifty-caliber rounds. Eten's blood painted the tarmac. The two BOET men and the remaining French security guard dragged Eten under the Falcon.

"Son of a bitch…son of a bitch!" Giacomo yelled.

He fired the last round, dropped his gun, and rolled on the cement to avoid the projectiles exploding around him. The concrete erupted as ammunition from the tools of death sliced through the earth. Debris from the onslaught struck Giacomo's left eye. Adrenaline flowing through his body, his mind sharp, senses awake, he didn't feel the pain. He used one of the dead bodyguards as a shield and grabbed the Uzi that lay beside the lifeless man.

The helicopter lunged to the right, rotating on its axis. Their target— Eten Trivette—hung on to life. The fifty-caliber ammunition continued to pepper the side of the plane. Empty shells cascaded to the asphalt in the unceasing attack. Giacomo stood and, with a sweeping arc of his arm, fired the Uzi. The bullets tore through the undercarriage of the chopper, striking the assailant dead. As the pilot maneuvered the damaged copter northbound, a ground-to-air missile launched from the White House destroyed the aircraft as it reached an altitude of eight hundred feet.

Chapter 13

The Abbey at Monte Cassino, Italy, January 20, 7 P.M.

Father Adinolfi ended the phone call without bothering to respond. The news of Eten Trivette's death allowed him to relax. He reached forward and grabbed a report written by Dr. Jackson Rift—Adinolfi was fascinated that he had contributed to Rift's discovery of the God genome, even though the testing was pushing the moral boundaries of genetic exploration.

> *We now can repair any major organ in the body using our regenerative tissue process. Our company is at the forefront of the medical technology industry, furnishing the world with biomechanical-engineered, 3D-printed human organs for study and transplantation. Our scientists have conquered the fifth complexity, the true regeneration of nerve, glial, and neuron cells.*
>
> *The techniques have garnered immense success in the restoration of nerves in spinal cords. Preliminary results from our studies have been astounding. Of the 150 quadriplegic animals treated, 98 percent regained full functional capacity within the two-week treatment schedule. At present, we are interviewing subjects from the United States Department of Defense for upcoming human trials. Using the CRISPR tool to splice and edit DNA to alter the human genome has surpassed our expectations.*

Adinolfi closed the folder. He reached for a brown leather sheath. Inside the case was, an ancient papyrus, dated 33 AD. The priest pondered the inscription with the hope the words would change the way humanity viewed Christianity. He smiled and translated the scripture aloud to himself, "The last hour for humankind has arrived."

Adinolfi imagined the secular board members' faces as they read the fraudulent text: the handwritten note of the Christ. He questioned whether the two-year painstaking procedure of manufacturing a relic would convince the inquisitors. A lie for the sake of a greater truth, that God was using him to propagate the faith for the one global rule—heaven on earth. The parchment paper established God's kingdom on earth, even if the words were scribed a week ago.

Dressed in a monk's brown tunic, Adinolfi walked to the far corner of his cell. A simple tapestry of a dove with the phrase *Spiritus Sanctus* embossed underneath the symbolic bird hung on the wall. He slid the needlepoint to the right, revealing a white stone block with red splotches. Carved on either side were two rectangular holes. He inserted both hands in the gaps, and with a grimace, removed the thirty-pound slab. A spasm in his lower back caused him to wince as he positioned the mass on the floor.

Inside the centuries-old hiding spot, a safe with an illuminated display flashed red and orange. The lights flickered as his fingers glided over the keypad, pushing a sequence of numbered buttons. The vault's door swung open. He moved aside Paolo DeLaurentis's first journal and the copy of his second. Adinolfi placed the fraudulent prophecy next to them. He paused for a moment before withdrawing a similar, eleven-by-fourteen-inch leather sheath from the secured box.

Within the cover, a pair of plastic sheets protected the parchment. He read aloud a portion of the torn, incomplete document. *"From the family of Laurentis a sign will emerge, paving a path for the Savior's return."*

There were three deciphered, handwritten Hebrew-to-Latin copies in existence. Adinolfi had two, while Paolo DeLaurentis kept one. He shuddered at the thought. *Did he have it translated?* Of greater importance, *where did he hide it?* A fury built within Adinolfi as he rationalized the decisions he had made over the last six months.

How could God use someone like Paolo? Why him and not the Church? He and his family must be the devil's lie. We are the loyal followers of the Holy Spirit. We are the gatekeepers of His word. Over 500 years of obedience...betrayed by our Father in Heaven? Never.

Adinolfi held the untorn copy. *How could this be true?* Even though he couldn't answer the question, in his subconscious, he knew it to be a fact. *For wasn't that like God to use a pagan rather than His ordained priests to reveal His kingdom?* He winced at the consequences; the Church's existence shattered if Giacomo and Rio released the third copy of the letter.

A monk, trying to stop the Great Schism of 1510, had stolen the original and copies of the Hebrew text. In the day's twilight, the locals found his punctured body cast across the steps of San Lorenzo Church in Grosseto, Italy, confronted and murdered for his sin and disobedience against the rule of the Order. The assassins recovered two of the documents from the dead cleric's body.

Believing he was being led by the spirit of God, the holy man gave the original copy to an Austrian nun before he died. The prophecy, passed down over the next two centuries, found its resting place in the hands of the DeLaurentis family.

With care, Adinolfi returned the document to the concealed vault, double-checking that the safe remained secured. He walked across the room and opened the shuttered window. The Liri Valley spread out below, with the Lepini Mountains off to his right. He took a deep breath as the lights of the village of Cassino twinkled in the twilight sky. When he awoke in the morning to the rising sun, the town would be enveloped in a winter fog. He touched the hallowed wall as the history of the Abbey whisked through his mind.

Chapter 14

The Abbey of Monte Cassino sat atop a seventeen-hundred-foot mountain located eighty miles southeast of Rome. Benedict of Nursia established the religious site in the year 529. It was upon this hilltop among the cedars where he penned the rule of the Benedictine Order, a way of life for his brother monks. Within the structure lay the ultimate resting place of the saint—the original location known as the pagan temple of Apollo, the God of prophecy and oracles.

Plagued by destruction throughout the centuries, the religious house became a staple of monastic life. The Catholic monastery provided a respite for the devout. Then, on February 15, 1944, obliteration befell the site once again. The battle of Monte Cassino—one of the bloodiest of World War II—ushered in its near-complete annihilation.

*   *   *

Fall 1943, Three Months after the Allied Invasion of Sicily

"Francesco, *vieni qui, vieni qui*—come here, come here!"

The fourteen-year-old boy ran toward Father Pasquale. The cleric stood by a German Army transport truck in the town center of Cassino. Francesco Tortolano was thin, five feet, six inches tall, dressed in brown trousers and a white T-shirt. A piece of rope that held tight to the youngster's waist replaced his belt. His shoes were black hand-medowns from his older brother Gerardo, who, against his will, served in the Italian military.

"Yes, Father Pasquale."

"How many boys in the village can you gather?"

The teenager counted his fingers, "Six of us."

"Good."

"Why?"

"Go do as I say, and hurry."

"Yes, Father."

"Francesco, let them know they will spend a couple of days at the monastery."

"Yes, Father."

Operation Avalanche, the Allied incursion of the western Italian coast near Salerno, concerned the German High Command. Orders to establish a stronghold at the base of Monte Cassino fell upon Lieutenant Colonel Julius Schlegel, a Roman Catholic, and Captain Maximilian Becker, a surgeon, and a Protestant before the war.

The stance was part of the bigger defensive Gustav Line, a one-hundred-mile stretch from the east coast to the west shores of Italy. For the Germans, the mountain provided a strategic location. Panoramic hilltop views of Highway 6 and the Liri and Rapidio Valleys gave them the perfect perspective from which to stop an approaching attack. Schlegel and Becker convinced their superiors not to commandeer the monastery. The officers instructed their troops to dig into the rugged terrain below and wait.

Twenty German transport trucks drove the winding road from Cassino to the abbey perched on the mount. Black smoke spewed from the exhaust pipes as the older vehicles struggled along the route.

Francesco accompanied his friends and the men from the town who could not join the Italian military. They sat opposite one another, bunched in the back of an army troop carrier. The driver downshifted and grinded the gears of the engine as it climbed the steep incline.

An older worker inquired, "Pasquale, can you tell us more?"

"The abbot told me Colonel Schlegel convinced the German High Command to move the monastery's libraries and paintings to the Vatican."

"Will we get paid?" Francesco asked.

"Food and twenty cigs per day."

"Cigarettes!" He and his friends repeated at once. The five teenagers gawked at each other. They knew they could sell them on the black market.

The truck hit a hole in the road. Augusto, one of the younger boys, bounced off his seat and almost fell out of the vehicle. Mr. Figliolini saved him from certain death by grabbing the back of his pants and pulling him back into the moving van.

"Thanks, Mr. Fig."

Francesco patted his friend on the head, thankful he didn't die. The man thought nothing of it and remained silent as he continued to smoke his cigarette. Rumor around the village was he served as a member of the underground. One thing was certain…you didn't mess with him. They reached the abbey twenty minutes later.

*   *   *

The transportation of the enormous volume of books, codices, ancient texts, and Italian paintings took three weeks to accomplish. The German Army provided 217 trucks with security to ensure the artifacts' safe travel to the Vatican. Included in the shipment was a detailed memoir, a record of global conflicts financed by the FHS.

Francesco and his friends stockpiled over a thousand cigarettes. The money they received on the black market offered little solace for what was to come. Word filtered from the Germans to the sparse populace that the war, perhaps within days, would encroach on the village's doorstep. The monks were safe in Rome, while refugees from the town and one priest occupied the site of Monte Cassino.

Chapter 15

Francesco walked the empty corridors of the abbey amid the 230 refugees housed in the monastery. As the fear of an allied bombing increased, the population of the village of Cassino dwindled. Three days earlier, his parents and sister fled to Rome, where the threat of an attack was far less. The teenager persuaded his father to allow him to stay to protect their ancestral home.

With a stick in hand, he scraped the walls of the stucco structure. He turned right and climbed the staircase to the abbey's top floor. Francesco entered the unexplored hallway lined with doors. Voices echoed from the far end. Scared that they were German soldiers, the young man hurried to hide in one of the rooms. As he peeked down the corridor, he observed two familiar men walk into a monk's cell. The fifteen-year-old's curiosity propelled him forward. Loud, muffled voices escaped the room. He peered inside through a crack between the door and the frame. Mr. Figliolini and Father Pasquale stood in one corner. A stone block rested on the tile floor.

"Listen, the Allies will bomb the site within days. We have to move this to a safer location." He handed the priest a brown leather pouch.

"I can take it to Rome and store it with the others."

"No. We must ensure this remains a secret. We are the safekeepers of the document."

As the boy tried to overhear the conversation, he leaned forward and fell into the room. Figliolini rushed over, grabbed him, and threw him against the door.

"What are you doing here, kid?"

"Leave him alone, Fig."

At that moment, the destruction began. Overhead, the roar of 142 B-17 Flying Fortress bomber aircraft blocked out the sun of the crisp, blue winter day. The incessant, fear-provoking whistles falling from the sky followed by the explosive rattling thunder caused Father Pasquale to pee his pants in terror. The screeching of bombs produced panic among Monte Cassino's inhabitants, the tools of death forewarning their impending demise. As the structure shook, the curdling screams of those about to die echoed in the hallways.

A block of masonry landed on Figliolini's head. Francesco fell to the floor. One after another, after another—*boom, boom, boom.* The Allied air raid pelted the building. Black-and-gray smoke rose from the monastery as walls collapsed. The noise was deafening. Father Pasquale and the boy attempted to stand, but every detonation kept them from rising. The interior wall tumbled and crushed Fig. His blood sprayed the room. An unnerving silence ensued as the whistling threats stopped. Dazed, the priest stood and placed the leather case back in the hole. He struggled to lift the thirty-pound slab of stone.

"Father, we have to leave," Francesco cried out. His ears bleeding from the concussion of the bombs, he couldn't hear the clergyman yell at him. The priest's lips moved, and his hand gestures signaled for the teenager to join him.

"Help me with this," he screamed.

The cleric leaned over to hoist the stone. Francesco came to his aid, and together they placed the blood-splattered block in the hole, covering the rawhide pouch. Without warning, the hideous shrill of devastation traveled through the air. The cascade of destruction rattled the building. The floor split open, revealing the rubble caused by the instruments of murder and mayhem. Francesco and Father Pasquale, unable to stand, fell into the chasm, their faces frozen in fright as they perished in the debris. Cries from the 230 injured inhabitants trailed off to moans, followed by the eerie silence of death.

The abbey lay in ruins. Wisps of black smoke spiraled upward, dispersing the smell of the charred remains. Amid the wreckage, the corner of the priory where Father Pasquale and Francesco died stood intact. The secret writings remained unscathed by the havoc caused by man.

On that fateful day, over a four-hour period, the Allies dropped 1,150 tons of explosives and incendiary devices. The battle of Monte Cassino became one of the bloodiest battles of World War II. The FHS funded the reconstruction of the religious house during the last days of the war and used the monastic community as its cloak of invisibility.

*   *   *

"Father Adinolfi, excuse me, Father? Evening vespers in ten minutes." The knock on the door continued.

"Yes, yes, I'm coming." He covered the hole with the stone that still showed traces of blood spatter. A remnant of the bombing of World War II. Adinolfi shielded the block with the tapestry. He murmured, "The secular has no choice but to believe this is the truth. We will regain control. Soon the Kingdom of God will be here on earth." Monte Cassino was to become the priest's permanent home. His plan...fast on bread and water for forty days. Then wait for the voices in his mind to erupt, exposing the plan of the Father in Heaven. Guided by the taunts of the unseen, Adinolfi's conviction that he was the Chosen was clear and indisputable. He prayed that after the events of tomorrow, January 21, a new era of God's reign would begin. Adinolfi sat atop the mountain on high, the resting place of Saint Benedict, and reveled in the thoughts of destroying those who wished to betray the society's mission.

Chapter 16

Washington, DC, January 20, 4 P.M.

Giacomo reclined on the gurney as the doctor secured his new eye patch. Colonel Jason Vandercliff stood outside the pulled curtain.

"You'll be fine, Giacomo. Wear this for five days. You're a lucky man. It could've been worse."

"Yeah, thanks," Giacomo's voice was sarcastic.

"Have a great day."

"Sure."

The doctor turned and slid the drapery open.

"I love the pirate look."

"Funny, Jason." Giacomo fiddled with the eye covering. "Where's Trivette?"

"Dead."

"Well, at least it wasn't from my hand."

"You wanted to kill him?"

"Maybe."

"Not good."

"Ask me if I care?" Giacomo's voice had a sharp edge.

"You never carry. Why do you have a gun in your jacket?"

Giacomo caught Jason's gaze.

"Don't worry, I wasn't going to kill him."

"Sure, you weren't."

"I wasn't." Giacomo jumped off the examining table.

"I believe you."

"Is the car here?"

"Yes and no."

"Excuse me?"

"The President sent a protective detail to bring you to the White House."

"Our guys?"

"Yes, I will tag along."

"Where are they?"

"Positioned outside the ER doors. They'll escort us through the basement service areas."

"Why?"

"News media is waiting for you."

Giacomo nodded his head as he buttoned his blue oxford shirt and placed the diamond earring in his ear. "I wasn't going to kill him. I wanted to, but I couldn't."

"I know, my friend."

*   *   *

Giacomo and Jason sat in the back of a black SUV, the two BOET members up front. A similar vehicle with soldiers from the unit traveled behind them. They traversed the streets of the nation's capital on the way to the White House. Giacomo's reflection bounced off the darkened window as he stared into the distance, his mind numb.

I wanted to kill him. I wanted to watch him squirm as he fought for his life, the bastard. My children are dead because of him. I hope he's rotting in hell. Giacomo shook the thought from his mind. *We must forgive and love—my ass.* Again, he battled his sentiments of outrage and hatred. He clenched his fist and gnashed his teeth. *Rot in hell. You should all rot in hell.* His breath became labored; a tingling sensation started in his scalp and went down his arms. Anxious, his mouth was dry.

"General, are you all right?" The driver glanced at his commander in the rearview mirror.

Giacomo gasped as he pointed and spoke. "Stop the car."

The passenger door flew open before the vehicle came to a halt. Giacomo jumped into the road. Bowed at the waist, he grabbed his knees, taking large, gulping breaths as the anxiety and panic traveled through his body. Horns and screeching wheels rang in his ears while cars maneuvered to avoid him. A second and third secret service SUV pulled up to shield him from the traffic.

Jason exited the car from the opposite side. "Giacomo, are you okay?"

"Yes, damn it, I need a minute or two. Let me catch my damn breath," he squeaked out the words.

"Giacomo, Giacomo…" a female voice said.

The sound of high-heeled shoes clacked along the pavement. More cars came to a halt.

The agents from the second vehicle drew their guns. "Hold right there and don't move any closer—United States Secret Service."

The driver's door of the third SUV swung open. "We're good here, Bob," the man yelled.

Chapter 17

"Twice in one week. You're not stalking me, are you, senator?" Giacomo smirked.

"No…we were two cars behind you when you jumped out. I had to stop." She picked up her glass of Chardonnay and took a sip.

He leaned back on his bar stool. "I forgot to congratulate you on your reelection." He adjusted his eye patch.

"Thank you. I met with your friend Tom Maro. He's going to nominate me for Director of the National Security Agency."

"You'll do a fine job. How long has it been?"

"You mean since you broke my heart?"

"Not nice—I was upfront with you. You knew I was still in love with Emily. You took it to another level."

Lisa Hill-Rift's blue eyes sparkled. She was as beautiful as her mother, five feet seven, auburn-brown hair that hung below her shoulder blades, a gorgeous smile, and flawless facial features.

"Well, you didn't stop—it takes two to tango. You're right, I was young and maybe foolish."

"Foolish, no—young, I'll accept that." He laughed.

"You're a jerk."

"Nice vocabulary, Senator."

They sat at a round table by the bar in the lounge of the Hay Adams Hotel, which was empty aside from the bartender. Giacomo had recovered from his panic attack. Although he might not admit it, the voice of Lisa Hill soothed his being. She had been the one to suggest they go to the famous inn so he could compose himself. The secret service and the BOET men stood guard at the entrance.

"We had always talked, even when Em needed her space…"

"You're right." He changed the subject, "Where's your husband, Dr. Rift?"

"My wonderful husband…in Italy attending a meeting."

He noticed the roll of her eyes. Aware of the infidelity issues, he kept his opinions to himself.

"Sorry."

"Please, don't be. We live total, complete separate lives now. With his schedule and mine, we're lucky if we see each other once a week. He never wanted children…I did. He hated my political career…I disapproved of his research. We are on opposite sides of the spectrum. I'm sure a divorce is in our future."

"Won't be easy."

"Yeah, but what am I to do? That's life. How's Rio?"

"She's recovering, stubborn, shuns anybody's advice."

"So—normal?"

He snickered. "I guess so."

"My heart broke when I heard the news she had died. I tried to call you."

"I know. Your brother left me a message."

"He told me. What's going on, Giacomo?"

"Are you asking me as the future NSA Director or as a friend?"

"Kinda both?"

"I wish I could, but I can't discuss it with you, Lisa—under presidential orders." Giacomo raised his shoulders and twisted his hands.

"I understand. Where are you staying?"

"Why?"

"I have a spare bedroom," she offered.

"Thanks, President-Elect Maro has invited me to stay at the White House for the next week."

"Ooh…fancy."

Giacomo saw the surprise on her face. "Long story."

"Dinner?"

"Sure—I'll call you," his voice was tentative.

Jason walked into the room. "Sorry to bother you, General…"

"Time to go?"

"Yes, sir."

Giacomo stood. Lisa finished her wine as Jason held her chair.

"Thank you, Jason."

"My honor, Senator."

Giacomo circled the table. The two friends hugged. He kissed her on the cheek and whispered in her ear.

"Be careful tomorrow. I'll see you at the inauguration."

"What?"

Giacomo noticed Lisa's perplexed glance as he walked away. When he reached the door, she shouted, "Wait! I don't understand."

"You will." Turning to Jason he said, "Let's go."

Chapter 18

Giacomo walked down the center corridor of the Executive Residence to the dining room. The inauguration was eighteen hours away. Packed boxes of outgoing President Jerry Richardson's belongings lined one side of the hallway. Along the other wall sat the personal effects of President-Elect Thomas Maro. With the actions of a well-oiled machine, the White House staff would move the items to their rightful place within hours of the swearing-in ceremony.

Two secret service agents stood at the doorway to the room nestled in the northwest corner of the White House on the second floor. Giacomo entered the dining area; his military instincts were on full alert as he surveyed the surroundings. *Why was the table set for four?* The presidents huddled by the window above the north lawn with a third person. Tom Maro pointed as he spoke to the unknown guest obscured from the general's view.

"Sorry I'm late."

"No issues, my friend," Tom said.

The three turned toward him as he approached. Giacomo stopped in shock. Tom and the visitor came closer while Jerry hailed a server.

"Giacomo, can I get you a drink?"

Stunned, he answered, "Pepsi, please, Mr. President."

"General, let me introduce you to my nominee for secretary of state, the good senator from Connecticut, Lisa Hill-Rift."

"Wow, twice in one day?"

He noticed the puzzled look on Tom's face.

"A pleasure to see you again, Giacomo." She moved forward, gave him a hug, and kissed him on the cheek.

"I guess you two know each other?" Jerry spoke as he placed his glass of malt whiskey on the dining table.

"I'd say so," Lisa said.

"Secretary of state?" Giacomo's eyes fixed on Lisa's as he felt a flash of disdain cross his face.

"Yes, President-Elect Maro asked me before you arrived."

"Interesting. I thought you said director of the NSA?"

Tom responded, "I believe her talents are best served as secretary of state."

"Smart move," Giacomo nodded. Absorbing the many coincidences, his military mind became vigilant to his surroundings and every word being uttered. Jerry handed him his glass of Pepsi.

"Thank you, Jerry. I see you recovered from your hand injury."

"Yes. I'll tell you, Giacomo, when I knocked the bastard to the ground, it was one of the greatest moments of my presidency—damn, my entire life. Please sit."

Giacomo recalled the incident between the president and Dean Essex, Tom Maro's chief of staff.

*　*　*

December 27, One Month Earlier

A breeze whipped around the fallow White House Rose Garden. The air was crisp; the blue sky sparkled with winter sunlight. Jerry Richardson sat in the Oval Office. Jason had been there earlier, his search revealing six high-frequency listening devices.

The door to the president's sanctuary opened. Giacomo and Arnaud, dressed as utility workers, entered. Richardson said nothing. He shook their hands and accompanied them to his private study. Jason was seated in the corner and he stood to greet them.

An hour later the intercom buzzed, "Mr. President, President-Elect Maro and his chief of staff are here."

"Please send them in."

Richardson stayed behind his desk.

"Mr. President."

"Please, Tom, call me Jerry." A broad smile crossed his face.

"Mr. President—a new secretary?" Dean Essex said.

Richardson ignored him. He smiled. "Please sit," he said, pointing to one of the two facing couches. He sat opposite Essex.

"With less than a month to go, Tom, I thought I would give you the fifty-cent tour. Sorry it had to be so early in the morning."

"I wish I had known. I would've arranged for Mrs. Maro to be here," Essex said.

Maro's tone was condescending. "When the president and I spoke the other day, he suggested it should be just us men."

Essex was bewildered and shocked. He fidgeted.

"Dean—I don't need to tell you everything. Besides, you've never been in the Oval Office, or have you?"

"Of course I've been here, Tom."

"With me, right?"

"Of course." A bead of sweat on his brow.

"Ever been here without me?"

Richardson smiled as Essex squirmed.

The cockroach tugged at his left ear. "What do you mean, Tom?"

"Well let's see, I believe the first time was—Jer, do you remember?"

"Oh, do you mean when Stalworth was in office?"

"I think so, Jer—a journal?"

"Yeah—you know the journal, don't you, Dean—or is it *Foster*? I'm confused as to your real name, you little piece of shit."

Essex's right leg bounced, his eyes darted. He unbuttoned the collar of his white shirt, loosened his blue silk tie.

"What's the matter, Dean? Is it hot in here? I'm comfortable—and you, Jer?"

"I'm comfortable—and you, Dean? I can open a window?"

The toad squirmed as he tugged on his left ear again. A door opened to his right, his head swung toward the sound.

"Hello, Dean."

Essex sat on the couch, stunned, as Giacomo approached him.

"Let me introduce myself—I'm Giacomo DeLaurentis."

The chief of staff rose from the couch. "I…I…"

With his opened right hand, Giacomo slapped Essex in the chest. He fell backward onto Tom. The president-elect shifted and allowed the traitor to sit by himself.

"You're surprised to see me, Mr. Essex?" Giacomo's sarcastic, cold voice shattered the traitor's demeanor. "Could it be that your assassin failed again last night?"

Essex said nothing for a moment, but then lashed out with spunky arrogance. "If it'd been my men, you'd be dead. Whatcha gonna do, DeLaurentis, kill me? You stupid moron." He jumped up, eyes ablaze, face red, a bead of sweat dripping from his chin.

"No, I'm going to leave that up to the Italian government."

"I'm an American citizen, you can't take me away!"

"Oh, he can and he will," President Richardson said. "You're a threat to national security, so by executive order, I have agreed with the Italian government to release you to them."

"By the way, you little shit, how did you know I was in DC?" Giacomo's voice roared.

With contempt, Essex said, "Why, your little sister, of course—she can't keep her mouth shut—what an imbecilic wench."

Giacomo stepped back. He cocked his arm, his clenched fist ready to smash the toad, when he remembered his promise to Andrew not to hurt the man.

Essex snarled at Richardson as he rubbed his left ear. "You can say goodbye to your family—they'll be gone by the end of the day."

"You pissant." Richardson rose and with a quick right, punched Dean Essex squarely on the chin. Essex collapsed, falling backward on the couch, unconscious. Blood ran from his mouth, splattering his pristine white shirt.

"Damn, that hurt," Richardson said. He shook his hand as he tried to rid himself of the pain. "But it felt great."

"Damn, Jerry—a hell of a punch."

"It was, wasn't it, Tom?"

*   *   *

Giacomo recovered from the recollection and said, "I believe you called him a pissant?"

"I did, the damn traitor."

"That he was," Tom Maro said.

The three men caught Lisa's questioning gaze.

"Once it becomes declassified, Giacomo will tell you the story," Jerry said.

Tom sat to Giacomo's left, Jerry to his right, and Lisa opposite him. The room was absent of personal photos or memorabilia. A fireplace glowed, adding warmth to the frosty atmosphere. The three men dressed in blue jeans and button-down shirts. Lisa wore a black pantsuit with a pearl-embroidered, white silk blouse. Giacomo sensed her uneasiness.

"Giacomo, what the hell? Trivette dead, you almost killed, and tomorrow—*damn*." Tom shook his head in disbelief and with a curious look, pointed, "How's the eye?"

"Not bad. I have to wear this pirate patch for a while. I'll be fine." It occurred to him Lisa had never asked about his injury. *What does she know? Why is she here?*

A waiter with white gloves served French onion soup in white bowls with the seal of the President of the United States emblazoned on the side. For the main course, beef tenderloin placed on a cabernet reduction with a drizzle of bearnaise sauce on top, accompanied by roasted potatoes and green beans almondine. Giacomo waited in silence and observed the polite conversation until a vision overtook his thoughts.

He stood on a pathway. The colors of his surroundings garnered his awe. A flourishing landscape in brilliant hues of vivid green. A mountain range in the distance upstaged a lush, yellow meadow before him. The inexplicable brightness caused him to catch his breath at the beauty. His skin tingled, and his being filled with an extraordinary joy. Confused, he questioned where he was. He swiveled, absorbing the vision. A conflict arose in his mind, then disappeared. In the field lay a hospital bed. He thought he recognized the patient. Wait…was it him? He heard his father's voice. 'I can't allow this…we can never change our fate.'

"Giacomo, care for another Pepsi?" Jerry asked.

He faltered. "I'm sorry. What was the question?"

"A Pepsi?"

"Sure, thank you." Giacomo focused on the conversation as he tried to wipe the vision from his thoughts.

"So, Giacomo, how do you know Lisa?" Tom asked.

Giacomo glanced at Lisa. "Simple, my father married her mother."

Tom sat back, astonished. "Your mom was Sydney Hill?"

"Yes."

"Whoa," Jerry commented. "Then you're aware of Giac—"

"No, Mr. President," Giacomo interrupted. He felt the onset of another panic attack. Giacomo sprang from his chair, stood, and took a deep breath. A secret service agent reacted and hustled into the room.

"We're good here, return to your post," the president said.

"Are you okay?" Tom asked.

"Yeah, fine."

As Giacomo walked over to the window, he sensed three sets of eyes observing him.

"You realize, gentlemen, I'm not one to pull punches." An inner rage boiled within him. "What the hell is going on here?" When he turned, his face was red. "Don't give me this line of bullshit. You weren't aware of the connection between Lisa and me?" Giacomo spotted Lisa's surprise, perhaps from the way he addressed the outgoing president and the soon-to-be commander in chief.

"Giacomo, I never told them." Her eyebrows rose.

"We knew nothing about your relationship," Jerry chimed in.

"I wasn't aware," Tom said.

"Then what is she doing here, gentlemen?"

On high alert, he scrutinized the minutiae in the room. He trusted no one. Jerry and Tom locked eyes and conversed in silence. Lisa sat with a puzzled look on her face.

"I invited her."

"Why, Tom?"

"Why don't you sit down, Giacomo, and I'll explain."

"Yes, Giacomo, please." Lisa tried to stand as Jerry touched her arm.

"Your drink, sir." The white-gloved attendant handed Giacomo his Pepsi.

The secret service agents stood at the ready, their hands on their guns.

"Thank you. I apologize. I've been a little paranoid of late."

"You should talk to someone."

"Don't have time, Tom. I have to overcome it."

"PTSD?"

"Likely so, Jerry. No matter what I try to do, I can't shake the memory of my wife and children being killed."

He saw Lisa wipe a tear from her eye. The sorrow on Tom's face penetrated him. Jerry bowed his head in sadness. The server broke the awkward silence as he placed a sliced New York cheesecake topped with strawberries by Jerry.

"That looks yummy. One of my favorites," Lisa said.

"May I get you a piece, Lisa?" President Jerry Richardson enjoyed serving his guests. He couldn't stand the pomp and circumstance of the office.

"Yes, please. How wonderful."

Giacomo observed the glint in Lisa's eyes as she flirted with Jerry. He smiled and said, "Secretary of state? Excellent idea, Tom."

"Thank you. I'm glad you approve. It's important." Tom removed his napkin from his lap and positioned himself so he could speak to Giacomo. "Let me explain to you why she is here. Jerry and I have discussed the transition in great depth, and we consider you vital to this process. Lisa is not privy to the events that occurred over the past several months. It's imperative that she's here tonight; you will work hand in hand during my administration."

"I don't understand?"

"Giacomo, I am nominating you for the chairperson of the Joint Chiefs of Staff."

Surprised, Giacomo sat back in his seat. "I don't know what to say." He thought for a moment. "To be honest, I'm not sure I'm interested in the job."

"You are the ideal candidate and an excellent choice for my administration."

"Giacomo, you're the perfect person for the position. We must bring a new spirit to our military and our country. Tom's presidency needs you, and America needs you."

"Thank you, Mr. President. Tom, I'll give it serious consideration."

"Please do, Giacomo."

"One question—Lisa's nomination. Do you think there will be an issue with her confirmation because of our relationship?"

"No. Given the current political climate, it won't be a problem."

There was an uneasy silence before President Richardson spoke. "What news do you have about tomorrow?"

Giacomo watched Lisa place her fork on her plate as he asked, "We can talk with the senator present?"

"At your discretion, Giacomo," President Richardson assented. "You can speak with no restriction, if you wish."

Giacomo's head was down as he fiddled with his silverware. He understood the comment to mean that she wasn't—at least, not yet—aware of his paranormal gift. "There will be an assassination attempt on Tom Maro's life tomorrow."

Chapter 19

January 21, 4:00 A.M.

Because of financial cutbacks, the lone officer from the recommissioned DC Police Air Support unit walked on South Capitol Street southeast toward Potomac Avenue. Tonight's tour of duty took him to the padlocked Washington Nationals baseball park, then back to headquarters. His job was to patrol the area and report on any suspicious activity. Should he encounter wrongdoing, the officer on duty had instructed him to call for backup. Protocol prohibited him from intervening unless his life was in peril.

Located two miles from the Capitol Building, the helicopter squadron provided air support and tactical aid for the inauguration. This evening, the seven choppers remained grounded as maintenance crews checked and verified the vehicles were in flying order. At the light of dawn, the flight crews strapped in their aircraft would wait for the signal to launch into the morning sky. Their mission: provide active surveillance on the estimated 1.7 million people gathered in the four-square-mile area. Their flight patterns were centered on the inaugural parade route and the Capitol grounds, and the swearing-in ceremony of the next President of the United States.

The seasoned pilot/police officer turned right on Southeast Potomac. He strode along the sidewalk next to the river. Concrete barriers piled six feet high surrounded the stadium. The blockade didn't stop the graffiti artists. Written across the main entranceway of the ballpark, a slogan denounced the corrupt government of America.

He leaned against a lamppost at the waterway's edge and lit a cigarette. The orange glow of the burning tobacco penetrated the darkness. His ears zeroed in on the sound of the leaves crackling nearby as he pulled back his black shirtsleeve: *4:15.*

The veteran officer needed to return to the station in forty minutes. He was required to clock out at five, enter one of the seven bunkrooms, and sleep for three hours. Then, after a quick cup of coffee, walk to the flightline and climb aboard his helicopter with a member of the secret service who served as second-in-command. The agent was there to shoot him or his co-pilot if they attempted to kill the president. He found it to be unnerving at first until he realized he and his co-worker each carried a gun.

To his right was the entranceway to the DC police dock. Tied to the pier during daylight hours were patrol boats that cruised the Potomac River. Tonight, a twenty-seven-foot Boston whaler occupied the spot. His cell phone rang.

"Hello, honey. You getting ready for work?"

"Yeah, having my first cup of coffee. It'll be a marathon day."

"Tell me about it."

"When do you think you'll be home?"

"After the parade. How about you?"

"As long as nothing happens, six."

"Good. I need to go, hon. I have to make my way back. Love you, Liz."

"Love you too, Fred. Be careful."

"Of course."

He ended the call. His wife of twenty years was a nurse whom the government mandated work at the hospital during the Presidential Inauguration. This was her fourth time. The officer returned the cell to his pocket. A sound to his right caught his attention. He moved his head toward the noise. Placing his fingers on his gun while feeling for the clasp, he released the holster strap.

"Damn it. The gate's locked," someone said.

The police officer crept closer to the voices, slipping into the darkness as he crouched by the wrought-iron railing. He reached for the radio transmitter pinned to his lapel and called for help as he listened to the conversation.

"Shit, where the hell is Charley? He's late."

"We can climb over the fence."

"Backup. Station forty-three. Two perps," the officer whispered.

There was no response in his earpiece. He tried again. The blackness was instantaneous. He felt no pain other than a pressure at the base of his neck. The silencer made a puff of noise as the fifteen-year police veteran toppled forward.

"Sorry I'm late. I couldn't leave the station. The secret service is being a real cramp in my ass."

Charley walked over and unlocked the gate.

One man pointed, "Did you kill the cop?"

"Yeah, he was calling for backup."

"Did he contact anyone?"

"No. Take the body with you. Here are the directions. Make sure you place them at the correct locations."

Lieutenant Charles Basset handed the leader an envelope and a box that contained four fifty-caliber laser-guided bullets.

*   *   *

Basset arrived back at the station at five in the morning. The lieutenant was a short, well-built man, balding, with a pug nose. They often referred to him as "Bulldog," but never to his face. Tasked as the flight operations manager, he ensured the helicopters were ready for immediate dispatch at a moment's notice. As the commander of the unit, he also served as liaison to the secret service. He placed a Dunkin' Donuts bag on the night dispatcher's desk.

"All for you, Del. A glazed and an old-fashioned."

"Thanks, Lieutenant."

Basset walked over to a security door, entered his five-digit access code, and went to his office, where he tapped in a six-digit alphanumeric cipher. He sat at his desk and pushed a button by the phone, locking him in his secured and soundproof workplace. His computer screen came alive. Opening the flight department schedule, he removed the dead officer from the roster. He waited for his instructions—the next steps to engage in the plot to assassinate the next President of the United States.

Chapter 20

The White House Residence, 6:00 A.M.

Giacomo awoke to the sound of men moving furniture. He got out of bed and did some stretches, sit-ups, and push-ups. After the exercise routine, he walked to the bathroom, showered, and shaved. Scheduled to attend a private breakfast with Jerry and Tom at seven, he stood before the mirror and combed his hair. Today was the day. The vision plagued him.

The air is icy—a light snow appears. Tens of thousands of people gathered. The Capitol before me—Tom Maro gives me a smile. President Richardson smiles. Overhead, six fighter jets fly in formation, their afterburners glowing bright. A commotion begins—I hear the screams. Oh my God, oh my God.

There was a problem with the vision—today the skies were a vivid blue and no snow in the forecast. Giacomo knew this discrepancy was going to be a topic of conversation when he met with the president and president-elect.

"Good morning, Giacomo."

"Morning, Mr. President."

President Jerry Richardson placed his newspaper on the dining-room table. He grabbed a silver coffee pot.

"Coffee?"

"Sure."

Giacomo sat down next to him. The soon-to-be-former commander in chief poured the black brew into a white mug.

"Thanks."

"No problem, son. I have to say you blew the socks off your—sister, stepsister? I don't know your…"

"Friend."

"Yeah, sure?"

"She just about fainted when you blurted out the attempt on Tom's life."

"Yeah—shit, it scared me."

President-Elect Thomas Maro walked into the presidential residence dining room.

"Good morning, Tom. Coffee?"

"Sounds like an excellent idea, Jerry—since it might be my last day here on earth."

"Let's hope not."

"I'll ditto that, Giacomo."

While the men sipped their java, Jerry reached down and grabbed a red folder marked "President's Eyes Only." He removed the top-secret, classified document and handed a copy to Tom.

"Gentlemen, the Freedom Brigade is active again—I received this during the night."

Maro read the intelligence briefing aloud. "At 5:08 AM we intercepted a communique between two parties discussing an assassination attempt on the president and vice president elect. Our analysts determined the call originated from Italy. However, we could not establish a definite location. The receiver was in the Washington, DC metropolitan area, and the conversation ended with the recipient's response, 'We won't fail this time. America is ours.' It's our opinion the Freedom Fighters Brigade (FFB) is active again and intent on overthrowing the United States government. Our conclusion: an assault will occur today."

"Well, looks like your premonition bears some fruit."

"Maybe," Giacomo became hesitant. "The issue is the skies are blue, but in the vision, it was snowing."

"So, the attack won't happen?" Tom asked.

"No, it will," with a blank stare, his gaze rose to the ceiling.

"You said to expect snow. The weather reports are saying the opposite."

"You're correct. Doesn't mean they won't try to kill you, Tom. Even the FBI believes you're in danger today."

Confused by the inconsistencies of his vision, but resolute in his thoughts, Giacomo knew Tom's life was in peril. He pondered whether his imagination was getting the best of him. *Was his friend Andrew, now the Pope, correct? Was it possible the visions had meaning not intended as reality? This apparition was different—he knew it to be genuine.* "Tom, even if what I foresaw is wrong, you're still in danger."

"I have my doubts." Tom shook his head.

Giacomo recognized the skepticism in the president-elect's eyes. *Perhaps the vision wasn't true?*

"We should reevaluate our security measures," Tom said.

"We could, but I recommend against it."

"I disagree with you, Giacomo. We should leave it alone and follow the normal inauguration protocol." Tom's voice was adamant.

Jerry stood. He walked over to the window and leaned against the pane. Giacomo took a sip of black coffee, placing the cup on the saucer with a clang. Tom's face was pale. Giacomo's eyes followed the movements of the secret service agent who set another sterling silver coffeepot by his seat.

Jerry spoke, "Tom, we should move the swearing-in ceremony indoors."

An awkward silence fell across the room.

"I could agree with that. Giacomo, what do you think?" Tom asked.

"I've taken the steps to implement if need be."

Giacomo smiled at Jerry and Tom's curious expressions.

"You have?" They asked in unison.

He glanced at his TAG Heuer watch. "Yes. What I require from you, Mr. President, is your authority to move forward."

"What about the people?" Maro asked.

"They'll understand, Tom. We'll issue a statement, explaining that because of security concerns, we had to change to an inside venue. Your press secretary will inform the media at 11:15, no earlier. It is vital that our enemies don't catch wind of what we're doing."

"Why, Giacomo?"

"To keep them from regrouping, Tom. We continue to move forward with the outdoor ceremony. This will keep them at bay. Our crews revamped the west front of the Capitol building. The grand staircase and the lawn will be vacant for security reasons. We've installed enormous television screens throughout the National Mall for the people. They'll understand."

"I agree with you, Giacomo. Tom is in danger, and we need to protect him at all costs." Jerry leaned forward and said, "Let's make this formal. I authorize you, General Giacomo DeLaurentis, to do what is necessary. I'm sure I'll be getting a couple of nasty phone calls."

"Without a doubt you will, Jerry."

As Giacomo departed the room, he heard the president issuing the order to the commander of the Joint Task Force of the Capital Region to obey the directives of General DeLaurentis.

Chapter 21

Capitol Building, 9:30 A.M.

Giacomo, Jerry Richardson, and Thomas Maro gathered around a conference table in a room off the main chamber.

Tom pulled the sleeve of his cuff-linked white shirt, exposing his Citizen watch. "Nine thirty." He paused. "I want to move the inauguration to an outside venue."

Giacomo raised his eyebrows. "That's a mistake, Tom."

"We can't surrender to a terrorist threat. Our people need to witness my swearing in live. Thousands of our fellow Americans are waiting in the cold. They're not here to watch me taking the oath of the presidency from a television screen. I've thought hard, and I am adamant about this, gentlemen. I will not yield. The citizens of the world *and* our enemies are watching. We will not succumb to these monsters who wish to destroy our democracy. Your vision or whatever you saw won't happen today. You said it yourself—there's no snow in the forecast."

Tom's stern comment didn't go unnoticed. Giacomo grew frustrated. Was it because Tom rebuffed him? *I don't need this. Go kill yourself.* He reconsidered. He knew Tom was correct; the prognostication wasn't the same. *Maybe he's right.*

"I can see the displeasure on your face, my friend. Don't be. Life events change. Today is one of those days…"

"You're taking a risk," the president said.

"Jerry, it's a calculated chance. Look at the facts. There's a blue sky, no clouds; different from Giacomo's vision."

They could not dispute the truth—the weather didn't conform to the prognostic event. They had ninety minutes until the start of the inaugural program, and Giacomo needed to make a decision. Indoors or outdoors? Making his displeasure visible, Giacomo gave the command to revert to the normal protocol.

"I'd be lying if I didn't tell you, you're making a mistake."

"Tom, I agree with him."

"I appreciate the concern, Jerry. What about the press?"

"Not permitted access to the Capitol grounds and they're pissed off," Giacomo said.

"We need the media. They have to be visible."

"I see your point, Tom, but I insist we confiscate their cell phones for security reasons."

Tom hesitated. "Fine, but I'm not happy."

Jason entered the room, Giacomo stood.

"Jason, glad you're here. We have a change of plans."

Chapter 22

Five American flags flew between the pillars of the Capitol Building behind the west steps. A maintenance worker aligned the presidential seal on the podium, then adjusted the microphone. "Testing…one, two, three," she said. With the inaugural platform in place, other workers scurried to complete the arrangement of chairs for the limited honored guests, which included the many blowhards of Congress. Snipers with their AK-47s at the ready perched at the base of the dome. Bulletproof glass, double paned and eight feet high, surrounded the guest area on all sides. Army personnel with German shepherds patrolled the grounds, the dogs sniffing for explosives.

By ten o'clock, 1.9 million people crowded the National Mall—200,000 more than estimated. Fifty-four TV screens, each thirty feet high, dotted the park. Two men traveled unfettered across the west front lawn carrying a ladder. They clandestinely adjusted laser-equipped cameras on three of the oversized monitors, completed their task, and entered a black van with darkened windows parked on Garfield Circle. They drove through the security checkpoints unrestrained.

Throngs of citizens lined the one-and-a-half-mile parade route from the hallowed halls of the government to the White House. After the congressional luncheon, the new president's armored limousine made the ceremonial journey down Pennsylvania Avenue. Against the advice of the secret service, Tom stopped and exited the car three times along the fifteen blocks as he greeted his supporters as well as those who believed democracy had failed.

Under Giacomo's order, additional security personnel had been added to the 32,000 police officers and FBI agents. He stationed National Guard troops by the perimeter to provide extra protection during the proceedings. Five hundred BOET—Black Operations Elite Team—members infiltrated the crowds, alert for suspicious activity. Giacomo had disregarded Tom's recommendation and informed his commanders of the assassination attempt. He had Jason sequester them to an operational control center in the Capitol Building.

The sky was a pristine blue with no wind. Low-hanging clouds formed fifty miles to the west. As the time for the inauguration approached, exuberance fanned through the crowd. The anticipation of a new government revitalized Americans' hopes. An administration that promised a unified Congress and the protected rights of the people.

Chapter 23

Lieutenant Charles Bassett trotted out to the flight line. His first officer, Harry Burke, and secret service agent Ken Dickey stood by the American Eurocopter MH-65C, classified as an AUF—Airborne Use of Force—its armament stripped for the day's mission.

"Are we ready?"

"Yeah, we're all set, Chuck."

"Ken, you got the box."

"Stowed on board."

"Good. I received the go call twenty minutes ago." He reached inside his flight vest, pulled out two one-inch-thick envelopes, and handed one to each man.

"You both know the plan. We'll hover at eight hundred feet over the National Mall by the Monument. Harry, you activate the remote for the rifles when Maro steps up to the podium. Four seconds later, the lasers mounted on the Capitol TV will light up the targets. Six seconds after that, the guided bullets will be on their way. Once we accomplish the mission and return to base, we go our separate ways."

"Will the laser distract Maro on the dais?"

"No. New tech—it's invisible to the naked eye."

"Cool. Roger, Chuck."

"Stop calling me Chuck, will ya?"

"Yeah, sure."

The three men entered the helicopter. The Turbomeca Arriel turbines started. With the rotor blades engaged, Bassett lifted the machine into the air and headed west toward the Washington Monument. The time was eleven o'clock.

Fastened to the roof of the southwest corner of the Nationals Park baseball stadium were four fifty-caliber rifles. Camouflaged, the instruments of death remained undiscoverable from the ground or the air. Loaded with specialized laser bullets, they stood in abeyance, waiting for the digital signal to launch the miniature missiles at their painted target 1.09 miles away.

The military developed the unique $20,000 ammunition during the Afghanistan War. Nanotechnology allowed the finned projectiles to spin instead of tumble, providing an accuracy of two millimeters— assured of hitting their target.

A nation would soon be in crisis.

Chapter 24

Giacomo stood to the side of Tom, his wife, and his children. His earpiece came alive. "Giacomo, we've picked up a high-frequency transmission. Trying to pinpoint its location now."

Jerry Richardson tapped Tom Maro on the shoulder. With his arm outstretched, they shook hands. President-Elect Maro responded with a smile. Without warning, a strong wind swept through the crowd. The American flags battered the aluminum poles, the clanging sounds carried away by the intensity of the gust.

Voices from the enormous mass of people voyaged through the air. The cold temperature materialized their breath into millions of small puffs of vapor. Fear rustled through Giacomo as he turned his attention upward to the now-dark-gray, ominous clouds racing over the city.

His heartrate increased as a sickening dread overcame him. In the distance, he could see the black exhaust of the approaching F-22 raptors. His scan moved to Maro. He observed the man's face drain of color, changing to a pasty pale, as the blue sky turned to the gloomy gray of the vision. Within moments, the heavens wept. Snowflakes floated to the ground.

*   *   *

Bassett maneuvered the helicopter over the ruins of the Washington Monument. The iconic structure had toppled after an earthquake and was never rebuilt due to Congress not approving the funds to restore the obelisk. The crowd behind the president stood.

"Eleven fifty-seven," the lieutenant said. "Are you ready?"

"Yep."

Harry opened the silver aluminum case containing an array of instruments, switches, and four tiny monitors. He connected a USB wire to the electrical panel. The system powered on, awaiting the operator's commands.

The helicopter hovered. While the nose of the vehicle, with its treasonous crew, pointed downward, they set the plan in motion. It was now eleven fifty-eight. The gunpowder exploded, pushing the fifty-caliber missile through the barrel. Four miniature fins opened as they exited the muzzles. The tiny cameras began their search for the invisible laser beams focused on the victims of the attack. Microprocessors gathered the signal and homed in on their target. The projectiles climbed twenty-five feet, overcoming the obstacles in their path.

*   *   *

11:58 A.M.

Giacomo watched as President-Elect Thomas Maro walked to the area where the swearing-in ceremony was to take place. The Chief Justice greeted him. Tom's wife held the Bible. They exchanged pleasantries. "Giacomo, we've detected a second and a third wavelength."

"Have you pinpointed the signal location?"

"Washington Monument. Repeat, Washington Monument."

Giacomo's body swiveled toward the secret service agent, then back toward the impending attack. Giacomo saw the hovering aircraft.

"Holy crap!"

"What is it, Jason?"

With a scourging roar, five F-22 fighter jets flew over the National Mall, and on cue, they began their meteoric rise into the overcast sky. The afterburners' blazing flames spewed from the tails of the planes' engines. A sonic boom encapsulated the spectators. The throngs of people within the mall cheered, pointing at the military hardware. In the instant prior to the swearing in of Thomas Maro—as in the vision—a commotion erupted. Giacomo pointed to a trail of white smoke emanating from the top of a building. At 11:59:30, as Tom Maro raised his right hand, General Giacomo DeLaurentis took action.

*   *   *

12:01 P.M.

"Harry, what's going on? Where's the president?"

"Down. He's down," Bassett yelled.

"Damn, it worked. Gentlemen, our mission is complete. Cabo San Lucas, here I come," Burke said.

Bassett maneuvered the helicopter as it swiveled on its axis toward its escape route. The celebratory Air Force jet flyby caused a shockwave that rattled the chopper.

A surface-to-air missile scorched the horizon, its target the fifth F-22. With a thunderous explosion, the airplane plummeted out of the sky. The remnants floated and crashed into the crowd, missing the Capitol dome by a hundred feet. A chunk of the right wing corkscrewed, clipping the rotor blades of the unsuspecting copter. Bassett struggled to keep the aircraft upright, to no avail. Doomed, he released the controls. The lives of the traitors ended in a ball of fire.

The panicked throngs of onlookers scrambled to escape the ensuing carnage. With nowhere to go, they stood and watched the scene unfold, hoping to survive the chaos. Several people pointed to the gray sky as a parachute appeared—the pilot of the F-22 escaped unharmed.

The stiff wind carried the aviator across the lawn. Applause erupted. The enormous TV screens flickered and came alive. The protective bulletproof glass surrounding the presidential podium lay in shards on the ground. Security and medical personnel surrounded President-Elect Maro and the chief justice. An eerie silence engulfed the populace. The major news anchors waited for the go-ahead to confirm the death of the elected president.

Chapter 25

Italy, January 21, 5:57 P.M.; Washington, DC, 11:57 A.M.

A royal-blue Alfa Romeo Giulia traversed the winding thoroughfare of the Tuscan countryside. The driver's destination was an Italian villa nestled atop a low-rising hill. The entrance to the property appeared innocuous. He realized, though, that once he drove onto the estate, hidden cameras with mounted machine gun turrets tracked him with the intent to kill. Any false movement or act of aggression sent a command to destroy the car and its occupants with a plethora of fifty-caliber bullets.

Sergio took a deep breath, reached for his wallet, and placed the billfold in the cup holder. He resolutely turned right onto the four-mile, white-stoned private road. Tall green Lebanon Cedars provided guidance as he negotiated his way to the orange-rust stucco, gray-shuttered, twenty-room mansion.

Three security guards aimed their guns at the car. They surrounded the vehicle. Two mercenaries inspected the exterior of the automobile, while one kept the driver in her sights. The woman motioned with her head for Sergio to exit the Alpha Romeo. He stood with his arms above his shoulders. One man frisked him while the other searched the interior. The protocol never changed—no exceptions.

Encircled by the soldiers, Sergio was escorted to the house. The door swung open to a marble-tiled foyer. A security checkpoint with a metal detector stood to the left.

"Empty your pockets," a man said in a heavy Middle Eastern accent.

Sergio removed a Montblanc pen and his cell phone and placed them on a table.

"Over here. Palms on the wall, spread your legs."

He obeyed the command. The guard searched him a second time. *Do I have the guts to speak my mind without getting killed?* His mission was to conclude the business ties between Adinolfi and the assassin.

Accompanied by armed personnel, Sergio approached a fortified door. He understood that at any moment, his life might cease. The first guard entered his five-digit code. The second person input her four-alpha sequence. Once the six lights above the key lock turned green, the visitor entered his password, transmitted by a computer-generated voice. The encryption changed on the hour.

The steel door hissed as it cracked open, then disappeared into the wall. Sergio stepped through the entryway into the thirty-by-forty-foot room. Once inside, the opening sealed shut with a clasping noise. The guards remained in the hallway. To his left, an array of twenty-five monitors displayed various camera angles of the secure facility. A familiar hissing sound caught his attention. Turning right, he saw her in the hidden archway.

"It has been a while, my cousin."

"Circumstances have kept us apart."

"I'm surprised you're here."

"Adinolfi wanted me to ensure the payment met with your satisfaction."

She said nothing as she walked to a computer. The woman typed a set of commands. The monitors went blank. A second later, eight screens in the center of the wall came alive.

"This occurred thirty-five minutes ago. Look—observe the destruction of the American government."

Sergio gasped in horror as he beheld the assassinations of the United States President-Elect Thomas Maro, Chief Justice Thelma Blair, and his dear friend whom he had betrayed, Giacomo DeLaurentis. A wave of nausea overcame him. He grew unsteady and grabbed the desk.

"Are you all right?"

"Yeah, it's hard to witness the death of a friend."

"Cousin, the death of DeLaurentis is of no surprise to you. You're not that stupid. Besides, my fee was well worth the expense to your organization. What is happening with Adinolfi?"

"He's at Monte Cassino, still convinced the prophecy will ring true."

"The boys?"

"He didn't say."

"Hmph."

"What do you care if the boys are alive or dead?"

"Watch your words, my cousin."

Sergio bowed his head. "I apologize."

"That's your problem—always apologizing. You should have my attitude...I don't care what people think or do. My job was to kill DeLaurentis. I was more than happy to oblige. The death of their president was an added benefit. By the way, he was one of us, a pawn played in FHS's quest to achieve global rule."

Stunned to hear that Tom Maro was a member and that Adinolfi's successor stood by, he tried to conceal his reaction. Sergio handed her a piece of paper with instructions on how to access the remaining €24 million owed for services rendered. He picked up a picture of an antique wooden maple clock.

"Put it down, please." The woman grabbed the photo of the 300-year-old, handmade Swiss timepiece and returned it to the shelf.

Anne Fortunato Richler was sixty-seven and stood five feet, nine inches tall. Attractive, with piercing blue eyes, she radiated a cunning persona. Her gaze could terrify the hardest psychopath. The murderer adjusted a silk scarf that covered a scar from her right ear down to the base of her neck. Once a ruthless freelance spy for Dr. Colin Payne, the NSA traitor had tried to destroy the world and kill Giacomo's father, Paolo DeLaurentis. She earned the nickname *the Chechnyan Assassin*. Presumed dead, Dr. Anne Fortunato Richler touched her disfigurement as her mind replayed the tragedy of that fateful day.

Chapter 26

Virginia, April 2002

Paolo DeLaurentis stood near Bill Conti's gravesite at Arlington National Cemetery. Today marked a year since the murder of his friend in Venice, Italy, a tumultuous 365 days filled with angst. His misinterpretation of the persistent vision of the crumbling World Trade Towers. His roller-coaster relationship with Sydney. Compounded by Dr. Colin Payne, director of the NSA, who tried to destroy him. The thoughts caused his head to pound.

Paolo was determined to bring the murderers to justice, his mind set on a course of revenge. He made the trip to the nation's capital in secret, not wanting to share his grief. A day of solitude filled with memories of the life and death of his childhood friend, Bill.

With one knee on the ground, Paolo pulled a handful of green grass from the soil. He held it for a moment, brought the blades to his nose and inhaled their scent, then tossed them into the warm spring air.

"Hello," he whispered into his cell phone, as he stood and walked back to his waiting car.

"Paolo, I've got news about the killer."

His senses perked, but his heart still ached. "Go ahead, Mike. What do you have?"

"Remember the picture Bill showed you?"

"Payne and the Chechnyan woman?"

"Yes. Well, she's not dead, and she's not Chechnyan."

"I don't give a crap what she is—where can I find her?"

"Austria."

"I want you there ASAP. I want all the information you can get on her."

"No problem. I'm already here in Salzburg, and you will not believe this one."

"She's a doctor."

"How the hell did you know?"

"I just do."

"You amaze me."

"The truth is, I couldn't stop her from killing Bill."

"What do you mean?"

"It's a long story. Arrange a meeting between her and me."

"Of course."

The driver stood by the door as Paolo approached. Before he entered the car, he nodded his head and continued the conversation.

"You can't use my name."

"No kidding, Sherlock."

He spoke to the chauffeur: "To the airport."

"Where are you?"

He ignored Mike's question. Paolo remembered the picture of the assassin, and within moments he could remote-view her. The seer found himself in Fortunato's presence. The gifted man immersed himself in her surroundings as she studied a photograph.

"Are you there?"

"Yes." He withdrew himself from the scene. A moment later, his thoughts shifted back to reality. "Our doctor friend is a buyer of antiques. She's in search of a Swiss clock. It has meaning for her. I'm emailing you the clock's location and owner. Mike, I don't care how much the damn thing costs. I want it. What's her name?"

"Anne Fortunato."

Paolo said nothing and disconnected the phone call. He murmured, "I'll get you, you son of a bitch."

"I'm sorry, sir. Did you say something?"

"No, talking to myself. What's our ETA to the airport?"

"About twenty minutes."

"Thank you."

He opened his cell's contact page and called the captain of his private jet. "Danny, change of plans. I want to go to Milan tonight. Any issues?"

"No. I'll let Jim know."

"Good, we'll depart out of LaGuardia."

"No problem, Paolo."

"Danny, pack your bags for a couple of weeks. We'll end up in Salzburg, Austria."

"Should we carry?"

"Yes."

Hired on the recommendation of a friend, both Danny and Jim were ex-secret service agents, now serving as Paolo's bodyguards and personal pilots of his Gulfstream Five.

*   *   *

Twenty-one days later, with arrangements in place, the aircraft landed at W. A. Mozart Salzburg International Airport in Austria. Onboard the airplane with Paolo was Mike Quinn, his in-house investigator. Secured to a seat was a Swiss-made clock, circa 1700, worth $3 million. Paolo paid double that amount to get hold of the antique.

Paolo DeLaurentis stood and grabbed his blue sports jacket. He rubbed his four-week-old beard and touched Mike's shoulder. "Do you think she'll recognize me?"

"No. With you dying your hair gray and the growth on your face— no way. Even if she does, we'll handle the situation as it arises."

"Yep." He bowed his head. *Am I going to do this?*

"What's the matter, boss?"

He took a deep breath. "No, it's nothing."

Danny opened the cabin door that isolated the passengers from the cockpit.

"I arranged everything, no worries." He walked down the aisle and handed Paolo a manila envelope. "Inside is your new identity. Your name is Rob Abrams, a reclusive antique collector."

"I like the sound of his name. Reminds me of an old dear friend." He removed the fraudulent American passport and flipped through the tarnished pages. "India?"

"And Russia, and China, and last week you were in Ethiopia."

"Nice job, Danny."

"No problem."

Paolo watched as the broad-shouldered ex-secret service agent walked back to the cockpit.

"He's a good man."

"Yep, he is, Mike." He held up the passport. "He has unbelievable connections."

Chapter 27

May 2002

Snow spewed from the overcast sky. White crystals wafted through the air, coming to rest with a silent puff. Pedestrians strolled the streets of Salzburg, leaving footprints in the powder. The wintery weather was unusual for this time in May, Mother Nature's means of creating postcard memories for the unfazed inhabitants.

Paolo stood in front of the window. The hotel lay on the outskirts of the old town district. His third-story corner room provided spectacular views of the Salzach River. He touched his chin, observing the bustling morning traffic of the city. The locals and tourists promenaded the cobblestoned streets. Paolo tapped the face of his Rolex as he whispered, "It's 2:00 a.m. back home." Six weeks earlier, he had been in Colorado Springs with Sydney, the love of his life. Their last conversation was ten days ago.

*   *   *

"When will we talk again?"

"Whenever you want. You're the one who's keeping the secrets."

"Syd, I'm sorry. I'm in Salzburg on business."

"No problem—call me when you have time."

Preoccupied with finding Bill's killer, torn between love and his shrouded life. Sydney's sarcasm broke Paolo's heart.

*   *   *

He tried to remote-view Anne Fortunato throughout his three weeks in Salzburg, with no success. Prior to his arrival in Austria, he saw with clarity what she wanted. Stymied by his inability to use the paranormal gift, he wondered if his thoughts of revenge were the cause.

"Yes, come in."

Paolo's three men walked into the suite. He turned from the window, rubbing his face. He took a deep, labored breath.

"What time is the meeting?"

"Thirty minutes," Danny said.

Paolo shook his head. "Humph."

"Nothing to worry about. I'll be inside with you. Jim outside guarding the door, and Mike will wait for us by the archway."

"Archway?"

"Yeah, the old town is for pedestrians, no vehicle traffic. Fortunato's storefront is nearby. Not too far from Mozart's birthplace."

Paolo stared at the three men. He heard their voices, but the words didn't register in his mind. The clairvoyant's gaze was irate—focused and intense. His eyes met Danny's. Paolo knew at that instant an unspoken bond united the two, the ex-secret service agent willing to place his life on the line for him if necessary. Paolo watched Danny rub the back of his head.

"Damn, your stare scares the shit out of me. The hair on the back of my neck stood up."

Paolo touched his shoulder. "Sorry."

Chapter 28

Paolo gazed out the window as Mike Quinn maneuvered the black Mercedes sedan. He stroked his beard, turning his glance to Jim for a moment, then stared straight ahead.

"Danny, be careful today." He reached forward and touched the man's shoulder.

"Believe me, I will."

The car came to a stop. The disguised man opened the passenger door as an Audi streaked by, honking its horn. He saw Mike flip the driver a vulgar hand gesture. Paolo's senses were on high alert. The gray-haired seer exited the vehicle and went to the trunk. Inside lay a wooden box holding an antique clock. He motioned to Danny to pick up the vintage time piece.

Paolo, Danny, and Jim walked through the archway toward Getreidegasse, a popular street in the historic old town. The baroque buildings were atypical—thin and tall, with a pleasant flare of centuries past. Remove the tourists and the vast modern stores, and you'd believe you were in the seventeenth century.

"Mozart was born over there," Jim pointed to a dark yellow building.

"I can read the sign," Danny replied with a caustic attitude.

"Ass."

"Thank you."

Jim and Danny walked on either side of Paolo, his head bowed low to avoid detection.

"There's Fortunato's store."

The storefront was in a recessed alcove. A bow window that faced the street bordered an oak door decorated with the number six, written in gold-leaf lettering below the words "Antique Clocks: owner Anne Fortunato Richler, PhD." Showcased in the storefront were various watches as well as two large, wooden pendulum pieces.

Paolo followed Danny as they entered the establishment. A bell chimed. The musty scent of the shop caused him to cough. The owner had decorated the quaint emporium with an assortment of timepieces. Glass cases formed a square in the center of the room, sheltering an array of intricate antiquities. A man behind a counter closest to the front doors observed the customers. An attractive woman with piercing blue eyes walked through an opening next to a maple bookshelf along the back wall.

Paolo recognized Fortunato. His blood boiled. The hidden anger he'd stifled for a year now engulfed him. A hatred he never experienced overtook his mind. He turned toward the window, for he feared the look on his face betrayed him.

"*Guten morgen,*" said the man behind the glass counter.

"*Guten morgen.* I'm Rob Abrams. I have an appointment with Anne Fortunato."

He noticed how the assassin's eyes darted between him and Danny as she drew closer.

"Hello, Mr. Abrams." She stretched out her hand and cocked her head. "Have we met?"

Bile rose in Paolo's throat. The deceptive action of shaking the murderer's hand made him sick. *You're mine now, you bitch.* He brushed off the feeling. "I don't believe so."

The murderer was about to speak when she noticed the wooden box. Her eyes brightened. *You're mine,* he thought. The seething desire for justice besieged him.

"Care to take a peek?" A broad smirk crossed his face as he took the container from Danny.

"Yes, please. Fritz, can you help… How rude of me. This is my husband."

Paolo eyed him as he grabbed the container and placed it on the counter, after which he walked out from around the glass encasement. Danny took a defensive posture.

"Do you mind, Mr. Abrams, if I examine it?"

"No."

Paolo watched as Fortunato opened the container, gawking at the timepiece surrounded by a blue velvet cloth. He noticed her hand trace the keyhole carved into the base of the antique.

"You've had this for a while?"

"A short period."

"How did you find it? I've been searching for this antique for years."

"I have my ways."

"I'm sure money helps?"

"Yes. May I ask, Mrs. Richler, what's your interest?"

"I've always had a fondness for vintage pieces of history."

Paolo's eyes followed Fritz as he walked to the front of the store and locked the door. Attentive to the surroundings, he observed Danny placing his right arm behind his back. He imagined Danny removing the nine-millimeter Beretta. The husband returned to the encasement.

Justice and vengeance converged as Paolo reached for the thin garrote in his coat pocket. His fingers fondled the circular handles. Infuriated, he visualized the tiny tear in Anne's neck as the oozing blood squirted and she fell to the floor, gasping for air. He tried to shake the feeling of wanting her dead, but he couldn't rid his mind of his desire to watch her struggle for her life, writhing in agony and succumbing to death.

For wasn't revenge sweet? But, at that instant, he understood vengeance would not resolve the injustice, the outcome leading to heartbreak and a darkening of his soul. Paolo stepped back. His anger welled as a momentary sense of remorse overcame his fury.

The assassin reached for a silver chain draped around her neck. Secured to the necklace was a key. Fortunato's evil smirk sounded an alarm in Paolo's mind. His thoughts replayed the remote-viewing sessions of her desire to buy the antique. He scowled; Fortunato had played him.

Enraged, Paolo eyed Fortunato as she rotated her wrist to the left. The clock face popped open. With her fingernail, she pulled something toward her. Within the timepiece was a hidden compartment with a door. Fortunato's eyes exploded wide. Arching her back, she stood tall. Inside the chamber was a brown parchment.

"Mr. Abrams, it seems forever that we've had to wait for this piece of paper. We knew you couldn't resist finding the clock. Vengeance does not look good on you. You have fallen right into our hands, you fool. This is a note written by a priest in the fifteen hundreds, all about your bloodline, Mr. Abrams…or is it Paolo DeLaurentis? It's a shame today is your last."

Paolo grimaced at the assassin's condescending smirk. In a simultaneous motion, Danny and Fritz pulled out their guns. Danny ran the couple of steps and placed the nine-millimeter at the base of Anne's head.

"One move, Herr Richler, and your wife's brains will paint your shirt."

"*Leck mich am Arsch.*"

"Yeah, right, you can kiss mine too. Now put down the freakin' gun."

Paolo became immersed in the scene; the action felt surreal. Danny applied more pressure to Fortunato's neck. Her face smeared on the glass, held down by Danny's hand. Fortunato was quick. Her right leg kicked backward. He reacted faster and sidestepped. There was a pop. Fritz shot him in the left arm. Without hesitation, Danny pulled the trigger on the Beretta. The bullet whizzed past Anne's ear and struck the German in the heart.

Paolo's protector fell to the ground. Danny rolled to his right and sprung back up on his feet after seeing the six-inch switchblade in her hand. With blood dripping down from his arm, a martial arts move secured the knife and slammed the woman's face into the encasement. She lay motionless in the broken shards of glass. There were three pops at the front door before it burst open. Jim came running into the store.

"Damn, I can't leave you two alone. Let's go. It's time to depart the area."

"Danny's hurt."

"I'm fine. Bullet went through the flesh of my arm."

"Paolo, we have to go."

"Not yet. Help me move her off the counter." He recognized the incredulous look in his men's eyes.

"Jim, let's get her to a safe place until help arrives."

Danny wrapped his wound to stop the bleeding. Paolo and Jim placed Fortunato on the floor. A piece of broken glass protruded from her neck, a gash running to her right ear. Blood squirted from the open cut. Paolo ripped his shirt and stuffed the cloth into the laceration.

"You can't help her…she's gonna die."

"I know, but I have to try."

Jim shook his head. "Let's go."

"I've got the clock and the key. Couldn't find the note," Danny said.

"I have it." Paolo felt sorry for the dying woman on the floor. The approaching hand of death was out of his control. He whispered, "Revenge is never sweet."

Chapter 29

"One hell of a story." Sergio gazed at his wristwatch. He had to stretch his meeting with his cousin for another fifteen minutes.

Fortunato repositioned the picture of the clock and stood back. The knowledge that Giacomo, the son of the man responsible for the death of her husband, was dead and his daughter Rio was now a blithering idiot brought a smile to her face. *Revenge was indeed sweet…for the wicked.*

He pointed at her neck. "Is that why you wear a scarf? To hide the scar?"

She rubbed the healed wound and shot him an irate stare.

"So, the clock was a trap to kill Giacomo's father?"

"Yes, and no. The FHS under Adinolfi hired me to assassinate him, but they also wanted the antique."

"Why didn't they just buy the damn thing?"

"They tried for years, unable to convince the owner to sell. But when they realized the fact Paolo could remote-view…"

"Remote-view?"

"Yes, his consciousness could transport him to another location in real time, an extraordinary gift. Anyway, they suggested I stage a scene of me trying to purchase the clock. I did this every day. Paolo's tenacity to find his friend's murderer proved to be his downfall. We figured he'd use his power to remote-view. After six months of performing, we sucked him into our web."

"How did he buy it?"

"He used another one of his paranormal gifts…he persuaded the owner to sell. What I didn't expect, though, was his wrath. His eyes were blistering cold and if my husband hadn't died, I might have told Adinolfi to scratch his ass. As I mentioned to you, Paolo saved my life."

"So, you destroyed his son and daughter in retaliation for your husband's death?" Sergio said, a hint of sarcasm creeping into his voice.

"Watch what you say, or you'll end up like your son Alessio."

Sergio's blood surged with anger. *Be patient.*

"I believe you have something you wish to share?"

"I do. Let me forewarn you, my cousin. Be careful of Adinolfi."

"Why?"

"He killed Alessio, didn't he?"

The broken man stared at the assassin. His brow creased as his eyelids closed. A flash of remembrance of the day at the abbey gripped his heart.

"You don't have to remind me. The priest is a treacherous bastard who believes he's fulfilling the will of God through his actions. It's a bunch of crap when you consider his and Rift's genetic research. Their plan to alter the human genome is sinister." Sergio shook his head. "Adinolfi is delusional. His idea that the Holy Spirit chose him is nonsense. The man is evil."

"I don't dispute what you're saying. Are you aware of his research lab in the basement of Monte Cassino?"

"No."

"Well, go there. What he's hiding will surprise you."

"What do you mean?"

"Like I said, take a ride, my cousin. You'll thank me."

"Sure, I have every intention of paying him a visit to make amends. What else do you have to say?"

She flashed a sardonic grin. "Two things. First, Adinolfi doesn't know I have a photograph of the original parchment."

"The prophecy?"

"Yes."

"How did you get it?"

"My people were the ones who stole the journal from Rio's house. Equipped with live cameras, I followed their progress from here. To my pleasant surprise, when they scanned the room, there it was: the clock. I directed one of my men to open the secret compartment and photograph its contents."

"So, Rio has it?"

"She does. Let me tell you this, cousin—the second item you need to hear: there are others above Adinolfi who have grown tired of his antics. Time is short for the priest. They're moving the nations in a different direction. The priest's days are dwindling."

"What do you mean?"

"There's a new FHS leadership. Gone are the ways of old. Religious beliefs no longer hold the authority they once did. Their desire is for domination and global harmony, which is a joke. You can't remove the greed and ego from humanity. Peace…will never come."

Surprised at her comments, Sergio didn't care if what Fortunato spoke of was true or false. The fact was his son and now Giacomo were dead, murdered by this bitch's hand. Soon they'd all pay. "How do you know this?"

"They tried to recruit me. Enough. I'm tired of talking about them. Care to see the prophecy?"

"Why not?"

She rubbed the nineteen-year-old scar on her neck and handed the photographic copy to him. He read it. His eyes could not escape the truth of the words.

From the ancient village nestled in the mountains will arise a family from an orphaned child. The infant saved by a globe of light from the murderers who wished to destroy God's mercy for humanity. His kin, who will foresee future events, whose voice will go unheeded in the New World. The light shall surround him and his heirs.

Twins from the family of Laurentis will precede the Savior's arrival. The Third Trumpet shall rise to a position of authority. His children, the Gemini, by their absence, will usher in a binary future. Along with their father, the existence of humankind will continue. The death of the unexpected will awaken...

"You realize Giacomo's boys are the Gemini," Sergio said as he examined the photo.

"What are you looking at?"

"There's a fold in the paper with additional writing. Your people never unfolded the rest of the parchment. You don't have the complete message."

"Who cares? The prophecy is irrelevant. Adinolfi has the twins, and their parents are dead."

"What a tragedy. How long ago was this written?"

"The 1500s, could be earlier. I accomplished my mission. I can live my life now."

"What do you mean?"

"I told you I'm done. We've destroyed DeLaurentis and his descendants. My ties with the FHS are severed. My mind is peaceful."

Sergio glanced at the clock on the wall. "Time for me to leave."

"Why the rush? Stay, have dinner with me."

"Not today. I need to find Adinolfi."

"Very well." She walked over to her cousin, kissed him on each cheek, then stepped back and glared at him. "Remember, we must all account to someone for our actions. I'll pay for what I have done. Sergio, I sold my soul for this sweet revenge. Believe me, I will exact my retribution on those above me. Their time is approaching. Evil will continue to exist. Maybe I can slow it down a bit."

The monitors on the wall flickered, and one screen came alive with an image.

"No, this can't be! He's dead. I saw him fall myself."

Sergio shook his head and smiled. "I guess you failed." He moved toward the door. With a final look, he turned as his dumbfounded cousin stared at the television. In her anger, she took the picture of the antique clock and smashed it to the floor.

Escorted back to the Alfa Romeo, Sergio strode with a purpose. He pushed the start button; the engine awoke with a rumble. He reached up and pressed the switch to open the moon roof. With his arm outstretched, he waved goodbye to the mercenaries.

He placed the car in drive and drove down the Lebanon Cedar-bordered private road. At the gate, he turned left onto the unpaved street. His attention diverted to the roar of four cruise missiles that flew overhead. The thought of leaving behind his pen and cell phone, which housed the remote transmitters, caused him to grin.

Chapter 30

Paolo DeLaurentis sat behind the cherrywood desk at his home within the Brewster Estate. A brown white-tailed deer drank from the lake of the twenty-two-acre private residential community. Paolo twirled the brass key between his fingers.

He felt troubled by the events in Salzburg. The redundant tick-tock of the clock mesmerized him and echoed his thoughts. *How could this happen? How did I allow my feelings to take control? Why? Why?* He washed the agonizing thoughts from his mind. The anger was replaced with remorse and caused his eyes to well with tears.

Paolo inserted the key in the centuries-old clock. With a quick twist of his wrist to the right, the drawer opened. *Empty.* He reflected for a second, returned to the compartment, and rotated the locking mechanism in the opposite direction. The face of the timepiece sprung open, swinging on its hinges. Intricate wheels spun in rhythm to the beat of the sweep hand. He reached forward, slid the secret hatch down, and carefully removed the tattered brown parchment.

Paolo unfolded the prophetic document. He read the transcribed words. A single tear rolled down his cheek and dripped off his chin. In slow motion, the droplet splattered on the paper and stained the number *34*. Penned before the numeral was a Hebrew phrase translated into Latin—*anno domini*—followed by *copied in 1510*. Written a year after the death of Jesus and copied over a century later. A postscript inscribed on the lower fold read: *In time, the messenger will realize the error.*

Paolo sat back, stunned. A vision transported him to the future. There for a second, eyes wide in shock, unable to comprehend what occurred, the seer returned the parchment to its coffer. He never viewed it again; he didn't need to…the words imprinted on his soul. *Will I make the right decision? Am I a modern-day architect of life tasked with saving humanity? Why did I believe my visions gave me the ability to change the world? What if I am wrong? Fate governed by God, left to one human being to change the course of civilization?*

Chapter 31

From the window of his library, Speaker of the House Alfred Ramsey gazed at the inaugural crowd. He placed the FBI report marked "President's Eyes Only" on the table. Ramsey was surprised at the news that Maro had continued with the outdoor ceremony. He glanced up at the wall-mounted clock; he was moments away from becoming commander in chief. Ramsey smiled at the thought. The disruption of the inauguration provided him the opportunity to exercise the privilege of the President of the United States. The pause in the proceedings set into motion a plan to unite the populace of the planet under a true, singular global government. A supreme court justice and member of the FHS waited in abeyance in the outer room to administer the temporary oath of office.

Ramsey heard the roar of the F-22s approach. In a matter of minutes, he'd assume the presidency. His first act as president would be to sign secret Executive Order number 14964. The directive exempted a division of Marines from the normal military protocols. Once he executed the document, a trusted courier of his choosing would transport the edict to the Office of the Federal Register for publication.

"Hello?"

"Have you signed the order?" the anonymous voice asked.

"No. I'm waiting to be sworn in. Our contact at the OFR will ensure the file remains hidden until needed."

"Very good."

"And Adinolfi?"

"We have him under control. We cannot fail, Alfred, or should I say, Mr. President?" Ramsey ended the phone call. He sat back and wondered about the consequences of his treasonous act. The supreme court justice entered the leader's sanctuary with a Bible in hand as two successive explosions erupted and sent a shockwave through his office. A loose book from a shelf fell to the floor. Startled, he grabbed the remote and turned on the closed-circuit TV. He was aghast at what he saw. "Shit, he's not supposed to die." Ramsey reached for the phone.

*　*　*

Capitol Steps, 11:58 A.M.

Giacomo wasted no time. The vision was now a reality. At the sound of the exploding F-22 fighter jet, the military man spread his arms as if for flight. He sprung forward with his legs parallel to the ground. With a pulverizing force, he knocked President-Elect Maro and the chief justice to the floor. The air bristled from the onslaught of the four fifty-caliber bullets. It was a sound he recalled from his service in Afghanistan, followed by the dread of watching his fellow soldiers fall victim to the audacity of war. The protective glass around the podium shattered, the shards peppering those nearby. He heard shouting, "What the hell is happening?" and "Oh, *shit.*" Secret service and BOET personnel rushed to surround the fallen men.

"Tom, are you okay?"

The president-elect groaned, "Yeah, what happened?"

"They tried to kill you. Tom, we have to clear the area and get you out ASAP."

"No, damn it. I will not allow these bastards to win. Democracy will not cease on my watch."

"Tom, this is not a good idea."

"Giacomo, they will not stop me. Do you understand, General?"

"Yes, sir," Giacomo responded. He rolled over, touched his head, and stood. A nine-millimeter Beretta in hand, he waved an agent over to assist Tom.

Then, chaos...

"The chief justice has died, General."

Giacomo gazed at the standing members of Congress while the invited guests tilted their heads back to witness the carnage in the sky. As the noise faded, a senator pointed and yelled at the downed president-elect. "We are under attack. Maro's dead." The crowd on the Capitol steps panicked. To Giacomo, they resembled a herd of frightened animals trying to escape an oncoming wall of fire. The stampede began. Screams of the trampled echoed in Giacomo's ears.

"Jason, we need to get the people under control," he screamed into his microphone.

President Richardson ran to the podium. "Please calm down. He is alive."

His words did little to restrain the masses. As if a cowboy wrangling a herd, Jason commanded his men to fire their AK-47s into the air. The cowards of Congress stopped and fell to the ground. An eerie silence cascaded over the crowd, broken by the reassuring voice of Thomas Maro through the loudspeakers.

The new president and vice president stood abreast, their hands over their hearts, as they finished the Pledge of Allegiance to a roaring throng of citizens. After the attack, Thomas Maro refused to leave the Capitol steps. Surrounded by the military and secret service, a supreme court justice at forty-five minutes past twelve performed the swearing-in ceremony of Thomas Maro. His second of the day. The populace became silent as he approached the microphones to give his inaugural address.

"My fellow Americans, once again, we have come under assault. On a personal note, I want to thank the secret service agents whose courage saved my life. Thank you for placing your lives on the line to protect our democracy. I am outraged at this attempt to destroy the fabric of our country, the foundation that our forefathers built. We are the land of the free and the brave! A unified people! A defender of rights and justice! The world looks on in shock. America must lead the way in restoring peace. I say this to our enemies: the time for discontent must end. We must work toward reconciliation and healing for our nation and our world.

"What lies ahead, I do not know. What I realize…there's no greater country than these great United States. I pray that my fellow citizens understand this and keep faith that it will remain true. To those members of the FFB, let us discuss the issues.

"My first proclamation as President…" Maro took a deep breath as he gazed at the vast crowd. He grabbed the podium with both hands and spoke. "I hereby give the Freedom Fighters Brigade and its followers amnesty from prosecution for this latest assault. The time has arrived to reestablish harmony and stability in our homeland. We can accomplish this outcome through unbiased listening and reason. Again, I implore the Brigade leaders to stop this senseless violence. Come to the table of reconciliation. Together we can make a better America."

Chapter 32

Surprised by Tom Maro's words, Giacomo couldn't escape the nagging sense that other players were involved. Although the evidence supported the FFB's involvement, Giacomo believed this was a two-pronged strike by separate foes, unified in their hatred of the United States government. Prepared to retaliate against those responsible if the vision transpired, Giacomo and his second-in-command, Jason, left nothing to doubt. To Giacomo's astonishment, the attack came from a foreign entity. His earpiece squawked.

"We're ready."

* * *

Commander in Chief Thomas Maro, General Giacomo DeLaurentis, former President Jerry Richardson, Secretary of State Lisa Rift, and select members of the intelligence community huddled around a computer in a conference room within the Capitol. Their eyes focused on the monitor.

The coastline of the Italian countryside materialized in the distance. The missiles continued their trek. Equipped with cameras, they captured the scene of the rolling hills of Tuscany. Quaint villages passed by at a rapid pace as the tools of destruction traveled at 540 miles per hour at a height of one hundred feet.

"Giacomo, are we sure?"

"Yes… We have confirmation that the phone call made by Bassett was to the Villa."

"Any survivors in the helicopter?"

"No, sir."

"Right, you told me that. Sorry, I forgot."

"No worries, Mr. President. I've been there."

"General, one minute 'til impact."

"Thank you, Colonel," Giacomo said.

A live satellite picture of the mansion replaced the camera view of the missile's path.

"Mr. President, thirty seconds."

"Continue."

"What the hell?" Giacomo said. The explosion of the building was immense—a blaze filled the monitor's entire screen.

"Looks like our weaponry worked, Giacomo," Tom patted him on the shoulder.

"Our missiles haven't reached the target yet."

"Then who destroyed the Villa?"

"I have no clue, Tom…none," Giacomo said.

Chapter 33

Ottati, Italy, January 21

Rio walked the road from the Church of Cordanato to her residence in Ottati. The house of God sheltered in the fields below the ancient village. She enjoyed the evening stroll as the sun set over the mountain town. An old Fiat trailing dust slowed to a stop next to her. The driver rolled down the window.

"*Signora?*"

Rio approached the car. The man handed her a cell phone.

"*Pronto.* Hello."

"They have destroyed the villa. Nothing for you to fear anymore."

"I don't understand, Sergio."

"You will in time."

Puzzled and confused, she replied, "*Grazie.*"

*   *   *

Sergio reclined in his office chair. He adjusted the monitor as he watched the drone image of Rio walking down the dirt road.

He placed his hands over his face. *Did he have the courage to fight the evil that existed in his life? His son dead. His friend's children's lives were at risk. For what? An ideology of a fanatic who believes The Almighty is speaking to him. I and I alone can do the bidding of God? Bullshit.* Sergio knew he had means to resolve this wrong. In doing so, he provoked the wrath of Adinolfi and the Society. He was in a lose-lose situation, and there was no escape.

Chapter 34

Washington, DC, January 21, 1:30 P.M.

As the attendees left the room, Giacomo noticed President Tom Maro's penetrating stare.

"What the hell happened?"

"I don't know, Tom. Someone beat us to the punch."

"I guess so. We've destroyed our cruise missiles?"

"Yes."

"Any collateral damage?"

"No, sir. We redirected them out over the water and executed the self-destruct mechanism."

"Call your counterpart in the Italian government. Maybe they can provide the answers?"

"I will, Tom."

"Mr. President," a secret service agent interrupted, "we need to get you to Statuary Hall for the inaugural lunch."

Giacomo watched as Tom Maro pulled the cuff of his shirt up and gazed at the time. The president's face grimaced as the wrinkles around his eyes tightened and the physical side effects of holding the Office of the President overtook his facial expressions. After the occurrences of today, Tom Maro's body had aged two years.

*   *   *

"Ladies and Gentlemen, please welcome the President of the United States, Thomas Maro."

Giacomo and Lisa shadowed Tom into Statuary Hall, the amphitheater that once accommodated the House of Representatives, noted as the most visited room in the entire Capitol complex. Statues of notable American citizens interspersed the columns that lined the perimeter. The black-and-white marble floor resembled a checkerboard.

Tom proceeded down the line of invited congressional members, accepting their greetings and congratulations. He walked up to the Speaker of the House, Alfred Ramsey. They shook hands.

"Glad you could make it, Mr. Speaker. I heard you were ill."

"Thank you, Mr. President. Feeling much better now. Stomach issues."

"I see."

Alfred Ramsey was a man of diminutive stature. Troubled by years of ulcerative colitis, his body withered from the lack of nutrients. His face prematurely wrinkled, when he smiled, his jowls folded into deep creases. He wore a blue vested suit that did not hide his frailty. A four-term member of Congress, the well-liked gentleman from California ruled the House with a fair but iron hand.

"I look forward to working with you, Mr. President. Your tenacity and devotion to serving the American people, considering the events of today, is inspiring."

"Thank you. We can't allow our country to fall into the hands of these violent anarchists. They have a desperate wish to destroy the foundations of our Constitution." He paused to gather his thoughts. "We must not be deterred, Mr. Speaker, from adhering to our democratic right of elected government. I'm sure you can agree that we can't kowtow to their despicable acts of violence against our democracy. We need to move forward and overcome this foe for the American people."

"I agree, Mr. President. I admire your insistence on finishing the inauguration. Such a terrifying time in our history. I understand you provided amnesty to the FFB?"

"Yes, I did. It's important, that we listen to our adversaries. I believe we can achieve peace with discussion and not violence. On another topic, how did you enjoy being commander in chief for forty-five minutes?"

The Speaker smiled as his jowls creased. "I wish I'd known," he laughed. "I'd have signed a couple of executive orders."

"You never lose your sense of humor, Mr. Speaker."

"Sometimes you have to laugh, Mr. President. Nothing else to do."

"Yes, indeed, Mr. Speaker. I'm looking forward to working with you. Thank you for attending."

Chapter 35

Exhausted from the tension of the day, Giacomo tried to nap. His mind replayed the events. A bittersweet wave of elation that the vision became reality caused him despair. *Why me? Why do I have the gift?* Disgusted, he dismissed the feelings.

Giacomo felt honored that the president nominated him for Chairman of the Joint Chiefs, but it didn't ease his concerns. Scheduled to appear before the Senate in three days, his mind rambled. *Do I even want the job? Who wanted Tom dead? The loose ends of the investigation… Who killed Em and the twins, as well as the whereabouts of the prophecy, its meaning, and his father's second journal? Why was Eten Trivette attacked? Who destroyed the villa in Italy? Did the FFB shoot down the F-22 fighter jet? His wife and sons buried in the cold ground. His sister's mind fragmented. What was the point? Was his focus lost? Could he continue? Was it time to disappear?* His cell phone rang.

"Hello?"

"Giacomo, it's Lisa."

"Mrs. Rift, what can I do for you?"

"Mrs. Rift? So formal."

"Okay, how about, Madame Secretary?"

"Oh God no," she laughed. "Giacomo, I need a favor?"

"Sure."

"Will you accompany me to the Presidential Ball tonight?"

Giacomo was reluctant to attend; after the debriefing and what appeared to be endless meetings, he'd hoped for a quiet evening alone with his thoughts. But he couldn't refuse Lisa. "Hubby still away?"

"Yeah, he's in Monte Cassino, Italy."

"Interesting…"

"You seem surprised?"

"It's the third time this week I've heard the town's name."

"Well, do you want to go? I'll even pick you up at the White House."

"Sure, why not? But I moved to the Willard."

"I thought you'd like the residence. Rubbing elbows with the President."

"I needed privacy."

Chapter 36

Rio sat at the kitchen table in the house her father had bought. Her hands surrounded a mug filled with Italian coffee. A cool mountain breeze entered the room through a cracked-open window. A noise from outside focused her stare on the workers repairing the pergola on the portico.

After Emily's funeral, and against her brother's wishes, Rio elected to return to the picturesque village to recuperate instead of seeking treatment in the United States. Two armed men guarded the entrance of the centuries-old residence. Unaware of the world news, she opened her laptop and waited for the Wi-Fi connection. The squeak of the opening front door startled her.

"Who's there?" she barked. Rio stood and ambled her way to the stairs leading to the foyer.

"*Principessa*, it's me."

"Sergio, what a pleasure!"

She stayed at the top of the landing as he climbed the steps. He greeted her with a kiss on her left cheek, then the right. He held her arms as he leaned back and studied her. A tear formed in his eye.

"What's wrong?"

"I'm happy you're safe."

"I'm fine. Come in, Sergio. Can I make you an espresso?"

She followed him as the two made their way to the kitchen. Rio pulled out a chair from underneath the table for Sergio. "Sit," she instructed, as she went to the marble counter. "Sugar?"

"No, thank you."

She poured a cup of the Italian brew and placed it before him. Rio patted Sergio's shoulder and sat down next to him. She stared at the clock on the wall.

"You're here early."

"I couldn't sleep. I wanted to make sure everything is fine with you."

"Aren't you sweet? You could've called me." Her eyes reflected on a memory. "Didn't we talk the other day?"

"No."

Rio saw Sergio lower his head. "Humph, I thought we did. What brings you here?"

"Just checking in and seeing how you're feeling."

Her right eye squinted as she smirked. "I'm good, no worries."

"You look like Giacomo."

"Yes, twins often look alike..." she teased Sergio. "I believe he's back in the States?"

"He is, yes. He left a couple of weeks ago."

"I remember. Jeez, Sergio, am I that bad?"

"No, no. Have you spoken with him?"

"I did." She paused for a moment. Her eyes shifted to the right. "I think it was Tuesday or Wednesday. He was on his way to catch an airplane to Washington."

"So, you haven't seen the news yet?"

"No, why?"

"There was an assassination attempt at Tom Maro's inauguration."

"Holy shit! Was Giacomo there?"

"Yes, but he's fine; nothing to worry about."

"Thank God. My brother is amazing."

"He is, Rio, and so are you."

"I have my doubts, Sergio. My mind is more confused than ever."

"What do you mean?"

"I have befuddled thoughts—as if I'm a different person."

"I'm sure it will pass."

"It is better. I spend my days walking the village, wondering who I am. At times I feel lost."

"I'm sorry, my dear."

"This is not your fault, Sergio."

Rio's eyes widened. A smirk replaced her saddened face as a memory morphed into her subconscious. "Are we prepared for the next assault?" She grinned as Sergio pushed his chair back.

"What do you mean?"

"Don't be coy with me. You know." She leaned on the wood table and leveraged herself to stand. Pointing her finger at Sergio, she said, "You damn well understand."

A wave of fright traveled up his spine. Flustered, he said, "What are you talking about?"

Rio glowered at him; her face turned red as a bead of sweat dripped from her chin. She stammered and fell to the floor. The sound of her skull hitting the tile caused Sergio to feel sick. His movements froze from the terror of the noise.

Is Rio dead?

Her moan snapped him from the dire thought.

Chapter 37

Washington, DC, January 22, 4:00 A.M.; Italy, 10:00 A.M.

Giacomo opened the car door as Lisa entered the stretch limousine.

"Thank you, kind sir," she said with a giggle.

"You're most welcome, my lady."

They both had a slight buzz from the evening's alcoholic beverages. The crisp, pre-dawn morning air helped ease the symptoms. They plopped into their seats. The senator removed her high heels with a sigh as Giacomo unbuttoned the jacket of his tux.

"Looks like you spilled a little champagne on your dress?"

He gave her a tissue and watched as she swiped the spot off her silky black Versace gown. He noticed the tight fit around her waist. Giacomo reached for a bottle of water by his seat, twisted the cap off, and offered it to Lisa. She grabbed it, took a sip, and handed it back.

"What did you think?" she inquired. She fiddled with a string of white pearls around her neck.

"This life is not for me. I had more smoke blown up my ass than the spitting plumes from Mount Etna."

"Come on, Giacomo. You've done this before—military balls, dances. You know how to play the game."

"True, but this is politics… I'm not a fan."

"Yeah, I know, it's a lot of BS. It's the cause, the ideology of helping our people that motivates us."

He raised an eyebrow and grinned.

"What, you don't believe me?"

"Come on, Lisa. Maybe you, but the rest, they have their own agendas. I doubt most of them care about their constituents."

She sighed. "You're right."

Giacomo watched as she swept her hair from her face.

"I have my doubts about accepting the job. The government will tie my hands with protocol and bureaucratic bull. There are questions I need answered. I'd need to be independent and uninhibited to investigate and obtain information on those who killed my family." He turned his head to the window. A homeless person moved a grocery cart along the sidewalk.

"You can always resign."

"Not my style."

Giacomo shifted his body while Lisa stretched her legs, placing her feet on the seat next to him. An amorous sensation rushed through his body. He pushed the notion from his mind. *How could this be? My wife hasn't been dead a month.* Giacomo felt troubled and guilty by a memory of kissing Lisa during the time he and Em had taken a hiatus from their relationship. *It must be the alcohol.*

"Are you all right?" she asked.

"What? Yeah, I'm fine. I had a thought."

"You want to talk about it?"

"No. So, Madame Secretary, are you prepared for your confirmation hearing?"

"Yes, I am. And please, enough with the titles."

Giacomo laughed. Lisa kicked him in the thigh. He grabbed her leg.

"You going to give me a massage?"

Without realizing it, his thumb rubbed the arch of her foot. There was a moment of awkwardness. The car came to a stop.

"General DeLaurentis, the Willard hotel."

He removed his hand and took a swig of water. The smile on her face caught Giacomo's attention.

"Do you want company?"

The driver exited the limo and waited by the curb to escort Giacomo.

"It's a nice thought, but I think the alcohol is talking. Truth is, I can't. Besides, you're married."

"Another time."

"Perhaps."

Before he left, he leaned over and kissed her on the cheek. "You're still beautiful." He saw Lisa smile as the chauffeur closed the door.

Giacomo entered the lobby of the Willard InterContinental hotel. He walked past the golden-brown, swirled-marble columns. His polished black Italian leather shoes shuffled across the floor. Exhausted, he tapped his fingers on a round maple table. As he got closer to the front desk, he became more aware of his surroundings. To his right, a man sat in an ornate antique chair. He caught the stare of an Asian woman peering over her glasses while reading a magazine. His senses heightened as his eyes scanned the area. He rounded the corner.

"Sir?"

A military attaché appeared. Dressed in Air Force blues, she approached Giacomo.

She saluted. "General DeLaurentis, you're needed at the CIA. Your car is waiting for you." The captain handed him an envelope.

"Give me fifteen minutes. I need to clean up."

Chapter 38

Sala Consilina, Italy, 10:30 A.M.; Washington, DC, 4:30 A.M.

Sergio held Rio's hand as the paramedics pushed the gurney through the emergency entrance of Centro Medico Dianum. Rio awoke after being sedated during the hour-long drive.

"All is fine, Rio, you're safe now." Tears welled in his eyes. *"What have I done?"* he whispered with the caring voice of a parent.

He paced the waiting room. Forty-five minutes passed and still no word on Rio's condition. The door to the hallway squeaked open. A tall, thin doctor wearing a surgical gown appeared. Sergio's face gripped with worry and concern, his lips taut, brow creased. The physician approached.

"I'm so happy to see you, Mr. Prime Minister."

"I wish it were under different circumstances."

Sergio embraced Maria and, as was the European custom, kissed her right cheek, then the left.

"How are your baby girls?" Sergio inquired with a smile.

"Not so little anymore. Twenty-one and twenty-three, both at the University of Rome."

"And your husband?"

"He's fine, thank you, busy with his research." Doctor Maria Panzetta folded her arms. "Our friend is up to his old tricks."

"I'm afraid so. He murdered my son, and now this. You're lucky you got out."

"If it weren't for you, Sergio, our lifeless bodies may have ended up in cement footwear."

Sergio's eyes grew distant as he remembered the day twenty years ago. "Do you think you can help Rio?"

Maria inhaled, then let out a sigh. "How much time do we have?"

"I don't know. I never considered the issue."

"When did Adinolfi begin the process?"

"This past August."

"And she has had repeated episodes like today?"

"Yes."

"Well, that's a good sign. Her mind is fighting back. We might have a chance."

"He kept her in a coma."

"Yes, I read the report. Thanks for sending it to me. For a reversal to occur, we need similar DNA. Any siblings or a surviving parent?"

"Mother and twin brother."

"Are they here or in the States?"

"In the US."

"There's a doctor friend of mine in Washington who's had success in re-engineering the human genome. I'll contact her. I'm sure she'll help. Can you get blood samples from her family?"

"Yes."

"Good. We'll retrieve Rio's genetic material and send it to my friend's lab. We should have the amended genes within ten days. After testing, we'll start an aggressive therapy regimen. This should repair the damaged DNA. I'm confident we'll be successful."

As Sergio exited the hospital, the late morning sun drifted above the mountain, casting squat shadows. Relieved by the possibility that Rio could be cured, he blessed himself. The sounds of two doves cooing in a nearby tree brought a smile to his face. He gazed skyward and watched as a wave of clouds bristled overhead. A cool breeze rustled his jacket as he walked.

His resolve to pursue his vendetta against Adinolfi became paramount. Though overcome with remorse, he could no longer hide. Thoughts of his deception caused his stomach to churn. Sergio had betrayed himself and his wife and his remaining children. His actions resulted in his own son's death. Now Rio, the daughter of his late friend, Paolo DeLaurentis, was suffering at the hands of a lunatic. He reached for his cell.

"Giacomo, Sergio. We need to talk. I'm taking a flight to the States. I'll call when I arrive." He ended the voicemail by pressing the pound sign. His cream-colored blazer flapped in the breeze. He placed his phone in his inside jacket pocket. *How did life go so wrong?* A siren wailed in the distance. As he turned right into the parking lot, keys in hand, he pushed the remote start for his Alfa Romeo. He saw the flash turn into a fireball before the sound of the explosion met his ears. Sergio's mind went dark as the volatile force lifted him off his feet and propelled him into a parked car.

Chapter 39

The Abbey at Monte Cassino, Italy

A dinolfi read the message on his cell phone. The text said, "He's dead. Car exploded as planned." He paused for a moment, typed, *"Are you sure?"*

"Yes, the vehicle detonated when he turned on the ignition. His body is burned beyond recognition."

"We need to return the patient to Monte Cassino for further research."

"We have to wait until tomorrow. The authorities are still here."

Adinolfi shook his head in disbelief. *Why? Why did you think you could stop the spirit of God? May you rest in peace, Sergio.*

* * *

1964

Adinolfi's indoctrination within the FHS had begun at the ripe age of six. Placed under the tutelage of Brother Marco Rinaldi, the monk's mentoring molded the future priest-physician's thoughts. A local nunnery cared for the orphaned child prior to his admission to the monastery of Monte Cassino.

"Alphonso! *Vieni qua*—come here."

Now ten, the boy kicked a soccer ball against the wall of the abbey. Adinolfi adapted to his surroundings and enjoyed the protective care of his mentor. He gathered the red, white, and green-checkered sphere and ran to his superior.

"Yes, Brother."

Marco kneeled and tussled the boy's hair.

"Alphonso, it's time for prayer."

"Do we have to?"

"Yes. It is the essence of our lives."

Alphonso dropped his head in resignation. He walked at a slow pace as they moved toward the chapel. The monastic stood six feet, five inches tall and weighed 280 pounds. He turned, smiling at the boy, his dimpled chin widening. Raising his enormous hand as if to make the sign of the cross Alphonso scratched his Roman shaped nose. A gentle soul, he had given his life to God after the death of his wife and daughter.

"I have a surprise for you," he said, as he turned toward the youngster.

"You do?" The child's short legs carried him to his mentor. He tugged on the cassock. "Tell me, tell me. What is it?"

"Patience, my son."

"Oh, please," he pleaded.

"After dinner."

"Ugh."

Brother Marco chuckled as he reached over to pat the boy's head. Alphonso rebuffed him with an abrupt physical withdrawal; the youngster pouted and folded his arms in disappointment.

"Now, now, Alphonso—anger isn't healthy for a child of God."

The boy stamped his feet and ran away from his mentor.

*   *   *

Alphonso sat in his room, admiring the black cassock he wore. The mirror reflected the inner joy he felt. Now part of the community, someday he'd be a priest. His heart jumped at the thought. There was a knock.

"May I come in, Brother?"

"Of course, Brother Marco." His voice resounded in the delight of his new title.

His mentor moved a chair, propping the door open. The abbey rule stated, "Whenever two monks are together in a cell, there must be a clear passageway." Alphonso noticed this wasn't always the case.

"I have a gift for you."

With reverence, he accepted the book. "*Liturgy of the Hours*?"

The Breviary contained the official prayers recited during the day. All priests and brothers within the monastery were obligated to recite them at the appointed time. The young boy leafed through the pages. He enjoyed the feel of the thin paper.

"Yes, your very own. You know how to use it?"

"Yes, yes, I do."

"Good. Remember: Always pray to the Holy Spirit for guidance, so the words will speak to your heart. Sleep well, Alphonso."

"Thank you, Brother Marco."

The door to the room closed. The young boy dropped to his knees in prayer. With fervor, he asked to hear the voice of God.

His prayer was answered at twenty-six—a year before his ordination to the priesthood.

Chapter 40

CIA Headquarters, McLean, Virginia, January 22, 5:30 A.M.

Giacomo followed his aide into the building. He grabbed his cell phone on the other side of the body scanner. Glancing at the screen, he noticed a missed call. He retrieved his voicemail and listened to Sergio's recording. Puzzled, he squinted. *Why was Sergio traveling to the States? What the hell has happened now?* He tried to return the call, but it could not connect. Moments later, an intense fear traveled through him.

"General DeLaurentis, you don't look so good. Everything—"

"Yes, I'm fine, Captain."

Giacomo's footsteps echoed as they walked down the hall to a secured conference chamber. He undid his bowtie and pulled it from his collar, placing it in his tuxedo pocket. When he had gone to his hotel room, he decided not to change his clothes. Instead, he washed his face and brushed his teeth. At least his breath didn't smell of alcohol. *What am I doing here? I'm not confirmed. I don't even know if I want the job.*

As chairman of the Joint Chiefs, Giacomo reported to the president. There was no intermediary. He served as a member of the NSC, giving him access to classified *presidential eyes-only* information. His influence wielded power.

They approached a double maple-wood door. Positioned to the right, a marine sergeant saluted and turned the handle to allow Giacomo entry. Seated at the table were five people, one female and four males—their eyes fixed on a large screen where a fireball rose in the sky with nearby cars sailing through the air. The woman aimed a remote at the television, and the video disappeared. She stood and approached him.

"Welcome, General DeLaurentis, I'm glad you made it."

"Sorry for the delay, construction on the George Washington Parkway. What do you want?" Annoyed, he didn't apologize for his abruptness.

"No issues. We weren't going anywhere. We appreciate you meeting us here."

Giacomo eyed the woman as she stepped closer to him. Her chestnut brown hair flowed over her shoulders. She had olive skin and captivating eyes. She reminded him of Sophia Loren. He figured she was about forty-five years old.

"I'm Maryann Costatino, CIA, Italian station." She held out her hand. She introduced the men by their first names as specialists for the counterintelligence service and NSC. "Please have a seat."

Giacomo pulled the brown leather chair from under the table and sat. Annoyed, he said, "What's so urgent?"

"We thought this might interest you." She aimed the controller at the screen.

A wrenching ache struck Giacomo's heart as he saw his friend's car blown to oblivion. Horrified, he said nothing for a moment. "He's dead?"

"No. Sergio is alive and will recover. He used his remote to start the car..."

"When did it happen?"

"Less than an hour ago."

"How did you get the video?"

"After the death of your friend, Alessio, the Italian government requested our help in surveilling his father, your business partner. We've had him under observation for the past couple of months."

Maryann slid a manila folder across the table to Giacomo. The paper came to rest under his hand. He glared at the CIA operative while his fingers played a drum roll on the file. *Do I want to know the contents?*

"I take it I was under surveillance?"

"On the contrary. Our explicit instructions were to keep you out of the investigation. We believe you can help."

Giacomo took her nod as instruction to open the dossier. Inside, the top page of the three-quarter-inch thick report was a photo of Dr. Alphonso Adinolfi.

Chapter 41

"Why do you have a file on Rio's doctor?" He held the photo in his hand, then leafed through the dossier. Highlighted in yellow throughout the document were the names of his friends—Sergio and Alessio. As he read further, the phrase "Followers of the Holy Spirit," accompanied by the acronym "FHS," jumped out at him.

Giacomo was furious. His fists clenched while he continued the painstaking task of reading the file. The room was quiet. He was oblivious to his surroundings as he delved deeper into the report. Giacomo's jaw clamped tight with rage. Words on the paper blurred as he struggled to process the information.

"General DeLaurentis, sir?"

Devastated, he fixed his eyes on the CIA agent. His chest rose as he took deep, amplified breaths, the anxiety traversing through him. Giacomo glowered with fear. He pushed away from the table. The four specialists stood, and one reached for his nine millimeter.

"General DeLaurentis?" Maryann raised her hand, holding the men at bay. She approached him, touching his shoulder. "Relax, Giacomo, all is good."

The soothing words eased his convoluted mind. His rational thought process restored. *How could Sergio betray me?*

"I'm fine," he retorted. "Just need some space." Giacomo's stomach erupted in a wave of nausea. He stopped the bile from rising in his throat.

"Get him some water."

The specialist who had reached for his gun poured Giacomo a glass. He took a sip. "Thanks." His livid voice penetrated the room. "Adinolfi and Sergio are responsible for the death of my wife and children?" As he said the unbelievable words, his stomach churned. His body wracked with sorrow and rage at the betrayal.

"Yes and no. Our intel shows the ex-prime minister was not aware of Adinolfi's plan until after the fact. We're confident the priest orchestrated this attempted assassination in retribution. Giacomo, your friend was trying to save your sister's life."

"What do you mean? Rio's in Ottati."

"She was. Sergio went to visit her this morning. From what we can gather, Rio had a seizure."

Giacomo's eyes widened. "Is she okay?"

"Yes, she will be fine."

His mind grappled with questions, he strained to comprehend what he heard and what he read.

"Your partner transported your sister to a hospital in Sala Consilina. A friend of his, Dr. Maria Panzetta, contacted me."

"Why you?"

The hesitant gaze and sigh of the CIA agent garnered his attention.

"What's the problem?"

"My answer involves national security issues that you—"

"Yeah, so what?" Giacomo stood. The palm of his hands planted on the conference table. "Let me explain something to you, Ms. Costatino. You and your operatives are playing with fire. You'll tell me everything. I won't put up with your intelligence bullshit." Giacomo's voice boomed with the veracity of his military title. He scanned the room. The penetrating eyes of the agents caused him no concern. Giacomo recognized that Maryann remained calm. Her gaze never wavered as her face remained emotionless for a moment. Then she smiled at him.

"What's with the grin?"

"Relax, Giacomo. We have no desire to keep you out of the loop. I was going to say, my answer involves national security issues that you may not want to hear. Our concern is how you will react. The purpose of today's meeting was to inform you that Rio is traveling to the States, where she'll be treated and returned to normal health."

Giacomo shook his head. *Do I want to hear this?* "What do you mean *treated*?"

Maryann drew herself close to the table, folding her hands. Her brown eyes sparkled, and her white teeth glistened. Her tongue parted her lips. Captivated, Giacomo threw the impulse to kiss her from his mind.

"It's not what it seems."

Giacomo's eyes narrowed.

"It's not what it seems," she repeated, unperturbed by his stare.

"I've heard those words before."

"We know."

Giacomo tilted forward, placing his elbows on the table as he recalled the first time he heard the phrase.

"The monk in Rome who tried to warn me…he was yours. CIA?"

"Yes, he was. We didn't realize he reached out to you."

"Interesting…"

"We assume he contacted you because of your sister."

"What do you mean?" Giacomo noticed the quizzical gaze.

"I gather from your reaction, you missed the section about Rio."

"I guess so."

Anxiety arose within his body. The tingling sensation traveled down his arms. *What other deceptive information do they have?* He tried to relax. Giacomo needed to control himself and his outbursts. He saw Maryann flinch and observed the men take heed of her motion. *Am I ready for this?* He grabbed the dossier and riffled through the pages, his heart racing. Distraught, he closed the report and said, "Tell me."

"Dr. Adinolfi and his associates have perfected a way to re-engineer the human genome via DNA splicing. We have strong intelligence confirming that he altered your sister's."

Giacomo froze, stunned. "DNA? What are you saying? My sister is no longer my sister?"

"Correct. They bio-modified your sister's brain functions and thought processes. However, our scientists can repair the genetic material, and we are confident that the real Rio will recover."

He wanted to vomit. *How could this be?* "Sergio was aware of this?"

"Yes, at some point he discovered what Adinolfi did. He was bringing her to Dr. Panzetta for treatment when Adinolfi retaliated. Panzetta, her husband, and a doctor here in the States have been working with our government to perfect a reversal process."

Giacomo rubbed his face. *I'm in a nightmare; none of this is real.*

Maryann moved closer. She touched his hand. "I understand this is difficult, and I'm sorry you had to learn about Rio in this manner. But we had no choice. We had to bring you in prior to your confirmation. Your sister will arrive in Connecticut in about five hours. We've arranged transportation for her to Yale New Haven Hospital. I have spoken with your second-in-command, Colonel Vandercliff, to provide armed security."

"You said her condition can be reversed?"

"My understanding is yes."

"Sergio…where the hell is he?"

"He is under our protection, with one of our operatives, who we resurrected from the past. A friend of yours."

"Who?"

"Frank."

"Why him? He has his own life."

"We don't know who to trust, Giacomo. Frank was a safe bet. After our investigation began, we uncovered two organizations that use the acronym FHS, Fidelis Hereditas Sapien and Followers of the Holy Spirit. Our ensuing inquiry discovered that the same leadership controls both factions. In our due diligence, we found that the groups' tentacles influence global Fortune 500 corporations, world, national and local governments, and, of course, religious institutions."

"Do you have proof?"

"Not yet. We're working on it. We believe at one point the FHS was a single spiritual organization, and over the years, they split into two independent organizations. The strife within the group has propelled their leader to reestablish control."

"Adinolfi?"

"Yes. By accident, we intercepted a communique between him and a subordinate about the President of the European Union."

"Trivette was involved in this, wasn't he?"

"No. Adinolfi manipulated his mind, the same way he's trying to influence your sister's thought process."

"That son of a bitch."

"Rio is in expert hands, she'll recover."

The statement provided little comfort to Giacomo. Exhausted, his brain scrambled for answers. Without warning, he pushed his chair back.

"Thank you, Ms. Costatino. I'll call you later today. I need sleep and time to think. May I take the dossier?"

"Yes, of course. And please, Maryann."

"Very well, Maryann."

Chapter 42

Sergio's ears rang and his body ached as he awoke to the rhythmic beep of the heart monitor. Befuddled, his mind recalled what had happened. He remembered pressing the remote start switch, followed by a flash. He tried to scratch his nose. An IV tube inserted in his arm hampered the movement. He focused on what appeared to be an indignant person sitting in a chair by his bed. The broad-shouldered, bald gentleman with a goatee stared at him.

"*Chi sei?*" Sergio's voice crackled.

"Speak English."

"Who are you?"

"I'm here to save your ass. Don't ask me why? If it was my choice, you'd be dead." The man withdrew an envelope from his shirt pocket and threw it at the patient. The paper landed on his chest.

"Can you help me sit up?"

"Push the button on your bed."

The rudeness of the man shocked Sergio. *Was this one of Adinolfi's people? No, if that were the case, I'd be dead.*

"Who are you?"

"I'm not your friend. Read the note."

The ex-prime minister of Italy adjusted the hospital bed. His head pounded and his heart rate increased when he saw the familiar moniker of Paolo DeLaurentis scrawled on the back flap. Beneath his signature, the imprinted date: September 30, 2002. He pulled the handwritten piece of paper out of the envelope and let it rest on his lap. Afraid to read the words, he fumbled. His callous protector frowned and nodded.

"I'm not going anywhere."

Sergio closed his eyes, sighed, took a deep breath, and perused the text.

My friend, the time has arrived to stand for justice and correct the wrong. The two boys must be returned to their father. Frank—the person before you—is a colleague of Giacomo's. He'll assist you by any means necessary to accomplish the task. Fear not, Sergio. I forgive you.

Sergio dropped the paper onto his lap as he cried.

"There's a tissue on the nightstand. Wipe your face, old man. Your doctor friend Panzetta filled me in about Rio and Adinolfi. Tell me about the boys."

"How is she?"

"What do you care? She's here because of you. Now tell me, who are the boys?"

Sergio hesitated. He knew his actions had consequences from which he could not escape.

"They're Giacomo's sons."

Frank stood rigid, his hands clasped on the bed rail. His facial expression became severe as his biceps and chest flexed. "What? Are you kidding me? They died with their mother. No way they are alive."

Sergio's eyes widened in fright at the hulking person scowling above him, the knuckles of his fists white with anger. The heart monitor beeped at a rapid pace, causing an alarm to ring. A nurse rushed in and pushed Frank away from the bed.

She grimaced. "What did you do?"

Frank's hands turned palms up; he replied in a nonchalant manner, "We were just talking. I guess he didn't like what I had to say."

"Leave, get out."

He did what he was told and stood beside the doorway. Fifteen minutes later, she left the room. With a disdainful scowl, she said, "You can go in. I gave him a sedative. He'll be asleep for a while."

Frank walked across the hall, humming a melody he had written. *He's not going anywhere.* He pulled a piece of paper from his back pocket. The ex-Delta Force member read the words as he sat on a two-seat couch.

> *Frank, don't concern yourself with right or wrong. The important point is that you complete the task before the combined holiday of Passover and Easter. Sergio is an old friend of mine who was duped. It's not our job to judge or seek revenge. I absolve him. For whatever reason, we must keep the information away from Giacomo. Frank, trust our friends back in the States.*

He folded the paper as he said aloud, "Yeah, maybe you can forgive him, Mr. DeLaurentis, but can your son?"

"I'm sorry, did you say something?" Dr. Panzetta asked as she walked up to him.

He stood. "No, I was talking to myself. Is Rio ready to travel?"

"Yes, she's comfortable. The return flight to the States shouldn't affect her. Your men are going to accompany her?"

"Yes, with an army nurse and doctor."

The physician reached into the front pocket of her white coat. "Here are instructions, should a medical issue arise on the airplane. They'll know what to do."

"Thank you. I'll give the directions to my people. Sergio's release date?"

"In a day or two."

Two men walked over to Frank, one whispered in his ear.

"Are you sure?"

"What's going on?" Dr. Panzetta asked.

"We have people inquiring about Rio."

He turned his attention to his men. "Take them out but keep them alive."

"Yes, sir."

"As we guessed, Adinolfi knows she's here. It's time to move."

"What can I do?"

"Do you have a discrete room where we can interrogate the intruders?"

"Sure, you're not going to kill them, are you?"

"No, just ask them a couple of questions, then hand them to the authorities. Is the ambulance ready to transport Rio?"

"Yes."

"My men will escort her. I'm staying here until you release Sergio."

"He's a good man, you know. He saved the lives of my husband and children."

Frank said nothing as he left Dr. Panzetta and hurried to Rio's room.

Chapter 43

Adinolfi's emissaries lay unconscious from the thrashing they endured by Frank's men, who guarded the corridor. Frank and Dr. Panzetta stood outside the intruders' hospital room. The ex-Delta Ranger was unfazed as he watched three nurses attend to their injuries. A phone chimed. He reached into his pocket and answered the call with a simple acknowledgement.

"I'm listening." After hearing the response, he returned the mobile to its rightful place.

"Rio is airborne. Thank you for your help, Doctor."

"You're welcome. She'll receive the proper treatment she needs in the United States."

His cell rang again. Annoyed, he responded, "What…understood." The call ended. "Well, Doc, we're finished here. Don't need these two scumbags. We have notified the authorities. My men will stay until they arrive. I'll be leaving with Sergio in the morning."

* * *

The Abbey at Monte Cassino, Italy

The bewildered Adinolfi read the text. Rio escaped to the United States. His men failed him. Enraged, he slammed his fist on the desk when he discovered his former protégé, Dr. Maria Panzetta, and her husband had assisted in Rio's liberation. *How is this possible? Aren't they dead?* He tried to stay resolved and focused on his plan to maintain his position as chairman. Time moved slower. Four days had passed since he stopped taking his pills. The quiet demons vowed to return to narrate the story inside his head. *The intonation of the Holy Spirit. God's plan could not be thwarted.*

Adinolfi's failure to manipulate Eten Trivette further eroded his control within the organization. A member of the secular unit presided over the EU, infuriating the man. Adinolfi may have lost the battle, but the war was still his to win. The voices in his mind prompted him to fast and pray until the annual meeting of the board of directors.

The tormented man laid out the sequence of events in his mind. Before the vote, with eyes focused on him, he'd press a button on a remote control—the curtains behind him opening to reveal a glass case that contained the parchment prophecy. The board, in awe at the discovery, would surround him with praise, thus solidifying the religious importance of his and the FHS's role in the salvation of humankind. First on the list: recover the original and remove his enemies who wished to defeat him.

Rio had been absconded to America, but not for long. She could not escape his grasp. His agenda for her, to be the President of the United States under his authority, was the catalyst needed to establish the new Heaven on earth. In twenty-five years, she would take the oath of office. By then, her nephews, Arnaud and Paolo, will have completed their indoctrination to become the future leaders of the Church and one-global-rule government.

Adinolfi grinned at the knowledge Giacomo's twins were alive and safe in a nunnery. Their location remained a secret in his being.

Chapter 44

Giacomo returned to the hotel at seven in the morning. Disillusioned, he attempted to read the dossier. In an outburst, he threw the file across the room, then sunk into disheartenment as he tried to escape the crushing hurt of the deaths of his wife and children.

The betrayal by Sergio and his son Alessio compounded the agonizing pain. *Why? I don't understand. Will Rio be her old self again?* Giacomo's thoughts became fragmented. *What do I do now?* His resolve to kill Adinolfi and his friend Sergio made him sick to his stomach. In the quiet hours of dawn, he made his plans. He fell asleep steadfast in his belief that he didn't care who or what he'd trample to carry through with his goal.

When the phone rang, he answered with a preoccupied, "Hello?"

"Good morning, Giacomo. Did you sleep well?"

The exhausted man stumbled for words before he realized who was on the line. "Hi, Lisa. What time is it?"

"Eleven fifteen, I'm surprised you're not out of bed. You didn't drink that much. You alright?"

"I could be better."

"You want to share?"

"Not now."

"I wanted to remind you that our meetings on the Hill for our confirmation hearings start at three o'clock."

"Yes, I know. Jason reminded me."

"I can pick you up, say two thirty?" Lisa said.

"Sure…thanks."

Giacomo showered and dressed. He gathered the scattered papers from the floor and carried the dossier to the safe. Hungry, he went downstairs to the hotel restaurant for coffee and a snack. As he waited for the black brew and a BLT sandwich, he reached into his pants pocket and withdrew a piece of paper. Fury returned as he read the words he had written. *Monte Cassino, FHS, Sala Consilina, Genome, DNA, Dr. Panzetta, Sergio, and Adinolfi.* Thoughts of revenge consumed him.

"Excuse me. Do you mind if I sit?"

Giacomo folded the note as he eyed his visitor. The Rome section chief of the CIA unbuttoned a bluish-gray winter coat and removed the matching velvet scarf wrapped around her neck. Underneath, a black business suit highlighted the exquisite curvature of her body.

"Of course, Maryann. Care to join me for lunch?"

"Thank you." She sat down opposite him.

"What brings you here? I'm sure it's not by accident."

"You're correct, Giacomo. We need to tidy up our conversation from this morning to make certain we understand the implications."

"And what may that be?"

"The repercussions should you go rogue."

"What makes you think I will?"

Giacomo saw her eyebrows rise and the smirk on her face.

"Come on, Giacomo. We know, or I should say we *believe*, you'll set a course of vengeance into motion against your business partner and Adinolfi."

"I won't lie, the thought has crossed my mind."

"I'm asking you to refrain and allow the authorities to bring them to justice."

Giacomo's frustration brewed. "Why?"

"You have too much to lose. We need you here in the States. It's important you stay focused on your future appointment as the chairman of the Joint Chiefs. Through your efforts, we can make a united front to stop World War III and prevent another attack on our country."

"What the hell are you talking about?" He struggled to quell his irritation.

She reached for her purse and pulled out an envelope. Giacomo recognized what it was. A sense of peace fell over him—he wasn't alone. He pointed as he said, "My father?"

"Yes. A courier delivered it to my home in Georgetown this morning. I'm perplexed. My understanding is your father died."

"He did. May I see it?"

She handed it to him. On the front were the words, *Please hand-deliver to Giacomo.* He turned it over and, as was customary, his father's signature was penned across the torn flap, along with a date: March 3, 2003.

"Less than a year before he passed."

He removed the note and read Paolo's remarks.

> *Maryann, the planet is in great peril. World War III beckons on humanity's doorstep. It is vital my son Giacomo remain in the United States. His allies are few. A purge will begin.*
>
> *Remember when you were a child after the death of your parents? Remember the sense of being so alone? Your aunt and uncle rescued you and protected and guided you through your tumultuous teenage years. Their loyalty and love for you was unwavering. They gave everything they had to ensure you a pleasant life. You came to understand the meaning of your existence.*

Giacomo gazed at Maryann. His empathy for the woman tugged at his heart. The sadness entrenched within her being did not differ from what he suffered. He continued to read.

> *My son, I realize you are in pain, and the betrayal you endure is devastating. I beg of you not to follow your instinct for revenge.*

It is fruitless, nothing to gain. It is imperative you stay in the States and unite the two brothers. After they meet, peace will ensue. A picture is worth a thousand words. Rio will be fine. Remember, what is hidden will be revealed in time. I apologize for the riddles, but you'll understand when the time comes. Love you.

Dad

Giacomo folded the paper and placed it next to his coffee cup. His right hand gravitated to his nose as his forefinger tapped the corner of his eye. He sighed—conflicted about his father's request to remain in the country. He touched Maryann's arm.

"Sorry for your pain."

"Such a long time ago. I'm fine now."

Giacomo surmised she wasn't being honest. He understood her woundedness. He held her gaze as she looked away from him.

"How did your father...?"

"He had a gift of knowledge, he was...empathic."

"We could have used his talent in the CIA."

"I'm sure you could have."

"This letter..."

"How?"

"Yeah, he wrote this such a long time ago. How did he—"

"No idea."

"Are you going to heed your father's advice?"

"Maybe. One thing I know about my father, he was never wrong. Whether I will comply? We'll see. I'm dining with the president tonight. I'll ask him to approve your being available in my pursuit to apprehend Adinolfi. Any issues?"

"No. I look forward to working with you, General DeLaurentis."

"Thank you, *Miss* Costatino."

They both chuckled.

Chapter 45

The White House Residence

"Giacomo, did you enjoy the dinner?"

"Yes, Tom. Thank you."

"How did your meetings on the Hill go today?"

"The leaders of both parties believe I won't have any issues with confirmation."

"Excellent."

"I have to be honest," Giacomo turned his head. "I'm not sure I want the job. This is a great honor, and I thank you for the nomination. But I think I can best serve you if I keep my current role."

The president folded his hands, placing them on the oak table, and leaned forward.

"I'm aware of the betrayal of Sergio and the horror Adinolfi has inflicted on you. I understand your desire for revenge. But listen to me as a friend—retribution is never sweet. Vengeance will not free your soul or ease the pain in your heart. We need you here. Remember, Passover is right around the corner and your vision…Paris going dark? If your vision is true…we are facing a calamity of unknown proportion."

"Wow, how did I forget? I'm sorry to say I have nothing to contradict that the vision will become reality." Giacomo rubbed his face. His mind was tired. *Do I care that the earth's civilizations are coming to an end? Or is my grief so unsettling that relief from the agony is death? What hope do I have?* The thoughts ended with his realization that the vision was true; Paris was going dark. This time, Passover's meaning was different. The Almighty withdrew his hand from the inhabitants of the earth. The judgment was not God's choosing—rather, man's desire to be God.

"Giacomo, you okay?"

"I've been better, the stress is wearing me down. I'm having a problem putting life into perspective."

"My friend, you've experienced the tragedies of our human existence more so than any one person could manage. Life is tough for you, but our country, our world, is counting on you. Your role as Chairman of the Joint Chiefs needs to come to fruition, and you must remain here in America."

"Please, Tom. I don't need smoke blown up my ass."

"I'm serious, Giacomo. You're a key to our survival as a nation and a democracy. How did your father say it? A...trumpet? You've sounded the horn...warning us all."

"And what did that accomplish? I lost my wife...my unborn sons...my friends deceived me. And for what? To know the future? To manipulate the outcome?"

"Yes. We have a responsibility to try to thwart the catastrophes, or at least prepare for them. Our duty is to halt the evil in our country and the world. Your vision is going to happen. We have an obligation to prevent the devastation."

"How can I do that if I'm sitting behind a desk?" Giacomo stood, walked to the window, and scanned the White House grounds. He turned and leaned on the pane. A secret service agent appeared and handed a note to the president. "Another message from my dead father?"

"No, on the contrary. Your sister is safe, and Jason is with her."

"Damn, Rio. How could I forget?"

Giacomo recognized the compassion on Tom's face. *I have to pull myself together.* He needed to refocus his energies and realize his grieving had to wait. Giacomo believed, even through his psychological torture, he had an obligation to prevent the demise of the multitudes of innocent people. He needed to put an end to his struggle to overcome grief. *Revenge might be the answer, followed by saving the planet from destruction.*

"Your confirmation hearing is in two days. No doubt you'll breeze through the approval process. From there, your term will commence February twenty-seventh, a month from now. Return to Connecticut and put your life back in order. My friend, we'll get these bastards, I promise. But I need you to stay here. The laws and hands of the United States government will serve justice. Do you understand?"

"Yes, Tom." Giacomo's words conflicted with his desire for retribution.

Chapter 46

New Haven, Connecticut, January 29

Giacomo sailed through the confirmation process, while Senator Lisa Rift had a more arduous time. An irate president squashed a disagreeable partisan-charged debate over her secretary of state nomination. Tom Maro called the leaders of both parties to the White House and admonished them with an unbridled ferocity. He demanded that the political division cease. The country's perilous road toward separation ended that day, but according to one politician, a gauntlet had been thrown, the duel was about to begin, and there would be severe consequences for the loser.

Giacomo sat in a brown leather chair in his study. He placed the pamphlet describing the seven stages of grief on his desk. What hope could there be for him? He fought off depression. *I can beat this. I don't have to accept this feeling. I need to keep myself busy.* He refocused his mind on the morning sun glinting through the bay window; his gaze fell over the backyard. Deer tracks pressed in the fresh, fallen snow trailed over the white lawn. Across the front of his massive maple desk were five twenty-one-inch monitors. Giacomo wiped the dust from his computer screens as they awoke and displayed flickering images from his unmanned aircraft. The aerial videos of his house and the surrounding neighborhood piqued his curiosity.

Because of a conflict of interest, Giacomo needed to divest himself of his company, Remote, LLC, before February 28. The corporation operated from four secret facilities, two in the United States, one on the island of Corsica, and the last in Rome. Giacomo's firm could be the roving eye of any government who wished to pay for the shadowing services. Their computers housed an elaborate array of facial and vehicle recognition software. The plan had been to relinquish control to Sergio.

Instead of transferring ownership, he informed his employees of his intention to cease business operations on February 27. To curb their disappointment, he provided each worker with two million dollars severance pay, tax free, on the stipulation they stay until the end of the month. Although he agreed not to travel outside of America, nothing could stop him from tracking Adinolfi and members of the FHS.

The doorbell rang. His cellphone flashed a photo of a woman standing by the door.

"I'll be right there," Giacomo announced through the video speaker. As he walked to the front door, he noted her casualness. Dressed in blue jeans, boots, and a tan suede jacket with a white fluffy collar, she carried a brown leather flap briefcase over her shoulder. Her eyes sparkled at the camera.

"Good morning, Maryann. Come on in, please. Can I take your coat?"

"Yes, thank you. I love your home."

"It belonged to my parents. I bought the house from my mom when she remarried. Care for a cup of coffee?"

"Sure."

He guided her to his study. "Have a seat; I'll be right back. Sugar, milk?"

"A touch of cream, if not, milk is okay."

Giacomo entered the kitchen. As he did so, he scrolled through the screens of his phone. A picture of his office appeared. Maryann sat on the couch, changing the position of her legs. He saw her scan the room. She checked her cell and fiddled with her hair. He grabbed a mug, filled it with java, and added a splash of cream, his eyes never wandering from the display.

"Thanks for stopping by. Here you go." He placed the cup on a coffee table and sat opposite her.

"No problem. It was on my way. I have a meeting in Boston."

"Where are you from, Maryann?"

Giacomo noted that the question surprised her.

"Connecticut, close to here. North Haven."

"My friends Bunny and Fran Lynch live there."

"Small world. I attended high school with Bunny."

"Ah. She heads counterterrorism for the Northeast."

"Yes, I know. We've talked and traded information, but I haven't seen her in years," she said.

Giacomo smiled. "Great people. I hope you don't mind my asking. I like to know who I'm working with."

"Not at all—as long as you don't ask me my weight."

"Funny. I promise I won't."

"Quite the setup here."

"Thank you. I oversee my business assets from that desk."

"You mean your drones?"

"Yep. Care to look?"

"Sure."

Giacomo watched Maryann move to his workspace and take a seat. He followed and stood behind her, placing his palms on the back of her chair. He noticed the luster in her hair. The smell of her perfume reminded him of Emily.

"On the center monitor is the live camera image of the Abbey of Monte Cassino, the last known location of Adinolfi."

"He's not there anymore?"

"No. I have a video of him leaving yesterday morning, and as yet he hasn't returned. My software tagged his car and face. He won't get far."

"Why is this screen blank?" Maryann pointed to a second monitor.

"No video feed because the drone is on loan to the FBI. They are conducting surveillance in the area. I'm sure you're aware that the CIA has used my remote drone technology."

"Yes, they informed me."

Giacomo walked to his wall safe and withdrew the counterintelligence agency dossier. He returned to the couch and sat. Maryann followed.

"I read your report. I'll be honest, the document is riddled with gaping holes, with no basis but conjecture. It's vague on the secular FHS. They appear to be a legit corporation with vast real estate holdings. Adinolfi...I want him dead. I couldn't care less about the organization."

"I understand your feelings. We believe the consortium's goal is to manipulate the nations' governments and economies."

"Any supportive information?"

"A theory, at the moment. But we're getting closer to the truth. Giacomo, there are way too many coincidences. Adinolfi is a cog in the group's wheel. Their ideology, from what we can gather, is to control the nations and impose FHS beliefs on the global populace."

He listened. A picture flashed in his mind. He fixed on the thought.

"Everything alright with you?" she asked.

"Yeah, I'm fine. The Roman empire returns."

"Your father..."

"Yes, what about him?"

"Giacomo, we retrieved the second journal."

"What! How?"

"Our team found it on Trivette's airplane."

Giacomo sat in amazement as Maryann reached for her briefcase and pulled out the composition tablet.

"The director and I have read the prognostications. He's not a fan. He calls it a bunch of crap. I, however, believe that what your father wrote will happen."

"Why?"

"The letter I received convinced me. And when you mentioned the Roman empire...well, here."

Before she could pass it to him, Giacomo grabbed the notebook. He recognized his father's writing. With his fingers, he found the paper-clipped page.

The ancients of the church waited in the abyss for chaos to blossom to strike humanity. A priest with voices that rattle his mind, the one who embraces the parchment, will deceive the masses if the powers can't stop him. The Roman Empire shall rise again. They'll propagate a united world with a false peace, but devastation awaits their plan. The angels weep in silence for the sorrow of humankind. He holds the Gemini close. Their presence brings forth the favor of God.

"How did you know?" Maryann asked.

"A gift handed down." Giacomo shrugged and decided not to elaborate.

"Giacomo, what does this parchment mean, Gemini? Angels?"

"No clue. I've been racking my brain trying to imagine what it implies. Time will tell, I guess."

"But is there *enough* time?" The quizzical look on her face caught his attention.

"Good question. We are in the heart of a dramatic change, and I don't believe it's a pleasant one."

"I heard you saved the President's life."

"I helped."

"You're modest. It was more than a little help."

"When I get to know you better, I'll tell you the story."

"I'm always up for hearing a good tale. You know Frank is with Sergio?"

The mention of his ex-friend's name caused him to feel ill. "Yes, I am. What are they doing?"

"Your partner, Sergio, wants to make things right."

"Good for him."

"I appreciate your hostility toward him. We will use the former prime minister to gain access to Adinolfi."

"How are you going to do that? He thinks Sergio died in the explosion."

"We have our ways."

Giacomo sensed he wasn't being told the whole truth. "I guess we both have secrets. I'd have no issues if he turned up dead."

"I understand that." She grabbed her coffee cup and stood. "Can I put this in your kitchen? I have an appointment in Boston in three hours."

"No, leave it there on the table."

"Giacomo, please consider helping us dismantle the FHS; it might be the best way to capture Adinolfi."

"Dangling the carrot?"

"Your words, not mine. Thanks for taking the time to chat."

He walked her to the front porch and watched her enter the waiting black SUV. Closing the heavy oak door, he returned to his study. He scanned the room for electronic eavesdropping devices—there were none.

Giacomo was reluctant. *Should he tell her about the prophecy, his visions, what had transpired over the last four months? Could he trust her?* He'd stopped the attempted assassination of Tom Maro. What else did the future hold? The knowledge that Adinolfi killed his wife and children spurred his desire for revenge. That thought alone sent him into despair. He felt tired, worn out, and the spirit of retaliation eroded his rationale. Adding to the stress was his sister Rio's well-being. He was scheduled to meet her doctor this afternoon.

Chapter 47

Giacomo parked his Land Rover in the garage on Howard Avenue, locking the doors as he exited. He pressed a button on his cell phone, activating the cameras to the SUV's surveillance system. A black GMC Denali pulled into the parking spot across from him. Giacomo gave the thumbs-up to his security detail in the vehicle. The protocol would have two additional men on the street, watching for any ominous activity. The winter air was crisp, and the sky blue. A hotdog stand was to his left. The owner kept himself warm by drinking coffee.

"Dog, mister?"

"No thanks, maybe on the way back."

Giacomo waited for a car to pass, then crossed the street. A five-story building, part of the Yale New Haven Hospital campus, stood before him. He climbed the six steps to the front door and entered. To his right, an armed BOET soldier was waiting for him.

"General?"

Giacomo turned and smiled. "Colonel."

"Why so formal?"

"Well, you called me 'General' first. Thanks for being here, Jason."

"Giacomo, this is where I need to be, my friend."

The men hugged.

"Your sister's on the fifth floor. Hunter five. Elevators are over here." Jason walked him down the hall.

The person who stood guard by the lift saluted both men.

"I see you haven't been to a barber yet. Soon, you'll be able to put your hair in a ponytail," Jason teased.

"Hilarious, my friend, you should consider comedy. I'll have my locks for a couple more weeks. Prior to my swearing-in ceremony, I'll get a buzz cut or a trim. We'll see how I feel. Tell me about security."

"This is the one elevator with access to the fifth level. An armed man positioned here twenty-four seven. Six men guard the roof, and they occupy the floor at the stairwells and entrance. For added protection, I posted a sergeant outside Rio's room. Nobody is getting in without us knowing about it."

"The cameras?"

"All entrances and exits."

"Face recognition?"

"Yes, the feed goes to BOET headquarters."

"What about hospital personnel?"

"Vetted. We scan everyone before entering the floor for weapons and electronic devices. No cell phones allowed."

"That must've gone over well?" Giacomo raised an eyebrow.

"Some issues, but when they were told of their compensation, they rejoiced at placing them in the safe."

"Nice job," Giacomo patted Jason on the shoulder. "How is Rio?"

"Sedated. The doctor will be here in thirty. Her plane from Washington landed a few minutes ago."

"Her name?"

"Dr. Paige Leavitt."

"Hm…" *That name sounds familiar.*

Chapter 48

The Fishing Village of Nerano, Italy, February 2

Frank stopped the car by the dock. He scanned the surroundings and tapped the hood of the vehicle, giving the all-safe sign for the former prime minister to exit. They had made the two-hour, twenty-minute drive in silence. Sergio slept while Frank kept his brooding thoughts to himself.

A fishing vessel waited to transport them to Ostia, a town on the outskirts of Rome. The route traveling north hugged the Italian coastline of the Tyrrhenian Sea—toward the island of Capri, around the peninsula to the cliffs of Sorrento, with Pompei to their right as they navigated the tip of Naples on the way to their destination.

Sergio and Frank walked the dock, their feet giving way to the rising swells as the wood creaked. Two deckhands untied a Riva Italian speedboat. The captain powered the dual 400 Volvo Penta engines. The wind carried the rumbling noise. A ship docked at the pier rocked as the waves slashed its port side. A British flag hoisted on its mast fluttered in the breeze.

"Come on, we're going over there."

A five-foot-ten-inch, broad-shouldered man jumped off the craft and approached the two men. A powerful wind blew his jacket open, revealing a shoulder harness with a nine-millimeter pistol.

"Frank, good to see you."

"Yeah, you too, Anthony. How long to Ostia?"

"Three days. We're set up inside for the interrogation."

"Unnecessary—he doesn't know where the twins are."

A wave crashed into the dock and sent a spray of mist over their heads. The wind howled as the sky became overcast with ominous clouds. The men gazed upward at the distraction. Then they heard the roar of a boat's engine as the Riva broadsided the wharf. Anthony and Frank stumbled as they tried to grasp the railing on the pier. Sergio, prepared for the onslaught, turned in the vessel's direction as two sailors jumped off with AK-47s pointed at his captors.

"Thanks for the lift. Frank, I must solve this by myself. I need to make it right."

Frank stood and watched with a grin as Sergio's men helped the former prime minister board the speedboat. The captain pushed the throttles forward, and the ship gained momentum and headed toward Positano. Anthony pulled his Beretta and aimed at the departing vessel.

Frank held up his hand. "No, let him go." He reached for his cell phone and called CIA agent Maryann Costatino.

"He's on his way. The plan worked."

"Did you plant the tracking device?"

"Yes." He ended the call.

"Thanks for your help, Anthony."

They shook hands. Frank walked from the dock to a waiting Mercedes sedan, the driver ready to take him back to Naples. From there, his schedule dictated he board a flight and return to the States. Frank's job was finished for now. Sergio was under surveillance with the hope he'd lead them to Adinolfi.

Chapter 49

The waters crested over the bow of Sergio's boat. He sat astern, troubled that Giacomo was aware of his betrayal. The thought that Adinolfi had tried to kill him invigorated the former prime minister in the pursuit of finding Giacomo's sons. His gratitude to Dr. Panzetta for aiding him in his escape didn't ease his disillusionment with his immoral behavior.

The day before his discharge from the hospital, he had given the doctor a folded yellow piece of paper. Inside were detailed instructions to call a trusted contact within the Italian government to come to Sergio's aide. His plan: find the twins, then destroy Adinolfi. Could Giacomo ever forgive him? What Sergio didn't know, however, was the physician who had assisted him was a CIA operative.

Sergio held fast to the boat while the captain navigated the treacherous seas. The roller coaster ride lasted forty-five minutes. Rain pelted the vessel as it docked at a pier in Positano. Two men waited.

"*Buongiorno*, Mr. Prime Minister." The six-foot man with bright, emerald-green eyes fixed his gaze on Sergio.

"Raphael, my friend, thank you for doing this for me. It's been a while. I understand you've tracked Adinolfi to Perugia?"

"Yes, sir. Adinolfi caught us off guard. Our last report indicated he left Monte Cassino in a hurry. His original schedule showed him in Monte Cassino until the annual meeting."

"I'm confident Adinolfi is hiding the boys in Perugia. Do we know where he's staying?"

"No, but he contacted an FHS member within the Italian government, looking for protection."

"Can we use one of our men?"

"Yes, this is Monsignor Luciani. He'll be our listening post."

"*Buongiorno.*"

His face was familiar. The priest towered over him. The man sported a close-cropped haircut. His powerful brown eyes and vice-grip handshake made Sergio wince.

"Have we ever met?"

"No."

"Are you a monsignor?"

Luciani looked toward Raphael to answer the question.

"No, Prime Minister, Mr. Luciani will be Adinolfi's bodyguard under the guise of the priesthood."

"How did you arrange his cover story?"

"Adinolfi recruited a private security firm for protection. We intercepted the call. He'll meet with him in Perugia."

"Why isn't he there now?"

"I wanted to introduce you to him before he left, in case you had further instructions."

"Yes, I do; find and rescue the two infants."

"I will, Mr. Prime Minister."

"*Humph.* Do you have a first name?"

"Warren."

Chapter 50

I-84 outside of Hartford, Connecticut, February 4, 5:30 A.M.

"Costatino. Yes, I'll hold."

"Good morning, Maryann. Thank you for taking my call."

"Please, Mr. President, I'm honored."

"Can you give me an update on Giacomo and the investigation? I am concerned he might take matters into his own hands."

"Yes, I agree. My fear is he's a loose cannon. I have the sense that he will flee the States and end up roaming the streets of Italy. I'm worried he'll screw up our probe. With that said, we discovered Sergio in the city of Cassino, at an Italian safe house. We presume he is waiting for Adinolfi to return to the abbey. Our man has contacted Adinolfi in Perugia, where we believe the boys are being held."

"My understanding is our operative is a civilian, a friend of Giacomo's father."

"Correct. Did you receive a copy of Mr. DeLaurentis's letter?"

"Yes. We must find the twins, Maryann. Do whatever is necessary."

"Yes, sir. Mr. President, these letters—"

"No idea where they came from. What I'll tell you, Maryann, is Paolo has never been wrong. A couple of days ago, Giacomo told me a story I found unbelievable...believable, in the way a fairytale is. The story was about how he reunited his father with our new Secretary of State Lisa Rift's mother, Sydney Hill. When the party ended, his father whispered in Giacomo's ear, and to this day he doesn't know what he meant. Paolo said to him, 'I have seen the future of humankind; will I be able to stop the cataclysm to come?'"

Chapter 51

New Haven, Connecticut, February 6

Followed closely by his security detail, Giacomo finished his run from the Yale Bowl to his house on Alston Avenue. He reminisced about the times he and his dad walked down Chapel Street. As a ten-year-old, his imagination propelled him to play the soldier scouting the road ahead…the simple days. He had believed in a future that included strolling this path with his sons. "Wasn't meant to be," he whispered as he entered his home.

Giacomo shook his head as the depression gripped his heart. He draped his military forest-green zipper jacket on the coat stand next to the door. His head bowed, he ventured to his office, feeling hopeless. Isolated in his thoughts, he slumped on the couch as he held back tears of grief.

Without warning, his mind whisked him away. The vision of the memory erupted into a full-scale motion picture of the October evening of 2003, where he witnessed the reunion of his father Paolo and Sydney, the love of his life, in the mountain village of Ottati, Italy.

*   *   *

The guests milled about the patio as the sun set. Tall outdoor heaters were lit to warm the patio area as the night air cooled. With wine glasses in hand, the invitees enjoyed a light appetizer of cured meats and cheeses. Italian music played in the background.

Paolo tapped his water glass with a spoon. "Ladies and gentlemen, I'm so glad you're here. Please, sit down." A police siren echoed through the streets, fading. The voices of the party quieted. Maria said, "Sounds like the polizia are in the piazza. Roberto, my husband, get more wine and make sure the restaurant is all right."

"I'll go help you with the wine," Giacomo said. The two men left.

"Wow, you can see the blue flashing lights in the valley."

"It's nothing," Paolo said to his nurse, Marge. "Come on, Rio, let's go check on the food."

"Okay, Dad."

"I will come with you, mi amore," Maria said.

Paolo and Rio glanced at one another and smiled.

Five minutes later, Paolo, Rio, and Maria returned to the patio. A fresh, familiar scent wafted across Paolo's nose in the cool night air. By the tile stairs stood several familiar faces—one wore a beret and had a cane in his hand, the other two were Jim and Rami.

A broad smile crossed Paolo's face. "Oh my God, what are you three doing here?" In the same breath, he added, "Where the hell are all my guests?" Like the great sea parting, the three men stepped aside.

Paolo stumbled forward and grabbed a chair. Rio was behind him. "It's okay, Dad, it's not a hallucination."

There in the sparkling light of the moon stood Sydney Hill. Paolo wept. "I'm not hallucinating?"

"No, Dad, you're not."

"Oh my God, oh my God. How?"

Sydney walked to Paolo. He met her halfway. As the rays of the moon surrounded them, the two embraced. In the darkness of the alley, the villagers clapped and cheered.

Arnaud walked to them. "Bonjour, my friend. I hope you are as happy as I was that day when you returned Emily to my arms."

Paolo could say nothing. Speechless, he looked into Sydney's face. The dazzling green eyes captivated his soul once again. "I don't understand. I don't understand. Are you okay?"

"I'm fine, my love, I'm fine." She rubbed his face and kissed him.

"But you're dead."

She pulled back from him, took his hands, and placed them on her face. "No, I'm not. See? I'm real."

"Dad, why don't you sit down?"

"That's a good idea. Rio, can you get me a glass of wine?"

"Sure, Dad."

Everyone piled onto the patio. As if it were Christmas Day, joy and laughter filled the air. The village of Ottati came to life. Maria sent her staff over to the restaurant to get more food. Wine flowed as people chatted away in Italian and English. The celebration ended by ten, the doors to the patio closed.

Paolo hugged Giacomo. "Thank you, son, thank you." And in the silence, he whispered in Giacomo's ear, "I have seen the future of humankind; will I be able to stop the cataclysm to come?"

The vision swept Giacomo to another place.

Three people stood before him: their faces unrecognizable. A sense of fear, anger, then peace filled him as a new image formed. A distant tree overshadowing a meadow of bright green grass. Its leaves changed color to the orange and red hues of fall. An adolescent boy sat nestled between the overgrown roots that stretched to the horizon, his knees pulled to his chest. He gazed out over the pasture. His twin approached him and whispered in his ear as he pointed to their father.

They climbed the oak and perched themselves on one of the thick, sturdy branches as they waved. Giacomo returned the gesture and moved toward them. The wind howled as the bottom of his coat fluttered. The unknown people reappeared, posing a threat to his offspring. He tried to run forward, but the arduous gale held him in place. Their faces remained unrecognizable. Two of the thugs kidnapped the children while the third raked the fallen foliage. He heard his name and turned. Dad? In the field was a hospital bed. He thought he recognized the patient. Is it me?

* 　 * 　 *

The chirping of Giacomo's cell phone pulled him away from the vision. He shook his head and stood, walking to the window in the corner of his office, eyes fixated on an evergreen tree. Numb from what he had witnessed, he answered.

"Hello?"

"General Giacomo DeLaurentis?"

"Yes."

"Dr. Leavitt. I'm here with your sister. We're going to wake her from the induced coma. Could you come to the hospital? It's important she sees a familiar face."

"No problem. When?"

"How about an hour?"

"Sure, I'll be there." A glimmer of hope made him smile.

* 　 * 　 *

Giacomo arrived twenty minutes later. He called his mother to keep her apprised of his sister's condition. Unable to be with her daughter due to a knee replacement, she was grateful for the update and told him she continued to pray for Rio. Security still in place, a BOET soldier escorted Giacomo to Hunter Five.

"The fourth door on the right, sir."

"Thank you, sergeant."

Giacomo stood in the doorway and observed the interior of Rio's room. A two-drawer cabinet next to the hospital bed held a telephone and a remote control for the TV. An overhead light cast a soft orange glow. To his left, louvered blinds were closed. The usual monitoring equipment beeped, tracking her physiological state, accompanied by the hissing sound of a blood pressure cuff inflating. By her bedside, a woman placed a stethoscope on the patient's chest and listened to his sister's heart.

When she finished her assessment, Dr. Paige Leavitt crossed her arms and read Rio's medical chart posted on the monitor. The stunning thirty-eight-year-old woman stood five foot seven. Her beautiful facial features reminded Giacomo of Emily.

The day before, Jason had forwarded the doctor's curriculum vitae to Giacomo. She had earned her doctorate in biogenetics by the time she was twenty-three. After six more years of study, she received her medical degree with a specialty in neurodegenerative disorders and was on her way to becoming the world's leading authority on using genetic engineering to rehabilitate the spinal cord.

"Dr. Leavitt?"

"Yes. You must be…?"

"Giacomo."

She approached him with her hand outstretched. "A pleasure to meet you, sir."

"How is she?"

"Resting. We've re-engineered her DNA and treatment will begin today, provided she's stable."

Giacomo walked to the hospital bed. The brother leaned over and kissed Rio on the forehead.

"Good morning, little sister." He paused in quiet thought. "Will it work?" he asked the doctor.

"In theory, yes. She has undergone serious brain trauma, which, of course, is concerning. We—"

"We?"

"Dr. Panzetta and I. We've collaborated on a procedure to reverse the damage by re-splicing her genome to its original sequence. Giacomo, there's no reason to believe the therapy won't be successful."

"I can count a thousand reasons why it won't be."

"Have a little faith, Giacomo. Your sister will have questions when she wakes up. I suggest you avoid telling her about Adinolfi's treatment at this point."

"Why?"

"She may not want to be her old self. Rio has become acclimated to her altered brain chemistry."

I never thought about the consequences. Giacomo needed his sister back, not this changed version. *What if Rio was comfortable, and she didn't want to change? Shouldn't she have a choice?* Frustrated, his mind weighed the moral implications. Revenge entered his consciousness, and he thought about how he wanted to watch Adinolfi die and Sergio right behind him.

"I see. What do I tell her?"

"Affirmation that she will be okay and recover."

A nurse arrived with a medical cart. She stopped at the foot of the bed, unlocked a drawer, and removed a syringe.

"Hello, Dominique."

"Good afternoon, Doctor."

"Let's wake up Rio."

Fifteen minutes later, the patient was sitting up and alert. Brother and sister were alone. Giacomo hoped for a healthier conversation between the two than the one in Italy…

"Hi, sis."

Rio's eyes darted back and forth.

"You're safe, Rio," Giacomo touched her arm.

"Where am I?"

"Yale."

"What happened?"

He held nothing from her as he explained the events that brought her home.

"So, Sergio rescued me?"

"Yes."

"Where is he?"

"I'm not sure."

"He's your partner. You don't know where Sergio is?"

"Somebody blew up his car at the hospital…"

"Is he alright? Who's responsible?"

Giacomo tried not to reveal his fury. Inside, he roiled with emotion. His psyche screamed for justice, with hatred for the man he'd called a friend. How could he feel depressed one moment, then angry in the next?

"I don't know, and I couldn't care less about him." He saw the puzzled face. "Let me rephrase. I'm more concerned about you."

"Sure. How bad is my brain?"

"You're going to be okay. My understanding is you'll recover and be your old self again."

"Are you telling me the truth? I'm not going to die?"

"I am. You're going to be fine."

He noticed Dr. Leavitt standing in the doorway. "Hello, Miss DeLaurentis, you will be fine." She introduced herself.

"When does the treatment begin?" Giacomo asked.

"Today."

Rio's face turned red. "What the hell are you talking about? I'm not sick. Get me out of here."

"Rio, relax. You need to stay."

"No, I don't, big brother. I want to go home! Damn it, listen to me." She tried to lift herself out of the bed. Falling back on the pillow, she passed out. Giacomo felt the touch of Dr. Leavitt's hand.

"She'll be alright…her mind is confused."

He stood by as the nurse injected a sedative into the IV port. Giacomo, frustrated, controlled his emotions. Now, more than ever, he wanted revenge. He watched the shallow breathing of his sister. "Do what you need to do. Keep her comfortable. Money is not an issue. I'll be out of the country. Please text me with updates."

Chapter 52

Monsignor Warren Luciani walked beside Father Adinolfi. He scanned the piazza by the Hotel Brufani and recalled the letter Tony had given him at Katz's.

> *Warren, my dear friend, the favor I ask of you may seem dire. Please trust that no harm shall come to you. Tony has arranged for your transportation and your contacts in Italy. Observe and listen. The importance of what you hear and monitor will help decide the course of action to recover the boys. I warn you, do not venture out on your own. Your life will be in jeopardy if you choose to follow your desire for revenge and justice.*

Warren accepted the task, no questions asked. He wondered who the children were. Before his departure, a man whom he understood to be ex-secret service injected a nano-chip beneath his skin. The device monitored and recorded his voice communications. The secondary GPS component tracked his every move.

The last two days with Adinolfi had proved interesting. Warren often discovered the priest conversing with non-entities, mumbling words that made no sense. He questioned him about his bizarre behavior. The disturbed man responded by gazing to the sky and saying, "The Holy Spirit and the angels of God hear me."

Both men dressed in civilian clothes, forbidden from wearing the pastoral frock. They finished dinner at La Taverna, a restaurant hidden off the steps of the old city. Warren had feasted on a rack of lamb, while Adinolfi enjoyed an Umbrian bolognese sauce over papardelle pasta. For dessert, they shared a selection of fruits and pastries.

"Tomorrow I have a meeting at Saint Agnes Monastery. You can have the day off."

"Is that a good idea, Father?"

The priest tilted his head to the sky. "Yes, this is what we wish."

"We?"

Adinolfi turned his head toward Warren, his eyes blank, his voice ignited. "Do not question us. We walk in the steps of The Chosen One. You will abide by our decision."

Warren bowed in supplication. "I am sorry, Father."

*   *   *

The following morning, a CIA asset observed the priest entering the small monastery. A Franciscan nun greeted him with a bow of her head. Adinolfi walked through the entrance, then stopped with a startling abruptness. He turned. His eyes, filled with evil, fell upon the agent as she sat in her turquoise Fiat. He closed the door and mumbled "*Et tu spititu sancti*"—the Lord be with you.

After he entered, CIA agent Maryann Costatino removed an earbud. The wicked expression in the priest's eyes caused a chill to travel down her spine. She tried to shake off the eerie feeling.

Chapter 53

Chapel Street, New Haven, Connecticut, February 12

The man stood outside his car, dressed in a long, navy-blue London Fog overcoat, a cell phone glued to his ear and a cigarette dangling from his lips. He inhaled as the sun rose and the darkness vanished. The smoke encircled his head before vaporizing into the crisp morning air. The private investigator had tried to hide the automobile behind a tree as he kept a wary eye on Giacomo's house. A light flickered on upstairs, followed by others downstairs.

"It appears he's awake. He'll be out for his run soon: 7:15—time for me to leave." He started the vehicle.

Giacomo listened to the conversation. With the President's approval, he dismissed his security detail with the hope that his enemies would pursue him. He'd shored up his personal surveillance security and used a silent drone to hover over his house at an altitude of two hundred feet. The video software tracked all outside movements and conversations within a three-block radius. After the discovery, Giacomo called Jason to make certain his stalkers weren't part of his protection unit, who might have been under the direct orders of his friend and second-in-command.

A vehicle and driver huddled in the same spot for the past four nights had caught his attention. Giacomo viewed the screen and tapped his royal-blue Montblanc pen on the desk. He prepared a list in his mind of the items needed for this evening's jaunt to meet his adversary.

*   *   *

The Next Day

Giacomo's clock displayed the time—3:00 a.m. He made a quick phone call. Dressed in black, he affixed his night-vision goggles over his eyes. He checked the safety on the nine-millimeter Beretta holstered behind his back. Pissed off that he delayed his trip, he couldn't wait to question the spy. Incensed, Giacomo hoped to control his zeal for answers, not to push the boundaries of interrogation. He didn't need to spend the night in jail.

Giacomo exited his English Tudor house through the French doors to the backyard and darted past the pool. He climbed over the stone wall, landed on his neighbor's patio, and slipped on a sheet of ice. The agile man rolled to his left and stood. *Ten minutes until I meet my adversary.*

Giacomo trotted down Woodside Terrace and took a right on Woodbridge Avenue. A right on Alden, and up Edgewood. A dog from a nearby house barked as he passed. The circuitous path now placed him behind the prowler, between McKinley and Alston. A lone blue light illuminated the occupant of the car. He guessed his stalker was looking at his cell phone. Adrenaline pumped through his veins as he heard the driver's window descend. A yellow flame flickered. A puff of smoke escaped, the white wisp hovering around the automobile. The smell of the burning tobacco reached Giacomo's nostrils as he withdrew his gun and released the safety latch.

"Put your hands on the wheel."

The cold metal of the gun's muzzle pressed against his head caused the intruder to drop the cigarette on the floor. "This can be easy or difficult. Answer the question, and you'll be free to leave. Who do you work for?" Giacomo shoved the pistol into the man's skull. "Who's your boss?"

"Screw you."

"Do you think I'm joking? I'll plaster your brains all over the windshield. One more time; tell me your employer's name." Giacomo shuttled a round in the chamber. His military training kicked in, the use of force a moment away.

In the corner of his peripheral vision, he noticed the police squad's SUV approach. The red-and-blue lights emitted their colors as the vehicle screeched to a halt.

"Move away and drop to the ground." The officer's voice was loud. Two other unmarked cars approached and blocked the street.

Giacomo did as he was told. He withdrew from the car. With his arms above his head, he fell to his knees and placed the weapon on the sidewalk. Gun drawn and pointed, an officer maneuvered toward Giacomo as the others stood at the ready. They had defused the scene… until the driver stepped out of the car and started firing. A bullet grazed a cop in the arm. The officers responded in kind and killed the intruder with a barrage of bullets. Amid the chaos, Giacomo removed his face gear as a bright light shone in his eyes.

"What's going on, General DeLaurentis?"

Giacomo stood and addressed the police officer. "Lieutenant May, thanks for showing up." He pointed to the dead man. "He's been running surveillance on me for a couple of days. The time arrived for us to have a brief chat. I guess that didn't work. I appreciate you covering my back."

"No problem. Glad I could help."

"Do you mind if I peek inside the car?"

"No, sir."

Giacomo searched the vehicle under the watchful eye of a New Haven officer. With their permission, he removed the man's cell phone and placed it in his pocket. He walked back to his house as a police SUV trailed behind him at a slow pace. The lights of nearby homes dimmed as Giacomo's frightened neighbors went back to their beds.

Giacomo entered his house through the garage. Turning the hallway light on, he stopped. Stunned, he recognized the shadow of a woman holding the hands of two children. His heart raced. "Em?" The dark reflection released the hands of the boys. "Paolo, Arnaud." He fell to his knees with his arms open to receive his sons. "No, you're dead. This is not real." The silhouette of the children disappeared.

Chapter 54

Perugia, Italy, February 13

"We might have a break. I transported five men to Saint Agnes's Monastery last night. Adinolfi is meeting them this morning. I had to rent a van for one of them."

"Sounds good, Warren. You'll handle the vehicle?"

"Yes."

Maryann placed the cell phone in her pocket as she exited the Fiat. Discouraged that the past seven days of surveillance proved worthless, she hoped for better results today. Maryann needed a break in the investigation. She expected Adinolfi to return once again to say morning Mass. Her sights focused on the side entrance to the monastery.

With an air of impatience, she waited for her contact to greet her. *Where is she? I hope I didn't blow my cover.* Then the centuries-old, cracked oak door squeaked open. A nun wearing a humble, chestnut-colored cassock with a white rope tied around her waist and dangling rosary beads emerged and nodded. Maryann followed her in silence.

They descended a darkened staircase dotted with dim lights. The downward spiral was precarious. She held the guardrail that at times gave way to the rusted bolts anchoring the banister in place. Dirt-stained stone walls smelled of mildew, which didn't seem to bother the CIA agent. The women arrived at the basement floor. Maryann followed the religious woman as they turned right and entered a cabinet room filled with relics, boxes, and vestments. The sister went to a closet, withdrew a habit, and handed it to Maryann.

"How do I look?" she whispered.

"Great. You should consider becoming one of us."

"Hmm…no, thank you."

Maryann smiled and considered her statement. She wondered if God existed, and if so, why He allowed His people to suffer. As a clandestine agent, she witnessed firsthand the atrocities committed by the governments of the world. *Was she at fault for her own complicity? Could she be forgiven?*

"I will take you to the chapel, where you'll be able to listen to his conversations without being noticed."

"Thank you."

The nun, an American stationed in Italy, was the daughter of a visiting CIA agent. Her father, an astute man, had recognized Adinolfi conversing with the Mother Superior. He called in the sighting and arranged for his reluctant offspring to meet with Maryann.

They exited the basement through another set of stairs leading them through the kitchen, down a hallway, and into a private chapel reserved for the cloistered. The room was sparse. Four pews, two on either side, each sat six. Placed to the right of the tiny altar was an image of Saint Francis. A brown wooden crucifix loomed overhead. Directed to a pew closest to the wall, the nun reached over Maryann and slid open a one-way window shade.

Maryann rested on the hard seat and watched Adinolfi recite the sacred mysteries of the Mass.

*   *   *

Father Adinolfi raised the ornate chalice as he proclaimed the rite of the Last Supper professed at every Catholic service. A few moments later, he recited the closing prayer. In the pews were five men. The priest bowed before the cross and walked down the aisle into the sacristy. Each man exited their pew, genuflected, and followed him.

"Yes, yes, yes, I know. Of course, we will not allow that to happen."

"Did you say something?" one man queried.

"Not your concern. Gentlemen, we have good news." Adinolfi glanced toward the ceiling. His face became animated as he listened to the voice in his head.

"Adinolfi, what's wrong?" a man with a French accent asked.

"Yes, yes, I'm fine. I was listening to the essence of God, my brothers. The Gemini are safe. Our conspirators misguided us with their words that the brother and sister were preparing to thwart our preparations. Through the guidance of the Spirit, our actions have placed them in our hands. We must protect the twins at all costs. They should never discover their ancestry." He paused and pitched his head upward. "We'll raise them as our own. When we provide the evidence to the others at our annual meeting, they'll have no choice but to follow our way of life, not theirs. We will ascend to our rightful place. The Followers of the Holy Spirit will shepherd in the promise of our almighty God."

Adinolfi reached for his briefcase. He unclasped the brown leather bag and pulled out an envelope. "Here," he handed it to the Italian. "We have moved the Gemini to this location. Proceed to the village and arrange protection for the two. Our sources have informed me the US government is searching for them. Our mole reported their father has no idea they are alive. Gentlemen, he must not learn of their existence. Do I make myself clear? Under no circumstances will you leave the twins unprotected."

The five men bowed in unison.

"Go! I must listen to the Spirit."

As the men left the sacristy, Adinolfi pulled the Italian aside and whispered in his ear. "If they compromise you, send the boys back home to God our Father. Do you understand?"

The monk nodded and exited the room.

Chapter 55

Maryann left the Abbey the same way she entered. The sky was now overcast, a slight chill permeating the air. She tilted her head to button her navy-blue coat. A person sneezed in the distance. She glanced upward for a moment. Not threatened, she continued to walk to her automobile. She opened the driver's door, buckled her seatbelt, and started the Fiat.

"You look funny sitting there."

"Yeah, thanks a lot. Do you think next time you could get a bigger car?"

"Were you seen?"

"No, I waited until he left. I got your text about the others."

"Any problem?"

"All good. I attached the GPS monitors to the van. Any information about the boys' location?"

"Not yet, but Adinolfi is aware we're looking for them."

"How does he know?"

"I don't have a clue, Warren. This is more than a religious order. What did you find?"

"Adinolfi is a lunatic. He imagines he's talking to God, and the good Lord is telling him what to do. The priest is schizo."

"You mean a schizophrenic?"

"Yeah, that's what I said…he's schizo. I overheard a telephone conversation that might give credence to your statement of the magnitude of the organization. He mentioned he needed the financial statements for the board meeting scheduled in two weeks with a detailed analysis of the corporation's holdings. Adinolfi also requested a written summary from 155 CEOs."

"Shit, if this is true…when is he receiving the summaries?" she asked.

"No idea."

"Do you think you can access them?"

"Yeah, shouldn't be a problem. Also, I discovered he has a hidden office at the abbey."

"Where?"

"I plan on finding it when we return. I eavesdropped on a conversation he had with the voices. In the hotel's corridor, Adinolfi argued with himself, saying he protected the prophecy. It's in his room and he didn't want to keep it locked in his office. Let me tell you, Maryann, this guy is a loon. Adinolfi kept repeating, '*It is a secret. I know where the paper is hidden. They won't find the safe. I concealed the parchment in my cell.*' He was so outraged and flustered that at one point he pounded a table screaming, '*Stop, stop, stop!*' Then he muttered something about salvation and Passover. '*They can't control us…*' The priest is a lunatic. He babbled on about the parchment and other gibberish crap."

"Wow."

"Yeah, he's a freaking weirdo."

Maryann maneuvered the car into the bus station drop-off area. "Thanks, Warren, keep me updated."

"Will do."

Chapter 56

The Oval Office, Washington, DC, February 14, 8:00 A.M.

Thomas Maro's expression was intense, his mind focused on the discussion. The corners of his eyes and forehead creased as he listened to the speakerphone.

"Maryann, what you're telling me is he believes the Spirit of God is talking to him."

"Yes, that is correct, Mr. President."

"Wow. Do we have a medical dossier on him, by any chance?"

"No, sir."

"Any luck in finding Giacomo's children?"

"I'm afraid not. Adinolfi has given them a code name of Gemini, and he's aware we are looking for them."

"How does he know?"

"Your guess is as good as mine. And one other issue, Mr. President. He sent a security force to guard the twins and prevent them from being rescued. I'm forwarding the transcript of the conversation by diplomatic courier. The document should be in your hands later today."

"Excellent idea. Who knows who we can trust? What can you tell me about this guy, Adinolfi?"

"He's a priest and a physician and the leader of a group called Followers of the Holy Spirit, FHS. Information about the organization tells us there are two divisions, one religious and the other secular. Our people have been working with extreme diligence to unmask the consortium. Our intel revealed Adinolfi is involved in genetic alteration—you've seen the memo."

"Yes, it's quite disturbing, and what he did to Rio is disgusting. Is the FBI engaged in the investigation?"

"Yes. Oh, I forgot one additional item, Mr. President. Adinolfi mentioned Passover. I don't know if there is any significance to the holiday and his agenda. Can I pass that info on to NSA?"

"No problem. What are your plans?"

"I'm going to rescue Giacomo's children."

"Your words to God's ears...best of luck." Tom ended the conversation. He pressed the intercom button. "Cameron, can you get me the Pope?"

A few moments later, he heard on the other line: "Mr. President, how are you?"

"I'm fine, Your Holiness."

"Please, my name is Andrew, for I am just a man."

"Me too." Tom chuckled. "Thank you for taking my call. Are you familiar with a group called Followers of the Holy Spirit?"

"Yes, a religious sect originating in the thirteenth century and disbanded after the schism of 1510."

"Do you suppose they are still active?"

"They might be."

The president pondered. He swiveled his chair to face the credenza. He lifted a tattered photo in a glass frame. It was a picture of him with his father, taken forty-plus years ago.

"Our CIA is investigating a group by that name."

"Shall I have my people investigate the organization for you?"

"That would be helpful. Thank you, Andrew."

"You're welcome. How is Giacomo? I haven't heard from him."

"Our friend is struggling. He's angry, frustrated, and depressed, which is understandable."

"Yes. I continue to pray for him."

"I'm sorry to have taken your time."

"Anytime. I hope you'll visit the Vatican soon."

"I plan to, thank you. I'll have our State Department contact yours."

The phone call ended. The acronym FHS caused Tom to whisper, "Is it possible they are the same?" He thought nothing more of it as he placed the photograph of himself and his father back on the credenza as he said, "Boy, he sounds so familiar."

*   *   *

Vatican Secret Archives, 6:00 P.M.

Pope Andrew entered the library where a collection of ancient documents, books, periodicals, and church secrets were housed. Closed for the day, the Holy See provided access to scholars and scientists upon request. The Vatican librarian escorted Andrew to an enclosed space in a corner to the right—the chamber reserved for His Holiness, the librarian, and anyone approved by the Pope. Andrew withdrew his keycard and swiped the lock. The tumblers clicked, and the door popped open with a whoosh. They walked into the sealed, five-hundred-square-foot space that housed the archives.

"What are you looking for, Your Holiness?"

"Nothing, I can escape here. I need to be alone."

"Then I shall leave you to your time."

Three hours later, he found the hidden rudimentary accounting record. He brought the register to the table where he'd first seen it. After his conversation with Tom Maro, his mind's eye flashed a picture of a green ledger with the letters FHS embossed on the cover. He searched his memory. *Where had he seen the book?* Then he remembered—five years ago, when he'd visited the secure room with the previous pope. What did the journal contain?

Andrew opened the register to a tattered, brown-lined handwritten document. The first ten pages, from what he could gather, were an accounting of funds received beginning in the year 1510. They continued through 1618, then there was an initial dispersal in 1619. The ensuing years showed copious amounts of increased receivables. What caught his attention further on in the book was a legible summary detailing the exploits of the FHS. The synoptic statements appeared to be written starting in the 1700s and concluded with the 2022 Russian invasion of Ukraine.

Pope Andrew stood, trying not to vomit. The sect financed the American, French, and Russian revolutionary wars, World Wars I and II, the Korean conflict, and the Vietnam Campaign, to name a few! The entries seemed endless. His Holiness grew more nauseous as he realized the enormity of the destruction and death the organization had been sponsoring for centuries. In total, the FHS bankrolled and manipulated sixty-seven wars.

The remaining pages outlined political elections, assassinations, government overthrows, uses of biological weapons to control populations, and the related monies used to secure the outcomes. Stunned at the chronology, he grabbed his phone and snapped photos of the information. Ten minutes later, an ashen-faced Pope exited the Holy See.

*   *   *

Archbishop Renaldo Benavequa watched the closed-circuit TV monitor. He reached for his phone.

"He found the ledger."

"How? I thought we destroyed the damn thing."

"I have no explanation."

"Did he take the book with him?"

"No. He photographed the pages with his cell phone. I tracked him to the papal apartment."

"We'll handle the situation from here."

Chapter 57

New Haven, Connecticut, February 14, 6:00 P.M.

Unable to recover information from the dead man's cell phone, Giacomo packed a travel case. When he finished, he moved to his desk to retrieve a pen. He slid open the right drawer. A Valentine's Day card sat on top of a stack of papers. The sight of the item he purchased months ago, professing his love for his now-deceased wife, riled the emotions of anger and hate he'd been trying to tame. He snatched up the image of the couple holding hands and, allowing his despair and rage to conquer him, tore it to pieces. Haunted by the betrayal of Sergio and Adinolfi, he again vowed to exact his revenge.

A prisoner to his own mind, he laid out his plan. His primary objective: to find Adinolfi without anyone discovering he'd left the United States. Giacomo whispered, "Adinolfi, you're going to pay for what you did to my wife, children, and sister. The sheriff is coming to town, you bastard."

Giacomo's security system alerted him that his ride was in the driveway. He grabbed his bag and exited to the garage.

*   *   *

On board Tony's new Gulfstream 750, Giacomo read the report Jason sent him. Jason had arranged for a false passport and identity as an American businessman and had ensured Giacomo's entry into Italy through military diplomatic channels. Scheduled to land in Rome by 6:00 a.m. the following day, he settled in and prepared for the journey, making sure the supplies he needed would be waiting for him upon his arrival at the Marriott Flora Hotel. He'd rest, then drive to Monte Cassino in the pre-dawn morning hours of the next day.

The plane touched down with a squeak of its wheels. His rental car waited at the bottom of the stairs. Wisps of rain hung from the clouds in the overcast Roman sky. Anxiety gripped Giacomo. *Would it ever end?* Two months had passed since he and Emily were in Rome. His mind became hollow except for the raging fury that overwhelmed him. He clutched his bag stuffed with surveillance equipment and camouflaging outerwear. Focused, he made his way in search of his adversary.

Chapter 58

The Abbey of Monte Cassino revealed itself as the fog dissipated. Ominous clouds rose over the Benedictine monastery. The sun's rays showered the white stone structure as the mist drifted above the tower at the far end of the ancient home of the FHS order.

Sergio remained holed up in a one-bedroom apartment on the third floor of a multi-dwelling complex. The living room comprised a small couch and a chair. A single window with green shutters cast its sights on the priory. He went to the closet and grabbed a hanger. Draped over it was a monk's brown cassock. With Adinolfi away, his time was now.

Dressed in the friar's robe, Sergio arrived at the monastery at dawn. The rising sun peeked over the horizon, soon to be hidden by a broken, cloudy sky. All of the brothers were attending morning Mass, affording him the perfect opportunity to enter the Abbey unnoticed.

He traversed the pathway, observing two groundskeepers trying to remove a rope that hung down from the structure. The chapel bell rang—the call for prayers. Sergio approached the gate and saw the procession of monks and priests making their way to the church. Fog emitted from their bodies as the warmth of their breath shocked the frigid air.

Surprised his passcode still worked, Sergio entered and climbed the three flights of stairs to the restricted area. He ambled through the hall. As he got closer to his destination, his gait slowed. The memory of seeing his son Alessio laying on a stretcher with a gaping bullet wound in his head stirred nausea.

Resolute to make the wrongs right, Sergio strode with intent to destroy Adinolfi and locate the twins. The floor was empty, and the entrances to the private cells closed. The route funneled toward a room at the end of the corridor. White stone walls stained from the passage of time surrounded him. Trepidation surged through his body. He noticed the door was ajar. He peeked inside. A friar dressed in a brown garment with his back to Sergio lifted a cornerstone.

Sergio leaned on the oak molding. Losing his balance, he stumbled upright into the room. The commotion startled the monk, who turned awkwardly to him, his head tilted down to the left, his chin resting on the collarbone. The invalid walked toward Sergio. One of his legs dragged behind, making a scraping noise. The ex-prime minister froze; his face went pale as he recognized the brother. Sergio fainted, cracking his skull as it landed on the stone tile. The man approached him, stepped over the body, and exited the room.

Chapter 59

The Abbey at Monte Cassino, Italy, 5:00 A.M.

Under the cover of darkness, Giacomo scaled the stone wall. He tied a rope to the eaves of the monastery in case he needed a quick escape. Twenty minutes later, he sat on the roof, peering out over the village of Cassino. The lights of the houses beneath him flickered as the inhabitants awakened in the pre-dawn morning. Across the landscape, the illumination cascaded from one house to another. The fragrance of wood fire wafted up the mountain from smokestacks built on the orange-tiled roofs from the valley below.

Giacomo positioned himself by the bell tower. He reached inside his backpack and grabbed a bottle and a chocolate power bar. He squatted, placing his back on the cement steeple as he took a slug of water. The emergence of the morning sun was fifteen minutes away. As he waited for the opportune time to begin his search, he focused on trying to suppress his feelings. His emotions traveled the gamut of bitterness, angst, depression, and sadness. He mumbled to God. "Why didn't you take me? I should have died. Let's make a deal, my life for my family?" Giacomo knew he was talking nonsense. There was no hope in his family's resurrection…they were gone. Within moments, a vision overrode his thoughts.

A distant tree overshadowing a meadow of bright green grass. Its leaves changed color to the orange and red hues of fall. An adolescent boy sat nestled between the overgrown roots, which stretched to the horizon, his knees pulled to his chest. He gazed out over the pasture. His twin approached him and whispered in his ear as he pointed to their father.

They climbed the oak and perched themselves on one of the thick, sturdy branches. Emily appeared and spoke to the boys. They descended, stood before her, and waved at Giacomo, who returned the gesture and moved toward the three.

The wind howled as the bottom of his coat fluttered. He tried to move, stuck in place by the arduous gale. His wife patted the boys' bottoms, directing them to go to their dad. They leaped forward, and as they drew close, the gale repelled Giacomo backward. Prevented by an unknown source, he struggled to reach them. His heart ached. The twins were so close, but he could not quite touch them. A sense that they were a lifetime away beleaguered him. He heard his father's voice. 'We can never change our fate.'

Clanging bells brought the apparition to an immediate conclusion. Alarmed, he jumped to his feet and covered his ears. A raucous anxiety overcame him as he attempted to escape the noise. Giacomo jogged toward the far side of the building, stopping at the edge.

He leaned over, placed his hands on his thighs and took deep breaths to calm himself. His heart raced over the deafening clatter until the chiming ended. As his body relaxed, the recollection of the vision returned to haunt him. Vexation caused his mind to erupt into violent images of what he wanted to do to Adinolfi. *My wife and children are dead because of him.* Giacomo so wished to rid himself of the hateful thoughts. Without mercy, they clung to him.

He descended the stone staircase to the third-floor entrance, where the sight of a push-button lock stopped his progress. *A monastery with a security system. Why?* The astute military man felt confident this was where Adinolfi lived. Giacomo examined the control pad, noticing three numbers discolored from usage. On the fourth attempt, the door unlatched. He peered through a small opening. A monk whose leg trailed behind him departed through an exit at the opposite end of the hallway.

Giacomo paused before entering. Cautious, he gazed down the corridor and counted eleven rooms, six to his left and five to his right. He exerted restraint as he moved forward. Spotting a twelfth hidden cell in the corner with its door open, he froze. Alert, he made a quick assessment and decided it was a communal room for the brothers to meet outside their cells.

His search for Adinolfi continued to his dismay. Every chamber was identical: a kneeler beside the bed, a crucifix, an image of Saint Benedict on the wall opposite a sink with a mirror. Frustrated that he couldn't find Adinolfi's sleeping quarters, Giacomo closed the last door.

A groan and sounds of sobbing shattered the silence and caused Giacomo's adrenaline to kick in as he considered his escape options. He turned to what he believed was the communal area. There, he spotted a friar sitting on the floor, his hand covered in blood. Giacomo's empathic sense focused his attention on the man. Tears welled in his eyes as he felt the person's inner torture. Perplexed by this overwhelming awareness, he approached.

Chapter 60

Perugia, Italy

The old town was above him. People stood by railings snapping pictures of the valleys of the Umbrian countryside. Warren climbed the stairs through the medieval fortress Rocca Paolina. He exited the building. The imposing man turned to his left, where he saw Father Adinolfi dressed in his clerical clothing, gazing at the sky, mumbling.

"Father, are you alright?" asked the doorman of the Hotel Brufani.

"Yes, yes, yes, I'm fine." He turned and entered the lobby.

Warren scanned the area. Surprised to find the troubled man wearing his priest garb, he walked to a café to his right. The server approached, and Warren ordered an espresso and sat at one of the outside tables. The scraping of a chair against the cobblestones next to him caught his attention. The person sat close to Warren.

"Can we trust Maryann?" Frank asked.

"Yes. She's intent on finding the twins. Aren't you traveling to the States?"

"Delayed, Giacomo's in Italy."

"Not good."

"No, it isn't."

"Where is he?"

"They dropped him off in Rome. Last I knew, he rented a car and drove to Monte Cassino. Thought you should be aware."

"Damn, we return there tomorrow. He's after Adinolfi?"

"Yep," Frank stood. The old friend patted Warren on the shoulder. "I've called in some favors; my people are on their way. They'll watch his ass."

"We have to get Giacomo back to New Haven."

"We're working on it."

"Tony's airplane still in Rome?"

"Yes. I gotta go. I'll see you at home."

Warren waited several minutes before he returned to the Hotel Brufani.

Chapter 61

The Abbey at Monte Cassino, Italy

To Giacomo's surprise, what he'd mistaken for a communal area was another cell—living space for a priest, a monk. An overwhelming sense to assist the friar sitting on the floor propelled him to move forward. Not aware of Giacomo's presence, the man sobbed.

"Can I help you, Father?"

"No, leave me."

He turned and began his walk to the exit, but stopped. The voice was familiar.

A wave of revulsion traveled through Giacomo's body. An eruption of resentment clutched him. A fury journeyed through his being as he reached for his nine millimeter. He turned and looked at the old man. Blood dripped from the friar's head. Giacomo removed his hand from his armament. Sergio sat before him, eyes red, cheeks stained by the salt of his tears. He appeared older; life's consequences had withered him. Immobilized, unable to move or respond, the men were caught up in the shock of seeing one another.

Giacomo reacted to the clank of a gun as a bullet entered the chamber. Then he heard the explosive detonation of the pistol. The impending death projectile ricocheted off the stone wall to his right. He spun as he withdrew his Glock 19 from his back holster and fired two rounds. The assailant lay in a pool of blood.

Sergio still sat on the floor.

"Are you hurt?" Giacomo asked. He grabbed the withered man by the collar of the tunic and lifted him. "Are you injured?"

"No."

"Good. If you're going to die, I want it by my hands."

"Shoot me now, please. I can't take it."

"Can't take it? You bastard. My wife and children are dead. And Rio…" He tried to suppress the hatred. "Let's go. More are on the way."

"Wait."

"Screw you, old man. I'll kill you where you stand."

Giacomo grabbed the betrayer by the throat, pinning him against the wall. *Could he stop the all-permeating need for revenge?* His empathic sense again swept over him. Filled with remorse, inches from Sergio's heartbroken gaze, he stumbled backward. The sorrow was so strong that he wept.

"Why, Sergio…why? How could you do this? We were family." He released his grip as the devastated prime minister slumped to the ground. Giacomo felt ill as he watched Sergio gasp for air and grab hold of the cell's desk. His former friend's eyes filled with dread, his neck red from Giacomo's vengeful, strangling hands.

"I'm sorry, Giacomo, I am so…" his weeping drowned out his words. "They sucked me in years ago. I didn't understand who they were until Adinolfi killed my son."

"What do you mean?"

Sergio told him about his first encounter with Father Franco as prime minister, how Adinolfi beckoned him to the monastery to see Alessio's dead body carried out on a stretcher, and his discovery of a research lab in the Abbey.

"Giacomo, your sons—"

A crash from the adjacent entrance jolted them.

"Sergio, hide behind the bed," Giacomo said as he reached for his gun.

"General DeLaurentis, AFSOC 7. Make yourself known, sir."

Giacomo shook his head in surprise at the sound of his name. *Who knew he was in Italy? Was the intruder from the United States Air Force? Adinolfi's men?* His military mind set to high alert, there was no time for feelings of anxiety and remorse. Trapped in the murderer's cell, their lives were in peril.

Giacomo assessed his alternatives. His options were limited. Escaping down the corridor was fruitless. The better choice: wait for the assailants to walk past the room. Once the aggressors were in sight, he could pick them off. *Do I have enough ammunition?*

He positioned himself so he had an unobstructed view. As he outstretched his arm to take aim, the opposite door down the hallway shattered open. Trapped, his departure from life was moments away. Two men with Uzi submachine guns opened fire. Bullets whizzed past Giacomo, ricocheting off the stone walls. He fired back. Within seconds, the attackers lay dead, drenched in their own blood.

"General, Frankeee says all is good."

The way the soldier stretched Frank's name out was Giacomo's clue the United States Air Force Special Operations Command unit was there to protect him. With his adrenaline pumping, he continued to hold his pistol at the ready. The soldiers rounded the corner.

"In here, gentlemen," Giacomo shouted.

"Sir, Major Nick Drew."

Three men with rifles aimed down the hallway flanked the six-foot, two-inch soldier.

Giacomo returned his gun to the holster. "I imagine you're here for me?"

"Yes, sir. My orders are to bring you home."

"How much time do we have?"

"Helicopter is five minutes out."

"There's a research lab in the basement I want to visit."

"Might be difficult. The site is not safe."

Giacomo gave the soldier a hard stare as he turned to his left. Sergio's lifeless body planted in a swamp of blood. A man he loved as a father, whom he hated and wished dead moments ago, now lay wasted, no longer in pain or turmoil. Not knowing what else to do, he leaned over Sergio and closed his eyelids as he said, "Rest in peace, my old friend."

"Let's go, Major."

The Air Force Ops team escorted Giacomo down the stairs, one soldier positioned in front and two others in the rear, the major by his side. Their rifles at the ready. The sound of a helicopter's rotor drifted through the halls.

"I recommend we not proceed further. Even though we have moved the residents to the church, there is still a potential danger, sir."

"You understand who I am, Major?"

"Yes, General, but—"

"No buts. Let's go."

"Sir."

They arrived at a basement door. A soldier placed an endoscopic camera under the entranceway.

"We have a hallway with two doors. They wired the first one with a retinal scanner, the second a janitor's closet. No enemy or civilians around."

"Copy. You stand guard here," he commanded the subordinate. "General, once we're inside, you have five minutes, then we need to leave."

"I agree. How will you bypass the security?"

"With this." The Major reached in his pocket and pulled out an electronic gadget. A square box with a high-tech camera and a data-transfer chip.

"How does it work?"

"We hack into the scanner's database and download the secured retinal images. We then reverse the process and enter unannounced."

With caution, they approached the secure entrance. The remaining soldier attached the device and implemented the procedure to gain access to the records. Within seconds, the door popped open. They executed another endoscopic search before entering.

"Clear, Major."

"Stay here and stand guard."

"Sir."

Giacomo entered first. The facility was a replica of a hospital floor. There were ten rooms to his right, and on his left, three operating theaters. Against the far wall, a group of stainless-steel doors. A doorway in the distant corner had a sign posted that read "*Crio.*"

"What is this place, General?"

"Your guess is as good as mine. Sergio told me…" The conflicting emotions of remorse and wrath toward his friend stabbed him in the heart. "He said it was a research lab. This is where Adinolfi has been conducting human DNA testing. I'm here to kill the bastard for what he's done to my—"

"General, you're best to leave the justice to the authorities."

"Yeah right, Major. If I get the chance, the bastard's dead. You go left, I'll search this side."

Giacomo arrived at the third room. The first object he saw was a picture of Sergio and Alessio. Puzzled, he investigated further. In the closet was a monk's tunic and shoes. He departed the sparse room and ventured to the wall with the stainless-steel doors.

"General, I'll do that. The Major lifted the handle. As the door opened, a light cast an eerie glow inside the compartment. He pulled out the unzipped body bag.

"Well, I guess we found the mortuary." Giacomo tilted his head to the *Crio* entrance. "Do we have time to explore?"

"Two more minutes. The helicopter is waiting."

The door to the *Crio* room creaked open. Startled, the men withdrew their pistols, aiming at the monk who appeared.

Chapter 62

Perugia, Italy

Warren settled on his bed for a quick nap, his arms outstretched above his shoulders. As he drifted off to sleep, he heard banging.

"Father, Father! We must leave. We must go now!"

He peered through the peephole. Adinolfi appeared to be in a state of panic. Warren watched the man walk down the hall talking to himself, tilting his head, listening to the voices.

"What is wrong?" Warren asked as he cracked open the door.

"We need to return to Monte Cassino…terrible events have taken place." His demeanor changed from confusion to focused, purposeful thought. "Get your ass moving, Father. I'll meet you by the car."

Warren watched the disturbed man enter his room. He reached for his cell phone.

"Maryann, we're leaving Perugia. Something happened at Monte Cassino."

"Do you know what?"

"No, but he's confused and agitated."

"Why?"

"He mentioned terrible things had occurred at the monastery. He was rambling, then the next second he was telling me to move my ass."

"Okay, Warren, keep me posted."

"Any luck with finding the boys?" He wanted to inform her about his suspicion that Giacomo was involved in whatever had transpired in Monte Cassino.

"Not yet."

*   *   *

Ten minutes later, Warren waited by the car for Adinolfi. He calculated a three-hour drive with an estimated arrival time between 5:00 and 5:30 p.m. Walking briskly, Adinolfi exited the Hotel Brufani.

"Drop me off at the airport. You stay here in Perugia. I might need you to transport people to the abbey."

"Yes, Father." Warren prayed Giacomo was long gone by the time Adinolfi arrived.

Chapter 63

The Abbey at Monte Cassino, Italy

Giacomo stood in shock. *How is this possible?*

"General, are you alright?"

"Yeah." His eyes were wide, not knowing what to think.

The monk who entered the main chamber froze at the sight of the men. He mumbled something unintelligible.

"Who is he?"

"An old friend who's supposed to be dead. Do we have space in the chopper?"

"Yes, sir."

"Good, he's coming with us."

Giacomo approached him. He spotted a patch of gauze on his forehead. Sergio's son Alessio moved backward. His eyes reflected the fear within him.

"You don't recognize me, do you?"

He tried to speak, but the words were incoherent.

"It's alright, Alessio. You have nothing to be afraid of." Giacomo glanced at the major. "Let's get the hell out of here." He directed Alessio out of the building and grabbed his cell phone. "Andrew, I need to see you." He yelled over the noise of the helicopter's rotor. "I'm in Monte Cassino. Can we land at the Vatican?"

"Of course. What's going on?"

"You'll understand when we arrive. We're twenty minutes out."

A wave of nervousness surged through Giacomo's veins as the view of Saint Peter's Basilica grew on the horizon. The flashbacks of him and Emily walking the Roman streets to the Piazza Navona replayed in his mind. Distracted by the memory, a tragic event in his life's journey, he held his grieving emotions in place.

Alessio, who sat across from him, garnered Giacomo's attention. *Why did he and Sergio betray me? What did Adinolfi promise them?* The brain-damaged man stared out the window as he pointed, mumbled, and grabbed at the pocket of his cassock. His eyes were empty, his face blank. Every five minutes, he repeated his movements. Giacomo wanted to retaliate, to throw him from the chopper and watch him plummet to his death.

He sighed at the acknowledgement that Alessio was no longer the man he knew. Still, he couldn't shake the intense emotion of revenge within him. The array of feelings coursed through his veins: a moment of anger, followed by thoughts of retaliation, shadowed by a deep remorse, and sadness. Giacomo's mind became a convoluted mess of ruminations. Depression engulfed him. Was there a solution to this madness? He knew of one...

Major Nick Drew exited the helicopter first, offering his hand to help the traumatized man leave the aircraft. Hesitant to move forward, Sergio's son scrutinized the bleak and cloudy sky. Giacomo reassured him. "Alessio, you're safe here."

The frightened look in his eyes caused Giacomo's heart to ache. *What happened to him? Sergio said Adinolfi shot him in the head and the wound confirmed as much. How could he be alive?* He believed Alessio recognized him, yet he didn't seem to know him. A papal vehicle waited. The passenger door opened. Pope Andrew smiled at Giacomo and stood to greet his friend. He walked to welcome him, then stopped cold in his tracks.

"Andrew, thanks for meeting me here."

The quizzical gaze on Andrew's face caught Giacomo's attention. "Yeah, I assumed he was dead, too."

"Alessio, I'm so happy you're alive."

Giacomo replied, "He doesn't recognize us. You and I have to talk." His voice stern and pragmatic. "If you don't mind, I'd like to walk. My brain is going to explode. I need to figure this shit out, sorry."

"Of course, of course."

Giacomo walked the Vatican gardens to the papal residence. His brain was immersed in fog as depression and confusion overtook his thoughts. *Life has no meaning. I wish I were dead.* The gripping, wrenching feeling around his heart caused a deep pang of loneliness. His head lowered, tears cascaded from his eyes, leaving a trail as he made his way. The sky was blue and the winter sun cast its glow upon him, but it could not penetrate the darkness within him.

Chapter 64

The Abbey at Monte Cassino, Italy, One Hour Later

Adinolfi didn't hesitate in exiting his car. Five *polizia* vehicles were at the entrance of the monastery. The commander approached him.

"How bad is it?"

"Six dead. What's going on, Father?"

"I wasn't here, you tell me. This is a tragedy."

"Why do you have armed guards?" he asked, his eyes fixed on Adinolfi.

"We have priceless relics."

"I see."

Three silver SUVs with black-tinted windows halted four feet from the two men. The doors opened, and nine members of the Italian militia exited the vehicles and established a perimeter. Someone jumped out of the passenger side of the third automobile. He gave orders to his agents to stand by.

"Father Adinolfi, at the request of the AISI, we are here to assist you." The captain pulled a sheet of paper from inside his vest and handed it to the police officer in charge. "This is a state matter; you are no longer needed. We will take control of the investigation."

The indignant police officer grabbed the document and read it. Furious, he summoned his men and departed.

*   *   *

Adinolfi and the captain from the AISI climbed the stairwell. They stepped aside as two bodies were being removed. As they reached the third floor, monks were cleaning bloodstains off the walls. The priest went to his room. He saw the feet of a dead friar by his bed. He approached.

"Sergio, what are you doing here? It appears the car explosion didn't kill you." He stopped, tilted his head. "Yes, yes, leave me alone."

"Did you say something, Adinolfi?"

"No, no, we were talking."

The captain's eyebrows raised as Adinolfi continued his conversation with an unknown entity.

"Yes, you're right. I know, I know…stop bothering me." Adinolfi cupped his hands over his ears, trying to quiet the demons in his head. After a moment, he folded his hands across his stomach and turned to the shocked, gaping AISI agent.

"Go to the first-floor security office. Review the video footage and find the people responsible. And remove this traitor."

The captain obeyed his instructions and grabbed Sergio's feet, dragging him into the hallway. Adinolfi closed the door and walked to the tapestry in the corner. He moved the needlepoint aside.

"Yes, yes, leave me alone. I understand. I shouldn't have left the prophecy. No, it is not my fault. No, no, no, stop it! I am beholden to him whom I serve. What? Who are you?" The disturbed cleric smiled as he listened to a second voice. "Thank you. Why, my Lord, do You allow him to attack me? I am Your faithful servant. I abide by Your commands. Yes, I realize what I have done. I shall be obedient to Your wishes." The voices departed, the torment ended for the moment. Adinolfi removed the stone that covered the safe. He punched in the code, and the door swung open. He peeked inside the secured container. His right hand moved the two journals and the pistol. He panicked. *Where were the plastic pouches?* His mind's captors' roar erupted in his head. *We told you. You shouldn't have left. We told you! We told you!* Adinolfi covered his ears as he screamed, "Stop, stop!" The door burst open. The AISI captain stood at the entranceway.

"Are you alright?" The captain approached the crazed man.

Adinolfi's eyes were bulging, filled with hatred. His face red, he emptied the safe and threw its contents on the ground. The gun made a crashing noise. The agent took no chances, picked up the weapon, and placed it in his belt.

"Where are they?" he yelled. He fell to the floor. On his knees, he rummaged through his possessions.

"Can I help you?"

"No, no."

The voices exploded, taunting Adinolfi. *We told you, you're an idiot. What are your plans, child of God?*

His eyes devoid of emotion, he sat on his haunches. The tormentors gone, he gawked at the fear-stoked captain.

"They stole a valuable item from my safe. What did you find on the video?"

The captain took out his phone and showed Adinolfi the downloaded photos.

"DeLaurentis! He's supposed to be in America." His cell rang. "What? Are you sure? Keep him there. I'll call later."

Chapter 65

Papal Conference Room, Vatican City, 6:00 P.M.

Giacomo paced as he waited for Pope Andrew. His depression was no longer at the forefront of his consciousness, at least for the time being. He paused at a credenza adorned with three framed photos. One was Andrew's father and his five-year-old stepbrother, whom Andrew had never met. The second photo was of Andrew's mother. And the third a photograph of Andrew, Emily, Rio, and himself.

Disturbed by the image, he walked to the window. The Vatican gardens lay below him, the hills of Rome in the distance. If a priest had instigated the treacherous events against his family, was Andrew involved? *Adinolfi, who had treated Rio at the Papal City apartments—a physician recommended by the Holy See...was this a coincidence?* The notion made his stomach churn.

The papal conference room door squeaked opened as the widower continued to scowl out the window. "Did you know?" Giacomo asked, as he turned around. His eyes betrayed his thoughts.

"About Adinolfi? No, I didn't. I am as outraged as you are. The CIA dossier you sent me is troubling. I'm appalled that one of our own is behind this tragedy against you and our family. We have launched an investigation and if we, the Church, are at fault, then…"

"Then what, Andrew? You'll bring my wife and my children back? Repair my sister's brain? What the hell are you people doing?"

"I understand your anger—"

"You *what*? Are you serious? You don't have a clue. Those responsible need to die. I want Adinolfi dead. That bastard will pay for what he did and if you're—I promise you will suffer the consequences, too."

"Giacomo, calm down. I am not a party to this. You are my family." Andrew's voice was soothing. "Please, my friend, sit."

"How did this happen? A Vatican doctor—a priest—one of yours. You told me Rio was safe. Damn it, my wife, my children, how..." Distraught, he pulled a brown leather chair from the conference table and sat. Tears rolled off his chin. "Why, Andrew?"

"I have no answers for you. We are gathering...evidence."

Giacomo met his friend's gaze. His fixed blank stare caused the Pope to bow his head. In a flash, Andrew's soul lay bare for the heavens to see.

"Giacomo, what happened?"

"What do you mean?"

"Just now. Your gaze penetrated me, then your face changed and I...I...I...saw your father staring at me. My being transfixed..."

Giacomo didn't reply. The men sat together, not saying a word. There was nothing to say. A spiritual event had transpired, one for which there was no explanation. A tranquil sense swept them from reality to a realm away from the chaos of Giacomo's existence. Fixed in time, the passing minutes were suspended, as if no longer following the laws of nature. Giacomo saw the tears in Andrew's eyes.

The door to the conference room sprang open as two plainclothes Swiss guards entered, their guns drawn.

"What are you doing?" Andrew demanded, appalled at the sight of the firearms.

"A bright flash came from the room. Are you safe, Your Holiness?"

"I am fine," he smiled. "We're good. It was the hand of God."

Puzzled, the men holstered their pistols and retreated.

Giacomo was silent for a moment. He placed his fingers on his face, drawing them from his forehead to his chin. "My father...you saw my father?" A forgotten sense of hope traveled through him. A feeling that everything was going to be okay.

"Yes."

"I'm sorry for what I said, Andrew. I'm stuck in this world, a place where I don't belong. How I wish I were dead. What should I do?"

"Time will heal your pain, Giacomo. Go back home. Let the authorities exact your justice. You have important work to accomplish in the States."

"What about Alessio?"

"I'll find a place for him. We've sent him to a hospital in Rome."

"Someone should inform his mother?"

"We'll notify her after we have examined him. Giacomo, Adinolfi and his people are playing God. Their atrocities will not go unpunished."

"What evidence do you have?"

"I discovered disturbing information in the archives about the FHS."

"Yeah, what?"

"I'll let you know when I can. You need to trust me."

Giacomo felt the uneasiness in Andrew's voice and accepted his answer.

"What happened to Sergio?" Andrew asked.

"He's dead."

"Did you…?"

"No, I was with him when he died. He'd already sustained mortal wounds when I found him in Adinolfi's room at Monte Cassino this morning."

"What was he doing there?"

"The same reason I went to the abbey—to kill the bastard. He wanted his revenge for what Adinolfi did to his son and Rio. Sergio confessed his betrayal to me. He mentioned the FHS had been keeping tabs on us since he was the prime minister."

"Why?"

"From what I understand, a prophecy about my family. Though it makes no sense to me. We don't live in a world of fantasy. This is not a movie. No happy endings—it is life, and it sucks."

"I agree with what you're saying, Giacomo. To tell you the truth, I'm skeptical. Remember, throughout man's history, there have been gifted people who witnessed the future. The relevance of a foretelling document could be valid."

"Bullshit, Andrew. Sorry, humanity is nothing but a group of lunatics who live within the rationalizations of their own minds. Someone had a prophetic message about my family. Ugh, what a bunch of crap. Why are we different from anyone else?"

"You're not seeing the complete picture. Do you agree your father knew events before they happened? And let's not forget what happened to us a few minutes ago."

"You have a point."

"Then tell me why you can't believe."

"It makes no sense."

"Because it's true?"

"Yes."

"Perhaps the prophecy is valid. One thing is sure: Adinolfi believes the message is authentic and that you are a hindrance. Whether it's true is of no consequence to him. You are in danger, my friend."

Giacomo covered his lips with his forefinger as he contemplated Andrew's words. His eyes scanned the room. *Could he be correct? Why can't I accept what is true? What has changed?* "I guess the future will show where wisdom lies."

"And it will, my friend."

"Yeah, sure."

"Why don't you stay here for a couple of days?"

"No, thank you. I have to close the office in the city."

"How about if I arrange an apartment for you here in the Papal Palace? You'll be safer."

"Like my sister?" Giacomo noticed that his sarcastic comment caused the Pope to flinch. "I'm sorry, Andrew. That was uncalled for. I'll be fine on my own."

"Are you staying at the Marriott?"

"Yes. Maybe dinner or lunch in a couple of days. I have to close my office here in Rome."

"When do you plan to leave?"

"Probably the twenty-second. I need to get back to the States."

"Make sure you give my secretary a call. I'll clear my calendar so we can get together."

"I will." Giacomo looked at the ceiling.

"What is it, Giacomo?"

"Before the attack on Sergio and me, he mentioned my sons. I'm puzzled as to why? Anyway, I'll call you in a couple. Have a good day, Andrew."

Chapter 66

The Abbey at Monte Cassino, Italy, February 18

Adinolfi knelt under a painting of Saint Benedict looming high above him. The voice in his subconscious continued its torment: *You failed. Your ineptness has caused the angels to cry. You fool! The twins must return to the Father in paradise. We command you to obey. Your time is running short. We told you! We told you!*

The tortured priest covered his ears as he screamed. "Stop, stop, you're wrong! I did not fail."

The Gemini must die. You failed, you insipid loser. You've lost favor with your God.

"No, I have not. I do the bidding of Him whom I serve. Away from me, I command it. I, the FHS, will save the Church. We'll rescue His people. The others cannot take control."

The tormentor laughed with menacing rancor. *No, no, we won't allow it.*

In a serendipitous change, a calm voice spoke. *Don't permit the demon to enter. Go to the twins. They are paramount. Raise them as your own. Your plan has failed.*

No, no, they must die…Yes, yes, they must.

Adinolfi succumbed, steadfast in his rationale. The religious order— not the secular — will show the people the favor of God. He realized, now that fourteen days had passed without the pills, the voices continued to harass his mind. Wasn't that his fate since the beginning? God the Father created him this way. Man gave him the medication. He understood by depriving himself of the drugs, his rational thought process journeyed into a cacophony of convoluted images and voices—the reality of life dismissed by the delusions within his consciousness. He held the bottle containing the miracle pills, which kept the demons at bay.

Adinolfi pondered the end of his torment. He gazed at the open safe, void of the parchment, the mystery of its disappearance solved when an associate based at the Vatican discovered the ancient papyrus in Alessio's pocket. Maybe Adinolfi could resurrect his plan?

He was scheduled to meet Dr. Rift at the abbey to discuss Giacomo's boys. Should the prophetic message turn out to be true about the twins, they could harvest their DNA. As a medical student, Adinolfi believed that the bodies of the saints had a unique genetic marker, a potential key to their divine powers. Able to authenticate the validity of his thought with the modern capabilities of DNA extraction and analytical equipment, he empowered Dr. Rift to examine the preserved corpses and remnants of Saints Francis of Assisi and Padre Pio. Rift's discovery proved a chromosome strand aberrant to the human genome. *Did Giacomo's twins have a similar link?* Adinolfi texted Rift the new location of the Gemini now that the facility had been compromised.

Chapter 67

D r. Rift reached for his briefcase, placed a manila folder into one of its compartments, and exited the building. He slammed the passenger door of his silver Mercedes AMG. The doctor had controlled his anger as he walked to the driver's side of the vehicle but couldn't hide his disgust as he gazed back at the CIA building while getting into the car.

Fortunately, the US intelligence community had presented him with a get-out-of-jail-free card. Unable to display his outrage in the director's office, he now grabbed hold of the leather steering wheel. His knuckles turned white from the intensity of his grip. Powerless to control his fury any longer, he screamed in defiance: "How dare they? Do they realize who I am? I have restored human life!" His mind filled with thoughts as the consequences of his actions broadsided him. *Does my wife know? I need to escape. What choice do I have? Screw—*

His burner phone chimed.

"We need you back here now."

"For what, Adinolfi? The board meeting isn't for another—"

"Don't question us! Do as you're told."

Go scratch your ass, Rift was about to say. *What was wrong with this guy?* The last time they met, he found the priest talking to himself. He suggested Adinolfi seek help. Rebuked, he was told his psychological well-being was none of Rift's concern.

"Relax, I'll catch a flight tonight. Why do you need me?"

"To perform a DNA analysis on a set of twins."

"Can't you have your people do it?"

"No, we trust you. The boys might have the *God genome!*"

"Incredible…" Rift's voice rose in excitement. "Are they at the abbey?"

"By the time you arrive in Rome, they will be."

"If it's true, we can harvest the chromosome."

"I had similar thoughts. We could create a modern Messiah who will bring the Church to its rightful place."

"Yeah, sure."

"Don't dismiss us, doctor. Remember, without our funding, you're nothing. The FHS comes first, then you can conduct your Frankenstein research projects. Do you understand?"

"Yep. I'll see you in a day or two."

Rift called his secretary.

"Yes, doctor?"

"Where's Paige? I've been trying to reach her. She doesn't answer her cell."

"Dr. Leavitt isn't here."

"Why?

"She phoned in, saying she had an emergency and won't be back for a couple of days."

"Damn it. I'm traveling to Italy tonight. If she calls, let her know."

The doctor ended the call before he got a response. He had plans to meet his wife, now secretary of state, for supper. Tensions between them were bad enough, and now this. *Screw her too.*

He called Lisa as he drove his Mercedes on I-95 to their house to pack a suitcase for his 10:00 p.m. flight to Rome.

"We still having dinner tonight?"

"What's the matter with you? You can't say hello anymore?"

"Don't start with your crap, Lisa. I am not in a good mood."

"That's been your excuse throughout our marriage."

"Yeah, yeah, yeah. Screw you."

"You'd like to."

"I have. I got your money. Go kill yourself."

"You bastard. Expect to be served with the divorce papers. You and your little honey can move in together. Oh, one other thing—how was your visit to the CIA? You going to jail?"

The phone conversation ended. Rift bellowed, "Bitch, bitch, bitch!" swerving in and out of traffic as he stepped on the accelerator.

Chapter 68

Eight Years Earlier

Rift's introduction to Adinolfi came after he gave a speech to members of the European Union Medical Association. The topic was nerve regeneration and the ability to change the genetic makeup of a human being. His discourse on the development of CRISPR and its capacity to alter a person's DNA piqued Adinolfi's curiosity.

Unable to continue financing his research projects himself, Rift negotiated with Adinolfi to sell Genome Labs, LLC to a convoluted consortium of hedge-fund companies that fell under the umbrella of the FHS. The money sucked Rift into a game of playing God—transforming the evolution of humanity from the natural to the scientific. With twenty million dollars deposited into his personal bank account, Rift began his quest to change human biology. Adinolfi placed a caveat on the agreement: he tasked Rift with examining the chromosomes on the remains of Saints Francis and Padre Pio, both of whom had had mystical powers.

In a clandestine operation, members of the FHS broke into the crypt of Saint Francis of Assisi and withdrew bone fragments from the burial chamber. The shrine of Padre Pio proved more difficult; the religious scientists had enclosed the mystic in a hermetically sealed crystal coffin. This caused major consternation among Adinolfi and his followers. *How to open the sarcophagus and keep the saint's body preserved?* By a stroke of luck, the Vatican requested Pio's remains for the celebration of the Jubilee of Mercy in Rome. Adinolfi's contacts within the Holy See had the technological means to acquire bone and skin fragments while preserving the body. No one ever discovered the defilement of Padre Pio.

Within the first eighteen months of his tenure, Rift—using the organic material from the two saints—discovered what he called the *God genome*: a strand of DNA attached to the double helix. He believed that if he and his associates could find a living donor with a matching God genome, they could harvest it and transplant the chromosomes into newborn babies.

Rift's hypothetical result was a superhuman species with a lifespan of 150 years and brain capacity and capabilities that mirrored a modern-day supercomputer. After Rift's discovery, FHS rewarded him with an endless stream of cash.

Four years and two hundred million dollars of research investments later, Adinolfi summoned him to Rome, requesting his presence the following day. Rift did as he was told and, the next morning, exited the Alitalia Airlines terminal, where his driver carried his bags to a waiting silver Mercedes sedan. Unfamiliar with the city, he observed the sights of the ancient Roman metropolis. The chauffeur stopped the car at the Marriott Flora. A doorman opened the rear passenger door as a bellman removed his luggage from the trunk. When Rift reached the curb, he was greeted by Adinolfi.

"You're surprised, Dr. Rift?"

"I didn't know, Adinolfi, that you were a priest."

"There are plenty of things you are not aware of, Dr. Rift. I promise today will be a highlight of your life. Later, I'll introduce you to the others."

"Others?"

"Yes, our annual executive meeting of the FHS."

"FHS?"

"The company that owns you. Here's your hotel key. You're in room 606. You'll meet the directors at two o'clock. I'm sending an associate to escort you to the conference at 1:45. Be ready by then." He turned on his heels and left Rift standing on the sidewalk.

Dr. Rift gazed out his hotel room window, taking in the landscape of Rome—the dome of Saint Peter's Basilica on one side and off in the distance, the Colosseum. After the initial shock at seeing Adinolfi in priest's garb had worn off, he opened his computer and searched the web for FHS. The result was a religious group called Followers of the Holy Spirit. Intrigued, he wondered why he was there and what the board wanted from him. A knock on the hotel room door caused Rift to glance at his Rolex. "Right on time."

His escort was silent as they rode in the elevator. When they stopped at the first floor, he said, "This way, sir."

A guard standing near the meeting room greeted Rift as he approached. "Good afternoon, Doctor."

Rift walked through the entrance. Inside were twelve men. As they turned to greet him, he recognized their faces and stopped. The renowned group held global positions of power and wealth. Four were the chairpersons of the largest Fortune Ten corporations in the world. Three were the Prime Ministers of England, China, and Italy. Next came the President of the European Union, and three well-known American politicians from both the United States Senate and House of Representatives. The remaining man, he didn't recognize...a monk.

"Come in, Doctor." Adinolfi approached with his hand outstretched. "Gentlemen, please sit. Dr. Rift, I'm sure you are familiar with our Board of Directors?"

"I am, with the exception of the friar."

"Ah yes, our soon-to-be papal librarian, Father Benavequa."

Chapter 69

The Office of the Speaker of the House, Capitol Building, February 19, 4:00 A.M.

Alfred Ramsey picked his nose as he read the intelligence briefing. He rejoiced in having been victorious in ushering in Executive Order 14964. The secret directive established a military protocol that isolated a division of the United States Marines. Under the authority of the Speaker, the commander of the unit could make unilateral decisions without presidential or congressional approval.

The Marine task force's job was to protect members of the new government and its capital and ensure adherence to the new international constitution: America and its global partners—ten regimes joined as one, a unified earth with the primary goals of peace and equality. Their combined strength was enough to unify the soon-to-be-broken landscape. The American generals were all on board, except for General Giacomo DeLaurentis, who was supposed to be dead.

Ramsey was fortunate not to be implicated with the past House leadership, who had tried to overthrow the government. He remained in the shadows. A representative of the FHS for two decades, Ramsey was slated to take the reins of the global society in a few short weeks. The transfer of authority couldn't happen fast enough. Adinolfi's beliefs had become an impingement to the unification of the world's political parties. The priest's infatuation with a prophecy was leading the organization to a quick demise.

The consortium's fifty-year plan was to pit two major superpowers—China and Russia—against each other. The FHS and Chinese philosophies were not much different. China believed in a slow, methodical approach to proselytizing its ideology by becoming an economic superpower—thus, securing a major foothold by providing financial and infrastructure support to the democratic nations and the impoverished countries. The beginning of a one-world order. During those five decades, the FHS was able to install its own people within the communist party and government. They waited in abeyance for the right time to strike.

While the European Union was economically sound and on its way to bringing the United States under its wing, Russia was failing and becoming isolated. The Soviet Union's desire to reunite the USSR countries provided the catalyst for the FHS to implement its plan for a one-government global rule. Fueled by the invasion of the Ukraine, the FHS put its resources into funding the Ukrainian military with the hopes that the remaining hardline Chinese communists would see an opportunity to solidify their alliance with Russia while excluding the free societies of the world.

After bailing out the Russian government to the tune of one trillion dollars, China believed the Russian populace would be grateful. The opposite occurred when the Soviets defaulted on their loans and snubbed the Chinese, setting up the conflict the FHS needed to move forward: China attacks, the Russians retaliate, both governments destroyed. Secondary targets included Iran, Iraq, Libya, Venezuela, India, Pakistan, and Cuba. On a particular date privy to select members, certain events were scheduled to take place in rapid succession: the assassinations of the Chinese and Russian presidents, the issuance of nuclear launch codes destroying Moscow and Beijing, followed by the detonation of multiple EMPs—electro-magnetic pulses—decimating electrical components capable of disabling communication, flight, and missile launches. The world would come to a stop.

Within thirty-six hours after the attacks, the leaders of the FHS would signal its members to emerge from protective shelters and assume the succession of power by rescuing the terrified citizens of the world. Safeguards had been put in place to prevent a financial collapse while stabilizing global chaos. Five hundred years of patience and strategic positioning led to the coming moment—the comprehensive unification of the republics as a one-rule government.

Within a week after the downfall of the nations, the FHS would authorize the military powers of its member countries to take action, in a primary decree to maintain peace and promote freedom for their citizens. Then, the ultimate phase of the plan: destroy Washington, DC, while Congress sat in session and establish the new continental United States government with its capital in Philadelphia.

Ramsey observed the clock on his desk and murmured, "ten fifteen in Paris." He reached into a drawer for his secured satellite phone. Ramsey dialed the number and waited for the others to gain access. The roll call began.

"US here," Ramsey said.

"Germany online."

"Italy."

"France here."

"England."

"Australia."

"Brazil."

"This is Spain."

"Israel."

"Saudi Arabia."

"Russia."

"China is present."

When the final national representative announced himself, the German delegate spoke. "First, Adinolfi has gone missing. Three hours ago, we were notified of an incident at Monte Cassino. We discovered the *dummkopf* had a separate side venture in human genome modification. I will transmit the details to you later today. America, we'll need your help. It involves your CIA."

"Understood," Ramsey replied.

"We have scheduled the attack to start a week before Passover, maybe sooner if we can rid ourselves of Adinolfi. Our Chinese and Russian counterparts have secured the final EMP transmitting devices."

The French delegate interrupted the German. "What is the impact on Europe?"

"There'll be power disruptions as far east as Paris. Our scientists have assured us the outages will last three days, maximum."

"What about my country, Russia?"

"At least two months. This should give your multinational troops in Serbia adequate time to reach Saint Petersburg, the new capital. I believe we have completed the construction," the German representative said.

"Yes."

The Chinese delegate chimed in, "We've moved the summit of the National Congress to the epicenter of the attack. We protected members of the new contemporary government in Taiwan."

"We've calculated that the nuclear fallout shall be minimal in the Middle East, South Pacific, and South America."

"How many expected casualties?" the Italian representative asked.

"The number doesn't matter. We must remember, ladies and gentlemen, that the sacrifice of life is necessary to ensure global peace."

Chapter 70

"Thank you for the information. I'll put you in my schedule. Let's meet after the security briefing." As the conversation ended, President Thomas Maro's private phone alerted him to a recent voicemail. He gazed at the calendar on his computer monitor, dotted with notes for topics of discussion. The president placed the cursor over the plus sign to add an appointment and typed in his meeting with Speaker of the House Alfred Ramsey. Tom preferred to handle his own schedule and not leave it up to his chief of staff or his secretary. He turned his attention to his cell phone and returned the call of the CIA's Rome Section Chief, Maryann Costatino.

"Maryann, Tom Maro."

"Mr. President, the CIA director asked me to return to the States."

"Why?"

"I was told I am being promoted to the Directorate of Operations."

"Congratulations, I'm sure you'll do an outstanding job."

"Thank you, sir, but we haven't found the boys yet. And there's another issue. Giacomo is back in Italy."

"I surmised as much. I didn't expect him to hang around in New Haven. Where is he?"

"On his way to the Vatican. There was an incident at the Abbey of Monte Cassino earlier today."

"What happened?"

Maryann explained the details. "Mr. President, are you still there?"

"I am. Is this part of the group we discussed?"

"Yes, the FHS. We're hoping to have their leader in custody within the next two days."

"Adinolfi?"

"Correct. We've discovered the organization is a cover for a multinational conglomerate with vast holdings in real estate management funds, financial institutions, arms manufacturing, as well heavy investments in aerospace and food production."

"I know."

"You do?"

"I received a report from the FBI and the House Intelligence Committee outlining their assets. There was also a statement from FHS's board of directors condemning Adinolfi."

"Why?"

"He diverted funds to finance his DNA research."

"Interesting…makes sense."

"What do you mean?"

"Giacomo found a secret research facility at the abbey."

"I wonder what Adinolfi's agenda is?"

"Excellent question. I'll tell you this. One of our agents says he's a schizophrenic."

"Any medical proof?" Maro queried.

"No. Mr. President, can you call the director and postpone my appointment? We're close to finding Giacomo's sons, and I want to see this through."

Tom paused for a moment. "Is that a prudent idea, since he is not aware of your mission?"

"True, but…"

"What about your men in the field—Giacomo's associates? How resourceful are they?"

Maryann hesitated. "No problems with Frank; he's ex-military. However, Warren lacks the experience."

"Hmm, we can't risk not bringing you back. Remember, Maryann, we don't know who our friends are, and my guess is they're few and far between in our government." Maro grabbed a manila folder from the desk, opened it, and leafed through the classified papers.

"That's true, Mr. President. Still…"

"When are you supposed to return?"

"Two days."

"Then let's hope you and your team can find Giacomo's sons in the next forty-eight hours."

The conversation ended and Tom read the confidential briefing.

> We must terminate Adinolfi. His actions thwart our desire for a global government. He is no longer useful to our cause.

POTUS placed the folder in his briefcase, making a mental note to shred the document upstairs in his private residence.

*   *   *

Westover Air Reserve Base, Massachusetts

"In accordance with Executive Order number 14964, your mission is to assassinate Dr. Alphonso Adinolfi. His last known location is Monte Cassino, Italy. Godspeed, gentlemen."

The Marine Colonel exited the military airlift command aircraft as the engines started their whine.

Chapter 71

Leonardo da Vinci–Fiumicino International Airport, Rome, Italy, February 20

The CIA's Rome Section Chief Maryann Costatino waited for her passenger to arrive. The three-and-a-half-hour ride from Perugia proved disconcerting. Her team had failed to track Adinolfi's men; their efforts found his van deserted in an alley, giving credence to her suspicion of a CIA mole. To add insult to injury, the president's decision not to rescind the order for her to return to the States increased her frustration. Maryann's heart ached with disappointment, dismayed at the inability to find the twins. She questioned whether there could be a break in the investigation in time. *Where are Giacomo's sons?*

As she arrived at the airport, she received a phone call from her assistant.

"Are you positive?"

"Yes, ma'am. We intercepted his conversation with Adinolfi. Dr. Rift's plane is scheduled to land in Rome in forty-five minutes."

"Do we know what terminal or airline?"

"No."

"How the hell are we going to locate him?"

"Good luck."

"Yeah, thanks."

The news renewed Maryann's hope of finding the infants. She grabbed three agents and drove to the airline terminal.

"Park over there," Maryann pointed. "I'll get out here. I'm confident someone is picking him up. I'll track the driver. You two stand by customs. Let me know when Rift arrives."

*   *   *

Rift exited the customs-and-immigration door, followed by the two clandestine operatives. His cell phone chimed. He took a cursory look at the screen, shaking his head. Maryann approached her target holding a sign that read "Dr. Rift." She had convinced the limo driver, with 300 euros, that he had a new assignment, and she was his replacement.

"I'm Doctor Rift."

Maryann did not hesitate. "CIA," she flashed her badge. "I'll take your phone." She snatched the device and read the message.

"Don't come to the abbey—twins at 42.71N 12.11E, seven churches, the third da—"

Rift grabbed the phone and slammed her in the chest, causing Maryann to lose her balance. He bolted back inside the airline terminal. Chased by two CIA agents, he ran up the escalator to the second floor. The doctor removed his brown sports coat, tossed it into a trash can, and blended into the crowd. He entered a coffee shop and hid in the corner. The operatives sprinted past him. Confident he had eluded his captors, the scientist exited the passenger departure area.

"Don't move, Rift."

He stopped and turned.

Maryann stood ten feet behind him, her nine-millimeter Beretta drawn and pointed at his head. "Stay where you are, or I'll splatter your brains on the ground."

He snarled and ran across the Kiss-and-Go car lot. Vehicles sped by, beeping their horns at the man in the road. A crowd of onlookers lined the sidewalk in front of the terminal. Maryann fired two rapid gunshots into the sky. The gathered people screamed, causing confusion as they dispersed into the shadows of the Alitalia departure area.

"Stop! I'm warning you," she shouted. She took aim at his leg. Trapped, Rift stopped at the guardrail and glanced at the traffic twenty feet below.

"Don't do it, Rift." The agent squeezed the trigger. A blue Renault slowed in front of her, blocking Maryann's shot. The bullet ricocheted off the front bumper. She waved the gun at the driver who froze at the sight. Maryann ran around the car. The sound of tires screeching sliced into the morning air. She banged her fist on the guardrail as she saw the sprawled, broken body below.

Chapter 72

For the past five days, Giacomo's mind was occupied with his business, which needed to be dismantled per his agreement with the Department of Defense. Exhausted from the day, he entered his hotel room at the Marriott Flora. He had hired a trucking company to haul the furniture from the Rome headquarters of Remote, LLC to a storage facility. Being in the office complex had fueled his grief. Dismayed by Sergio's betrayal, he tried to put it behind him.

Giacomo sat on a couch by the coffee table. He reached for a file next to an empty glass, pushing aside the pamphlet on the seven stages of grief. Shaking his head, he read the doctor's report Andrew had sent him. The medical dossier stated that the patient's brain cells, destroyed by the point-blank gunshot, were healing themselves. No explanation was given as to how or why Alessio's brain was recovering. *Did the scientific quest to restore the human body cross moral boundaries? At what cost? Alessio was not cognizant of who he was. He would be better off dead.* Giacomo placed the document on the nightstand by his bed and answered his cell phone.

Though the caller ID was blocked, he said, "Hello, Maryann."

"How did you know it was me?"

"Intuition, I guess. What can I do for you?" His hand fell on the grief pamphlet.

"Are you alright?"

"I'm fine. Why?"

"I understand you were at Monte Cassino."

"True, I was."

"What happened?"

Giacomo remained silent. He wished he could forget the last three months. *I need to be with my wife and my sons, to leave this horrific existence of anguish and despair.* The pain plagued his being. Was there no end to his misery? He knew the solution…death—if not by a combatant, then suicide. What choice did he have to relieve his agony?

"Giacomo… Giacomo…?"

"Yeah," his voice was subdued. Giacomo updated her on the outlandish events—how he located Sergio, and the disconcerting discovery of Alessio's resurrection.

"I'm sorry. A tough day for you?"

"Yes, to say the least. My anger got the best of me. Now all I want to do is…"

"Is what?"

"Doesn't matter. I don't care anymore."

"Giacomo, you don't sound well. You need to talk with someone."

"Yep."

"We have good news. We'll be taking Adinolfi into custody in the next couple of days."

Giacomo's interest piqued. "Bring him to me. I'll kill the bastard for you."

"Giacomo, you know I can't hand him over. Listen, I'm heading back to Washington. They have promoted me to Directorate of Operations."

"Congratulations?"

"The opportunity couldn't have come at a worse time. A plane is standing by to take me home tomorrow. Come with me? It's vital you return to the States."

"Why?"

"For your safety and for the sake of national security."

"Here we go again. It's always national security with you folks. What a bunch of crap. I can take care of myself. What information are you keeping from me?" As Giacomo's frustration intensified, his despair vanished.

"Giacomo, we are weeks away from dissolving a global organization, which has far-reaching implications. I'm sorry, but this is more important than your personal desire for revenge."

"I beg your pardon? Do you realize who you are speaking with?"

"So now you're going to pull the power card? Just because you hold the title Chairman of the Joint Chiefs doesn't mean you can obstruct justice—"

"How dare you!" Giacomo walked to the window as his voice erupted. His resolve stoked his irritation to avenge the death of Em and the twins. Maryann's antagonism flooded his consciousness. "Let me explain something to you, Maryann. By my own will, anytime…" He gritted his teeth. The corners of his lips pursed while his eyes blazed. "And I mean anytime, I will exact my revenge, whether it be today, tomorrow, or next year. This is a warning—no, it's a promise. If you or anybody else gets in my way—"

A brilliant flash of light caused Giacomo to cover his face as a muffled explosion rocked the Marriott. He fell to the floor as detonations shook the building. The hotel window imploded. Shards of glass pelted the room as his vision went dark. Cell phone still in his hand, the last thing he heard was Maryann calling his name.

Emily walked toward him. Giacomo's heart raced. "Em, what are you doing here?" The two embraced. How he had longed for her touch, her kiss, and now, they were together! He didn't know where he was, the colors vibrant. Then he saw his father, Paolo. "Dad, Dad." Then Arnaud, and he realized he had died. He scanned the fields for his children. Why weren't they here? Filled with a sense of requited love, Em whispered in his ear, "Return and find our sons."

"Giacomo? Giacomo?"

His eyes opened. "What, what are you doing here?"

"I've come to take you home."

"Where is Em? Where did she go? My boys, where are they?" A tear, not from physical pain but from resounding heartbreak, traveled down Giacomo's chin.

They hoisted Giacomo onto a stretcher and carried him to a waiting ambulance.

"Maryann, Frank here."

"How is he?"

"A laceration on his forehead. He's in and out of consciousness."

"Can he return with me?"

"Shouldn't be an issue. Best to have a nurse or doctor on board."

"I'll arrange it."

"Maryann, he was mumbling about Emily and his sons. Giacomo kept repeating, 'I must find the boys.' I thought he didn't know."

"As far as I've been told, Frank, he doesn't."

"How bad is it there?"

"A nightmare. The entire Italian government is in a state of shock."

"I can imagine. My contacts informed me the president issued a 'combat readiness' to our troops stationed there. We also have disturbing news about our communist friends…Russia and China are on high alert."

"Interesting…any idea why?"

"Who knows? To be honest, Maryann, I can't wait to return to the States. I have a nasty feeling."

"Not yet, Frank—I need your help. We believe we are close to finding twins."

"Where?"

"In the village of Orvieto, at a local church."

"Shouldn't be too hard to find."

"Well, last count, there were at least seven churches. We also think they are moving the boys on a day-to-day basis."

"Freaking wonderful…"

"Listen, Frank, there's an airplane standing by at the Perugia airport for you. Warren will wait for you at the cathedral in Orvieto. Locate the twins and bring them back home."

"You make it sound so easy."

Chapter 73

United States Air Force Base, Aviano, Italy, February 21

"Gentlemen, looks like the gods are with us. We have briefed you on the attack on Vatican City. Our task is to command a multinational force that will surround the city of Rome. This will aid in our capture of Dr. Adinolfi. Our sources report he's *en route* to the Papal Palace. You'll air-drop here at the following checkpoints." The Colonel pointed at the map. "You have the authority over these units. After you apprehend the criminal, your orders are to notify me for further instructions. Questions? Very well, dismissed." The men stood and saluted the marine officer.

*   *   *

"What did you say, Father Adinolfi?" the limo driver asked.

"Nothing that concerns you. What's our arrival time in Rome?"

"Another hour, depending on traffic."

"Why the delay?"

"I'm not sure. It could be from the attack."

"What are you talking about?"

"The terrorist strike on the Vatican."

"What?"

"The attack on Saint Peter's and the Papal Palace."

"No, no, this can't be happening. Is the Pope alive?"

"He's missing."

Adinolfi panicked as he searched for his cell phone. His hands flailed as the voices overtook his mind. *You're a failure, what are you going to do, priest? Ha, ha, your church will never be under your control. How foolish you are to think you can thwart the spirit of God.* "Stop. Stop!" He covered his ears. "Stop, I command you to stop," he screamed.

The chauffeur swerved the vehicle, slamming on the brakes as it screeched to a halt on the right side of the highway amid the blaring horn of a speeding tractor-trailer truck. He exited the car and opened the back door. Adinolfi, his head down, mumbled words maniacally, imprisoned by his own tormented mind. He glanced up at the driver.

"What are you doing? Why have we stopped?"

"You told me to."

"Yes, yes, you're right. I can't find my phone."

"Father, over there in the cup holder."

"Oh yes, yes, thank you. Stay here. We might have a change of plans." Adinolfi grabbed his cell.

"Is the prophecy safe?"

"Yes."

"I'm on my way. Meet me in the square."

"I can't—they have evacuated Vatican City."

The tormentors continued their madness. *Ha, ha, you failed. You are nothing but a failure. Ha, ha, ha, ha, ha!*

"Adinolfi, are you there?"

Adinolfi tried to suppress the voices as he struggled to converse. The persecution stopped. His mind focused. "Yes, where can we go? Time is running out; I need the parchment today." He paused, struck by a revelation. "It's a perfect turn of events. The world will see God no longer protects the Vatican. Our time has arrived. The words of the prophecy shall console His flock. With any luck, our Pope is dead. Yes, yes, it's coming to fruition. This is God's plan."

Adinolfi heard two people talking as the car door opened.

"Excuse me, Father?" The driver said.

"Yes."

"The military has set up roadblocks around Rome. We could be here for another five hours before we enter the city proper. Also, they evacuated the Vatican."

"Yes, I know." Adinolfi continued his phone conversation, "Where are you?"

"Tivoli."

"Driver, how long to Tivoli?"

"The GPS says two and a half hours, provided I can exit the highway."

"I'll be there in a couple of hours. Meet me at the gardens by the waterfall." Adinolfi placed the phone back in the cup holder. He gazed out the window as the car exited the thoroughfare. Excited, he reached again for the cell and called Rift.

"Hello," a woman's voice said.

"Where's Dr. Rift?"

"Who's calling?"

"Put him on the line. And do it now."

"He's not available."

"Who the hell is this?" the priest growled the question. "Get me Rift."

"I'm sorry, he's dead…a tragic car accident. Is there something I can help you with, Dr. Adinolfi?"

It surprised him that the woman mentioned his name. He tried to focus on her words as he pushed the voices out of his head.

"Whom am I speaking with?" he asked.

"We know about the twins," the woman responded without answering his question.

The tormentors erupted. *Ha, ha, ha priest, you failed again.*

"Shut up, shut up!"

"I'm sorry, Adinolfi, did you say something? Or is it the voices in your mind?"

"What, what, who are you? No, it's the Holy Spirit. It's, it's…" His voice changed to a frightening demonic whisper as he said: "You'll never find the boys. They're mine. You will go to hell, you bitch." He threw the phone across the car, where it hit the windshield. The voices grew angrier. *You have to get the twins…they are more important. Kill the Gemini, and the prophecy ends.*

"Take me to Orvieto," Adinolfi barked at the driver.

Chapter 74

Province of Terni, Italy

The old city of Orvieto, perched atop vertical cliffs of volcanic rock, came into view. Frank circumnavigated the winding roads. He downshifted the forest green Renault and started the climb to the sixteenth-century papal refuge.

Blue signs guided him to a lot close to the Piazza Guglielmo Marconi. The muscular man locked the car, paid the parking attendant, and walked to meet Warren by the Duomo. He hoped they could locate the boys and make their way to the Perugia Airport within a day's time. *How hard could it be to kidnap two babies?* He reached for his cell phone.

"Maryann, I will need local police support to get these kids back home. I just realized, this is a kidnapping."

"Yeah, sorry, Frank, I should have mentioned that to you. We've arranged a military and law enforcement detail to escort you and the children to the airport once they're found. The men are being vetted today. We should have clearance by tonight."

"Another question."

"Yes?"

"How will we know if they are Giacomo's sons?"

"Simple. They'll be surrounded by a cadre of armed guards."

"Good point."

Maryann's phone chirped. "Hold on, Frank, I have a secured email. Let me give it a read." A minute later, she said, "We've had a lucky break. Our operatives got a visual on Adinolfi when he left Monte Cassino.

His chauffeur is one of ours. Adinolfi was traveling to the Vatican; he didn't know terrorists had attacked the city. Long story short, he's going to Orvieto. My guess is he's after the twins."

"Makes sense. We'll wait for him. Can you get word to the driver?"

"Yes. He will contact you when he arrives. If the situation warrants, it's a sanctioned kill."

Frank rounded the corner and walked toward the cathedral. Parked in front was a candy-apple-red tractor-trailer cab adorned with a large white bow fastened to the grill. Across the Piazza, people gathered. He saw Warren leaning against the wall of the Museo Etrusco.

"What's going on?"

"A wedding. Can you believe it, a wedding during the week."

"Yeah." He pointed. "That's a hell of a church—the marble mosaics and stained-glass windows. The colors are amazing. What's over there?"

"The entrance to a series of underground tunnels. Closed now, but they'll open for sightseers in a couple of months," Warren stated.

"Interesting. An FYI, we got Giacomo out; he should be back in the States."

"Good news. So, what's the story, Frank? What are we doing here?"

"Let's find a place to eat, and I'll update you."

The imposing men walked the village's narrow streets. Sidewalks were clear of the restaurant tables found during tourist season. The onslaught of visitors began in spring and ended in the late fall months. Foreigners inundated the town, feeding the local economy. The dreary days of February, however, brought few outsiders.

Frank and Warren drew the look of the butcher as he posted a closed sign on his establishment's door. The men's daunting figures appeared alien in the Italian village. They passed a lone couple who seemed to be window-shopping. The woman cupped her right hand above her eyes and pointed at the expensive, multicolored ceramic dishes. She tried to convince her husband to purchase the set. The men entered a pizzeria two storefronts down.

"We have to be careful that Adinolfi doesn't recognize me."

"I don't think he will, Warren. And if he does, so what? We'll apprehend the bastard, grab the kids, and leave."

"Sounds like an excellent idea. What about the bombing at the Vatican? What the hell is going on, Frank?"

"Your guess is as good as mine. Last news report I heard was that Chinese money was behind the Iranian attack on the Holy City."

"China and Iran? Makes no sense."

"Tell me about it. I'm worried this will not end well. I want to be stateside before the crap hits the fan."

"You're concerned?"

"I am. Warren, I think World War III is around the corner. The Vatican assault was a colossal mistake. People are pissed, bombing the Pope broke the camel's back."

Warren and Frank leaned back as the server placed two pizzas in front of them. Warren took a slice, folded the crust, and consumed it.

"Hungry?"

As he grabbed another, he said, "I am, I'm starving. Maybe some pasta later?"

Frank's mobile phone vibrated. He read the text. "Adinolfi is forty minutes out."

"Good."

"Not good—he's being followed by a helicopter."

"Ours?"

"No."

"Great." He nodded at Frank's pizza. "Eat. It might be a long day." Both men's cell phones chimed.

"What the hell?" Frank said.

Warren gazed at the news bulletin that appeared on his screen. "I can't believe this."

"Me either. Damn, the shit is gonna hit the fan, big time. China bombed Moscow."

"I thought they were allies?"

"Me too. Remember, China came to Russia's defense after the tragedy in the Ukraine. I heard the Russian government had enough of China's communist agenda for their country."

"Once you have experienced democracy and freedom, it's hard to return to the old ways," Warren said.

"Yep. Putin must be rolling over in his grave."

Chapter 75

"Father Adinolfi, sir?"

"What is it? I'm busy."

The driver glanced in the rearview mirror and shook his head.

"What is it?"

"We're being followed."

Adinolfi craned his neck as he stared out the back window of the Mercedes down the autostrada. "Which one?"

"Above us—a helicopter."

"Are you sure?"

"Yeah, I noticed it about twenty miles ago."

"Could they be following someone else?"

"I doubt it. I'll exit at Attigliano. We'll go off-road. Then we'll know for certain, if they're still there."

"How much longer?"

"Forty minutes."

*   *   *

"Colonel, they exited the A1," the helicopter pilot said over the noise of the rotor blades.

"Can you get a clear shot to take them out?"

"I'll try."

The pilot dropped the helicopter to an altitude of fifty feet. The downwash from the rotor blades stirred up the dirt on the road. They sailed through the sky, wedged between trees on either side of the highway. One of two side doors slid open as a fifty-caliber machine gun appeared. A soldier squeezed the trigger. The exiting shells peppered the road around the car.

"They're coming for us. Adinolfi, put your head down."

"What, what? How could that be?"

"Put your damn head down."

The surrounding ground erupted. A piece of the pavement recoiled off the right passenger door, making a clanging sound. An evasive move by the driver caused the car to swerve and graze a tree. Adinolfi covered his ears at the crunching sound of metal as the voices in his head laughed at his cowardice. Another aggressive turn to the left, as the chauffer stepped on the gas pedal then slammed on the brakes. He peered out the front window as the helicopter overshot them. The vehicle stayed hidden until the danger passed.

*   *   *

"Sir, this is too dangerous."

"Roger that, Captain. Nice job. I got word Adinolfi is traveling to Orvieto. Let's put a team in the village. We'll apprehend him there."

The officer reviewed a map of the city. "We'll drop our people here," he pointed to a grassy area. "Then, Captain, circle back to observe and communicate Adinolfi's position to the men."

*   *   *

"Good pizza. Not like New Haven, though," Warren said. "I think Sally's is the best."

"I like Pepe's," Frank replied.

"This is the type of pizza Paolo liked," Warren said.

"You knew him well, War?"

"Yeah, he was a great friend."

"I met him twice when Giacomo and I attended West Point." Frank tapped his watch. "Adinolfi should arrive soon. Let's head toward the cathedral. My car is close by if we need it."

Frank and Warren walked out of the pizzeria and started making their way to the church. The *wop, wop* sound of a helicopter caused the men to gaze up at the low-flying military chopper.

"Humph, looks like we have company, Warren."

"Yep. Let the games begin."

*   *   *

Adinolfi's Mercedes entered the city of Orvieto Scalo. He could see the vertical cliffs and the old village perched on the ancient volcanic rock.

"Stay to your left and turn on *della Stazione*," Adinolfi barked. The unseen voices rambled. G*et the boys and destroy them. Kill the Gemini, and the prophecy will never happen. The twins must die.* He shook his head to rid himself of the torment. "No, I can't." He reached inside his pocket and pulled out his medication. Adinolfi pondered consuming two pills to silence the raconteurs in his mind. *Put those away. You don't need them; you're fine. We'll leave you alone for a while. You'll see.* He did what he was told. His tormentors fell silent.

Stuck behind an old truck that sputtered, Adinolfi's driver swerved to the left to pass the lumbering vehicle. He sped up while maneuvering along the curved road as it ascended.

"There's a *piadineria* over there. Turn into the parking lot. I'm hungry." Adinolfi exited the automobile as it came to a stop. "I'll be back. Wait here." He slammed the car door shut. Still shaking from the helicopter attack, he walked to the restaurant.

The driver leaned against the hood, facing out over the valley below. Above, he heard the helicopter, and, to his right, he observed the *piadineria* and enjoyed the drifting aromas. To the left, a locked gate protected a set of slow-rising stairs that ended on a pathway of loose brown stone. The trail weaved its way through a heavy thicket of green trees and overgrowth. Beyond that, the imposing perpendicular volcanic cliff walls loomed.

Adinolfi, accompanied by a waiter, exited the side door of the building. They walked to the opening, pushing aside the bushes, and unlocked the entrance. The priest gazed at the sky, mumbled a series of incoherent words, climbed the shallow steps, and disappeared into the grove. The driver strolled to the outside window of the *piadineria* to purchase a bottle of water. He pulled his cell phone from his jacket.

Chapter 76

Frank's cell phone chirped. He read the text: "Adinolfi's arrived." Frank grabbed a map of Orvieto stowed in his back pants pocket. He unfolded it and pointed. "About twenty minutes ago, he was here having lunch, then he disappeared into this area of trees."

"Where the hell did he go? That's a solid cliff."

Frank and Warren hustled along the Via Lorenzo Maitani. The street emptied into the Piazza Duomo. The blue-and-gold mosaic tiles shimmered in the afternoon sunlight.

"My car is around the corner. We'll drive down and wait for him."

They walked at a hurried pace. The wedding party disbanded. People milled about the front of the cathedral, snapping photographs of the picturesque church. As they entered the piazza, Warren's arm swept across Frank's chest, holding the man back.

"What's the matter?"

"Over there, coming out of the archway, the hooded monk."

"Yeah, what about him?"

"It's Adinolfi."

"Are you sure?"

"Yes, I am."

"Did he see you?"

"I don't think so."

They observed Adinolfi climb the cathedral's stone steps and enter the oak door farthest to the right. A man stationed by the entrance escorted him into the house of God. Two additional men appeared from the corner shadows of the church. Their military personas were easy to distinguish—the chiseled, muscle-toned bodies moved with purpose. One stood by a short cylindrical concrete barrier, his eyes darting back and forth as he scanned the area. The other tried to gain entrance to the locked cathedral. Frustrated, he went back to his partner and huddled in discussion.

"Adinolfi's followers," Frank suggested.

"Yep. Look, you can tell they're wearing bulletproof vests under their jackets. And the guy who allowed the psycho into the church, I drove him to the monastery in Perugia. The twins are *here*."

"Warren, where did you say you saw Adinolfi?"

"By the entrance to—*damn*—the tunnels!" The epiphany illuminated Warren's face with an enormous grin. "C'mon, Frank, let's go. I read there's a labyrinth of underground passageways throughout the city. He's gonna make his way back here and escape."

Chapter 77

You have disappointed your father in heaven. You failed to restore the church. The twins must die. "Stop…stop," Adinolfi whispered. He genuflected before the tabernacle as he made his way to the sacristy. A baby's cry echoed in the house of worship. *You can't murder the children of God. Kill them. No, this is wrong.* The conflicting torment caused him to stop by a kneeler. *Death to the Gemini, and the prophecy ends.* The persecuted man shook his head to expel the demons. *Do not destroy the boys.*

His escort spoke. "Adinolfi, are you—"

"I'm fine. Where are the others?" Adinolfi leaned against the trim of the door frame to keep his balance. A sharp, agonizing pain erupted within his head, then disappeared.

"They are waiting for you downstairs," the man said.

The escort stood to the side to allow Adinolfi to enter the sacristy. Ornamental vestments of green, purple, and red hung on a rack in the room's corner. Wooden drawers and cabinets filled the dressing room. Amid the cabinetry was a door propped open that led down to the basement. A baby's cry resonated up the passageway.

Adinolfi walked to the entrance and descended the stone steps. Dampness and the smell of the centuries-old staircase pervaded his being. He held the wall with his right hand. A string of light fixtures highlighted his way. Trepidation filled him.

The side of his face erupted in excruciating pain. He stopped and composed himself, shaking off the unsettling sense. Adinolfi saw the final landing that headed to a hallway with an open door. His left leg ached as he felt his left cheek droop and his eyes close. *Ha, ha, you won't make it. You fool.* These were the last words assaulting the tormented priest's consciousness as he tumbled down the remaining stairs. His head seared and throbbed in agony...the voices silent as he lay dead at the bottom of the steps.

Chapter 78

Frank and Warren scrutinized a map of the underground pathways. The vast network of tunnels intersected with one another in many places, creating an endless maze that crisscrossed the city. The villagers had constructed and carved out the passageways in the third century. Filled with caves, wells, and the occasional wine cellar, the nobles used the underpasses as escape routes throughout the years of strife and discontent. Now, they were a tourist attraction.

"Look, a tunnel underneath the Duomo," Warren declared, touching his finger to the map.

"Yeah, but it's blocked. That's why he came through here." Frank pointed to a different location.

"So, we should wait 'til he comes back. Adinolfi's escape is through the tunnels."

"True…"

When they heard the echoing of police sirens, both men glanced at one another. The tourist center attendant ran to the window as the *polizia's* flashing blue lights lit up the room. Frank slapped Warren on the shoulder. "Let's go."

The scene around the cathedral evolved into a group of spectators and militia. Within moments, the officers barricaded the church's steps. Seconds later, an ambulance arrived, squealing to a halt. The door to God's house creaked open. A nun wearing a black habit appeared at the top of the stone stairs. She waved the men inside the church. The EMS personnel grabbed the gurney and hurried to meet her. Adinolfi's assassins took the opportunity amid the confusion to enter the Basilica. Warren and Frank followed, not far behind the hired killers.

"Warren, this could be a setup. They'll place the twins in the ambulance and escape."

The sound of gunshots rang out from inside the cathedral.

"What the hell? Are you kidding me? It's a freakin' church."

"Warren, stay with the ambulance and keep your head down."

Frank climbed the steps of the church, reaching for his nine-millimeter Beretta in his back holster. A police officer, aware of Frank's identity, followed with his pistol at the ready.

"I'm American military."

"Yes, we know. Let's go."

They held their guns above their heads. Their backs against the stone face of the cathedral, together they stood by the door. Frank used his fingers to count down: 3, 2, 1. Hands positioned on the weapon, he swept the muzzle, searching the church for the assassins.

The cavernous place of worship echoed with a baby's cry. Three nuns ran past the sanctuary, two of them swaddling children close to their chests. With fear as their fuel, they crossed in front of the altar. Their shoes resounded across the tiled floor. Five shots reverberated in the silence. Frank pointed his gun at the sacristy at the far end of the church. His counterpart acknowledged the gesture. They crept their way through the nave, using the pews for protection.

The Italian officer entered first. He jumped back. "Somebody is coming up the stairs." A voice crackled over his two-way radio. "It's over, they're dead."

Frank and the officer holstered their weapons, shook hands, and walked toward the front of the church. The deaths of the killers didn't calm Frank's nerves. *Did they lose the boys?* He opened the cathedral doors to the applause of the locals gathered by the ambulance. Frank smiled, relieved. Frank grabbed his cell phone and snapped a picture of Warren cradling Giacomo's sons.

Chapter 79

White House Situation Room, Washington, DC, February 23

President Tom Maro sat at the conference table. An 84-inch monitor displayed an expanded, split-screen satellite view of the cities of Moscow and Beijing, their skylines dotted with rising black-gray smoke. Seated with the president were four men: Head of the Senate Intelligence Committee; Head of the NSA; Alfred Ramsey, Speaker of the House; and his assistant, Scott Evans. Absent from the room were Secretary of State Lisa Rift and Chairman of the Joint Chiefs of Staff General Giacomo DeLaurentis.

"Where do we stand?

"Phase one is complete, Mr. President. Tensions between both countries will continue to escalate through March twenty-fifth, the first day of Passover—four weeks from today. China is condemning the attack on Moscow, denying their involvement. And the Russians repudiated the fact they retaliated," Ramsey summarized.

"Any chance the timeline can speed up?"

"It's possible, sir, but doubtful. We control the sequence of events," Evans added.

"You're sure of yourself. Did you consider, Mr. Evans, that the Russian and Chinese presidents might decide to take matters into their own hands?"

"Again, Mr. President, we dictate the actions. Our people are in place," chirped Ramsey.

"We must put our forces on high alert. I suggest we move to DEFCON One," the head of the senate intelligence committee interjected.

"A nuclear attack warning? I will not allow that. DEFCON three, no higher. We need to keep everyone calm. I'll play the diplomat between the two countries. In the meantime, inform the media that we have evidence the attacks are from rogue insurgents. Maybe we can restrain the Russian and Chinese leaders."

"As I stated, Mr. President, we control the events."

"Then what the hell happened at the Vatican, Ramsey?"

"We don't know, sir. The plan was to destroy the archives. We had no knowledge the Iranians bombed the Papal Palace. Believe me, we have dealt with those insolent bastards; they paid the price for their stupidity—which, by the way, ended up working to our benefit. The world is teetering and outraged. We established the money trail showing how China funded the Iranian militants." Ramsey smiled.

"Anything else?" the president asked.

"Our European counterparts have completed their tasks. We can speed up the timeframe if our plan unravels. I will disseminate more information to each of you as events unfold. Our goal of a singular global government has arrived. World peace is around the corner," Evans said.

"Glad to hear." President Thomas Maro tried to keep the disdain toward Ramsey's assistant out of his voice. He placed his palms on the conference table for leverage and stood. "Gentlemen, I have a country to run. Enjoy your day."

The four men gathered their papers to leave the room, acknowledging the commander in chief as they exited.

"Thank you, Mr. President."

"Mr. President."

"See you soon, Mr. President."

"Al, you and I need to have a conversation later."

"Yes, Mr. President," the speaker of the house replied.

After the men left, the president brought his attention to the speakerphone. "No turning back now…"

"What is happening, Tom?"

"I wish I knew. Whatever it is, I doubt we'll be able to stop it."

"Any idea what the plan is?"

"No, but I can assure you, Andrew, it's not good."

"We're taking a risk if we can't prevent it. Are you going to bring Giacomo into the loop?"

"Yes—in a couple of days, when he's released from the hospital. I'm glad you weren't hurt."

"Me too," Pope Andrew replied.

Chapter 80

Giacomo awoke with a pounding headache. An IV bag attached to his left arm dripped medication and nutrients into his veins. He lay despondent, his mind swirling with questions. *I died, and they brought me back to this shit. It wasn't a dream. I held Emily in my arms. My boys, where are they? Emily said, 'Find them.' Where are my children? They're dead, and I wish I were, too. Life makes no sense. How did I get here?* Yet somehow a sense of hope filled his heart. Maybe his children were alive? His memory was vague...*an explosion...the building shook...Frank was there.*

"Hey, stranger."

The voice was familiar. Giacomo opened his eyes. "Rio." He smiled.

She walked over to his bedside and sat in the adjacent chair. "How're you feeling?"

"Like crap. I take it I am back in Connecticut."

"And what gave you that idea, my brother?"

"Ah, my witty sister. How are you doing?"

"I wish the doctor would let me go home, but to answer your question—much better. An occasional outburst, but otherwise, I'm good. Dr. Leavitt said it's normal. The last test showed my DNA is repairing. I'm on a mood stabilizer to help with my temperament swings."

"Great. The doctor said your recovery could take a while but eventually you'd be your old self."

"Yes, the wonders of modern science."

Giacomo grinned. His eyes lowered. "How long have I been here?"

"Just a couple of days."

"Seems longer."

"At least you weren't in a coma, like me. My life disappeared."

"Sorry, Rio."

"It's fine. I'm better now. Time to move forward. I hear you're a big deal…Chairman of the Joint Chiefs?"

"Yeah…" Giacomo's head tilted as he stared into the distance.

"What's the matter?"

"What was Frank doing in my hotel room? Emily, the boys…" His thoughts scattered as he spoke. "The explosion. What blew up? How did I get here?"

"They didn't tell me."

"Well, what happened in Rome?"

"A terrorist group attacked the Vatican."

Giacomo's eyes went wide, afraid to ask. He saw Rio bow her head.

"Andrew's dead?"

"Unknown, he's missing."

Giacomo's heart monitor beeped faster as his blood pressure rose. He threw the sheets off himself as the door opened.

"And where do you think you're going?" a familiar voice asked.

Giacomo struggled to move as he crashed backward onto his pillow. Colonel Jason Vandercliff stood at the base of his bed.

"Jason, glad you're here. Help me. It's time for me to leave. We have to find Andrew."

"Relax. We got word today that the Pope is safe."

Chapter 81

Giacomo laid back on the bed, relieved to hear that his friend Andrew was safe. Jason positioned his chair out of the way as a nurse removed the IV from Giacomo's arm. Rio stood by the window.

"Are you alright, little sister?"

"Yeah, New Haven is beautiful in the snow. I can see our building."

"Did the doctor give you a discharge date?"

"Maybe next week."

"Glorious news," Jason chimed in.

"Sure is, Jason."

Giacomo spotted the brightness in Rio's eyes as she smiled. Happy she was on her way to a full recovery, his thoughts returned to his own near-death experience. Emily's voice still resonated in his mind: *Find our boys.* Hope surged within his being until the reality of despair struck him—*My family is dead.*

"What else have I missed, Jason?"

"Tragic news from Italy. Secretary of State Rift's husband is dead. Funeral services were today."

"What happened?"

"My understanding is a car hit him at the Rome airport terminal."

"Poor Lisa. My heart aches for her. The world is crumbling around us," Rio said.

"Their marriage was turbulent, from what I understand. I'm sure she is conflicted, bittersweet," Giacomo said. He'd disliked the man from the first time they met. Giacomo never understood why his senses guided him to despise Lisa's husband. *Could it be I am still attracted to her?* He shook the thought from his mind and addressed Jason, "Why was my friend Frank in Rome?"

"No idea. Military command told me he rescued you?"

"Yeah, I was on the phone when the explosion occurred. Next thing I remember is Frank staring at me… What the hell is happening? I need answers."

"I'm sure you do, Giacomo. But it's gonna have to wait. The battle lines are being drawn between China and Russia. And you, my friend, will be in the center of this mess."

"What do you mean?"

"According to the Pentagon, we are preparing for war. DEFCON 1 is being discussed."

"Holy crap, a nuclear attack," Rio said.

"The warning is imminent, Rio," Giacomo replied. His eyes went blank. A vision grew in his mind, one he had seen before. *The lights of the nations diminished in the darkness. One by one, the countries of Europe cascaded into obscurity.*

"Giacomo?"

"I'm fine, Jason," he shook off the prediction. "Looks like we have our work cut out for us."

"Yes, sir."

"Rio, are you going to be alright?"

"Of course, my brother. I am on the way to becoming my old self."

"Oh, boy. Watch out, world." Giacomo's smile transformed to a grimace as he shifted in the bed. The morbid dread of a nuclear war obliterating humanity lingered in his subconscious. Was this the last time he'd see Rio?

Chapter 82

The newscasters stared into their cameras as the TV screen split. Another reporter joined the group, making her way to the front of a police barricade outside Saint Peter's Square in Rome.

"World leaders continue to wait as the Italian military sifts through the rubble in search of survivors. In what we could describe as miraculous, the thousands of Catholic pilgrims who gathered to see Pope Andrew were unharmed, somehow shielded from the flying debris. The terrorists destroyed portions of the Papal Palace and the Vatican Secret Archives." The reporter turned and pointed, "As you can see, workers are fixing the gaping hole in the dome side of Saint Peter's Basilica. We expect Pope Andrew, who escaped from the wreckage, to give his first blessing this afternoon."

The television screen went blank. Three clanging horns sounded over the TV speakers. "This is an emergency bulletin; this is an emergency bulletin." The monitor awoke from the blackness as a dazed prime-time reporter blinked at a rapid pace. She waited for her cue to begin the broadcast. A map of the continents beamed behind her as she fidgeted.

She had a nervous cough as her voice wavered for a moment. "We have been notified by the Department of Defense that the United States has moved from DEFCON 3 to DEFCON 2. Governments around the globe have halted all air traffic. China and Russia continue their war of words, vowing military retaliation against each other. US Secretary of State Lisa Rift has contacted their presidents in hope of finding a resolution to diminish the escalating confrontation."

The reporter placed the paper on her desk. Her eyes welled as she tried to compose herself. "We are on the threshold of a catastrophic nuclear war between two superpowers. Military commanders are projecting a tragic loss of life that will reach historic numbers. Our world waits in silence and prayer, hoping our diplomats will achieve a peaceful solution. President Thomas Maro will speak to the nation later this evening."

In the upper corner of the television screen, street scenes of chaos were broadcast. As the news of the potential nuclear conflict spread, the population of the world shifted into desperation. No nation, town, city, or village went unscathed. Food supplies became nonexistent. In the poorest of towns, clashes arose, for this affected them the most as the wealthy hoarded their resources. Within a short period, the conflict between the rich and the poor escalated to bloodshed.

Secretary of State Lisa Rift placed the remote on the coffee table. She had buried her husband the day before. Sad, but not distraught, she knew in the end her husband got what he deserved. The arguing and mutual dislike had reached its tipping point over a year ago, although their marriage had ended long before. The arrogant scientist was married to his business, not to Lisa. *A shame we couldn't put our issues aside.*

"Madame Secretary, we need to get you to the White House," her secret service agent said.

"Yes, I know, thank you."

She looked around her living room. Life moves forward. With the planet on the precipice of nuclear war, she wondered if, by next month, she'd even have a home and bed where she could rest her weary bones.

Chapter 83

Giacomo entered his bedroom to pack a suitcase, for the DC members of the legislative branch they spent their days and evenings planning a doomsday scenario to ensure the continuity of the United States without regard for the safety of the American people. A deep uncertainty wavered in the hearts of its citizens, who believed their way of life was ending. An eerie, unsettling sense beckoned him. *Was Emily's spirit lingering in the house?* Within his conscience, he heard his two boys crying in their cribs, looking for nourishment from their mother. His eyes welled at the notion. *Where are my sons?*

Giacomo plopped himself down in one of the blue upholstered chairs and cradled his face in his hands. His body still ached from the bomb blast; he rubbed his left thigh. Disillusioned that he failed to find Adinolfi, now—with the world teetering on destruction—his hope was that his nemesis would endure a horrific death. There was a country and a world that needed to be saved. Giacomo had to return to the epicenter of trying to prevent World War III. He had to put his vengeful feelings aside. The people of Earth were more important than him. His doorbell sounded. *Who could that be? Secret service surrounded the house, and they—*

The bedroom intercom chimed.

"CIA Agent Costatino is here."

"I'll be right there."

Giacomo observed Maryann and his second-in-command, Jason, from the upper landing as they stood in quiet conversation. He descended the fourteen dark-blue carpeted steps.

"You two know each other?"

"We met during an intelligence briefing about a month ago," she said.

"Hmm, and what brings you here today?"

"I was checking to see how you're feeling."

Giacomo looked at her in confusion.

"You don't remember, do you?"

"I guess not."

"We were talking on the phone when the explosion occurred."

"Oh, yeah. Tell me, Ms. CIA, why was my friend Frank there?"

"Simple. We figured we could trust a colleague of yours, so we recruited him to keep watch on Adinolfi *and* on you."

"Interesting. And what information are you keeping from me now?" Giacomo observed Maryann's physical response. The question caught her off guard. His military voice resounded in the confines of the foyer. "We'll visit this at another time. We have bigger problems on our plates. I'll let it go for now. But believe me, Ms. Costatino, we will continue the conversation. Jason, we need to get going."

"It's not what you think. I bring news."

"I'm listening."

"Adinolfi is dead."

Giacomo registered the words. It surprised him that he didn't feel more elated. The emptiness and dread continued to eat at his heart. "Well, I guess that's good," he responded.

A secret service agent opened the front door. "Sir, we need to leave now."

"I'll be right there."

Maryann grabbed Giacomo's sleeve. "I have something else to tell you." She held her phone.

"I don't need to see a picture of Adinolfi dead..."

"No, no. Look." She handed him the phone.

Giacomo stared at the screen. His eyes darted to the photo, then to Jason, to Maryann, unable to comprehend what he was seeing. "Warren, what is he doing? What is he holding?" A tear streaked down to his chin, he knew, but he couldn't say it as shock overwhelmed him.

"Sir, I'm sorry but we can't wait any longer. We have to depart," the secret service agent interjected.

"Stand down," Jason barked.

Giacomo's eyes brightened as he smiled through his tears. "My sons? Are those my sons?"

"Yes, Giacomo, they are," Maryann chimed.

Giacomo felt Jason's hand on his shoulder. "My sons...Jason, how? Where are they? I want to see them now. They are alive, oh my God. How?"

"We don't know the details yet."

"Maryann, you are sure they're *my* sons?"

"Yes, we tested the boys' DNA."

"Please, sir, we have to go."

Giacomo watched Jason stare down the agent as he said, "I will be with you in a moment. Go wait in the car or this will be your last day. Do I make myself clear?"

"Yes, sir."

Jason opened the door for the agent. "Sorry, Giacomo."

"It's okay. He's doing his job. Jason, where are my sons now?"

"In Perugia, with Frank and Warren, under the protection of the BOET."

"My sons are alive. When all seems lost, a ray of hope..." He raised his head to the ceiling. "How can I get to them? I need to have my sons with me. I'll send an airplane." He reached for his phone. Giacomo raised his eyes and watched Maryann and Jason exchange glances. "I'm afraid..."

"It's okay, Maryann. I understand military protocols are in place and they shut down international airspace."

"Yes, the plan is for Paolo and Arnaud to be in your arms by next week at the latest."

Giacomo hid his consternation. Happy that his sons were alive, disappointed they were not with him. He asked, "Who was responsible for finding my children?"

"Maryann," Jason said.

"I was just doing my job."

Giacomo, overwhelmed with emotion, embraced Maryann's face with his hands. He held her eyes in a deep, penetrating gaze as he kissed her on the lips. *Why did I do that?* "I'm sorry. I didn't mean to…"

Maryann blushed, "No worries."

Giacomo noticed the twinkle in her eyes.

*   *   *

"Yes, it's true, Rio. I don't know how, and I don't care. My sons—your *nephews*—are alive. Listen, I just arrived at my hotel and I have to make a couple of phone calls," he lied. Giacomo needed time alone to process the news. "I'll call you later. Love you, too." Giacomo rode the elevator to the fifth floor. He entered his suite, leaving behind two BOET soldiers, who guarded the door. Elated and filled with hope, he poured himself a Scotch and sat on the couch.

"Em, our boys are alive… How I wish you were here." He took a sip from the glass and placed the alcohol on the coffee table. As he reminisced about the day, a bitter-sweetness tugged at his heart. He opened his cell phone to photos and stared at his boys. By tapping on the image, the picture became his wallpaper.

"I'd give anything for you to be here, Em."

The relentless grief for his wife overcame Giacomo's happiness that his sons were alive. Tomorrow he would begin his five-day indoctrination at the Pentagon—days and nights filled with policy and procedures. A saving grace for his troubled mind.

Chapter 84

"Giacomo, it's good to see you're up and about. And the news about your sons… I'm so happy for you."

"Thank you, Tom. Maryann briefed me on your involvement. I can't tell you how appreciative I am."

"You're welcome, my friend. They will soon be in your arms. I'm making sure of that. You've been through enough."

"Thank you again, Tom. The boys are my one shining ray of hope. Knowing they're alive helps ease the sadness of losing Emily."

"Please, sit." Tom offered him a chair in the presidential workplace.

"I like how you decorated your office." Giacomo changed the subject before the conflict of hope and despair consumed his thoughts. *The world was on the verge of a nuclear war. A ravaged landscape was not the place to raise his sons.*

"Thank you."

Giacomo studied the pictures on the president's credenza. A framed photo caught his eye. "I've seen this picture before," he blurted.

"Which one?"

"The photograph with the little boy."

"Yes, me and my dad. That was a year before he died; I was five. I am sure you saw it at my house in Baltimore."

"Maybe?" Giacomo tried to place where he'd observed the snapshot. His father's writings echoed in his thoughts: *A picture is worth a thousand words.* "I'm sorry, Tom. Life without your dad must have been difficult."

"Yes, I remember little, but mom always told me he treated her well. He was twenty years older than my mother. It's my understanding that I have an elder stepbrother."

"I guess you've never met him?"

He noticed Tom reflect on a memory.

"No, someday. Giacomo, right now we have serious issues we must confront."

The intercom chimed and a soft-speaking voice said, "Mr. President, Secretary Rift is here."

Tom pushed a button on his phone. "Send her in, please."

Lisa strode into the office, dressed in black. Both men rose to meet her. Giacomo approached and embraced her. "I'm so sorry to hear about Jackson. Anything I can do?"

"No, thank you. Rio called me earlier. She appears to be better, and the news about your sons... I'm thrilled for you."

"Thanks."

"My condolences, Lisa." Tom hugged her.

"Thank you, Tom."

"So, what happened?" Giacomo asked.

Tom and Lisa exchanged glances, which didn't go unnoticed by Giacomo.

"You two can discuss the details later. We don't have a lot of time to talk; I have the congressional leadership arriving within the hour." Tom motioned to them to sit.

Giacomo sat opposite Lisa on a matching tan suede couch. Tom walked to his desk and withdrew two folders from a drawer. He placed the documents on the coffee table. Giacomo leaned forward and reached for the manila files, handing one to Lisa. The president folded his arms and rested against the front of his credenza.

"As you both are aware, China and Russia are at odds, and within weeks, if not days, we expect World War III to erupt. Enclosed are two reports, and the NSA document will bring you up to speed with the latest intel. Please read the Vatican dossier first, though, as that file is of utmost importance."

Giacomo withdrew the report from among the papers, as did Lisa. He read aloud: "Since the failed coup on the United States and the assassination attempt on their President, we have exposed a complex plot with origins as far back as five hundred years. Begun as a spiritual organization named FHS or Followers of the Holy Spirit, this society built an empire of property holdings and corporate entities throughout the world. Today they control ninety percent of the world's Fortune 500 companies, as well as numerous governments and the President of the European Union. They composed their ranks of politicians, professors, religious zealots, military commanders, diplomatic overseers, and elite corporate leadership."

Lisa and Giacomo exchanged looks of astonishment.

"Is this for real?" Lisa blurted out.

"This reads like a novel, Tom. This can't be true, and if it is…I don't know what to say."

"Giacomo, read on," Tom said.

"It came to our attention that an internal strife occurred with its titular head, Father Alphonso Adinolfi. He disagreed with his secular counterparts over how to establish a singular global government. He also had a predilection for a so-called prophetic message. Coupled with his obsessive research of the human genome, his ideas became distorted—bordering on obsession. Our operatives discovered the man was schizophrenic. They found him dead in a church in Orvieto, Italy. Two American Marines hired to execute the priest died in the gun battle with the Italian military."

Giacomo stopped and said, "*Our* military? What the hell?"

"We're investigating. We received the information this morning."

"Do we know who killed the assassins?"

"Yes, the Italians. We had operatives following Adinolfi, who found themselves in the fray. I am happy to report they were unharmed."

"Humph." Wearied by the narrative, Giacomo took his finger and scanned the remaining portion of the dossier. He stopped at the last two sentences: *"It is our belief that members of this group have infiltrated every major government. This includes the United States."* He paused and watched Tom walk behind his desk and open a brown leather briefcase. He removed a blue three-ring binder and clutched it to his chest. Giacomo noticed the apprehension in Tom's eyes as he drew the notebook closer to his body.

"What is it, Tom?"

"This document contains the most disturbing chronicle of events I have ever read. We have not shared this with anyone.

"Pope Andrew, using his mobile phone, snapped pictures of a ledger he found in the secret archives. I received them moments before the explosion struck and the library was destroyed, as well as portions of Saint Peter's, and the residence at the Vatican. We believe the attack was both an effort to silence Andrew, because he discovered the ledger, and to destroy any other FHS evidence. Thank God he had no phone coverage in his papal apartment, or else he'd be dead. I'm sickened at the thought of Andrew losing his life at the hands of terrorists. Our world is imploding. Thanks to the Almighty, he suffered only minor injuries from a tree branch that fell while he was searching for a signal in the gardens. I have to be honest, though—His Holiness and I are hesitant to give this to you."

"Why?" Giacomo probed.

"Because the implication is dire, and our decision is grave."

Giacomo glanced toward Lisa. Their eyes locked. "Nuclear war, Tom?"

"Worse, total global anarchy. Laying in abeyance is a universal revolution which will destroy the nations' governments. In this notebook is a history of wars funded and manipulated by the FHS. The first entry that influenced our country was January 7, 1776."

"The Revolutionary War?"

"Yes, Lisa. They financed our independence, but at a cost to our so-called democracy."

"What do you mean?"

"They staffed our government with members of their organization so they could carry out their agenda."

"I thought that was the Freemasons," Giacomo queried.

"You're correct."

"They were a cell within the FHS?"

"Yes, the FHS controlled the Illuminati, the Order of Skull and Bones, Knights of the Golden Circle, the Black Hand, Knights Templar, and the Bilderberg Group…to name a few. Their initial intention was a global rule under a unified church. Over time, the organization became a secular consortium of individuals who believe that a single true world government will bring peace."

Giacomo was overtaken by a familiar vision.

Three men, their faces clouded by a haze. Two wore white robes—one with a frayed, discolored red hem and the other with a black collar—each held an earth in the palm of his hand. The third was dressed in sackcloth, his hands empty.

He strained to see who they were.

The man in the tattered robe squeezed the planet. As his grip strengthened, his fingers morphed into vices. The screams of humanity erupted. In slow motion, the malformed sphere dripped blood, and its life force splattered on the floor. The one in sackcloth appeared with a mop and cleaned the stained ground.

Giacomo's inner gaze turned to the person with the black collar and the planet he held. As the vision converted into a three-dimensional scene, he *saw above him the stars and the planet's place within the universe. Lights of the nations of the earth sparkled, then one country after another grew dark. The man in sackcloth took the sphere. He struggled to embrace it. He writhed from the heaviness of the new earth, falling to his knees, careful not to let it drop.*

The cities illuminated with a flicker. The creature in the frayed robes glowered with a fierce, seething rage. In his wrath, he snatched the orb and scowled at its inhabitants, causing chaos among the people.

The man wearing the black collar, his eyes full of fury, struck the aggressor. His physical appearance transformed, towering over the other two men. He reached down, picked up the assailant by his neck, and threw him into a dark chasm. The man's excruciating groans traveled throughout creation. With his might, he closed the abyss and shrank to his original size. His robe became a dazzling white. He grabbed the chaotic earth from the individual dressed in sackcloth, who protected the planet with his life.

Once more, Giacomo heard his name. Dad? Three people stood before him, their faces unrecognizable. A sense of fear, rage, then peace filled him, as a new image formed. *A distant tree overshadowing a meadow of bright green grass. Its leaves changed color to the orange and red hues of fall. An adolescent boy sat nestled between the overgrown roots, which stretched to the horizon, his knees pulled to his chest. He gazed out over the pasture. His twin approached him and whispered in his ear as he pointed to their father.*

They climbed the oak and perched themselves on one of the thick, sturdy branches as they waved. Giacomo returned the gesture and moved toward them. The wind howled as the bottom of his coat fluttered. The unknown people reappeared, posing a threat to his offspring. He tried to run forward, stuck in place by the arduous gale. Their faces remained unrecognizable. The two boys vanished. An entity called out for him, and he turned. Dad? In the field was a hospital bed. He thought he recognized the patient. Was it him? He heard his father's voice. 'We can never change our fate.'

In an instant, Giacomo made sense of the vision. The man in the tattered robe symbolized the FHS, the black collar represented the global government, and the remaining person stood for the citizens of the planet.

What did it mean? Why are my boys there? Who was in the hospital bed? Why my father's voice?

"Giacomo, are you with us?"

"Sorry, Tom." He shook his head. "Just a thought."

"Care to share?"

"Not yet."

Tom took the notebook and placed the repugnant document on the coffee table. He sat next to Lisa.

"Giacomo, come here. We will review this together."

The general did as he was told. The three lined the couch as Maro flipped the pages, allowing them to read the sinister timeline. Fifteen minutes later, an astonished Giacomo stood, as did the secretary of state. Giacomo sauntered to the windows behind the president's desk. Introspective, he rubbed his face as he watched Lisa pour a glass of water from a silver pitcher.

"Want some?" she inquired.

"After what I saw, I need a shot of tequila."

"Is it true? The assassination of Lincoln, Kennedy, Sadat, the wars, the conflicts…" she asked.

"As far as we can tell, yes."

"Who's we?" Giacomo's stare penetrated the president. An apprehensive sensation surged through him when he avoided eye contact.

"We're in big trouble, folks. In a matter of weeks, if not days, a nuclear conflict will erupt between China and Russia. To my regret, they will pull the United States into the fray."

Giacomo observed the president's movements as he continued to avoid Giacomo's gaze.

"I'm afraid tough choices await us. We need to prevent the catalyst to World War III from happening."

"What the hell are you talking about, Tom?"

"Giacomo, your tone," Lisa warned.

"No issues here, Lisa. I need you both to speak your minds. No titles or ranks, either. Giacomo, *I* am a member of the FHS."

Chapter 85

D r. Leavitt stood by the privacy blind draped around Rio's bed. "Do you need help?"

"No, thank you."

The curtain slid open. Rio was dressed in jeans, a brown sweater, and a pair of sky-blue walking shoes. She smiled at the physician.

"Are you ready to go home?"

"I can't wait, Paige. A new day, a new life." Rio grabbed her phone from her purse and tapped the screen. "My nephews, Paolo and Arnaud."

"They are adorable. Who's holding them?"

"A family friend."

"I understand your brother's wife died."

"Murdered is a better word…anyway, a new beginning. I can't believe how much weight I lost."

"A couple of days of pasta, and you'll be fine."

"Sounds good to me. A week of dinners at *Nataz* and I'll be good. Have you ever been?"

"Yes, excellent food."

"I cannot thank you enough for what you've done for me…" Rio stared past the doctor, trying to forget the memories of when she would awake from the induced coma, watching Adinolfi inject her with engineered DNA.

"In time, the ruminations should fade."

"How did you know?"

"The reflection in your eyes."

"What are your plans now that Jackson Rift is dead?"

"Yale offered me a position. I'm confident I'll accept the offer. I have no desire, Rio, to return to the private sector. My passion is research, and that institution will provide me with a better environment."

"Very exciting. If you ever require financial backing, please call me. I'd be more than happy to write you a check."

"Thank you, Rio."

A volunteer pushing a wheelchair arrived at the door. "Miss DeLaurentis?"

"I don't need that. I can walk."

"It's hospital protocol, ma'am."

She rolled her eyes at Paige. "Thanks again, Doctor."

*　*　*

The hospital's elevator doors swept open. With Adinolfi dead, there no longer seemed to be a valid threat to Rio's life. Giacomo had arranged for his father's longtime friend Tony to bring her home. Rio smiled when she saw him. She stood, pushed the wheelchair behind her, and walked to him. He kissed her forehead, and they embraced. Rio's head rested on his shoulders as tears streamed from her eyes.

"You look great, my dear," Tony said, as he held back his sniffles.

She patted him on the lapel of his jacket. "So do you. I see your book made it to the number one spot on *The New York Times* bestseller list."

"Yes, it did, thank you. My publisher was thrilled. You remember Danny, my pilot?"

"Yes, of course. How are you? Thank you so much for saving my life. I can't believe we all survived that crash. I understand it was you who carried me out of the aircraft." She hugged him and kissed him on the cheek, then shuddered as she recalled the harrowing experience of ditching in the bay of Naples after Tony's airplane was struck by a terrorist missle.

"Are you blushing?"

Danny gave the author a quick glance and said, "Let's go. The car is out front."

A light snow fluttered from the sky. Rio was quiet as she peered through the window of the royal-blue Range Rover. The familiar sights of downtown New Haven and Yale University filled her with an inner peace.

"When do you think you'll head back to work?" Tony asked, as they drove past her office, the Gold Building.

Rio was an attorney who fought for the downtrodden, and was a major benefactor to the poor and homeless. Accused of subverting the United States government, she was summoned to appear before a congressional hearing. Not one to mince words, she called the panel moronic a-holes, which she followed with: *I'm sitting in front of a pack of baboons whose only interest is their own agenda, not the American people. If I were you, I'd resign before it's too late. Yes, I want a revolution, but my revolution will abide by the Constitution. We'll vote you jackasses out of office.* Rio then stood to the rousing applause of the gallery and walked out of the hearing.

She gave Tony's question some thought. "In a week or two. My desire to right the wrongs has subsided. My concern after watching the news is that life as we know it will become precarious should the Russian-Chinese conflict escalate. There's more important work to accomplish. Maybe I'll just call it quits and take care of Giacomo's boys."

"That's a good idea. Let's hope our president can prevent the rising conflict, Rio."

"I hope so, Tony."

They rode in silence the rest of the way. The snow-covered sidewalks and streets provided comfort to Rio. She perked up when she saw Whitney Lake—they were within walking distance of her home.

Danny turned the vehicle into the compound. The car stopped at the guardhouse as security cameras scanned the license plate and the passengers' faces. In less than a minute, the black wrought-iron gates swung open.

The history of the property dated to the mid-1800s. A local industrialist named James Brewster purchased the land. Surrounded by a ten-foot-tall, three-foot-wide stone wall fortification, the twenty-two-acre estate was dotted with rolling hills and enjoyed an artificial pond and a thirty-room mansion. Servants' quarters flanked the two entrances. Brewster decreed that, after his death, the manor be demolished and the parcel of land bequeathed to the City of New Haven.

"I'll never forget the day your dad gave Steve and me the check to buy this property to develop. All he wanted in exchange was the home you are living in. He allowed us to keep all the profits from the sale of the subdivided estate."

"Such a long time ago, Tony."

"Sure was. I still shake my head at the thought he trusted us with $8 million. Your father was an unbelievable man. I loved him, you know."

"Yes, I do. He loved you guys too, like brothers. Did he ever say why he didn't purchase the property himself?"

"He disliked the limelight. Paolo often told me, 'I want to stay under the radar.'"

"Excellent advice. I should have heeded his guidance."

The 1850s-style streetlights flickered on as darkness approached. Danny navigated the vehicle past the pergola. A couple warmed themselves by the firepit as they watched their children play in the snow. Tony and Steve subdivided Brewster Park into twenty-one lots comprising individual townhouses, with an exclusive condominium complex in the northeastern section of the estate. The compound contained fifty-two private residences.

"Rio, are you going to be alright by yourself?"

"I'll be fine, Tony. I'm looking forward to being alone."

"We had your home cleaned up and painted. Everything should be intact."

"Thank you. Giacomo told me it was a real mess."

"Sure was. We updated the security at the house, too. Even if there's a power failure, the system will continue to function."

"If you say so."

Danny turned left into the driveway.

Chapter 86

The Oval Office

Tom Maro's words—*I am a member of the FHS*—horrified Giacomo. They circulated in his mind. *How could this be?* The news that the FHS had manipulated the governments of the world was devastating, as the extent of the monstrous treachery reared its horrid head. He eyeballed Lisa, her face shocked with surprise. An emptiness filled his stomach, a hurt in his being so deep he grew numb. How much more could he withstand? *Was it a betrayal? Did Tom play a part in Emily's death? No, there must be more to this.*

Not realizing where he was, Giacomo sat in the president's chair and rested his elbows on the Resolute Desk, a gift from Queen Victoria to then-President Rutherford Hayes in 1880. Tom continued to sit with his arms crossed. Giacomo fixed his concerned stare on the defensive posture of his friend. *Was Tom a friend or foe?* "I am at a loss for words."

"It's not what you suppose."

"Care to explain?" Giacomo's right eye twitched as his focus became more intense.

"I knew nothing about Adinolfi. They kept me at a distance."

"That's one hell of a distance, Tom. How many times have I heard that line of crap? And *you*, Lisa?"

"I'm shocked. They have manipulated us for hundreds of years—all the death, hunger…for what? We're not a democracy…I don't know what to say."

Giacomo watched Lisa walk across the room. She stopped and positioned herself by the desk, her arms folded. Giacomo reached forward and grabbed the president's fountain pen and irritably twirled the black instrument between his fingers. The Oval Office was silent, save for the breath and heartbeats of its occupants. *What is transpiring?* He inhaled deeply, then sighed. "Tom, if you had no association with Adinolfi..." He paused and scribbled on the president's stationery, then continued. "And, for some unknown reason, I'm inclined to believe you. After all, our goal is the same..."

"Yes, send these bastards to hell," Lisa interjected. Giacomo said nothing. He stood, walked to the opposite sofa where Tom was, and sat. He motioned for Lisa to join him.

"It is clear Tom struggled to share the horrific history of the FHS. He acknowledged they manipulated world societies, thus putting himself, his life, in peril. Which brings me to the question: Why, Tom, are you telling us this? Well?"

"Until I received those pictures from Andrew, I had no clue about the society's insidiousness. In fact, I was surprised as hell to learn Adinolfi and I belonged to the same organization. The acronym means..."

"Followers of the Holy Spirit," Giacomo finished.

"Yes, and no. According to the ledger, the Order founded in 1510 laid out a future for a one-church global rule. Over the centuries, the association converted to a more secular form of business operation. From what I read..."

Tom took the binder and searched for the page. Giacomo watched with a suspicious eye as Tom positioned the document for them to examine.

"After World War II, the FHS became Fidelis Hereditas Sapien, meaning *the faithful inherit wisdom.*"

"Which *really* means what?" Giacomo moved his head from one side to the other. The stress was tugging on his shoulder muscles, the start of a nagging headache.

"By being faithful to the order, you'll inherit its wisdom."

Giacomo rubbed his forehead and his eyes. "Yeah, that and ten dollars will buy me an espresso."

He saw Lisa give him a stern look. Giacomo's smoldering fury ignited into a slow burn. He tried to stay calm. The memory of his Emily as she died in his arms flashed through his mind. He felt Lisa touch his leg.

"Please, Tom. Tell me you weren't involved with my wife's death."

"Giacomo, I had no part in the killing of Emily." Tom's eyes welled with tears. "You must believe me that I am disgusted by what we've discovered. So much so that I am ready to resign from office. Our democracy is a farce. They have manipulated the American people since before the Revolution."

"Quit, Mr. President?" Lisa asked.

"Yes."

"How long have you been a member?"

"Since my nomination. During the campaign, I had an unexpected call from former President Arthur Waldron." Maro bowed his head. "May he rest in peace. As you know, he was my opponent at the time. We became close, as you're aware."

* * *

White House Residence, Seven Months Earlier, Three Days after Democratic National Convention

"Tom, so great to meet you," Arthur Waldron held out his hand.

"Mr. President, I'm honored."

Behind Waldron stood his Vice President, Jerry Richardson. "Mr. Vice President, I didn't know you would be joining us?"

"Not today, I'm here on other business. Mr. President, I'll be in my office if you need me."

"Thank you, Jerry."

"Please, we are on a first-name basis here. No need for titles."

"I have to say, Arthur, this is quite unusual for opposing candidates to meet, let alone in secret."

"Yes, it is. Our conversation is important for our democratic system, or what we refer to as democracy."

"I don't understand."

"Have you heard of the conglomerate FHS?"

"No."

"We are an organization that adheres to the autonomous principles of freedom. We date back to the Revolutionary War. Most of our country's presidents have been members of this group."

"How did the others get elected?"

"It was an aberration. The issue…they tried to move our country in a different direction. It's because of the actions of these outsiders that I attained the Oval Office."

"The overturning of the Electoral College?" Tom reasoned.

"Yes. Our democracy is at risk, Tom. I'll be frank, I don't want to do this job unless I have to do it."

"Why did you run for a second term, then?"

"Because I was told to."

"By whom?"

Waldron reached for a sheet of paper on the coffee table. "Here," he handed the letter to Tom.

> *Gentlemen—my name is Paolo DeLaurentis. Arthur, what you don't know is, the fraternal organization you belong to is determined to destroy the fabric of democracy. The inner workings of this collection of governments, societies, and religions have manipulated the global population. They brought about a division among and within the nations.*
>
> *It is imperative that you run for reelection and invite Tom Maro into the association. Together, you can defeat this evil. I don't know which of you will win. What I have seen is this: the*

world's landscape changing from green to charred black. These manufactured, cataclysmic events shall occur over the next four years, regardless of who holds the office. One of you can bring peace to this escalating conflict, created by a globe intent on war. Gentlemen, it is imperative you understand the FHS will attempt to sway you to an outcome that you must stop.

Remember, as the tongue of the serpent is forked, so is theirs. When the crucial moment arrives, and the citizens have given up hope, then we'll discover the solution. It won't be a straightforward decision. Caution: a singular global rule will fail because of the corrupt nature of man. Use the wisdom of the society to ensure its downfall. Do not share this letter or inform my son, Giacomo, until you witness the proof that the fraternity has split in two.

Paolo DeLaurentis, Sept 2003

"Do you believe this? He sounds like a conspiracy nut," said Tom.

"Look at the date he wrote the note. Question is, how could he know we were running for president? To be honest, I'm gonna listen."

"Could the letter be a ploy?"

"Excellent point. Do you recognize the name, Tom?"

"Yeah, I think he has a daughter, Rio, an attorney who advocates for the poor, and a son, Colonel Giacomo DeLaurentis."

"Yes, I remember him. I attended a conference at the United Nations where Paolo spoke. I have to tell you—his words touched the core of my soul. It is a damn shame no one listened, myself included. I was too arrogant. It won't hurt to heed his advice…what happens if he's right?"

"So, I guess it's better to believe than ignore?"

"Yes, Tom."

"What's the organization?"

"Fidelis Hereditas Sapien—the Faithful Inherit Wisdom. They are a powerful group who discuss solutions to the problems of the world."

"Doesn't sound too ominous?"

"Don't let the words deceive you. I am the president because their influence overturned the Electoral College. They realized it's better for the country than assassination. They're powerful, and we must work together to change this. To be honest, I don't believe we can. If what Paolo says here is correct, maybe there's hope."

Tom pondered the information. *If this is true...* He responded, "I'm in."

*   *   *

Giacomo turned toward Lisa. Her eyes were wide with bewilderment. He placed his hands around his face and rubbed his chin.

"Do you have the letter my father wrote?"

"I do," the president reached into his inside jacket pocket and pulled out the note. He handed it to Giacomo.

"Do you mind, Giacomo?" Lisa said, as she grabbed the piece of paper.

"What do you think?"

"Looks like your dad's writing. Here."

Giacomo took the message, read his father's words, then returned the letter to Tom.

"Yep, that's his signature. Has anyone approached you?"

"Yes, Speaker of the House Ramsey."

"Damn," Giacomo rolled his eyes. "Next you're going to tell me the pope is involved."

Tom hesitated and cleared his throat. "I'm afraid he is."

Chapter 87

Brewster Estate, Later that Afternoon

Rio wandered the townhouse after a long, hot shower. The smell of paint, a fresh beginning in life, filled the air. She removed the outdated calendar hanging on her kitchen wall as she traversed her way to her sanctuary—her library office. She drew in a deep breath, happy to be in a safe, secured environment, a home free from threat and harm.

Pictures stacked on her desk showed Mom, Dad, Giacomo, and Emily. She picked up each one, dusted them off, and placed them where they used to be. Her father's antique clock sat between her memo pad and Montblanc pen set. Books lined the shelves. A smile came to her face. She stood against the window with her cell phone camera and took a snapshot, then texted the image to her sibling. *Thank you, big brother. Everything is perfect!*

As she sorted her mail, she found an envelope with familiar writing.

"Oh, Dad, how I miss you." She turned it over. Across the seal were her father's signature and the date September 2003.

> *My Principessa, how I adore you, my dear. I don't know what you have endured. I wish I could have forewarned you, but I never seem to view enough to prevent these events or their causes. It pains me when my empathic senses embrace me with dread. I'm sure it was difficult. But I see a future for you, a beautiful life, which gives me solace.*

The world and its nations are about to endure a dramatic and painful change. You, my precious daughter, shall find yourself at the center of its morphing. Sad days approach for the billions of the earth's inhabitants and their lands. The Angels cry in heaven over the pain humankind is about to suffer. You are a strong and decisive person filled with compassion. The people will unite around you in the next year as the government rebuilds. Fear nothing, Rio. I have always loved you and, wherever I am now, my love shines on you.

Dad

Old tear stains dotted the note. Rio wiped her eyes with the sleeve of her shirt. She reached for her cell phone and called her brother.

Chapter 88

The Oval Office

The conversation bewildered Giacomo. *Could this get any worse?* He felt his cell phone vibrate.

"Andrew's a member of the FHS?" Giacomo had the urge to jump up. Instead, he held back and listened. *What could he do?*

"No, no, I'm sorry. I mean, he's involved in trying to find a solution."

"Damn, what a relief," Lisa said.

"You're talking about an end to the escalation between Russia and China?"

"No, bigger. A pathway to halt the FHS's involvement in our government and, if possible, the world."

"But what about a diplomatic resolution?"

"Sad to say, Lisa, diplomacy will fail."

"We can't try?"

"Of course, we can. And Lisa, you are instrumental in bringing forth a plan of peace. I still have my doubts. I am frightened, my friends. The problem is they've developed a global strategy, which we need to stop. And to be honest, I doubt we will prevent them from enacting their scheme without luck and a lot of help. I see a charred landscape on the horizon."

Giacomo noticed the worried face on the president. "What is their agenda?"

"Destroy the existing world governments, including ours."

"How is that even possible?"

"I don't know. I'm not privy to the scheme. My understanding, Ramsey is an architect of the implementation."

"Why not arrest him?" Lisa questioned.

"Because it won't stop the FHS from carrying out its mission," Giacomo chimed in.

"Sad to say, I agree. Believe me when I tell you I have no confidence or trust in our legislature. As far as I am concerned, they are all suspect. The infiltration runs deep within the country."

"What about us?" Lisa worried.

"Giacomo, I can count on. My hope is we can depend on you as well."

"I've dedicated my life to our nation and the Senate. I am not a traitor. By the way, nobody approached me."

"They didn't have to—your husband was a member. He kept an eye on you."

Giacomo watched Lisa's face turn red, her hands tighten as the tendons in her neck swelled.

"What the hell do you mean?" she barked the question.

"Lisa, relax."

"Relax? I don't appreciate your sarcasm, Giacomo. My husband was a no-good son of a bitch. We have to defeat and destroy these bastards."

He touched her arm. "Lisa, please calm down."

"Yeah right."

"I'm sorry, Lisa. I didn't intend to upset you," Tom said.

Giacomo saw Lisa struggle to rein in her composure. Moments away from a cascade of tears, she sat upright and spoke.

"What if we make it public, bring it to the news outlets, Tom?"

"The pope and I discussed releasing the information and yes, Lisa, it's an option. The problem is…we have no proof. Our concern is if we attempted to pursue a media distribution, we'd end up being their next assassination targets."

"Besides Andrew, who else is trying to find a solution?"

"No one other than you two, I hope."

"Can we trust His Holiness?"

"I have no reason to doubt him, Lisa. Giacomo, you're his friend. Is he trustworthy?"

"No hesitation, Andrew loves our country. He is loyal to us. Tom, do you believe it's possible to learn the details of their plan?"

"I am meeting with the Speaker of the House on the twelfth, four days from now. I'll press Ramsey. Maybe he'll share their agenda. In the meantime, Giacomo, can you put together a team you can trust?"

"Will do. I know you've been reluctant in the past to spy on our own without judicial authority, but—"

"What do you want to do?"

"Start clandestine active surveillance on the Speaker of the House."

"I have no objections."

"Good. I'm going to require the CIA Rome section chief Maryann Costatino, Jason, and certain forces of BOET are put under my control, including your security team."

"No problem, I'll arrange it."

"What about Giacomo's duties as chairman of the Joint Chiefs?" Lisa asked.

"I'll resign."

"No, you can't."

"Why?"

"You need unencumbered access to me in case the shit hits the fan. You'll work out of the White House. It's easier to explain—we are on a combat footing. You're my number-one advisor."

"Makes sense."

"And Lisa, you might have the most demanding job of all."

"What's that, Tom?"

"Help me prevent World War III."

Chapter 89

Giacomo and Lisa walked in silence from the Oval Office. They passed the workplaces of the chief of staff and the vice president. As they turned into the lobby, a marine guard stationed by the entrance of the West Wing stood at attention and saluted General Giacomo DeLaurentis. Giacomo returned the gesture and exited. A waft of cold air ambushed the two.

Outside, an army private closed the tailgate of a troop carrier after the last of its personnel had disembarked. The twelve soldiers took up their positions with their M16s at the ready. The home of the commander in chief had become a fortified military installation.

War beckoned. Was the American government falling into the hands of a kleptocratic society—a singular global rule where the elite use their power to steal the resources of humankind? Or had that always been the case?

A black SUV stopped at the entrance. Colonel Vandercliff exited the front passenger door. He saluted Giacomo.

"Madame Secretary, pleasure to see you again."

"Thank you, Jason."

"Who's driving?" Giacomo got down to business.

"Your pilot, Pat. Danny is securing a facility for us to work from. Where are we going?"

"Department of State, the Truman Building. Have the men scanned the vehicle?"

"Yes, and we've installed the jamming equipment. We are secure."

"How did you—"

Giacomo interrupted Lisa's question. "I'll tell you once we're in the car."

As they entered, Giacomo acknowledged Pat. "Are you ready for the task?"

"Yes, sir. Since we can't fly, I'd be more than happy to help."

Giacomo sensed Lisa's stare. Jason jumped inside, reached for a frequency jammer, and turned on the device. "All set." The door slammed shut.

"Drive the long route to the Truman building and light this baby up."

Pat flicked a switch on the dashboard, which flashed the red-and-blue lights within the grill. A siren emitted from the outside speakers.

"Giacomo, what the hell is happening? How did Jason know to be here?"

"Simple, I'm wired." He unbuttoned his shirt, exposing a raised bump under his left clavicle. "He monitored my conversation. I directed Jason to pick us up when I used the bathroom. Like Tom said, the infiltration runs deep. To be honest, can we even count on Tom?"

"And me?"

"I trust you with my heart, Lisa. That will never change."

He wished he could take back those words. *Why did I say that? I love my wife. Why do I feel this way?*

"Thank you, Giacomo."

"Four hits so far, Giacomo," Jason said.

"I don't understand," Lisa inquired.

"We are under active surveillance. Our enemies are trying to listen in on our conversation. Jason, what are your thoughts?"

"First time in my life that I'm afraid. If what the president said is true..."

"You can't imagine it. Can you?"

"It's surreal...numbing," the secretary of state added.

"When you consider the repercussions if the public ever finds out... the chaos." Jason shook his head.

"It's baffling to consider that the FHS manipulated the societies of the world for centuries. What do we do now, Giacomo?"

"I don't know, Lisa. I wish my boys were here." Giacomo glanced at his cell phone and smiled at the picture of his sons.

Chapter 90

President Tom Maro walked out of his study, attached to the Oval Office. He pulled up his sleeve, checking the time on his Citizen watch. His meeting with Speaker Ramsey was to take place within the next twenty minutes. Giacomo's men from the BOET command force completed their electronic sweep. They found no listening devices. With the president's permission, they installed a camera and a microphone.

"Giacomo, can you hear me?"

"Loud and clear. How about me?"

"Perfect," Tom adjusted the earpiece in his left ear.

"Ramsey is on his way, should arrive in ten minutes."

"Thanks. Any luck in changing his security?"

"No. We discovered he handpicked each of them. Too risky of a move to change his team."

"I understand."

"Sir, the secretary of state is on the line."

"Thank you, Louise, put her through." The Oval Office phone chirped as he placed the call on speaker. "Hello, Lisa."

"Good morning, I've arranged for a private summit with you, the Chinese Premier, and the President of Russia."

"Excellent. When and where?"

"Wake Island, three days. March 15."

"Not much time."

"No, sir."

"Giacomo, I need something faster than our 747. What do we have?"

"The Gulfstream 750 can do Mach 1.3."

"Get it done."

The door opened. Louise stood in the entranceway.

"What?"

"The Speaker of the House has arrived."

"Thank you. Give me five minutes."

He returned his attention to the conversation. "Lisa, you'll join me at Wake."

"Yes, sir."

Tom Maro ended the phone call, sighed, and straightened his tie as he waited for the traitors to enter the inner sanctum of the President.

*   *   *

Giacomo, Jason, and Maryann watched the screen as Alfred Ramsey made his way into the Oval Office. Behind him, one of his staff members shuffled in. Jason reached for the control panel and increased the volume on the speakers. They observed Tom as he greeted the men.

"Al, happy to see you again."

"Thank you, Tom. You know my assistant, Scott Evans."

"Mr. President."

They shook hands. "Please," he pointed to the couch. Tom sat opposite the two. Evans reached inside his pocket and withdrew an electronic device the size of a small cell phone. His hand swiped the face of the gadget, and a green light flashed.

"All set, we're secure, Al."

A buzz emitted from the monitor's speaker. *"Change channels and convert to the president's earpiece. Just as we expected, they're jamming the low-frequency spectrum. Tom, move your head side to side."*

A second later, Tom obeyed the command.

"I must have slept wrong. I have a crick in my neck."

"We're getting old, Tom," Al said.

"Yeah, without a doubt."

Ramsey leaned forward. "Where do we stand with DeLaurentis?"

"He's moving his office into the White House. He'll be my advisor, so we can keep a closer eye on him. And the other Joint Chiefs?"

"They're with us."

"Excellent, Al. Did you speak with Paris?"

"Yes, they denied the request for full access."

"Not good, Al. Why?"

"They want you to act as normal as possible in your role as the commander in chief."

"Makes sense. What's the status?"

"As of next week, all the preparations will be complete. With Adinolfi gone, we've moved up our timeline," Scott Evans said.

"Why?"

"It was something you said, Mr. President, something that made the committee rethink its decision."

"And what did I say, Mr. Evans?"

"Russian and Chinese presidents might decide to take matters into their own hands."

Al interjected, "The consensus among the board was not to leave the scenario up to chance. Communism and the collective governments of the world will cease to exist sooner rather than later."

"How is that possible, we're discussing catastrophic loss of life?"

"We often need the sacrifice of the people to accomplish the task at hand." Evans interjected.

"It's not as bad as you think. We've got safeguards in place to minimize civilian deaths," Al chimed in.

Tom was silent as he listened to Giacomo speak.

"Tom, tell them of your plan to meet with the Chinese and the Russians."

"Al, I'm contemplating a meeting with Presidents Chin and Polotny."

"Why the hell are you going to meet with them?" Evans barked.

"Excuse me? Do you realize who you're talking to?"

"Relax, Tom," the soft voice traveled to his earpiece.

"Evans, enough," Ramsey chastened, as he turned back to the president. "We must tread with prudence. It's important the escalation between the two countries continues."

"Al, if we don't engage in diplomatic peace protocols, they will shroud our country in a nuclear winter."

"I understand. Believe me, we have safeguards in place. We need both governments to be occupied with the threat of warfare."

"What better way to keep them engaged than by bringing them to the table? We can't stand by and do nothing, Mr. Speaker."

"He has a valid point," Evans assented.

"Alright, when is the meet?"

"The fifteenth. Three days, Wake Island."

Chapter 91

The door to the Oval Office closed. Giacomo and his team, holed up in the wood shop, watched the monitor as the president walked toward his desk. He waited for Tom to speak.

"This is bad, Giacomo. What's your opinion?"

"Their reaction to the Wake Island meeting was interesting. The sinister grin plastered on the Speaker's face was—"

"He was hiding something, like he had a change of agenda."

"Yes, Maryann, I agree. The smirk was frightening."

"What do you think it means?" Tom asked.

"He's a snake. That's one thing I'm positive about. Ramsey is a creep. I'm sending fighter escorts with you. We have to be cautious—this guy is evil. He's not going to catch us with our guard down. I'll have another contingency within twenty-four hours."

"Excellent idea, Giacomo."

"Mr. President, if you can't convince the Russians and the Chinese to deescalate, we cannot escape the impending doom."

"You're correct, Maryann, and believe me, I'm worried. The reach of the FHS is astounding. We are weeks, maybe mere days, away from the execution of their plan, a scheme we know nothing about. I wonder, do we have enough time?"

"We have to stop them." Giacomo reflected for a moment. "If the public discovers how the FHS influenced world history over the past five hundred years," Giacomo paused, "I promise you, anarchy will ravage the earth. The consequence if people knew…"

"Riots will erupt in the streets, governments will topple. Everywhere you turn, there will be a military coup—law and order thrown away in the trash," Maryann exclaimed.

"We do nothing," Jason interjected.

"What do you mean?" Giacomo gave him a hard stare.

"I think we have to weigh the outcomes."

"Truman decision," the president agreed.

They were silent for a while. Each of them understood what the president meant—the choice to allow a few to die to save the multitudes. It was a moral option with no winner. The very decision Harry Truman had made to stop World War II, when he gave the order to drop the first nuclear bomb on Japan. The countless innocent allowed to perish within the FHS's plan caused Giacomo's heart to ache. Would he ever get the chance to hold his sons? How could they allow disorder to become the law of the land? Could the FHS prevent global chaos?

"Do we have any idea the number of people involved?"

Maryann riffled through pages of a dossier prepared by trusted staff members. "It's estimated their membership exceeds eight million throughout the world, Mr. President. Our algorithm calculates ninety percent of the group are leaders on the international and national government stage. What's interesting, in the United States, we count seven governors tainted with the FHS ideology. There are two scary statistics: the first is that their associates hold positions of authority in every aspect of industry—healthcare, education, religious institutions, et cetera. The second is, if we consider their influence on relatives and friends, the membership then exceeds a hundred million. We also discovered they operate as individual cells, on a need-to-know basis."

"What's their goal?"

Maryann hesitated. "World peace and a singular global rule, Tom."

"Bullshit. People will die...*have* died. How is this even possible?" Giacomo stared at the ceiling as he continued to speak. "How do we stop this? And *can* we stop it?" He paused. "Chop the head off the snake. This is what we must do: apprehend Ramsey and question him. Get the truth from the bastard."

"You mean torture him?"

"Not quite. Drugs will open his mind to our questions, and he will give us the answers."

"No, we can't."

"Why not, Tom? We're in a no-win situation here. It's been done before."

"I understand, Giacomo, but we are better than that."

Giacomo studied the president on the monitor. Tom covered his face with his hands. He looked up at Jason, then Maryann. She shrugged. Despair and frustration were sweeping them up in billows of scattered thoughts with no answers. Giacomo walked across the room. With a burst of energy, he scrambled to the monitor and microphone.

"Tom, keep the meeting with the Russian and Chinese leaders."

"I have no intention of canceling."

"Good. The noose will get tighter. The time is approaching when we can no longer thwart their plan. We need to act. It's imperative we unite with our new allies, the current leaders of Russia and China."

"There'll be consequences…we'll be their next target."

Chapter 92

March 12

Giacomo swiped his security key card and entered his room at the Willard hotel. Tired and hungry, he undressed and showered. After he left the wood shop, the remainder of Giacomo's day was filled with endless meetings. He listened to the adamant wartime arguments of his fellow commanders. He tried to persuade the other Joint Chiefs to extinguish the warfare rhetoric. He failed in his attempts to quash their desires, and nuclear war was at man's doorstep.

The windows vibrated from the sound of helicopters as they circled over 1600 Pennsylvania Avenue, on guard for any disturbance requiring the aircrafts' artillery. All airspace was closed to civilian aircraft.

Concerned that Ramsey and the FHS might try to assassinate the president, Giacomo issued orders to fortify the area around the White House. A security stronghold encompassed a rectangular zone measuring 1.3 miles long, stretching from Lafayette Park to the grounds past the Washington Monument, by a half-mile wide, to incorporate the government's executive office buildings. The military blockade went into effect at 0500 the following morning.

At midnight, the Army Corps of Engineers would block the roads with concrete barriers and fourteen-foot-high, barbed-razor-wire fences, as trailers mounted with robotic gun turrets scanned the perimeter. Throughout the morning hours, the citizens of DC listened to the chattering, chilling sounds of America's war machine echoing through the empty streets of Washington. Convoys of tanks and armored troop carriers waited on the outskirts of the Beltway. Surface-to-air missiles stationed on rooftops strengthened the line within the protected space.

Any employee or visitor to the White House had to pass through two mandatory check points, both staffed by BOET military police. After passing through the final security zone, the military guard marshaled the privileged personnel to the south entrance gate, where they'd be escorted to their appointed fortified area.

Giacomo looked at the time: *7 p.m.… 1 a.m. in Italy*. He grew anxious that his sons still weren't home. He should have been cradling them by now. Due to the current situation in the world and the no-fly zones imposed, he'd have to wait. He arranged a video conference call with Warren and Frank for the following morning…at least he could see his boys.

Hungry, Giacomo ordered room service—a hamburger, French fries, and a Pepsi. His mind swirled with potential scenarios, but the outcomes never altered…destruction and death for humanity. Regret became his nemesis. What if situations overpowered him? *Could I have stopped the tragedies from occurring? If Rio and I had kept our father's journal instead of giving it to the president, might anything have changed? Or was it fate? Where did I go wrong?* A series of knocks on the door interrupted his thoughts.

Giacomo reached into his pocket and pulled out a ten-dollar bill to give to the server. "Come in." Flanked on either side of the dinner cart were his bodyguards. The hotel employee stood eyeing the soldiers. Giacomo noticed the trepidation emanating from her eyes, the frightened look of a child who'd lost her parents.

"Thank you, gentlemen." The men saluted their commanding officer and walked back to their post by the elevator. He read the waitress's nametag. "Please come in, Sonia. I'll take the tray." Giacomo handed her the money.

"Thanks. Can I ask you a question?"

"Of course."

"Are we going to be nuked?"

Giacomo placed the food on the desk and turned. He could see the terror in her youthful face.

"No, we'll be fine."

"It's sad. After all the centuries of civilization, we can't seem to get it right. Wars, hate, greed…"

"You're a perceptive young lady…you must be a history major?"

"I am." She avoided his eyes and said, "I'm afraid in the coming weeks and months, the horrific death that will ensue is going to plague us…and *humanity will be forever gone.*"

The morbid statement struck Giacomo. At a loss for words, he knew she was correct. Love ceased to exist in this world of hate.

"I wish you the best, thank you for the tip."

Giacomo walked the girl to the door. He had an unobstructed view of the hallway leading to the elevators. As the college student entered a stairway, she turned and faced him. Their eyes locked. A moment of sadness crossed his face. He whispered, "Goodbye, Sonia."

The hotel had been evacuated earlier in the day for security reasons. Giacomo's floor housed no paying guests. Tomorrow the hotel became a military barracks. A chime sounded as the doors to the elevator opened. The secretary of state emerged, and the soldiers escorted her to Giacomo's room.

"Can I come in?"

"Please. Are you hungry? You can have half of my burger."

"No, no thanks."

"What brings you here? Do we have another problem?"

"I'm afraid. I didn't want to be alone."

Lisa removed her brown cashmere overcoat. Dressed in blue jeans, a pearl-white knitted sweater, and a thin gold necklace with a diamond pendent that hung above the collar, she walked to the window.

"Eat your dinner. You must be starving."

"I am.

"It's been a hell of a day."

"You're not kidding." Giacomo took a bite of the burger. Overcooked. He placed the sandwich back on the plate. He drank the Pepsi.

"Bad?"

"Freakin' nasty. There's some vodka in the wet bar if you'd like a drink?"

"Any wine?"

Exhausted, Giacomo yawned as he walked over to the mini fridge. He pulled out a bottle and read the label. "Chardonnay?"

"Yes, please."

He uncorked it and poured the beverage into a crystal wine glass. "Here you go, my lady."

"My lady?"

"You prefer 'Madame Secretary'?"

The living area of the suite was decorated with modern furniture. Balanced by a gray couch and two matching sitting chairs, a rectangular maple wood coffee table was situated in the middle. The tan-colored curtains were parted. The reflection of alternating red-and-blue flashes from the security vehicles stationed by the building disrupted the blackness of the night.

"I'm afraid, Giacomo, the Russians or the Chinese will enact a doomsday scenario."

"I had a similar thought. It's a real catch-22."

Giacomo sat in one chair. Lisa was on the couch. Silence overtook them for a moment, isolated from the craziness of a city under military control. The steel treads of armored tanks squeaked and rattled as they took their positions on the once-busy streets.

"The president told me Ramsey assured him the FHS has safeguards in place."

"Come on, Giacomo, once they push the button…life ceases, humanity is annihilated."

"Let's hope you and Tom are successful at Wake Island. I don't believe we'll be drawn into the conflict, though I have debated the scenarios in my mind. What concerns me is what happens afterward."

"What do you mean?"

"Our country won't emerge from this unscathed. A revolution is about to explode throughout this nation. The days of the Wild West will return, and crime will run rampant. The FHS's goal is a singular global government. Whatever they've planned, I'm sure it'll backfire, propelling the world back in time to the Stone Age, our land scorched and blighted for a thousand years."

Giacomo pondered for a moment. "Maybe we were never meant to live in peace as we perceive it. Maybe all the different ideologies strewn among the nations balanced humanity. I can guarantee you, that revolution you talk about will occur. There will never be peace. We're better off leaving well enough alone."

"You mean to say nothing, do nothing? That's a ridiculous notion, Giacomo."

"If we inform the people about the FHS, we're doomed. Anarchy, unrest, you name it. It will happen…I don't know, Lisa…I'm babbling. I'm at a loss."

Giacomo watched the secretary of state stand and walk around the couch, positioning herself behind him. Giacomo felt the heat of her palms on his shoulders. He held her hand as she circled the chair. Their eyes met. She leaned forward to kiss him.

"I'm sorry, Lisa, I can't…"

Their lips touched. The softness and tenderness of Lisa's mouth excited him. He placed his hands on her hips as he pushed her back.

"I'm not ready, forgive me."

He caught the disappointed look on her face.

"Our lives are going to be cut short. Giacomo, I love you, I always have. I don't want to be alone."

"Neither do I, but…"

"Emily. I understand."

"There's another bedroom in my suite with its own bathroom. You can stay with me. At least we'll be together when the world falls apart. Sound okay?" He saw the disappointment in her eyes, and his heart felt for her. But he couldn't shake the thoughts of his wife. *It's not right… besides, I have my children to worry about.*

"Sounds good. Thank you."

Chapter 93

"Folks, I need to be back at the White House in thirty minutes," Giacomo said. He sat at a makeshift conference table made of plywood. The smell of burnt wood from a power saw pervaded the room. He was behind schedule after his video call with his sons, but it was worth it. A pride built within him. *I'm a dad. They need a safer world. I wish you were here, Em...*

Within twenty-four hours, Jason and his team had secured the one-thousand-square-foot carpenters' workspace. Jason, concerned about an EMP discharge, commanded his men to build a Faraday cage that surrounded a bank of laptops. A squad of data sleuths pounded their keyboards, gathering information. Their screens scrolled with furious haste through computer code as algorithms sifted through billions of bytes of information. They tied the equipment and surveillance paraphernalia into self-destruct mechanisms. Any unauthorized admission into the protected area ignited small explosive devices, destroying the critical spying apparatus.

To enter the facility required a revolving alphanumeric password that changed every fifteen minutes. Once the facial recognition software confirmed the person's identity, a computer-generated code was transmitted to their cell phone.

Seated at the table with Giacomo were Jason, Maryann, and newcomer Bunny Lynch, head of the FBI's Counterintelligence Division.

"Hello, Bunny. Glad to see you again. They filled you in on the bleak status?" Giacomo directed his attention to his old friend.

"Yes."

"No issues with you being absent from your post?"

"I'm often missing in action, so no worries."

"Good. As you know, tensions between Russia and China have escalated. Washington is one step away from enacting martial law. We no longer have weeks to restore peace; we are down to days, which will soon dwindle to hours and minutes. FHS sympathizers have besieged our country. They believe in the idea of a singular world government. We won't be able to stop them. Our job today is to prevent a catastrophic loss of life. We must try to keep our democracy intact, hoping our actions will not draw our people into the crosshairs of a nuclear strike." Giacomo noticed the grim faces of those around the table. Their eyes hardened with resolve.

Maryann spoke, "We have good news. Our sweep team in Italy scoured the abbey in Monte Cassino. We found a secret room connected to Adinolfi's research hospital in the basement. Inside was a treasure trove of information, written material, and two laptops." She handed Giacomo the forensic file she had prepared.

"We acquired a list of the FHS hierarchy from his computer. Your assumptions were correct. They have infiltrated our government with a fair share of the group's partisans. Our people here are trying to hack their secure site to retrieve more info. The additional data will allow us to build a more powerful algorithm to provide a more definitive idea of their cell structure and locations," Bunny said.

Giacomo surveyed the list of names and titles, nodding his head at the ones he recognized. Most were billionaires, government officials, religious leaders, military personnel, and directors of large corporations. "Wow. Are they all aware of the plan?"

"Don't know yet. We discovered a secured satellite phone network of seventy-seven individuals. Our analysts have retrieved information on thirty-eight. The remaining should be online later this evening.

We're cross-checking their internal communications. I hope we'll have their strategy in hand soon. To answer your question, my guess is all seventy-seven are in the loop. The rest don't have a clue."

"You agree, Maryann?"

"Yes."

"Why?"

"Because there's no leak. These bastards are keeping the information to themselves. They don't care about the loss of life. Their dedication to this ideology has overcome their sense of benevolence. I suspect they act on a need-to-know basis, but as we get closer to their deadline, they will pass the data to their subordinates—thus, allowing continuity of the organization and their prospects of global rule."

As Giacomo heard the words, his mind whisked him into the vision that haunted his subconscious. *Three men, their faces clouded by a haze. Two wore white robes—one with a frayed, discolored red hem and the other with a black collar—each held an earth in the palm of his hand. The third was dressed in sackcloth, his hands empty.*

He strained to see who they were.

The man in the tattered robe squeezed the planet. As his grip strengthened, his fingers morphed into vices. The screams of humanity erupted. In slow motion, the malformed sphere dripped blood, and its life force splattered on the floor. The one in sackcloth appeared with a mop and cleaned the stained ground.

Giacomo's inner gaze turned to the person with the black collar and the planet he held. As the vision converted into a three-dimensional scene, above him he saw *the stars and the planet's place within the universe. Lights of the nations of the earth sparkled, then one country after another grew dark. The man in sackcloth took the sphere. He struggled to embrace it. He writhed from the heaviness of the new earth, falling to his knees, careful not to let it drop.*

The cities illuminated with a flicker. The creature in the frayed robes glowered with a fierce, seething rage. In his wrath, he snatched the orb and scowled at its inhabitants, causing chaos among the people.

The man wearing the black collar, his eyes full of fury, struck the aggressor. His physical appearance transformed, towering over the other two men. He reached down, picked up the assailant by his neck, and threw him into a dark chasm. The man's excruciating groans traveled throughout creation. With his might, he closed the abyss and shrank to his original size. His robe became a dazzling white. He grabbed the chaotic earth from the individual in sackcloth who protected the planet with his life.

In an instant, the meaning of his vision revealed itself. The cleric wearing the tattered robe was the FHS. The black collar represented the global government, and the remaining person stood for the people of the earth. This time he heard a voice: *'You can't be an architect of life. We can never change our fate.'*

"Giacomo, Giacomo, are you listening?" Jason asked.

He shook his head to bring himself back to this world. Seeing the concerned faces of his team, he said, "No worries. Yes, yes, I'm fine. I had an idea."

"It must've been a hell of a brainstorm. Your eyes were blank. We thought you were having a seizure."

"No, no, I'm fine. Maryann, it's a gift. I enter a realm of clarity. Sorry it spooked you. Perhaps we broadcast what the FHS has done throughout the international community and provide specifics to the populace?"

"Big mistake, Giacomo, you need to consider the ramifications—such as chaos, discontent, and riots in the street. We'll damn our people to destroying each other over our choices; what we think is right," Maryann replied.

"What the hell do *you* suggest?" Giacomo took a breath. "I'm sorry, I don't mean to get mad. We are in a freaking catch-22. There is no good choice." Giacomo inhaled as he looked at his team. "We need to unify our country and destroy these bastards. They've controlled the population long enough." Giacomo's no-nonsense stare affirmed his position.

"Oh boy, you're scaring me, Giacomo," Jason chirped.

"Guys, the FHS has manipulated the world's economies for centuries. They have funded and fueled wars by pitting societies and religions against one another. Look at this list. I'll bet most of their members don't have any idea that they've been exploited."

"What you say could be true, Giacomo. The problem is, how do you change hundreds of years of ideology?"

"A valid point, Bunny. Hatred, greed, and selfishness are prevalent in our society."

"How do you break from the dogma when the philosophy becomes your mindset?"

"Good question, Jason. The answer is this: lay down your weapons and live in peace." Giacomo noted the astonishment on their faces.

"You're crazy. That will never happen." That was the collective response, except for Maryann. Giacomo noticed the gleam in her eyes. He shook off the idea as a picture of his wife held his thoughts.

Chapter 94

"I'm sorry Giacomo, we're still at Air Traffic Control Zero. No airplane travel throughout Europe. The good news is we are moving a deployed military unit to Italy in seven days' time. The Italian government granted permission for the flight to return to the US the following day. Frank, Warren, and the twins are expected to be on board. Per your instructions, they'll be landing at the Norfolk Naval Station in Virginia. There'll be another aircraft standing by to transport them to Connecticut. We have arranged an armed security detail for you to meet them when they land in Norfolk."

"Sounds great, Jason. Thank you."

He was unhappy he had to wait to see his boys. A mixture of emotions filled Giacomo: elation at the thought of his sons' arrival in the States, depression that his wife Emily was not here, and anxiety that he might never hold his children in his arms. Giacomo had to put a stop to the paralyzing dread and concentrate on the task at hand, even if it meant he could not be with his children.

*   *   *

The White House Residence

General Giacomo DeLaurentis, Secretary of State Lisa Rift, and President Thomas Maro convened in the president's library. A sixty-five-inch monitor hung on the wall. They were silent as they waited for the video conference to begin.

Giacomo studied his companions' faces. Tom's eyes were fraught with worry. His jaw tightened as his facial muscles flexed in and out, and his fingers tapped on his cherry-wood desk. Lisa was fidgety, crossing and uncrossing her legs. She stood, smoothed her dress, then sat back down. Giacomo felt unsettled as he considered the implications that lay ahead. His hands rubbed his face as he rose from the chair and paced the president's library.

"Damn, I hate waiting."

"I get it, my friend. It feels like we have no control," Tom empathized.

Giacomo tried to hold back his exasperation as he moved to the couch. He motioned Lisa to slide over. "Well, we better get our act together, and fast, or we're screwed." He felt Lisa's touch on his thigh. A sense of comfort filled him.

"Lisa, are you prepared for our meeting at Wake?"

"I am, Tom. Both leaders are eager to resolve the matter."

Tom grabbed a pad and a black marker. He lifted the piece of paper and showed it to them both: *Does FHS know about the change?*

Giacomo shook his head.

"Mr. President, your video conference is ready to begin."

"Thank you," he replied to the voice emanating from the speakerphone.

The screen came alive. Ramsey's face appeared.

"Are you enjoying your isolation?"

"Need to protect our democracy, Al. I signed the executive order today to enlarge the protective area around the Capitol. Soon you'll join me in seclusion."

"Yes, my office will be my home. I'm not looking forward to the lockdown. Are you prepared for your trip?"

"As ready as I can be, Al. You know the Secretary of State and the Chairman of the Joint Chiefs?"

"I do," Ramsey's voice was condescending. "Let us get to the issue, Mr. President. Members of the House are concerned your meeting with our enemies places the United States in the center of the China-Russia conflict."

"They're not at war yet, Mr. Speaker," Giacomo rebutted.

"Believe me when I tell you, General, they will be."

"Let's hope not," Lisa interjected.

"Al, as you and I have discussed, this is an appropriate action to take."

"Yes, I agree with you. There are others, however, who dislike what you proposed. In fact, a few minutes ago, a fellow member berated me when he discovered you were traveling to Wake Island."

"This is necessary, Al. We must try to initiate a peace agreement. I'm sure you read the intelligence briefing. Both sides are gearing up for surgical nuclear strikes. We are talking hundreds of thousands, dead and injured. This is not acceptable. Has history taught us nothing?"

"The House withdrew its support for your meeting."

"My administration is on its own, then?"

"Yes, Mr. President, you will be alone should you choose to move forward. One other point: the simultaneous transportation of three world leaders could prove dangerous."

Giacomo noticed the taunting gleam in Ramsey's eyes. A battle line was being drawn, one that could cost Tom his life.

"I understand." Tom grabbed the remote, and the screen went dead.

Chapter 95

Dismayed, Giacomo walked through the secured entrance. *How many will die? Who will live? Was there ever a democracy?* He gazed at his assembled team of people, who could decide the fate of the world. Disillusioned with the afternoon's events, which had brought further despair and loss of hope, he took a deep breath and gathered himself.

"General," the BOET sergeant provided him with a crisp salute.

"At ease."

"Sir."

Giacomo walked to the plywood conference table. Maryann joined him, followed by Jason and Bunny. Their expressions were grim.

"Can't be that bad?"

Jason took a chair, turned it around, and sat. Maryann stood next to Giacomo, while Bunny crossed her arms and paced.

"I don't believe we can stop them in time. Our last hope is the president's meeting at Wake Island. Even if he's successful, we will not prevent them from trying to carry out their plan," Jason said.

"We have to try, Jason."

"I don't disagree with you, Giacomo, but..."

"Doomsday for the world?"

"Not likely in the US and portions of Europe," Maryann answered.

Giacomo felt her touch his shoulder. A sense of longing overcame him. He grabbed his cell phone and gazed at the pictures of his sons. Giacomo was filled with a sense of hope of holding them in his arms.

Maryann riffled through a notebook and continued her assessment. "Russia and China will be a bloodbath, and the war hawks in our government won't object to the carnage and destruction of their societies. Over the last twenty-four hours, both countries have been amassing their troops at the border. Also disturbing is that the Iranian members of the FHS appear to be disregarding the hierarchy orders. We can expect a nuclear attack on Israel."

"Shit," Giacomo shook his head.

"Yes, our exact words," Maryann replied.

"We hacked into the FHS mainframe computers," Bunny said.

"I'm listening."

"We discovered that over the last five years, their leadership had splintered. Adinolfi being the root cause. The board tolerated him because of the European Union's success in controlling the global markets." Bunny sifted through her dossier. "According to an email dated August of last year, members became aware of his human genome research. That in itself is not alarming. What caused their angst was the testing. His researchers inflicted mortal wounds, hoping to resurrect the dead by altering their genetic code. This depraved mindset repulsed the rest of FHS. Of note, the priest-physician was a schizophrenic."

"Yeah, I saw the evidence. What about the seventy-seven?"

"They are the leaders who used their power and influence to revive the idea of a singular global rule. We discovered they tried to finance the failed attack on American soil several months ago."

"Interesting," Giacomo paused.

"Yes, according to a document dating back twenty years, they discussed the dismantling of the FHS," Bunny said.

"Why dismantle, Bunny?"

"Good question. Certain members discovered the organization had financed various wars. My guess, after they uncovered the information, they came to a similar conclusion: a world wracked with chaos. A representative who is now deceased brought the material to FHS's board. Adinolfi, who was chairperson, suggested the group parlay their monetary influence with his desire that the church govern the world, creating a peaceful global government. Fast forward to Eten Trivette and the EU..."

The sound of Trivette's name caused a flash of displeasure to surge through Giacomo, which didn't go unnoticed. He nodded for Bunny to continue the story.

Bunny wrapped up the briefing: "We still don't understand how Trivette influenced the economies. We're positive he had inside information, either that or a crystal ball."

Giacomo interrupted, "By chance, did their wealth increase?" He noticed the surprise look on Bunny's face.

"Yes, every one of these leaders increased their power and financial resources tenfold during Trivette's reign."

"From what you guys are saying—and correct me if I'm wrong—there are seventy-seven members who capitalized on abundant international tragedies. They united their authorities to change the world's political landscape, and by doing so, hedged their bets that the destruction of the communist governments could unite the world."

"Yes, the FHS imposed their influence on the socialist leaders by fueling their greed and clout to gain "freedom," Maryann added.

"So, what changed? Why do this now?"

"Two reasons."

Giacomo watched his team react to Maryann's statement.

"Let me guess. *Me?*"

"Yes, sorry to say. We found evidence dating back to your father's writings that caused a furor in Adinolfi's corner. There's a so-called prophecy about your family. Because the priest couldn't leave it alone, his intent to destroy you became his demise. That sped up the FHS timeline."

"Because of my investigation into the death of my wife and children?"

"Yes."

"The other reason?"

"The world is ripe for a change."

Giacomo turned to face Jason. "You agree?"

"To a point. That and four dollars will buy me a cup of coffee. We have to deal with the dire issue of nuclear war. Ramsey stated safeguards were in place. We need to uncover their plan. I fear one false move, and Earth as we know it will no longer exist."

The statement resounded within Giacomo. His mind returned to the familiar vision. *The backdrop changes, the sunlight is blinding, then plunges into the blackness of an abyss. Bright green auras rise high on the horizon, highlighting the heavens. The scene shifts to Paris. Commotion and disorder roam the streets; darkness envelops the City of Lights. He hears the words 'We can never change our fate.'*

"Jason, our intelligence services have a good idea where the nuke strikes will occur in Russia. Can we run an EMP scenario for Europe?"

"Yeah, no problem."

Giacomo watched his friend as he plugged the data into his laptop.

"Here you are. A blackout for the European continent."

"So, Paris goes dark?"

"All indications say yes."

Giacomo pulled the sleeve of his shirt up and tapped his smart watch. "The President departs in an hour. We have less than a day to unravel their plan. We need a break. I'll be back in thirty minutes. Jason, make sure the satellite feeds are up and running."

Giacomo stepped outside; the gray clouds overhead held back the tears from heaven. He gazed upward. Sorrow beat at his heart as he realized he would never see his sons. An army sergeant holding a suitcase stood by a black SUV. He saluted.

"You have the papers?"

"Yes, sir." He balanced the suitcase on his knees and withdrew the document.

Giacomo took a cursory look, grabbed his pen from his pocket, signed the five-page legal indenture, and returned it to the man.

"Thank you, Sergeant. Be safe."

Earlier in the day, he instructed his lawyer to draw up the necessary papers to facilitate the adoption of his sons by Rio. The doomsday clock clicked closer to midnight. Trapped in DC, a bullseye for a nuke, Giacomo accepted that his death was imminent.

Chapter 96

The White House, March 15, 5:00 P.M.

President Thomas Maro and Secretary of State Lisa Rift followed Jason and his BOET squad through the cellar shadows of the White House's underground tunnels in what they hoped was a well-executed escape plan from the presidential residence. Taking advantage of the layers of security in place, BOET dressed the two government executives in army camouflage.

To complete the ruse, agents hired to act as stand-ins remained in the living area sealed off in the president's quarters. BOET soldiers had moved Maro's wife and children to a safe location earlier in the week.

"How much farther, Captain?"

"Just a few more yards, Mr. President."

"I guess those stories about the secret passageways are true," Lisa said.

"Yeah, it was the first item on the former president's note to me. He used this underpass many times to escape the insanity of the Oval Office. He suggested I use it often to flee from the world of politics. I never thought I'd be traveling underground to prevent World War III."

*   *   *

One Hundred Miles off the Coast of Norfolk, Virginia, Later that Night,
11:00 P.M.

"Tom, are you ready?"

"As best I can be. Quite the circuitous route you've put me on, Giacomo. Helicopters, a submarine, two aircraft carriers, and two fighter jets. Damn, what's next, the space shuttle?"

"I know," Giacomo laughed. "Let's hope they don't discover what we did. We'll be monitoring your progress. How do you like your digs?"

"Interesting. These men and woman are remarkable."

"Godspeed, Tom." The secured satellite communication ceased.

The Ohio-class submarine, *USS Louisiana*, rose to periscope depth. Ten minutes later, the bow of the ship crested the waterline. A navy helicopter hovered over the submersible, ready to lift the president and secretary of state and transport them to the waiting aircraft carrier *Carl Vinson*. The light of the full moon glistened over the calm Atlantic.

Aboard the chopper, a BOET crew assisted the two with their flight suits. Tom and Lisa listened to a briefing on what to expect during a carrier takeoff and landing. They put on their helmets and lowered their visors, their identities hidden as they traveled to the floating airport.

The pilot landed the whirlybird with a thud on the rolling flight deck. Once secured, a crewman slid open the side door. A cool gust of wind, filled with the smell of salt water, wafted into the vehicle. Three BOET men jumped to the surface.

"This way, Mr. President, Madame Secretary."

"Sir, welcome aboard. Your aircraft is standing by." The commander of the ship saluted.

He was the lone officer privy to the visitors' identities. Tom nodded his head in acknowledgement. Two BOET members escorted them to the two twin F18F Super Hornet fighters. They hustled the VIPs into the back seats of the airplanes. As the *Vinson*'s helmsmen maneuvered the ocean airport into the wind, the jets powered up, waiting for the "go" signal. The pilot's left hand increased the throttle, and with the click of a button, the afterburners ignited. The trail of flame woke the evening sky, followed by the second fighter. Within seconds, the two were flying in formation. The supersonic voyage of 4,530 miles brought them to the carrier *USS Enterprise*, sailing south of the Bering Sea.

*   *   *

The Wood Shop, Washington, DC

Giacomo and his team gathered around two TV monitors. The left showed a satellite image of the three naval strike groups. The Chinese *Shandong*, the Russian *Kuznetsov*, and the American *Enterprise*. Separated by fifty miles each, they were battle ready and on a solid war footing. The second screen revealed the isolated airstrip at Wake Island in the South. The strip of land waited for the remote-controlled decoy aircraft.

"Do you think it'll work, Giacomo?"

"I hope so, Maryann."

After dismissing the rest of the staff, General Giacomo DeLaurentis, CIA Directorate of Operations Maryann Costantino, FBI Analyst Bunny Lynch, and Colonel Jason Vandercliff remained.

"Bunny, any communication between the seventy-seven?"

"No, they've been silent. But once they turn on a phone, it will ping our server. We'll capture their location and conversation."

"How far away is the president, Jason?"

"He's an hour out."

"And the planes to Wake Island?"

"The Russian and Chinese are twenty minutes out, and ours is twenty-five."

Giacomo paced the room. Time moved in slow motion as a sense of doom rattled him. Precious moments of life faded away as the hourglass emptied. The realization that humanity's existence would be upended by destruction, death, and mayhem caused a wave of queasiness. He took a deep breath and shook his head. He had to focus, no time for thoughts of family…the world was in peril.

"Giacomo, fighters have intercepted the remotes. They are making their runs now. The bastards destroyed the Russian and Chinese aircraft. They have departed the area and, as you thought, ignored ours," Jason stated.

"And we have three satellite phone pings."

"Where, Bunny?"

"One here in DC, Moscow, and Beijing."

"Interesting. Ramsey knows. We're screwed."

"Your CIA intuition?"

The seasoned military men's eyes locked. "Shit," they spoke in unison.

"What's the matter?" Bunny asked.

"Giacomo, call the president's plane back. Tell them to turn around now," Maryann shouted.

They tried to communicate with the president's plane, to no avail. An electromagnetic pulse blocked the frequency. Giacomo's head filled with dread. He folded his arms and watched in horror as the enemy annihilated the Chinese and Russian carrier groups, sending them into oblivion. A nuclear shock wave from the concussion rolled the *USS Enterprise* and the American battle group fifty miles away from the point of detonation.

Chapter 97

March 18, Seven Days until Passover

Tensions escalated beyond reason to a foreboding future of a world at war. In less than twenty-four hours, the devastating events in the North Pacific dragged the United States into the conflict. Ramsey's threat came to fruition. World leaders accused America of escalating an aggravated situation. They blamed President Tom Maro and his administration for the annihilation of the two aircraft carrier groups. Fifteen thousand Chinese and Russian military men had died in an instant.

Within days, panic erupted in the United States. Citizens hoarded food, water, and supplies. Lines of people wrapped around drugstores as local governments issued iodine pills for protection against radioactive fallout. The nation's fear grew tenfold as the sun set and rose. The nights cried out for mercy as the populace prayed. Churches filled while the earth traveled across the solar system. The emergent tragedy of a nuclear conflict crept closer. US officials prepared to ensure continuity of the democracy.

*   *   *

Presidential Emergency Operations Center (PEOC), the White House

The Cold War between the Soviet Bloc countries and the United States spanned the years from 1947 to 1990. The major powers teetered on the premise that a nuclear attack and associated radiation poisoning were forthcoming. Entrenched in the populations' minds were recollections of the gruesome atomic bomb detonations over Hiroshima and Nagasaki—images of the August horror of 1945 fueled the nations' anxieties.

Paranoia and uncertainty trembled throughout the world for decades to follow. People feared that the annihilation of humanity was at hand. The threat led to the construction of massive secret underground bunkers. The installations provided for continuity of government and succession of the American standard of life.

A select group of people were chosen to survive, the rest doomed to an instant death or one of prolonged suffering by radiation poisoning and starvation on a charred landscape. Such a shelter, designated the Presidential Nuclear Emergency Operations Center, was located under the East Lawn of the White House.

Giacomo and Jason entered a secure elevator to the renovated PEOC. The 175-foot descent took less than ten seconds and ended with a swish and a hush as the doors slid open. Two armed marines greeted the men with salutes.

"This way, sir."

At the far end of the steel, stone, and titanium hallway was a vaulted entrance measuring fourteen-by-twelve-by-eight-feet thick, large enough for a car to enter. Above it, a red light flashed next to an illuminated digital sign blaring the message "DEFCON 2." Giacomo acknowledged the ominous status. He shook his head in disbelief. Then a chilling thought made him sick to his stomach: *Maybe it's better if the boys were dead.* He'd entrusted their safety to his sister Rio, but it was little consolation.

Dressed in full army green, the four-star general's polished black shoes clacked on the tile floor. The disheartened man scanned his surroundings before entering the secured PEOC. Giacomo's name was announced through a speaker system. Once inside, an alarm beeped. The heavy door creaked as it moved on its hinges. Giacomo watched the massive structure close with a thud. The sound of the locking pins engaging was followed by an onslaught of rushing air as the room was sealed against any seen or unseen intruder.

"Good afternoon, General. The president is waiting for you."

Jason followed a step behind Giacomo. They approached a door marked "President's Residence." A BOET soldier stood guard. She saluted the two men. They walked into an apartment. The disillusioned commander in chief was drinking a cup of coffee at the dining table.

"Gentlemen, glad you could make it."

"I'm happy you're alive, Mr. President," Jason said.

"It was a terrible sight. We were making our approach to the carrier when the explosion occurred. We were able to outrun the shock wave, thank God. I am beyond disappointed and angry. Please." The President pointed to a set of chairs.

Giacomo pulled one out from under the table and sat. Jason followed military protocol and stood opposite Giacomo. "They played us for fools, Tom."

"Yep, I called Ramsey."

"How did that conversation go?"

"He was smug. He issued me a warning: I'd be next if I interfered again."

"What a son of a bitch. Let's take him out. I'll have BOET arrest him."

"Giacomo, it won't stop these guys. We're in a no-win situation. Ramsey guaranteed me the US would not get caught up in the fray. He said the safeguards are in place."

"And you believe him?"

"No."

Giacomo followed Tom's eyes as he gazed around the bunker. "You see this," he spread out his arms.

"Impressive. I've always heard stories about the hiding place."

"Well, I didn't. Did you know a similar one exists under the Capitol? Ready for this—the facility can shelter all members of Congress, staff, *and* their families."

Giacomo and Jason exchanged a cursory glance. They shook their heads.

"It's called continuity of government. The elite will survive while the American people die in the onslaught. I am under what I call house arrest. I'm here for the duration. In a matter of days, World War III will begin. We have one chance to stop this calamity, gentlemen. We need to go public about FHS to halt the coming catastrophic demise of nations."

"The consequences are immense, Tom. Chaos in the streets, a worldwide revolution, military overthrows, and deaths of innocent people."

"It's awful, but it's better than nuclear war, Giacomo. The Truman decision, my friend. We have no choice."

Stupefied, Giacomo pondered the scenario. *Was he right? The tragic loss of life caused by multiple atomic bombs versus complete pandemonium in the world...he knew the consequence of both scenarios...enormous numbers of casualties.* Thoughts circled in his mind. *What other option was there?*

"Can you do it?"

"Yes, Tom."

"Godspeed, son. Should we never meet again..."

"Mr. President, be assured we will."

Chapter 98

Giacomo and Jason entered the secure facility and walked to the makeshift conference table. Maryann and Bunny were waiting. The sound of the computers processing algorithms filled the silence.

"How bad?" Maryann asked.

"They secured the president in the PEOC. Tom is confident portions of the States will come under nuclear attack, though Ramsey still refutes it."

Giacomo saw Bunny's face turn ashen. "Our families… We can't allow this to happen."

"I know. Let's flood the internet with all the data we have on the FHS. We need massive news coverage to persuade the world this is true. What allies do we have in our government, if any?"

"From what we've determined, the assistant director of the CIA, some cabinet appointments, and just four members of Congress," Bunny replied.

Maryann continued the assessment. "The remaining Joint Chiefs are compromised. There are indications that a secret military force is amassing along the DC, Maryland, and Philadelphia borders. We discovered Ramsey issued an executive order when he was interim President after the assassination attempt. The marines' orders are to seal those areas, but we don't understand why Philly is being surrounded."

"Damn, they covered their bases well. Looks like we can't do anything with the DC area…it's too late now. What about the National Guard? Let's bring the governors into the loop. They can activate their troops and isolate the States. Move away from Washington rule."

"Giacomo, we're talking about civil war. Internal strife at that level will disband our country," warned Maryann.

"Yeah, but it will give us time to rebuild and get these bastards out."

"Predicated on the belief America won't enter the conflict. If we're attacked, our chance of survival, I'm sorry to say…stand behind the FHS global government," Bunny said.

A klaxon bell emitted from a laptop. "We're at DEFCON 1, Giacomo. A nuclear strike is imminent."

Giacomo heard Jason's words. Faced with impending doom, he recalled a memory that caused him to smile…

Thirty years ago, while he hunted for Dr. Payne in France, he received a phone call.

"Older brother, Pop's had a seizure."

"Is he alright?"

"For now, Giacomo. Come back to Ottati. I'm afraid he's going to die. We should be together."

"Believe me, Rio, he won't. I'll be there soon. We found the bastard. Are you ready for this? Sydney's alive!"

"Holy crap. Dad will be so happy. Bring her with you."

"I intend to."

Rio kept Giacomo informed via text. Two days later, their father, Paolo DeLaurentis, recovered.

Giacomo smiled at the recollection as he remembered his father's face lighting up with joy when the love of his life, Sydney Hill, walked onto the portico.

Giacomo gazed at the door with the expectation of seeing Emily enter. His arms waiting to wrap around her torso, tilting her chin for the lovers' kiss, he shook his head as a tear welled in his eye. Soon, soon he'd be reunited with Emily. He prayed his sons were safe. Giacomo stared at his cell phone for the last time, casting his eyes on the picture of his infant boys.

"The angels must be crying, my friends. We've done all we can do. It's in the hands of God now. Release the information to the media and…"

A vision swept through his mind as he saw the flash. *He stood on a pathway. His senses elevated as he observed the surrounding landscape. The colors were brilliant with an inexplicable brightness. The hues of flowers and trees made him catch his breath. Vivid greens, a deep blue sky, a mountain range in the distance, a meadow before him. His skin tingled and his being filled with an extraordinary joy. Confused about where he was, a conflict arose within him, and then it disappeared. In the field was a hospital bed. He thought he recognized the patient. He heard his father's voice. 'What year is this? What have I done?'*

The concussion of the explosive devices rocked the room. The door to the wood shop burst open. Red laser beams traversed the space. A team of marines scanned the zone with their rifles. Explosions sounded as the laptops self-destructed, catching the unsanctioned military unit off guard. The intruders let loose a torrent of gunshots. An orange glow of flames filled the area. Muffled yelling resounded in the victims' ears. Another rapid volley ensued. The sound of dead soldiers hitting the ground with thuds and cries of anguish.

"Let's move, gentlemen! This place is going to light up like dried tinder. Locate General DeLaurentis and his people and extricate them ASAP. Hell is about to break loose," the BOET commander barked.

The BOET members pushed the deceased armed forces to the side and began their search. Within a minute, they extracted the four. The Black Operations Elite Team captain removed his mask and examined the bodies that lay on stretchers.

Colonel Jason Vandercliff moved his hand over his burned chin. CIA Directorate of Operations Maryann Costatino took deep breaths, her leg broken. FBI Analyst Bunny Lynch touched her body and found no injuries. A tear traveled down her cheek. On the fourth stretcher, face swollen, was General Giacomo DeLaurentis. The officer in charge knelt beside him, placing his fingers on the commander's eyelids.

"Is he dead?" Maryann asked.

Chapter 99

T he morning breeze rustled the shutters. Paolo's nurse, Marge, held his hand. In and out of consciousness, two days had passed since his seizure. Words escaped his mouth as she transcribed the seer's words.

He stood on a pathway. His senses elevated as he observed the surrounding landscape. The colors were brilliant with an inexplicable brightness. The hues of flowers and trees made him catch his breath. Vivid greens, a deep blue sky, a mountain range in the distance, a meadow before him. His skin tingled and his being filled with an extraordinary joy. Confused about where he was, a conflict arose within his thoughts, and then it disappeared. Paolo called Giacomo's name. What year is this? What have I done? In the field was a hospital bed. It was him!

He stirred. A moan escaped his lips. His eyes opened to a slow awakening.

"I see you're awake. Welcome back," the woman said.

"How long?"

"Two days."

He took a cursory look at his surroundings. A moment lost, yet something gained. "Rio?"

"Her morning walk. Are you okay, Paolo?"

"I have cancer. How am I supposed to be?" He noticed her quizzical stare. "What?"

"I don't know where to start. I…"

Paolo watched as the trusted woman reached down and grabbed a yellow pad. "What's that?"

"You told me to write what you said."

"I did?"

"Yes, after your seizure. Rio left the room to call Giacomo. Your eyes opened wide, and you said, 'Marge, write what I say.' Then you had another seizure, and you've been mumbling ever since."

"You couldn't wake me up?"

"No. The doctor said he's never seen anything like this. He believes your cancer is spreading and you're…delusional."

"Don't cry, Marge. It's okay. Can you tell me what I said?"

"You were telling a story about Rio and Giacomo and the terrible events that were happening in their lifetime. You stopped the story and began talking about a patient in a hospital bed. And just before you woke up, you screamed, 'What year is this?' Followed by 'What have I done?' You have a brilliant book here." She tapped the pages with her hand.

Paolo watched Marge turn the sheets of paper while he listened. As he heard the words, he comprehended what had occurred. The visionary was a witness to his children's and the world's future, according to plans he had implemented. Devastated by his stupidity, he sat upright with purpose. *What do I do now? I can't allow my son to die before his time. We can never change our fate.*

"I want to have a dinner party tonight. Hand me my journal, please."

He detected the skepticism in her eyes as she reached for the book by his bedside. The seer wrote a few words, then ripped out a piece of the lined paper and handed it to her.

"I'm fine. Not much time left. Invite these people. And Marge, underneath the floorboard by the window is another journal; can you bring it to me? If you don't mind, I'll take the yellow pad." In a frenzy, he scanned the words Marge had transcribed and found what he hoped to be true. He reminisced about the vision of the evening's dinner party. *The sparkling light of the moon shed its white glow as*

*his guests parted and Sydney, the woman who awoke his soul, walked
to meet him on the portico.*

Humanity's future rested on the shoulders of Paolo DeLaurentis. His
revelations showed he needed to change the choices he made before
he died. Was he a gift from God to be an architect of life? On Earth to
show an unbelieving world that God exists? *Was it a vision or the brain
cancer? No, I'm certain what I witnessed needed to change.*

Could the messenger from God transform the world and save
humanity? Would the consequences of his actions change fate?
Death crept toward Paolo's doorstep. Plans, letters, people, and even
buildings put in place to guide the future had to change. Paolo had
it wrong. His friend Tony said the hardest part of writing was the
editing process. Did Paolo have the time to edit? Or was the future
sealed—carved into the headstone of humanity?

Chapter 100

Brewster Estate, January 20, 2004

P aolo's breath was shallow as the cancer progressed to his lungs. Mornings and evenings proved difficult with each rotation of the earth. The desire to maintain life diminished with every gasp. He prayed for the day the gripping agony would disappear. Time dwindled with each fleeting moment. *Days, maybe…*he reflected. Death loitered before taking him home.

Sydney, his soulmate, departed the house at eight to go food shopping. A necessary break to ease the pain of watching her husband wither away. Paolo's recollection of their wedding replaced the tortured thoughts of his demise. Married less than a month, the newlyweds' love never ceased. Whenever Sydney entered the room, his heart skipped a beat.

Marge, his nurse, sat nearby reading a book while Paolo adjusted the hospital bed to better see the snow-covered pine trees on the grounds of the Brewster Estate. A moment of solace. Two weeks prior to his rapid health decline, he signed over the deed of his house to his daughter Rio. Paolo pictured his last hours, loved ones gathered by his bedside as his pain-ridden life eroded into the peaceful realm of Heaven. Before his soul departed its temporal existence, he needed to make right the wrong he had done. Today Paolo waited for his longtime friends Tony and Steve to arrive to help rectify the misplaced act of his playing God. Troubled by the visions that haunted him since he was a child, Paolo took matters into his own hands. He believed he now had to act on the divinations. He foresaw their last meeting and at the conclusion of his pleas to convince Tony and Steve to correct his errors, the dreaded final heartfelt exchange of their last goodbyes to one another, concluding with, "*Until we meet again in a place where suffering no longer exists.*"

Concerned his thoughts overwhelmed his rational thinking, Paolo kept his mind focused. Alternate realities of space and time intensified his visions. He questioned the validity of the revelation he had in Ottati, unable to distinguish between prognostication and hallucination. Was his premonition a result of the brain tumor or his gift? Could he trust the predictions? What choice did he have? He decided to have faith in his buddies.

"Marge, do you have the new journal?"

"Yes, Paolo, it's here." She lifted it off the bedside table to show him. "Can I ask you a question?"

"Marge, please, have I ever said no?" Paolo propped the journals on his lap and read, saying, "I have to get it right this time."

"What I wrote in the diary for you…"

"Ah, yes…"

"But how? It was as if you were your son, Giacomo?"

"Yes, the empathic curse. It's possible for me to become one with the person living their life in the future. Even though it has not yet occurred."

"You're confident what I transcribed could happen?"

"Yes. Let's hope it doesn't. I believe they'll have enough time to change what I've put in motion."

"Will you tell Giacomo and Rio?"

"I can't, Marge. I wanted to, but my original idea was disastrous, leading to tragic consequences. Danny…you remember him? He's my pilot."

"Of course, I do."

"He's more than my pilot." Paolo's eyes wandered to the window.

Marge placed her hand on his. "You, okay?"

"Where was I?"

"Danny."

"Yes. At my behest, he enacted a plan I established prior to my sickness, hoping to save my children and the world... What you transcribed for me proves that my original strategy will fail. A messenger from God...perhaps. My sin—I am a coward, hiding behind my gift. My idea was to allow Giacomo and Rio to decide what to do with my prognostications. But, as you know from what you wrote, that notion contributed to countless deaths. The future I saw was incomplete. I presumed I was doing the right thing. The reality, Marge, I believe what I witnessed and felt during my seizure gives mankind a second chance. Am I an architect of life with the ability to manipulate fate? I don't know. I've witnessed both futures and...with the help of Tony and Steve...we can try to change a history that will destroy humankind."

"Paolo, you are far from a coward." She leaned over and kissed him on the forehead. "They're here."

"Thank you, Marge. Have I told you—"

"Yes, I know you love me. I love you too."

He smiled as a sense of peace and joy seized his being. Paolo's quest to share his unconditional love for all people earned him praise from many nations. Not one to revel in his accomplishments, he had but one wish: illuminate a world that grew darker by the hour.

Paolo understood the notion to be momentary, surmising the human condition could never change. Humanity was cursed to revert to its voracious and selfish ways. However, what he needed to say to his friends might transform the future. An alteration that could stop the charring of the planet. The stakes were high—death would pound on the doors of mankind if he failed to convince them.

Steve was the first to enter, and Paolo noticed the hesitancy in his walk.

"Glad to see you didn't kick the bucket yet."

"Nice. Knock a dying man down," Paolo chuckled and glanced at Tony, who came in shaking his head at Steve's comment.

"How are you, Paolo?" Tony asked.

"For a guy who will soon meet his maker—crappy. I can't wait for this to end. The holding on hurts Sydney and the kids. I need to become a memory so their lives can continue."

He saw the tears well in his friends' eyes. "It's okay, guys. We can't escape the truth. Sit, we must talk. Tony, take my pad and write this down: *An Angel's Cry*. And Tony, remember, *Fate can never be changed.*"

Chapter 101

Tony and Steve walked out of Paolo's house into the stark cold of the day. Steve grabbed a cigarette from his jacket.

"You know you got to stop smoking those things. They're going to kill you."

"Yeah, I know. What do you think? Is Paolo losing his mind?"

"Could be, you know the cancer is taking a toll on him. I'd be surprised if he lasted another month."

"Yeah, it's one hell of a story." Steve cupped the match in his hands and lit the Marlboro. He took a deep suck. "You could add that to your writing repertoire. He said you were going to write twenty novels."

"Yeah, we'll see. I love Paolo, and I knew he was special. But this…I don't know, Steve."

"Why not?"

"The future…he wants us to change the future. And what did he say? *Fate can never be changed.* To me, it sounds contradictory. Then again, when has Paolo ever been wrong?"

"Gentlemen."

At the end of the driveway, leaning against an SUV stood a familiar person.

"Danny, how the hell are you?" Tony reached out his hand.

"I'm good, Tony. Steve. How are you?"

"My friend is dying. Life is sad."

"I understand. I take it Paolo filled you in?"

"Yes. Where do we have to go?"

"Follow me to my house."

*   *   *

"Beautiful piece of property, Danny."

"Thank you, Steve. Right over here, guys."

"That's a hell of a garage."

"Yeah, it's where I restore my cars. Gotta keep busy."

The three men walked on a slate pathway. Danny led the way. He input a seven-digit code and the door popped open. As they entered the structure, the lights went on. A navy-blue 1965 Cobra with dual white stripes on the hood glistened in the building's corner. Interspersed within the 10,000-square-foot facility, a mélange of vehicles ranging from a classic Ferrari to Danny's pride, a 1968 yellow Trans Am. Positioned on a lift was an antique Bugatti motorcycle being restored.

Tony, immersed in thought, followed Steve and Danny to the opposite end of the building. Confident his friend was trying to grasp what Paolo had told them, Tony had his doubts as well. *Was it the truth? Or was it a delusion caused by Paolo's brain cancer?*

They arrived at a white wooden door. Danny tilted his head toward a camera as the machine buzzed while scanning his eyes. The ex-secret service agent entered a ten-foot by four-foot hallway.

"Gentlemen, are you coming?"

"Danny, what the hell is this place?"

"You'll see, Steve. Be patient."

The men crowded into the corridor as sensors examined their bodies for hidden cameras and recording devices. A humming motor activated the wall as the partition fell into the floor. Danny stepped forward as the awestruck Steve and Tony followed. The structure returned to its former position. Once Danny heard the final locking pin click into place, he took a step farther. Lights illuminated two flights of stairs.

"Damn, you got to be kidding me." Steve searched his pocket for a cigarette.

"I don't think you can smoke in here."

"No, you can't," Danny quipped. "We're entering a fireproof, bombproof steel vault."

The men descended the staircase. When they approached the entrance, Danny slid his thumb onto a fingerprint reader and punched in a numeric code with his other hand. The door swung open. He moved to his left, flipped a light switch, and glanced at the rows of shelves.

"Holy crap!" Tony said.

"Gentlemen, what you see here are 3,000 documents with 1,400 sealed envelopes that represent the writings and messages of your friend Paolo DeLaurentis."

"Yeah, so…"

"Steve, Tony—you've known Paolo a lot longer than I have. He's your friend, my employer. You are the people he can trust."

"What about Giacomo and Rio?"

"They are not ready yet. He thought they were until…"

"He saw their death."

"I believe he witnessed Giacomo's death. I don't know for sure, Tony, but close enough. He saw the nations of the world destroy themselves, the destruction of humanity, his son in a pool of blood and his daughter Rio's mind altered."

"What the hell…pinch me, this isn't real," Steve blurted.

"No, this is true."

Danny walked to a safe and withdrew two envelopes.

"Here."

Tony took the envelope marked with his name. Steve did likewise. The men opened their respective letters.

Tony and Steve read the message from Paolo. Their faces lit up with radiant smiles. A tear slid off Tony's chin.

"Don't start, you're gonna make me cry."

"How could he know, Steve?"

"I have no idea. We discussed this while we drove here."

"No more questions, I'm convinced," Tony said. "What do we have to do?"

"Paolo thought you'd say that."

Steve turned over the envelope. Written across the flap was Paolo's signature and a posted date of three days ago.

Danny retrieved a journal from the safe.

"He believes the reality that he saw for his children and his own cowardice to accept his gift will lead to the calamity of the world. This diary depicts the future, as seen through Paolo's visions. You are here to encourage his children and their heirs to move forward to change the history of humankind to prevent a catastrophic tragedy that will unfold."

"How are we to do that?"

"Good question, Steve. It's spelled out here and will take forty years to accomplish."

"I'll be lucky if I'm alive by then."

"Paolo said you would be."

Epilogue

Thirty Years after Paolo's Ottati Vision, 2034

Giacomo walked down the street. A memory of his dad from his childhood entered his mind. His father often brought him and Rio to Warren's annual pig roast that occurred on the Sunday before Labor Day. His dad's old friends, now in their late seventies, greeted him—Steve, Tony, Warren, and Wayne.

"Giacomo, glad you could make it."

"Happy to be here. It's good to see none of you are using walkers yet." The four men laughed. They embraced Giacomo. "Five years since I've been here. My Dad loved you guys."

"And we loved him."

"How long have you been retired?" Warren asked.

"Twenty-one months, but who's counting?" Giacomo quipped.

The forecast called for a bright sunny day with a high temperature of seventy-three. Giacomo strode along the field, soon to be filled with families and friends. The farm to his left, bordered by the brook and fenced in by trees, he approached the infamous pit. A 125-pound pig roasted over the coal fire as the younger generation took over the preparation and cooking responsibilities. Chairs lined the shaded stone wall area.

"Dad, dad!"

He turned and smiled as his sons Paolo and Arnaud ran toward him. The twins, now ten years old, rushed into his waiting arms.

"Can we climb the tree?"

"Sure, why not? Be safe, please."

Giacomo watched the boys scamper to the oak and ascend a thick branch that hung out over the field. He eyed the street. His beautiful wife Emily walked with her father, Arnaud.

He reached for his spouse. They embraced and kissed.

"Giacomo, I adore the way you look at me. It's as if you're falling in love with me for the first time."

"Em, I fall for you every day. I am grateful you're alive and we're together."

"Thank you, honey. I love you too."

Giacomo smiled and went to shake his father-in-law's hand.

"Dad, so glad you could make it. How are you feeling?"

"Excellent. With this triple bypass, I'm good for another twenty years."

"Remember, you can't eat everything—it's bad for your health," Emily cautioned.

Giacomo noticed the expression on his father-in-law's face and laughed. His loving wife punched him in the arm.

"Stop, you're enabling him."

"Yes, my dear."

A rumble turned into a roar as a military jet flew overhead. The three gazed skyward as a helicopter made its approach to the field. A small crowd watched in awe as Marine One settled on the grass. Paolo and Arnaud jumped out of the tree and ran to their parents. The chopper's blades slowed, coming to a halt as the door opened. A soldier stood at attention at the base of the stairs. Giacomo and Emily walked to meet the president. As the commander in chief stepped on the ground, the twins scampered past them, yelling, "Auntie Rio, Auntie Rio."

After hugging and squeezing the Gemini, she turned to Giacomo. "Hello, big brother."

"So good to see you, Madame President."

"Please stop with the bullshit. I understand you're traveling to the Vatican to visit Andrew." She hugged Emily and Arnaud.

"I am, and Tom Maro will join me. I still find it amazing they are brothers."

"Well, if it weren't for you, Giacomo, they never would have met."

"I still remember the day when I saw the picture of Tom and his dad and realized Andrew had the exact photo."

"They are wonderful, brave men. Their persistence motivated me to seek the nomination. I doubt I'd be President if it weren't for Andrew, Tom, and Jerry Richardson."

The siblings moved away from the helicopter and walked toward the pit. Rio's arm interlocked with Giacomo's. She whispered in her brother's ear.

"The FHS no longer exists, and we have dealt with the seventy-seven. With Sergio's help, Pope Andrew destroyed the ledger. Adinolfi is in an institution. Thanks to Arnaud, who stopped Trivette ten years ago, the world can now live in peace.

"Wonderful news, Rio. Nice job."

"Don't forget, you deserve the credit, Giacomo. I was the one who doubted Dad's journal. Thank God Tony, Steve, and Danny brought you to the vault with the letters and computer algorithms. I don't know where we—"

"That's a simple answer: in the thick of World War III."

"Praise the heavens, my brother. That is not the case."

"Amen to that."

* * *

January 23, 2054

In unison, the twins gazed at their digital watches. Their wives exchanged glances.

"I remember that day Auntie Rio gave us a ride in Marine One," Arnaud said.

"Yeah, a wonderful memory. I wish she were here."

"She will be," Tony said, as he closed his eyes. The door to the room opened.

"Dad, Mom, Auntie Rio, when did you guys get home?"

"A few minutes ago. How is he?" Giacomo asked.

"I'm sleeping."

"I see you're still alive?"

"Hilarious, Madame President, I see you haven't lost your sense of humor?"

"Hi, Tony. How are you today?"

"To be honest, Rio, I'm tired. My life in this world is over. It's time… maybe I'll see your father again soon."

Rio walked over and gave Tony a kiss on the forehead. His eyes opened and blinked closed. Through his pain, he smiled.

"What a century. My time has arrived, the job is complete."

"Patience, my friend," Giacomo said.

"Dad, is this true?" Arnaud asked.

"Tony's story?"

"Yeah," the twins replied in unison.

Tony's eyes opened wide and locked on Giacomo's as he grinned and fell into eternal, everlasting peace.